Operation Monsoon

Also by Shona Ramaya

Beloved Mother, Queen of the Night
Flute

OPERATION MONSOON

STORIES BY

Shona Ramaya

Graywolf Press
Saint Paul, Minnesota

Publication of this volume is made possible in part by a grant provided by the Minnesota State Arts Board, through an appropriation by the Minnesota State Legislature; a grant from the Wells Fargo Foundation Minnesota; and a grant from the National Endowment for the Arts. Significant support has also been provided by the Bush Foundation; Target, Marshall Field's and Mervyn's with support from the Target Foundation; the McKnight Foundation; and other generous contributions from foundations, corporations, and individuals. To these organizations and individuals we offer our heartfelt thanks.

Published by Graywolf Press
2402 University Avenue, Suite 203
Saint Paul, Minnesota 55114
All rights reserved.

www.graywolfpress.org

NATIONAL
ENDOWMENT
FOR THE ARTS

MINNESOTA
STATE ARTS BOARD

Published in the United States of America
Printed in Canada

"Video Crime," written by David Bowie, Tony Sales and Hunt Sales. Reprinted by permission of ARZO Publishing

ISBN 1-55597-387-6

2 4 6 8 9 7 5 3 1
First Graywolf Printing, 2003

Library of Congress Control Number: 2003101169

Cover design: Scott Sorenson
Cover photograph: Dean Batchelder; Model: Rachna Agarwal
Cover art: Kiyomi Talaulicar, *Fragment* (detail)

I've got dollars—I've got sense,
Wonder where the Third World went?

David Bowie, "Video Crime"

ACKNOWLEDGMENTS

Various people have helped me with these stories in various ways. I'd like to thank them all for their critiques and moral support: first, Raghu, Lisa, and Susan. My agent, Susan Raihofer, has been, and continues to be, just terrific in her dedication and commitment toward my work. Anne Czarniecki, my editor, has been wonderful all along; and I am grateful to all the people at Graywolf who have involved me in the entire production process of the book. It has been a pleasure to work with them.

I also want to thank Dean Batchelder, Rachna Agarwal, and Gita Desai for their help with the cover photograph.

And most of all, I want to thank Anthony Direnzo, my best reader and critic: without his advice and critique I would be lost! In the words of a famous poet, I see Anthony, or Antonio, as I call him, as: *il miglior fabbro.*

CONTENTS

GOPAL'S KITCHEN

I sat at the table and blinked a few times. Eggs, orange juice, my mother, my brother, the servants, the smell of warm, thick date syrup over toast, all shimmered like apparitions. "Eat something." My mother's voice was far, far away, weakly penetrating the dense fog squeezing my head. "You can go back to sleep . . . sleep your jet lag off . . . this is what happens when you make a seventeen-hour flight after six years. . . ." Scrambled eggs. A delicate hint of coconut and almonds, silken against my tongue. "Rajiv Gandhi assassinated . . . Tamil Tigers . . . God knows what kind of riots will start . . . Floods, prices going up . . . Who's to take over. . . ." Eggs melted in my mouth with that blend of secret spices only he knew—I dropped the fork and stood up startled, the grogginess vanishing for a few seconds, swept away by a roaring storm of light.

"Who made the eggs?"

"Don't scream so." My mother pushed me back into the chair.

"*Namaste, didi,*" I heard from the kitchen door.

"Gyan," said my mother. "Taken over, two years now."

He stood against the doorframe, bowing his head slightly, clasping his hands against his chest. His white *kurta* had a few turmeric stains. He shifted his weight from one foot to the other, smiled, touched his forehead. I nodded. He nodded back, swinging his lank, straight hair that fell across his eyes. There was something very gentle and calm in his face and about his slight form.

"Who's he?" I muttered under my breath.

1

"He's the one," my mother answered, touching my shoulder. She let out a nervous giggle.

"He's the one—the one—he got the kidney."

The fog coiled around my head, making me gasp. At the center of its steely haze, I saw a fresh green coconut.

Gopal's kidney. I lay on my bed and looked around the room I had abandoned eight years earlier. Rajiv was blown up the night I landed in Delhi. "India is finished," my brother said. "There's a strange calm all around, like a lull before a storm." Just like that day, years ago, when I came back from school and I heard my mother's shocked voice, "How could you?" And Gopal, bowing his head, asking her to keep it down, not to tell the children. That long scar across his back. But his face calm, a tired calm, in spite of it all.

My room had a petrified calmness about it this afternoon. Eight years ago it used to look like a cyclone had ripped through it. Clothes, books, shoes, cassettes scattered in heaps all around. Posters of twisted agonized faces and bodies screaming silent messages of chaos. Plants, half collapsed from lack of water, lying limp in pots as if ready to give up the ghost any second.

The books, the posters, the plants were all still there. The bed was in the same old place by the windows. My desk next to it, then the dressers. The rug had been cleaned and the reds and blues glowed bright. The paisleys on the rug turned into little kidneys from time to time as I stared at them. They turned green for a second, altered shape, became green coconuts. I wiped the coconuts off with one strong blink. Paisleys, kidneys.

So he had it now. Gopal's kidney. Gyan, then, was the murderer. And here he was how? why? bringing forth those exquisite scrambled eggs, Gopal's special.

For the next few days, lunches and dinners were spectacular. Gyan overwhelmed the table with Gopal's special lamb chops, chicken korma, biryani, all the different vegetable and fish concoctions, and the fabulous desserts that Gopal had been famous for. I chewed and swallowed cautiously, every mouthful a time bomb of flavors. Curling shrimp quivered at the end of my fork as if ready to explode. We ate, smiling, cracking jokes, bursting out laughing. "*Tatva-gyan,*" my brother said to Gyan. "Hey, Enlightenment, get more rice, *yaar.*" Gyan, quiet, shy, withdrawing, smiled and vanished into the kitchen. He didn't have Gopal's garrulous charm, his effusiveness. "I don't understand," I said to my mother and father. They smiled, shrugged.

"Well, it's sort of this way," my mother said. "He appeared just after *Holi* two years back. Said he could cook and wanted to work. Of course, I was wary at first. You know, he had never worked anywhere before, he said. There was no one I could call to inquire about him. And he refused, just flatly refused, to tell us where he was from. He begged for a trial run. So I let him cook for a day. Well, that was that. When we sat down to eat, we nearly passed out with amazement. Gopal's egg korma! Gopal's shrimp curry!"

"We found out about the kidney business almost a year later," my father said.

"The *mali* found out and told me," my mother added.

"How is it you didn't choke on the kormas and curries," I asked, "knowing that Gopal died of kidney failure four years ago?"

"But the food, sis," my brother rolled his eyes, "made us lose it, just swoon. Hey, *A-gyan,* rice!" Unconscious, my brother called him in jest, adding an 'A' to his name.

"What are we eating here?" I asked weakly, in spite of wanting to scream.

"Just delicious," my brother drawled, a snarl of a smile expanding across his face. "Let the taste seduce you."

The persisting jet lag ushered me clumsily back to my room half an hour after lunch on the fourth day at home. "Sleep it off," my mother said, poking her head into my room.

"Close the door," I said.

"Don't go raiding the kitchen in a couple of hours, now that your jet lag is wearing off and you seem to be getting into your old routine. Ring that bell next to the bed if you want a snack." Her head withdrew and the door closed. I regarded the gleaming white button above the headboard with surprise. Hadn't noticed it before. My room wasn't the same then. They had interfered with its internal mess. Established civilized communication. Or was it concern? I hadn't entered the kitchen, since I'd been back. The kitchen used to be my favorite haunt—when Gopal was there.

How to reenter that kitchen now? To sit in that familiar spot in front of the windows, three yards from the stove.

Gopal in his starched white *kurta* and white cotton pants, tossing glittering spices into pots and pans that sizzled and smoked like magic cauldrons. His slender hands flying around, snatching a pinch of this, a dash of that, and the smells changing from one delicious aroma to another.

The hot kitchen would become an enchanted cave, full of curling smoke rising from shining vessels, startling your eyes with sparkling cascades of spices, oils, herbs, fascinating your nose with a thousand aromas. You breathed in deeply, coughing, choking, laughing as if breathing in new life, awakening to a higher consciousness. Gopal looked at you quizzically through the glistening haze of smoke and steam as nature metamorphosed to art in a saucepan. Flames texturized flesh.

And through that kitchen window, through the mingling sounds and smells of food, spices, clothes and dishes being washed, detergent, mangoes, sandalwood incense, crows and sparrows fighting over spilled garbage, through the magenta bougainvillea, the flame-hot turquoise dazzle of the Delhi sky became a painful, mystifying brightness. Gyan—what about Gyan? What kind of enlightenment from a kidney?

"I will run away if you don't tell my why," I had screamed at Gopal.

"You can run away," Gopal had said, "but it runs along with you." That long, wry smile. "Come sit," he'd say, as my mother and father left for work. "Come sit here on this stool and let me tell you. . . ."

But all of a sudden, I couldn't remember a thing. So many stories—I once knew them all. They refused to surface. My mind was disobeying in the most hateful manner, swimming and blurring, my eyes closing in spite of my need to see, hear, remember. My body was not mine anymore, it seemed. Something else was interfering, making it give in, give in, lose—

"For you."

A smell of chicken and spice and lemon. I rubbed my eyes and rolled over toward the smell. A plate of sandwiches on a tray. Six wafer-thin two-inch triangles of white bread. "Masala chicken sandwiches. I know you get hungry at this time—three-thirty." The sandwiches had spoken.

I shook my head and looked up. Gyan, smiling shyly.

"What the hell are you doing in my room?"

"I knocked," Gyan said, his eyes apologetic. "I didn't want you to wake up hungry and then not feel good about going to the kitchen."

I blinked at the sandwiches. Damn it, I was hungry. I always got hungry around this time. But these sandwiches? "Who told you about these?" I asked, anger spiking my voice to a higher pitch. "How dare you come here, to work here. You're the cause of his death."

"Gopal would have never said that," Gyan cut me off, his voice calm, soft.

"Why not? How do you know?"

"I have to go make tea now."

I separated the compressed pieces of bread and stared at the meat. Lifting one open triangle of bread, I bit into it cautiously. That same special flavor. I ate the sandwiches slowly, chewing carefully so that nothing escaped down my throat, missing my teeth and tongue. I ate each piece reverently, with eyes closed, with the acute concentration of a yogi meditating, as if each of those neat triangles contained some hermetically sealed knowledge that could only be transfused through internal membranes, osmosis, blood.

The kitchen waited.

The corridors, rooms, stairs, all so quiet, darkened and cooled with thick drapes, unobtrusive air-conditioning, and everyone lulled to sleep with its low, languorous hum. The kitchen has remained frozen. That same stool under the counter, that same stunning light through the window. I pulled the stool to the window and sat down.

Gyan enters through the back door. "Tea?" he asks, a smiling inquiry in his sharp dark eyes. "Coffee?" I shake my head. "Idiots," he says softly, "asking Sonia Gandhi to take over. Of course she refused. Don't know which way we're heading anymore. Tea?" I want to ask him about himself. I want to know, desperately, how and where he learned to cook like Gopal. I bite my lips in frustration. What words will I use?

"I won't be here long." Gyan turns from the stove.

"Oh?"

"I'm not really a servant. Wasn't born one."

"I see." I look at him in utter bewilderment. So some are born servants, then.

"Gopal wasn't born a servant," Gyan adds.

"How does it feel, then?" I asked. "To cook here when you're not one of them?"

"Good." He nods his head vigorously. "But now it's nearly time to leave. Make some money, marry."

"Win a lottery or something?" How else do you make sudden money? Inheritance, bank robbery. . . .

"Oh, no," Gyan waves a knowing hand. "All that's wishful thinking. Will it happen, will it happen? Not that. I'm getting eighty thousand rupees. I'm going to donate a cornea."

He pronounced it slowly since it was an English word and a very alien one: c-o-r-n-e-a.

Why, why, why? I had railed at Gopal. Why did you do it?

He's given, donated, oh, God, sold a kidney! My mother gasping in the living room.

Why? I had asked, sitting right here. Gopal had smiled at me, shaking his head to say, Don't worry, I'm fine. "Why did you?" I persisted.

"Sometimes, you have to do certain things," Gopal said, a tired look coming over his face.

"What things?"

"Tch-tch." He poured the eggs into a frying pan on the stove and began to add his mysterious ingredients. "Want to see my scar?" He lifted his white shirt and turned his side to me. A dark jagged line—more than a foot long—ran diagonally from the middle of his back and disappeared under the waist of his pants. Someone had tried to slice Gopal in half with a huge battle-ax, I felt, with one massive crescent sweep. I could see that he had lost weight. His ribs showed and his shoulders had lost their bulk. He had developed a slight stoop that deepened the look of tiredness about him.

"You shouldn't have," I said. "It's wrong. Whoever asked you for your kidney should be shot. What'll you do if something happens to your other—" I started to cry. "How will you ever buy it back?"

"You can't buy it back twice," Gopal said, a faraway look coming into his eyes while he scooped the eggs onto a plate, added sauteed tomatoes and pieces of toast, and gave it to me. "I feel like I've paid back."

"Paid back what?" I set the plate down on the floor. "You tell me now or I'll run away." He put the plate back in my hand.

"Go to the table and eat."

Gopal was not going to talk. As the eggs and toast slid down to my stomach, a desolate, wrenching curiosity squeezed upwards to my throat. "I won't eat," I said pushing the plate away. "If you don't tell me, I won't eat, ever, anything you make."

Gopal came out of the kitchen. He had that long wry smile on his face again. "When you're hungry enough, you'll eat," he said. "Then you'll eat all right."

"Neither tea or coffee? Yet I know you like both?"

"Where is that kidney exactly?" I ask, staring at Gyan's middle.

"Oh, right here." Gyan lifts his shirt, lowers his pants slightly, to reveal a four-inch scar near his left hipbone. "Right in here." He pats the scar. I look at the scar, narrowing my eyes. Gopal's kidney—right there. A pelvic kidney. Dislocated so completely—could it turn into an ovary through this relocation?

Gyan fills the kettle, puts it on the stove. He slices a rum cake, makes delicate cucumber sandwiches. "I understand," he says, concentrating on the bread, butter, and cucumber slices, "how you must feel. Gopal told me a lot about you, all of you."

"You knew Gopal!" I clench my fists slowly.

"He told me not to tell anyone but you."

"What—"

"I was going to die," Gyan says. "I was resigned to my fate. But my father wasn't. I was the only son, you see, and he wanted me to take over his business. My father searched all over Murshidabad and West Bengal for a kidney donor, and after several months Gopal came forward."

"Did you meet him before—?"

"No. But I felt this need to meet him later. My father wouldn't tell me who it was. So I bribed the doctor who had performed the operation for the information. I met Gopal three years after he returned to his village. I was drawn to him in a way I can't explain. I forgot everything." Gyan pauses, turns from the sandwiches, his eyes haunted. "I told my father I didn't want anything to do with his business, that I didn't want to stay with him or my mother. They were like monsters all of a sudden, disgusting, greedy, unscrupulous monsters. Poison." He stops again, shuts his eyes tightly for a few seconds. "I found Gopal in his paddy field. I worked with him, lived with him. I felt happy, happy like I had never been before."

"Where were you when Gopal died?"

"Why, right beside him."

"And you didn't—"

"He wouldn't let me take him to Calcutta, to a hospital. I pleaded, yelled. He was adamant. He kept saying, It's time, it's time, something about scorching ash. I took care of him. It was terrible—being there, unable to do anything, not allowed to help—" Gyan covers his face. "It was my hell."

And hell had surely broken loose on that afternoon—yes, that dazzling afternoon, returning now with its stunning clarity. I was sixteen then, and Gopal had gone to his village on his yearly leave. But that year he went home for three months instead of one. He said he needed the extra time, but he wouldn't tell us why. I returned from school in the most joyous spirit the day he was supposed to come back. I knew he'd open the door as I ran down the drive. Our *ayah* opened the door and I heard agitated voices inside.

"How could you have done this?" my mother was saying to Gopal. She struck her forehead with her hand. "How could you? What are we going to do?"

Gopal raised his hand and shushed her as I entered. He looked tired. I'd never seen him look so tired before, or so dejected. "What's wrong?" I asked.

"Don't—" he said to my mother.

"Don't what?" my mother said, in an angry, whining voice at the point of tears. "It's you who shouldn't have. Oh, God, he's given away a kidney, given, sold, why, you idiot?"

"What kidney?" I asked blinking rapidly.

Was he going to die? Was he then not the same anymore, one kidney less? Gopal not the same anymore. Not special anymore?

"He told me about all of you," Gyan continues. "He loved you people like his own family. You *were* his family. He whispered recipes to me, recipes he created for you, and I sat near him with my eyes closed, a disciple before his guru absorbing mantras. I know what Gopal meant to all of you, especially you. I felt I took him away from your lives, even destroyed his. Gopal was special, God, I know Gopal was special."

"Do you? I wonder." I turn to face the window.

Gopal started working at our house long before my brother and I were born. Gopal was eighteen then. An old *khansama* had brought him to my mother because she had been looking for a cook. Gopal was with us for more than thirty years.

Gopal made sure we got to school on time, all fed and dressed, scolding our *ayahs*, my mother, checking our schoolbags to see if we had all our books, notebooks, pens and pencils, sandwiches. Had our shoes been polished till we could see our faces? Was my hair braided just right? Was my brother's tie quite straight, his laces tied? Our *ayahs* never lasted more than one or two years under Gopal's taxing reign. "They are not good enough," he'd snap at my mother, lifting his chin.

His imperiousness always made me squeal with laughter. Gopal looked so odd when he lifted his chin that way. He was somewhat awkwardly put together. He was of medium height; judging by the size of his head and his face, he should have been a small person. But he had big shoulders and a barrel-shaped torso. His arms and legs were strong, muscular, but his hands and feet were small, slender. He had a narrow face with a long aquiline nose and a trim mustache. He wore his wavy black hair short and swept back from his domed forehead. His long thin throat seemed at odds with his powerful shoulders. So when he threw his head back, lifting his chin in contempt, the rest of his body didn't seem to comply. But in spite of this slight ungainliness there was something regal about Gopal, and all the servants from the neighboring houses, the *malis*, the *dhobis*, all treated Gopal with a certain reverence, as if he were someone special. I even saw our *dhobi* touch Gopal's feet once. "Why did he do that?" I asked our current *ayah*. "For a blessing," she said to me. "Gopal has a special life." I asked her what she meant, but she wouldn't explain. She shook her head vigorously and touched her own forehead.

So there was something special about Gopal, something secret, unknowable, imperious, mysterious, that made all others pay attention, obey, including my mother. My father never raised his voice before Gopal or repeated a request. But then Gopal was quite irreproachable.

He ran the house like clockwork so that my parents could lead their own lives, forget about us, and not worry about the menu or the state of the house when corporate hotshots came to dinner. My aunt decided to bring up my brother the right way; she whisked him away to her house two or three days a week. That left me on a stool in the kitchen while Gopal worked.

He was special, all the servants said. He had never married. My aunt said he was continually having affairs with our friends' *ayahs*. Murderous husbands would appear with axes, she told my mother. But no rolling-eyed, foaming-mouthed husbands ever turned up. Instead I saw some of them bow their heads as they passed Gopal on the street. That small fine head and the barrel body, and the contemptuous lift of the chin.

He told me how weavers worked their looms, how they wove into their cloth stories of angry river gods sweeping away villages; resolute parents dragging their children back from the underworld; men and women leaping into pyres to burn away their weak flesh and be reborn as invulnerable beings of pure light. I learned how cocooned silkworms were gathered from mulberry bushes, boiled, the silk unravelled, spun. Climbing up date palms, slashing the trunks, tying buckets under the cut to gather the juice, and so sweet the stolen juice, so sweet off sticky fingers. Gopal's eyes glistened as he talked, as he unveiled the thrill of sneaking out of windows of mansions, scrambling over walls, up mango trees. Oh, to become orange-yellow with mango juice, stained purple from *jamun*. Then the thrashings would follow, and defiant laughter. "Your childhood?" I asked him, wonder making me whisper. Gopal smiled, looked out at the burning June sky. "Has she eaten?" my mother asked from somewhere. "She ought to get out of her school clothes."

"You don't have to tell me," he said to her, turning from the window.

"Gopal-*da*," we called him. *Da* for older brother. But I meant father, I think. When he took his yearly leave—a month—to visit his village near Murshidabad, a small town north of Calcutta, I used to roll on the floor and howl. "Take me with you, don't go, take me with you." I was a kid then. After I was twelve, I simply stayed at a friend's while he packed his bags and took his leave.

"So I will make this money and leave, and I will have a happy life." Gyan looks defiantly at the sandwiches.

"A happy life?"

"Yes. I found out the secret at the blood bank. I was waiting with a friend who was there to donate blood and this man came up to us...."

Nightmare—I rub my eyes. Were we returning to the beginning of the farce?

"One of his kidneys!" My father ripped his tie off and struck the bed with it. He made frantic phone calls to doctors and urologists that evening. "They're all doing it," he said to my mother, looking aghast. "For money, for happier lives! The whole damn country."

"Call my brother," my mother said to him. So our uncle the surgeon was called after midnight. "Why do they all say it's okay?" my father yelled at his brother-in-law. "It's not okay, thirty thousand or not, it's definitely not okay and it wasn't a relative either, some damn contractor's son!"

"Why didn't you give Gopal the money if he needed it?" I screamed at my father. He held the receiver away and turned to me with a scowl.

"Where do you get the idea that I can make donations of thirty thousand at the snap of your fingers?"

"You should have tried—if Gopal can give away a kidney, why can't—" My father stopped me with a glare.

"Is Gopal capable of any housework on one kidney?" he asked our uncle just as he had asked all the other doctors that night. "Can he lift bags, cook, take care of things as before?" Apparently, my uncle informed us, Gopal was fully functional. "This should be completely illegal," my father was saying. "Why isn't it?"

It was all voluntary, my uncle confirmed. Dialysis is expensive, uncomfortable, and if someone is willing to donate a kidney, and there are so many who really need kidneys, and have the precious money to buy, could a doctor say, no, he or she wouldn't do this?

"But there is an international ban on selling organs from live donors."

Not in India, we learned. People come from all over the world to certain hospitals to get kidneys. Alas, my uncle himself had done such transfers, fifty-seven to date, and prescribed tons of immunosuppressant drugs for the recipients so that their bodies didn't reject the shiny new thirty-thousand-rupee kidneys. "You criminal!" my father shouted into the receiver.

He was overreacting, my uncle said to my father. A kidney is nothing.

People are selling corneas, skin, even one eye sometimes, if both are perfect. People in the villages need money and a lot of people in the cities will die without kidney transplants.

At two in the morning Dad called the Deputy Commissioner of Police—an old school friend of his. We found out that organ-selling was going on like any other trade, selling potatoes, say, or like donating blood. Indeed blood donors were often propositioned by middlemen regarding even more lucrative donations. The police were never able to make any arrests because nobody complained or reported or testified. "Well, I'll testify," my father said. "I'm going to go donate blood, and if anybody propositions me, I'm going to drag him to the police station—no, to your office."

"Can you guys shut up," my brother was groaning from his room, "I can't sleep."

"But can Gopal still cook those wonderful meals?" my mother sighed. "Can he still take care of the house, move furniture, lift heavy things?"

"How can you be worrying if he can manage *your* life?" I yelled, bursting into tears. "He's had a major operation. We don't even know if he'll live or die—what if his other kidney fails? Why can't you kill the surgeon who removed Gopal's kidney?"

"I will, too," my father said firmly. "And the damn contractor and his son who got the kidney."

Next morning—thank God we didn't have school that day because one of our teachers had been crushed by a school bus—my father put aside his ad campaigns, although my mother had left for her Rotary Club meeting, and announced he was ready for the bastards at the blood bank, that he had a master plan. He would go to a clinic to donate blood; if anyone solicited him, he would throw a half nelson and grab the scoundrel, then drag him off to his police-commissioner friend's office. My brother and I accompanied him for this adventure, not because we thought anything was going to come of it, but simply because we wanted to see how our willowy father in his silk suit would get anyone in a half nelson. I needn't add that he was terrified of needles. A journalist friend told him about a certain clinic in south Delhi that had a shady reputation—many people had been propositioned there and had made small fortunes in the bargain. On the way to the clinic we repeated about a thousand times that the nurses usually manage to get a needle into a vein after ten to fifteen jabs. The drive over was jerky. The car stalled five times.

The line of blood donors stretched a quarter mile outside the clinic. Farmers from villages just outside Delhi, office clerks, college students, government officials, all stood in the hazy, humid September heat, wiping their faces, spitting out chewed *paan,* smoking, chatting, cursing government policies. Looking at the irritated, sweaty faces all around, I ran Gopal's words inside my head: If you're hungry enough, you'll eat all right. Why were all these people really here? Did they all want to make small fortunes through a simple, horrifying trade? To make ends meet? No, I don't think that's what Gopal meant. We ushered Dad to the end of the line. "I hate standing in lines," he said, making a face. "Why are they staring at me?" People were staring at him. Nobody went to a clinic to donate blood dressed in a silk suit. And people who wore silk suits and managed ad campaigns didn't bother donating blood.

We reached the clinic entrance after an hour and a half. Dad had removed his jacket and tie, handed them to us, and rolled up his shirtsleeves. Shortly, we entered the lobby and a nurse handed us some forms. We helped Dad fill out his, and turned the forms in to the man sitting at a counter marked REGISTRATION. Then we stood in another line outside a large room in which people lay on beds hooked to bottles. Dad turned pale at the sight of the redness filling up the bottles. "Why hasn't anyone propositioned me?" he asked, his voice shaking a little.

"You haven't donated blood yet," we said. "The organ brokers usually hang out at the back, like your journalist said. They find out the blood types and all that, and then they choose their guys."

"Then I've been waiting in the wrong line!"

"No. You'll be in that line soon, on the way out, after you've donated blood."

"But I don't really—I mean, I came here so that—I mean, I want to go—let's go out that way. If I hang around at the back of the clinic long enough someone is sure to come up to me. I look quite clean and healthy."

Since Dad's voice had cracked to falsetto, and his silk shirt was drenched and sticking to him, we ushered him out. We stood in the back alley and watched people walk out slowly. "Look!" my brother said suddenly, his voice excited. A man of about forty, dressed in drab brown clothes, had taken a man and a woman aside. The couple was definitely from a nearby village, judging from their clothes and dialect. The three were whispering under a tree. The man and woman shook their heads negatively.

"Got him!" Dad said, and shot forward before we could stop him. He grabbed the man's arm and turned him around. "What is it this time? A kidney? Two? An eye?" The man in brown freed his arm with a jerk, pushed Dad hard, toppling him to the ground, ran down the alley and vanished around the corner. My brother ran after the man, and I helped Dad up, dusted his clothes. The man and the woman huddled against the tree. "What did that man say to you?" I asked them. They shook their heads.

"We don't know," they said. "We must go or we'll miss the bus." They moved backwards, the woman pulling her sari over her face, the man half covering his face with one hand. "We must go." They shuffled backwards down the alley, looking furtively at us, a slow desperation filling their eyes.

My brother returned panting. "He got into a taxi and—" He shrugged and turned his palms upwards. "I tried." Dad was still gasping from shock. "I don't understand," he said twice. "Something's changed, beyond—beyond." He smoothed his hair gingerly.

We drove back home taking the most secluded of roads. "I'm speechless," my father said, sitting down heavily on a couch, and asked Gopal for a double scotch.

"Life changed then, completely, beyond my—beyond my—" Gyan lets out a sigh. "But this time I'll change things. Life will be in my hands." He places a frying pan full of cocktail sausages on the stove. "Life can be happy. You have to know what to do. Know the right secret."

To know the secret. Years passed, I graduated from high school, went to college, my brother made it to tenth grade without failing any exams, our parents continued to throw their dazzling parties, and Gopal managed everything as before, imperiously lifting his chin when required. But his hands moved more slowly, his eyes seemed weary, and his shoulders stooped. Everything was pretty much as before except for one difference: Gopal didn't take his home leave for two years. I spent less time in the kitchen and more afternoons with newfound college friends. But that dull, twisting curiosity about Gopal's kidney refused to subside. Summer holidays brought me back to my stool in the kitchen, to Gopal's stories about his village. I asked him if his staying away from his village had anything to do with his kidney, but he refused to talk about that. "Was it just the money? Just tell me that," I implored. "Please please. I won't tell. I'll keep it a secret till I die, I swear."

"No," he said gently. "Not just that."

I lay in bed at night, my mind wild, painting various scenarios in my head: Gopal wanted to save a long-lost love; some woman he could never have, now united through this kidney. Perhaps it was for an illegitimate child somewhere; perhaps he had left this woman, and now guilt-ridden, he returned to save their child. Why did he not visit his village anymore? Dad tried to track down the doctor who had performed the operation; but without any information about where it had taken place—Gopal wouldn't say—he got nowhere. He gave up.

The summer following my B.A. exams, Gopal announced that he wanted to visit his village. After five years! Two days before he left I sat in the kitchen and watched him prepare dinner. Once more in this cave of marvelous transformations. Wrapped again in the seductive smoke of this different planet. Here, anything could happen, here, in this world of continual metamorphosis. Here goats that destroyed spinach fields lay sizzling in strips with chopped spinach in incredible delicious harmony. A shower of grated almonds blessed their perfect union. All boundaries collapsed in this world as predator and fodder fell under the same shining blade in Gopal's slender hand. Catalyzed by the last rites of hot oil, cumin, coriander, bay leaves, cloves, cinnamon, a new entity was resurrected. It steamed rich green and brown on blue china.

"My grades will be out soon," I said, breathing in deeply this heady smell of reincarnation. "Dad wants me to apply to American universities."

"You must go," Gopal said. "You must make sure your future is bright, wonderful, successful. You can't sit in this kitchen forever."

"What about your future? Why are you going to your village after staying away for five years?"

"Future," he murmured, "future . . . for me there is only the past. . . ." his voice trailed off.

"I'm going to ask you for one last time," I said. "The secret."

He gave me a one-sided smile. "Sometimes it's best not to know certain things. Secrets must remain secrets."

"If I guess, will you tell me?"

"Guess?" Gopal laughed. "Will it be your story, eh, or mine?"

Voices, voices, delicious smoke, and a very hazy world, and I think I heard—

Many years ago, in a village hidden between a forest and a hillside sliced by silver torrents, was a large mansion. It had marble columns, a stone courtyard, and was sheltered by broken walls with mango and *jamun* trees all around. Inside this mansion lived a middle-aged *zamindar,* impoverished by high taxes and low-yielding crops, and his dying son, his only child. His wife had died of tuberculosis years before. He sat by his son's bedside every morning and touched the pale, limp hand near the pillow. He felt the pulse and exhaled slowly. The village doctor had given up hope. He didn't even know what ailed the fourteen-year-old boy. A city doctor had been called in. He, too, had shaken his head gravely.

The boy lay on the bed and stared out of the windows at the play of shadow and sunshine on the brick wall and mango leaves, and on the glowing skin of the weaver's son, who spent afternoons sneaking up those mango trees and stealing the ripest mangoes. The weaver's son—the same age as he—caught his eye many times, and winked and laughed. He appeared like a woodland deity, sometimes all yellow-orange with mango juice, sometimes stained purple with *jamun,* his dark body almost a part of that dark glossy tree. The *zamindar's* boy heard him shriek with laughter when the *zamindar's* men caught him and thrashed him for stealing the fruit. He flew kites outside the walls, and the *zamindar's* son tried to raise himself to see him, hearing his reckless laughter. He heard his father's men curse that weaver's son. He heard his father moan to the village priest, "It breaks my heart to see that healthy, strong weaver's son run around so while my son lies dying."

"I wish I could be like that weaver's boy," the *zamindar's* son said to the burning turquoise sky. "I wish my body would stop aching. I wish this awful tiredness would leave my limbs." The world outside trembled hot and bright.

"So many doctors," Gyan says, "and all shook their heads the wrong way. Only another kidney can save him, they said. So awful, all those months hooked up to that machine. A tube through my wrist every third day. All my blood going out into something then coming back in. Just wanted to die. Wanted them to let me be. Wanted my father to give up. Not that tube through my wrist. But he just wouldn't give up. Kept searching and searching for a kidney. My friends looked in once in a while, telling me about soccer matches. I would touch the ball they sometimes brought with them—that wondrous planet I would never have access to." Gyan sighs again. "Maybe I didn't want my father to give up—I don't know."

The *zamindar* continued to strike his head against the temple altar. He fasted and lay before the altar for three days. He performed innumerable rituals, called on every god and goddess he could think of, whispering, sobbing, "Don't take my son away, please, my only hope." He even carried the sweets he had offered to Vishnu to the Muslim sector of the village and offered them to the *mullah*. Some of his men, worried by such an act of desperation, fearing insanity, told him to go and find the *tantrik* who lived in the heart of the forest in the forbidden Kali temple. Perhaps he could give him a magic herb. But then the *tantrik* might also cut off the *zamindar's* head on Kali's altar. You have to take risks if you want to save a life they told him. So the *zamindar* went into the forest, shaking, desperate, sweating, muttering Hari's name for protection.

His men waited outside the forest for four days. The *zamindar's* head is rolling at Kali's feet, they said to themselves and returned to the mansion. The *zamindar's* son looked so corpse-like that the men decided to prepare a pyre of sandalwood. It's a matter of hours now, they thought. While they were busy piling wood on wood and collecting baskets of white flowers, the *zamindar* stumbled in through the enormous iron gates of the mansion followed by a tall, dark man in a red loincloth, grasping a seven-foot trident.

The *tantrik* had arrived! The *zamindar* was alive! The men gaped at the lean old man with fiery eyes. "Where?" asked the *tantrik* in a rasping voice, striking the ground with his trident.

The boy who had lain still as a corpse for four days opened his eyes when the *tantrik* touched his pale forehead with his trident. "There is only one way," the *tantrik* said. "Is there another boy, strong, healthy? And are you willing to accept whatever the consequences might be?"

"Anything," the *zamindar* whispered, "everything."

"We will wait for a moonless night," the *tantrik* said, and left.

Three days later the *tantrik* reappeared and lit a fire in the courtyard after dusk. The glow of the fire was the only light in the darkness as the sky was moonless and overcast. He poured butter and incense and flowers into the flames. Then he took a fresh green coconut and sliced off its top. "This will be the vessel," he said, holding out the coconut, and placed the sliced-off portion back on it like a lid.

Through that dark night rumbling faintly with thunder and frog calls, when all the huts were dark, and not even a dog or a cat could be found on the dirt roads, the *tantrik* walked toward the weaver's hut with the coconut. He held the coconut in one hand and the sliced top portion in the other. The *zamindar*'s men leaned out of windows to see him. They saw only the darkness. "It's Kali's darkness," they muttered, "and the *tantrik* has become part of it. Let's go to bed, close our eyes. We are not supposed to see or know what lies ahead. It's better not to know; then whatever the curse—for there will be a curse—will not be on our heads."

The *tantrik* walked like a black shadow toward the weaver's hut. Whispering mantras into the coconut, he walked on, almost floated. He blew over the water inside the fruit three times as he reached the weaver's hut. Closing his eyes, breathing deeply, he waited till that uncertain hour of hazy darkness between night and dawn. And then he called out.

The weaver's son, sleeping peacefully on a mat near the door, heard a strange sound. The voice of his beloved aunt who lived in the next village. She had taken care of him till she had been married off. His own mother was too weak and frail to take care of the children. He opened his eyes and sat up. She was calling, "Come out child, I haven't seen you for so long. Come out and see what I've brought for you. Your favorite sweets." His parents and sisters were sound asleep. Hadn't they heard? Again, "Come out child. Can you hear?" So plaintive that voice.

"Yes, I hear you," he cried out, "I hear you." He felt a burning ball of light leap out with his voice and vanish in the darkness.

His mother and father woke up with a start to see their only son clutch his throat, writhe, then lie still.

The *tantrik* clapped the top of the coconut back on the fruit as soon as the weaver's son answered, covering it, almost resealing it. "Now the soul is in here," he said to the fading night. "Once more my art has proved to be perfect." He returned smiling to the mansion. The *zamindar's* son was woken up gently. "Drink this." The *tantrik* held the coconut before his lips. "Drink up. Not a drop should be spilled." The *zamindar's* son drank all of the coconut water and collapsed on his bed. The *zamindar* howled and fell to his knees.

"You've killed him, too!"

"If he wakes up in ten hours, then he will live," the *tantrik* said. "I can make no promises My work is done. Give me the ten goats you promised, and the fifty gold coins."

After seven hours the *zamindar's* son made a moaning sound. He asked for water. Within the hour he sat up, asked for food. The *zamindar* ran to the kitchen himself, too amazed to yell for his servants, and brought back some warm milk. His son asked for meat, fish, rice, honey, mangoes . . .

It was as if the world had stopped and then started spinning the other way. It was as if the sun was rising in the West and setting in the East. The *zamindar's* son started to walk around his room, out into the courtyard, even step outside the gates, throw his arms up, smile at the sky, the mango trees.

The weaver and his wife and daughters carried their boy to the edge of the forest and set him on the pyre the *zamindar's* men had prepared for the *zamindar's* son. "Lucky we don't have to buy wood," the weaver muttered to his wife. The villagers gathered to watch the flames leap and curl round the limp form on the pyre. The *zamindar* sent more sandalwood, flowers, butter, and oil to the weaver. "It is a sad thing," he said to the weaver, "to lose the only son. But who can prevent fate, who knows who God will keep, who He will take? It's all a grand illusion. A sleight of hand you could say. A trick of something dark, uncontrollable. Take comfort in your daughters. I will provide you with their dowry. Don't lose heart."

Meanwhile the *zamindar*'s son ran around the courtyard singing, laughing.

"You must resume your studies," the *zamindar* told his son. "I will send for your tutor again. It's been a year and a half and you have a lot of catching up to do. You will be a lawyer when you grow up. And you have to be educated, trained, you have to go to the university. We'll be rich again once you're established." So the old tutor was brought back from Calcutta, and he greeted his pupil with tears in his eyes.

"How much better you look. I haven't forgotten how clever you were—are—how refined your manners, how princely your bearing. You will make a fine lawyer."

But the *zamindar*'s son puzzled his tutor and his father as days went by. He seemed to have lost interest in the classics, in mathematics, in philosophy, in science, in all books. He looked at the mango trees while his tutor lectured. His hesitant walk changed to a lazy heavy-footed stride. His frail, slight body developed muscles, became broader, tougher, while his face, throat, hands, and feet remained thin, small, delicate. His gestures lost their gentleness and became bold, aggressive, even coarse. He began to eat with both hands, stuffing food into his mouth eagerly, hungrily, dropping part of it on his clothes, part of it around his plate. He licked his fingers after eating while his father and tutor stared with their mouths open. The servants couldn't stop whispering when the boy was seen stealing sweets from the pantry. One morning the *zamindar*'s son couldn't be found anywhere on the premises. The tutor spotted him suddenly and screamed in shock.

There he was, swinging from the mango tree, hands and feet hooked around a thick branch. He swung violently for a few minutes, shaking ripe and unripe mangoes off the tree, then leaped down and landed on the ground on all fours. He looked up at his father and the rest of the household with a wide, imbecilic grin on his face. He scratched his armpits and his bare chest vigorously, spat on the ground, and clambered up the tree again. The *zamindar* let out a moan and passed out.

"I never understood it—the madness that took over, after the operation, the kidney put in right here," Gyan pats his left hipbone. "I got desperate to meet this man who had given me back my life. Don't know why. Wanted to know him, know what he knew, learn his life. My father refused to locate the person. Learn the trade, he said. Need someone to work with me, take over. But I was going mad from the smell of paddy fields swirling around me constantly. It came from nowhere, everywhere, brick walls, flowers, my hands, windowsills, clothes, cement blocks. I dreamed of living in mud huts, wading knee-deep in paddy fields. I smelled food, all kinds, fabulous smells, fantastic images of kormas, cutlets, pulaos, couldn't understand, wanted to touch cloves, cinnamon, explored kitchens, ours, other people's, secretly, when no one was around, smelling, touching, tasting, even mustard oil, salt, turmeric, spinach. It was as if I were rediscovering another life, like reincarnation, remembering who I might have been, becoming that other all over again.

"And there was this searing pain all the time in the middle of my palms, as if something was burning into my flesh, constantly. Water, lotions, ice, nothing would get rid of it.

"So gripping this burning pain tightly in my fists I asked the engineers about their lunches—to see them, feel the chapatis, the dal, the rice, try to figure out if the dal was the right texture—instead of inquiring about the structure of buildings, or testing the quality of cement, or checking out how reinforced the concrete really was. My father sent me reeling with a blow to my head one day when he caught me checking out a bewildered laborer's *rotis*. I had completely forgotten about the shipment of bricks, forgotten to make the payment. When my father asked about the bricks, I asked him to look at the *rotis*. He went crazy. After flooring me with the blow, he began to bang his head against the half-constructed foundation of the building."

For a few days, the *zamindar*'s son refused to come indoors. He stayed in the treetops, slept under trees. The villagers came to watch. Possessed, they muttered under their breath, or mad, or both. What's happened to my son? the *zamindar* wondered. "Perhaps he's just exercising," some of his men said, offering helpful shrugs. "Newly developed muscles, sudden revival." The *zamindar* stood under the mango tree and begged his son to come down and back into the house. "My golden boy, hope of my life, come and sit with me, come share these sweets with me. I'll give you anything you want, only come down here." The boy grinnned at him and made odd squealing noises. The *zamindar* beat his chest, slapped his head, and appealed to all the gods and goddesses.

A few days later, the *zamindar*'s son left the trees and ran down the red dirt road that led to the weaver's hut. The door was ajar, so he went in. Two girls sat in a corner playing with shells. On seeing him, they screamed and huddled together. He made whimpering noises at first and went toward them. They shrank against the mud wall. "Why do you look at me with fear, my sisters?" he asked. "Where are my mother and father?" The girls screamed and threw pots and pans at him. He ran out with a bleeding forehead, straight into a group of villagers who had gathered before the hut hearing the screams and the din of crashing pots and pans. "Where is the weaver and his wife?" the *zamindar*'s son demanded, wiping his forehead with the back of his hand.

"Why do you care?" they asked him sullenly. "Rich *zamindar*'s son, healthy and strong all of a sudden—what do you care?"

"The weaver's wife, my sister—so ill she was—do you know?" The village potter came up to him, shaking his fist. "Soon after they cremated their son, she gasped, choked, and fell on the smoking ashes. Dead. Just like that. Shock, grief, call it what you will. And then the weaver gets drunk and wanders into the forest. We found him this morning, his body swollen, black from a cobra's bite. So what are you going to do about it, eh, rich man's suddenly healthy son? Why have you been climbing trees like my nephew?"

"We spit on the *zamindar*," the *dhobi* said and spat at the boy's feet. "These two girls left here in this hut with no food, no money. Rich people think they can do what they like, yes? Poor people's lives, yes?"

The villagers spat at the *zamindar*'s son, kicked him, threw stones at him. He ran into the hut for shelter, only to be beaten out by the girls. "I'll take care of the girls," he yelled at the villagers.

"Oh? And will you perform the last rites for the weaver and his wife, too?"

The boy ran back to the mansion and asked his father's men to get sandalwood. He had the men carry the logs to the edge of the forest. There they built a pyre just like the one they had built before, right next to the ashes of the weaver's son. The *zamindar*'s son carried the swollen bodies of the weaver and his wife to the pyre and laid them on it side by side. The brahmin from the temple sprinkled holy water, flowers, incense, said the necessary mantras, and the *zamindar*'s son lit a torch and circled the pyre. He touched the bodies three times with the torch, the eyes, the mouth, very lightly, then lit the pyre. The dry logs exploded into flames. The *zamindar*'s son had to jump back, for the flames leaped viciously at him as if they wanted to brand him for some terrible mysterious crime. In the roaring pyre he heard voices crying out—Why why why? He covered his face and fell to his knees, screaming in fear and confusion. He felt a distilled melting pain, felt his own flesh scorch and burn, shrivel, melt off his bones, then his bones burn with a white heat down to white ash. He was nothing, nothing, just a handful of ash, and he stood there before the screaming flames holding in his cupped hands the hot white ash of himself.

After five hours of tending the flames, making sure every particle was reduced to ashes, the boy gathered the ashes in a clay pot and went to the mountain stream two miles outside the village. He dropped the ashes in the running water, bathed, then returned to the village without looking back. He shaved his head, as a son is supposed to after the death of his parents. For twelve days he ate fruit and boiled rice and slept outside the weaver's hut in the dusty yard.

The girls watched him cautiously for four days. Their aunt arrived to take care of them, the same aunt who had taken care of the three children until the day she got married. She cried when she saw the *zamindar*'s son, telling the girls their brother had returned from the dead and they should welcome him back. Hari had played a strange game with them, but they should be thankful all the same. They allowed him to enter their hut and eat with them.

The *zamindar,* beside himself with confusion and anguish, sent baskets of fruit and rice to the weaver's hut for his son. So they all ate well. On the thirteenth day, the *zamindar*'s son invited the brahmins for the final ritual. The brahmins, thrilled with the feast after the rituals and the gifts of clothes and money, blessed the boy, assured the villagers that a miracle had taken place, and that they should all try to accept fate and live in peace.

The *zamindar* fell at his son's feet and implored him to return with him to the mansion now that all rites had been observed. He swore to provide for the girls. "But you seem like a stranger to me," his son said to him. "I don't know what has happened. But I want to live here with them. Go away now, old man." The *zamindar* went back to his house shaking. He sat quietly for a long time by his son's empty bed. Then he ran into the forest to find the *tantrik* again. But instead he found a shattered, empty temple whose stones echoed his desperate footfalls.

Back in his house, he lay in his bed for days, refusing food and water. His men went to the weaver's house and pleaded with his son to come back home or his father would die. He came back with them to see his father. "I'll spend time here, too," he said to the *zamindar*. "But I cannot be everything you want me to be. I'll be what I am now." So the boy divided his time between the mud hut and the mansion, clumsily working the loom half the day and falling asleep while the tutor droned on about tax laws. He regained some of his old imperious gestures, a toss of the head, a shrug, and lost some of the coarseness he had developed. He went to bed at night overwhelmed by a fatigue that made him cry silently into his pillow.

"I couldn't live with this anymore. My father banging his head against that wall, screaming hoarsely. And this madness that was draining me—oh, the tiredness! Couldn't sleep. Just dreamed endlessly. From one pain to another—a strange journey.

"Something would have to change if I were to carry on. I told my father I was leaving, didn't want any part of his business, didn't want to be their son. I bribed the doctor who had done the transplant and got Gopal's name and the name of his village.

"My other life took over after that. Gopal understood."

It was the *zamindar's khansama* who realized the boy's dilemma. He is not going to be a lawyer, nor is he going to get anywhere with the weaving. And the boy is used to a soft life. "Come here," he called to the boy one day and took him into the kitchen. "I'll fix it for you," he said to the boy. "You listen and you watch. You are, after all, a *zamindar's* son, an aristocrat by birth. Strange things have happened—evil things have happened. Now you are paying for your father's misguided actions. You may have changed somewhat, but it is impossible for you to become a weaver's son—you do not possess a weaver's hands. Weaving is not for you, and alas, due to other people's evil actions, the law courts are not for you either. I have seen you grow up, made your favorite dishes for fourteen years. I have eaten your father's salt for twenty-five years. Now I see you cry at the loom and fall asleep before your tutor. Tears come to my eyes. Life is hard. I want to help you so that life is not too hard for you, so that you find a place in a rich man's house, so that you're treated kindly, with respect. Therefore I will teach you all my secrets, teach you to be the prince of cooks."

So began his new life. Surprisingly, he turned out to be a magnificent cook. *"Hai Allah!"* the *khansama* would gasp from time to time. "You were born for this. Perhaps all that has happened was meant to happen so you would become what you were meant to be—the prince of cooks! Who can tell how destiny unfolds."

Slowly, the weaver's daughters grew fond of him. The two girls, one eight, the other twelve, liked him in spite of all the vicious talk about the *zamindar.* The boy was sweet, gentle, soft spoken. He didn't pull their hair, hit them, or torment them the way their late brother used to. He listened attentively to everything they said, did whatever they asked him to do, including climbing down the dark well to retrieve balls the two girls tossed in for fun and just to test if this new brother was as compliant as he seemed. Stoically, he allowed them to torment him. The younger sister, more outspoken than the timid older one, declared she preferred this brother to the last one. The older girl looked down demurely at her toes, but nodded hesitantly, all the same.

Their aunt began to spoil him like she used to spoil her late nephew. Since she had been widowed recently by cholera, and her only daughter had died a few days after birth, she settled into her old family with a vengeance. Twisting her long dark hair into a coil on top of her head, "What?" she'd hiss, coming up behind him while he reached up toward the baskets hanging from the ceiling to steal the sweets. Her false sternness would vanish at the sight of fear sweeping across his face. "Here," she'd say, bringing the sweets down, "here," and feed him, ruffle his hair, hug him as if he really were the boy she had cared for for eleven years and loved fiercely.

The villagers—after much discourse with the brahmins—regarded him with a mixture of disbelief and awe as if he wasn't quite real, quite flesh and blood. They touched their foreheads when they passed him in the streets, wondering if he were a curse or a blessing.

Accepted, even loved, the boy wasn't allowed to escape guilt. "Not really your fault," the doting aunt said to him. "But things have happened. And there's no man in this family to take care of the girls. They have to be married off, their dowries provided. They must feel assured that there is always someone, a brother, really, that they can turn to in times of despair. Husbands, these days, are not quite reliable. Can you promise to be there, to help, really help, if there is ever a need?" The boy nodded vigorously of course, of course, of course. He felt his palms burn with that white ash again. When the cool spring water didn't wash the burning away he clenched his fists and held tightly to that melting pain. Never to lose it now, never, this desperate hot ash that fused him with a misery he couldn't understand.

The *zamindar* grew thin and weak year by year. Drought ruined the crops, and famine drove the villagers to beg in the city streets. They cursed the *zamindar* for their suffering. The *zamindar* commissioned a priest to stay at his house and read the Upanishads and the Gita to him morning and evening. "Did I sin?" he would mutter to himself constantly. "Did my desperate action bring about this famine? Are we cursed? Is there no forgiveness?"

One night he passed away in his sleep. His son performed the same rites as he had done for the weaver and his wife and fed the brahmins one more time. He sold the mansion and all the property and estates to the government and received very little money. He distributed the money among the servants and the weaver's two girls and their aunt. The villagers threw stones at him, asked him to sacrifice himself to Kali and get rid of the famine.

The *khansama* took him by the hand. "Come with me to the city," he said. "I'll place you with a good family, and then I'll return to my village in the south." The *khansama* was very particular about where the boy should work. For five months they explored many households until the *khansama* found the right one. The boy, eighteen then, became part of a wonderful family and worked for them for over thirty years. He visited his village once a year. He sent the girls money, even got them married.

Then one day, he got a letter from his aunt. "I have found husbands for your sisters' daughters," she had written, "but we don't have the money for the dowry." When he went to his village and sat with his aunt she laid it down quite plainly. "We need thirty thousand to marry off my two grandnieces. Their fathers were poor farmers, their prospective husbands are poor merchants' sons. The girls will be climbing up socially—and that's a good thing considering everything. Now their fathers didn't make any provisions—how could they? One fellow trod on a snake in the dark; the other wanted to get rich by growing opium and the government has spies everywhere. Won't get out of jail for the next ten years, that one." She caught his hands and pleaded, "We have to get the girls married—thirty thousand for dowry and other expenses—they don't have a pair of gold earrings between them—floods, famine, had to sell, you know, I've given my word—we'd never live down the shame— their lives will be ruined. What to do, tell me?" She struck her forehead twice. "Fate fate . . . but perhaps fate is in our favor, nephew. Right now," she said, an excited gleam entering her old foggy eyes, "a contractor is looking for a kidney for his son. Some men came to our village and propositioned us for kidneys. Thirty thousand, they said. So I wrote to you at once. You lived because my nephew's soul was given to you. You can sacrifice a kidney for the second life you received. I wouldn't have asked this of you—but then, we have quietly accepted everything that has happened. We have never asked you for anything. Whatever you gave us you did out of your own free will. We are all grateful. But now there is a need. Who else can we turn to?"

He looked at his hands. Every day of his life, of his new life, he had felt hot ash in his hands. To burn away the ash—to perform, finally, the very last rites, and be free at last.

I could believe anything in this kitchen. The smells and smoke lured me to a different planet where mystery was the essence of living and that hot white ash the core of life.

I saw Gopal lying on a mat on the floor, in pain, thin, frail, just like that boy had once been—

"Are you here then out of some odd sense of gratitude, obligation, guilt?" I ask Gyan. I see myself face to face with Gopal, shaking him, screaming, Why why why?

"At first that's how I felt." Gyan inclines his head, pauses. "But not anymore. That hideous feeling just drained away after a year. I feel no connection to the past anymore, to myself in that hospital bed, to my family, to Gopal, to those days in his hut. That's all gone, like cutoff hair. Don't know why. I like being here. I enjoy cooking. I do love living here with your family."

I see Gopal again, tired, looking older day by day, as if the thin stream of the water of life that boy had drunk had been drained out with his kidney. He left two days later, and after three weeks, sent a letter saying he wouldn't be coming back: he was getting old and tired, he wanted to grow rice, live in his village. I left for America two months later. Five years after I left, my father called to tell me about Gopal's death. Poor health, typhoid, bad doctors, finally kidney failure. I stayed away for eight years, unable to return, to face a Gopal-less home.

"So you said you would marry? Raise a family? Go back to your family?"

"My father disowned me when I left for Gopal's village. He won't take me back, and I don't want to go back. But I think I will marry. After I make some money. I want to build a house, a very small house—" Gyan stops, smiles, draws a house in the air with his hands. "Then only will the woman I want to marry marry me."

"And where will you build this house?"

"Oh, not very far away from here. In a small village in Haryana. Next year I will make the money I need for this house."

"I see."

"I met a doctor through that man at the blood bank, an eye doctor who's going to arrange for this money. I'll be admitted to a hospital for an eye problem. Nobody'll know anything. They'll give me eighty thousand—cash. They'll take my left cornea."

I took a deep breath. "If you donate a cornea," I said slowly, as slowly as he had pronounced *cornea*, "you will go blind in one eye."

"I can live with one eye. They both see the same thing anyway." He waved his hand, flicked back his hair.

"You absolutely must not do this." I said, my voice hard. "It is wrong, illegal. You will not donate your eye while you live. Do you understand?" He looked at me puzzled. "You are not starving, Gyan. You are not on the streets. Why do you have to do this?"

"My wife-to-be's uncle has sold a cornea. Eighty thousand rupees! He now owns a TV, a scooter, and a refrigerator. The gentleman who bought the cornea for his daughter was very generous. He even gave them two gold watches. My wife-to-be's friend's cousin and his wife have both given a kidney each and—"

"What's the big deal about a—" I stopped. I understood perfectly. I didn't have a clue. "You said yourself that you felt you had taken Gopal away from us by taking his kidney. How can you talk about corneas and kidneys so blithely now?"

"But this is different. I'm fine now. Gopal and all that—that's in the past. I don't even feel that burning in my hands anymore, except just once, the day you arrived. But it's gone now. So." There was anger in his voice and scorn. "I've burned the past away in this kitchen, you could say, performed the last rites to end one life. I'm going to start a new life now, truly free this time. Marry someone I want to marry, like I see them do in the movies."

"Don't do this, Gyan."

"Tea? Coffee? Sandwich? Cake?" he inquires with a weak smile. I get up and leave the kitchen.

The elections are over. Changes will sweep the country, I hear, like the cyclones sweep Bangladesh, Orissa. Gyan continues to take his daily dose of immunosuppressants and steroids. I think of that boy in that village climbing mango trees one summer afternoon. "Your story or mine?" I hear Gopal's laughing voice clearly. Who's to tell? And does it matter?

I wonder where Gyan's left eye will go. I wonder how it will perceive the order of things. Will it see the world the way the *zamindar* saw it when his son lay dying? Will it see an eye for a house, TV, scooters, a kidney for a daughter's dowry? Will it envision a new and wondrous world where special healthy people are kept in exclusive communes and bred for dazzling eyes, glowing skins, and shining kidneys? That stormy ball of light burns through my head. I feel hot white ash melting my palms. I see Gyan walking toward a river holding smoking ash in his cupped hands. A very different ash—or a very different Gyan, I don't know. He doesn't feel the scorching pain. He walks on smiling toward golden rice fields and roaring muddy rivers rising up to swallow the land. The ash in his hands implodes, particles rush closer and closer, density increasing, mass reducing to a small white ball with a dark spot that contracts with light. I'm afraid to look out of this kitchen window all of a sudden. A nauseating, gnawing fear of seeing a tall, lean shadow and a hand holding out a green coconut metamorphosing to a steel scalpel.

OPERATION MONSOON

"Terrorists are displaced in every sense," Jean V reads from his "seminal" paper on environment and terrorism. He frowns slightly at the faint clanging of slot machines and whirring of roulette wheels. With a well-practiced shrug at the background casino noise that refuses to be fully suppressed despite the soundproofing of the auditorium, he continues, "A terrorist's sense of place is a Dali landscape with no real sense of self. They exist in hyperreality. As in cyberspace, a lethal fractalization of the self occurs and any sense of shared destiny is replaced by a vague notion of mission. . . ."

Dizzy and mildly nauseous from a 6 A.M. flight, I stumble out of the convention center of the Hotel Tropicana. I had to wake up at three in the morning to make the flight from Logan. I am still dazed by the onslaught of slot machines and giant TV screens as billboards at the Las Vegas airport.

A long corridor stretches in front of me, leading to the casino floor, noisy with music and slot machines. In the sunken restaurant to the side, a bird show is going on. Macaws, cockatoos, African eagles, doing tricks for the gaming diehards at breakfast. My room won't be ready till one in the afternoon, they told me as soon as I arrived in the shuttle from the airport, through a nagging grey drizzle. Where are all the lights and fanfare of this money-spinning city? In broad daylight, it is rather ordinary. The rain hasn't managed to break the intense spell of the dry summer heat.

Where am I? The rest of the world disappeared into that shuttle's muddy wake. I feel stranded. No self, no destiny, just some vague mission? Everything is a blur. A flash scent hits me suddenly. That rainsmell of jasmine and litchis and diesel fumes, of Calcutta waiting, on the verge of rain. . . . A gorgeous Eurasian waitress offers me a tall frothy, fruity concoction, the Tropicana special of the day.

From the end of the corridor an enormous segmented TV screen glows at me. It's an ad for a newly released book, *Operation Monsoon: Interview with a Terrorist.* A striking black-and-white cover: a series of superimpositions, negatives on negatives, an averted face, a gun, a prison cell, newspaper headlines, a van on fire, all through a screen of rain. I blink twice to make sure I'm not imagining it all, especially the author's name. Beverley Newton did not tell me about this new book of hers. The publisher is a well-known mainstream press. I had received only a short e-mail from Beverley as I was preparing for this conference: "I'll be there, too. Let's try to meet for a change. We should talk. Rain check, remember? My new stuff is all about him. And I still can't figure out, even after twenty years, why he took all his clothes off in the middle of your living room. What that meant. . . ."

What that meant. *As if a magic lantern threw nerves in patterns on a screen.* . . . Through the tinted glass this drizzle outside shimmers silver much like the Calcutta sky before the rains. And this conference, like her intrusion into my life some twenty years ago, is about her all over again. This time, about the launch of her big book, kept secret all these years.

As always, I close my eyes, shut out the dull monotone of décor and weather, and return to that first thunderstorm that detonates the monsoons and splits apart the sun-dazed Calcutta sky. And as always, I see him, whenever I think of rain, ecstatic, lying on the terrace, surrendering to the rain.

"I still can't figure out . . . even after twenty years . . . why. . . ." I make my way to the ladies room. *You believe what you choose to believe,* he had said. Then one by one, the shirt, the jeans, the underwear, and that intensity of darkening rain clouds in his eyes, and in almost a whisper, *This is the first step, and they ask you and they ask you what is the truth, and you want the hard cement floor to crack under your feet, tear open, so you can hide hide hide, but it doesn't, so you close your eyes and dream of rain.*

When you bring on the rain, everything changes, my grandmother had said. It's not the same place anymore. The rain takes over.

This conference, the news of her book—like stepping on a land mine. Something you've tried not to think about for years suddenly explodes all around you.

June 1978: the flying shrapnel of actions and words springs up in my head, connected, yet unconnected, and all I see before my eyes is the blur of torrential showers, the flash of lightning, and eyes that smile, wink, and vanish into the rain.

June 1978: soaked to the skin by the Calcutta rain, eyes pleading earnest behind glasses, straggly brown hair pulled painfully back in a ponytail, Beverley Newton stands at the door clutching a broken umbrella, demanding *the goods*. The goods. We all wanted that. From the moment he blew into our carefully planned world. Holding our breath we had waited to find out what would happen to *us* when he arrived, not to him, just us.

I enter the ladies room, holding my breath again. What kind of goods was I? What kind of goods was she after all these years? Why had I come? For the same reasons that had brought her to our doorstep? I need to put my luggage down and sit and resume breathing.

It is quite lovely, this ladies room. A sanctuary, a charming old-world powder room, a secluded antechamber to the stalls. I drop my bag and laptop and stretch out on the incredibly long and comfortable mauve satin couch. The relief! Another stunning Eurasian waitress glides in and makes a call on her cell phone. Indeed, these Eurasian waitresses are the only glamorous creatures in this hotel. Molded spandex, flounced satin miniskirts, spangled tights. Interestingly, only a week ago I saw this hotel, Tropicana, in an episode of *Angel*. Very glitzy, with attractive people winning lots of money, and Las Vegas glittering and glowing all around them. But as I entered the hotel half an hour ago, it looked smaller, duller, and except for the waitresses in their sparkly clothes, all the people were fat, middle-aged or older, and anything but glamorous. This is not the Las Vegas I had expected. (So the ladies room is a relief. It reminds me of my mother's bathroom in Calcutta, a refuge in so many instances.) So much for expectations. Had he lived up to mine, my terrorist? Now Beverley calls him *hers*. Delusions.

That's what the department secretary indicated when I was printing out copies of my paper for this conference. Delusion*al*, to be precise, for an economics professor to deliver a paper at a conference on

"Terrorism." But economics, particularly Third World economics, has become multidisciplinary. We have returned to the ethos of Marx and Smith; we are philosophers, sociologists, political scientists, ethicists, and literary stylists, as well as economists! My own paper reflects on this shift—postmodernism's impact on all the social sciences. Questions of narrative and cultural values have a direct bearing on an economic system, don't they? In one of Beverley's earlier e-mails, in which she again urged me to explore Women's Studies or Cultural Studies—she flung Weber's famous treatise on Protestantism and Capitalism at me. A new generation of economists are more anthropologists than mathematicians, she insisted. And are you not one of them?

So here we are, Hotel Tropicana, casinos, terrorism, and all postmodern, post-everything, but am I post-Beverley yet? For over ten years, we have exchanged hostile e-mails; attended some of the same conferences, but made sure we never met; passed snide remarks to each other's acquaintances about each other's work. Beverley had published many articles and a long, boring academic book on terrorism in India. Painstakingly researched, but without any mention of the terrorist in question—the terrorist who now makes his debut, resurrected in this flashy book of hers, *Operation Monsoon*.

I am determined to face her this time, to force something, but I'm not quite sure what. She has decided to meet with me as well, and I can probably hazard a guess as to why. In her head I still hold the key to the great common mystery in our lives: *her* terrorist. Do I? I take out my wallet, and draw from it a piece of folded paper. It is old and worn. I look at it for a few seconds then put it back. And what do I want? Some kind of an apology, perhaps, some admission of guilt, defeat? I want to see this woman humbled. I want to throw her, not in a dungeon, but in an inescapable labyrinth forever.

But here she is, with her book jacket gigantically displayed, the heroine of a renegade movement. Ms. Marx pirouetting on the roulette table!

I get up, change my clothes, wash up. I can't stay here for the next three hours, waiting for my room to be ready, while Beverley Newton takes her bow.

Inside the convention center of Hotel Tropicana, people are waiting for the next session. Everyone has a scarf or a hat or a badge representing some subversive organization or another. A sleek blond head breaks away from the crowd and rushes to me, grabs my hands. "My God! You look just the *same,* except, my *God!* You look strangely, androgynously *like him.* Where *have* the twenty years gone? You don't *look* any older. I hope I don't look anywhere *near* forty-eight. Isn't this marvelous?" Her thin, pencilled eyebrows go up, and she gives me a frosted peach smile—the hot color this summer. Beverley Newton has shed her round glasses. Her eyes are a brilliant green instead of that original light brown. Her mousy hair now shines on her head like a pale gold helmet. Her face is subtly made up; her nails, French manicured. In her pale green Chanel suit she looks unnaturally elegant, ready to make a speech at some important fund-raising dinner. "I've done it," she smiles triumphantly. "I've *got him down* in black and white. Given him a voice. I have made the subaltern speak! And, my dear, I have got myself *an image."*

I'm speechless, so she continues. "This is a secret conference—well, everybody *knows* about it, but only a select few have been invited, the cutting-edge academics. We're examining terrorism and bringing out my book—that's why the conference is called *Operation Monsoon* as well. The time of year too—after all it's raining to drown the earth over there now, isn't it? We're doing brilliant work. The presentations are just fabulous. Jean V is here, and the Time Band. You'll see. This conference is *it.* Like a terrorist operation, we're hiding out here and putting together and sharing brilliant establishment-shaking discourses. "See there!" Beverley points at two men in dark suits. "FBI! That's how much of a stir we're creating. Hah! Let's get our seats. Jean V is about to expand on his paper on environment, on hyperreality, on fractalization. Forget Foucault!"

Contexts, contexts, so important, who is situated where. . . . "I've been *waiting* for you to arrive," Beverley whispers in my ear. "Must make up, join forces. Hey, no grudges after all these years, I hope? Sorry I lost my temper back then, and in spite of our vile e-mails over the years—but you *do understand?* I felt I had lost everything. We must talk later. Something really *big."*

That flash scent hits me again from nowhere. No, not her Shalimar.

"I'm *delighted* you're here," Beverley whispers again. "You'll enjoy the setting. After all, you're a living part of this. This is how the silent receive voices, buried histories are transformed to future events."

"The beginning is irrelevant, you mean?" I snap. I think it's the heat. The air-conditioning must not be working very well in this room with its nauseating color scheme of peach, mauve, and uncoordinating shades of purple. The strong fluorescent lighting suffuses everyone with an ashen pallor.

"He will arrive at any moment. Just wait, wait a bit."

And we had waited, for hours, twenty years ago, for him to arrive.

"He will arrive on the six-thirty flight and I'll pick him up on my way back," my father had said before leaving for work. While we waited, almost in a stupor, like Calcutta, heat stunned by the summer of 1978, six policemen with automatic weapons arrived at four and took positions around the house. Two at the gates as you entered the drive, two before the front steps leading to the porch, two at the back, near the servants' quarters. Earlier that day, three men from the special investigations branch had come to tap our three phone lines: one, the regular line; the second, the restricted line; and the third, my father's personal line, the hot line to the Chief Minister, the Governor, a few other state secretaries, ministers, and the Commissioner of Police. My mother, my sister, and I sat quietly and waited for our cousin, the terrorist, to arrive.

"Wonder if he likes cauliflower cooked with peas?" my mother asked anxiously. "Ram's made it too spicy today."

"Food will be the first thing on his mind, I'm sure," I said, rolling my eyes. "Do you remember what he looks like?" My mother shook her head. No, of course not. I ought to remember.

Six years earlier, I had peeped into the intensive-care unit of the most exclusive private hospital in Calcutta, while my father talked with the doctors. An oxygen tent. A shadow form hooked to tubes. He was then twenty-two, finishing a masters in physics at Calcutta University. He had been involved with the Naxalite movement. 1972, with Calcutta in the never-ending grip of bombings, murders, arrests, executions. Riots, protests, tear gas, all-night curfews, police massacres, horror stories of torture and death in police custody. He had been caught, spent seven months in prison. No serious charges at that time; he had flung a few homemade bombs. And then he went underground. Disappeared for three and a half months. He was arrested again, while raiding an armed vehicle with one of the leaders of the movement who had become a legend in West Bengal for eluding the police and who took credit for most of the terrorist attacks on government institutions and officials.

A call from my grandfather had rushed us over to his crumbling, palatial, north Calcutta mansion. My grandfather was lying back in his enormous, ebony chaise longue, all crisp in starched white cotton, gently pulling on his old hookah. A woman sat next to my grandfather. She didn't look up when we entered. She sat very still, her face partly veiled by her cotton sari, her hands resting on her lap. "Call the Police Commissioner," my grandfather growled at my father. "Get the boy out of the prison hospital and into a trauma center right now. He's been in custody for three days. They won't let anyone see him, not even an outside doctor. Let's hope he's alive."

So my father had picked up the phone and called the Commissioner, and within the hour, this "boy" was transported to the trauma unit of Bellevue with four of the best surgeons in India retuning his body. My mother had sat with this very special "boy's" mother in the waiting area, while I had followed my father to the intensive-care unit where our patient was finally wheeled in and hooked up. "Don't come in," Dad had said before going inside to talk to the doctors. I heard whispers, caught broken phrases. "Multiple pelvic fractures . . . pleural rupture with laceration of the right lower and middle lobes . . . severe rectal trauma . . . splenic rupture with hemo-peritoneum . . . second-degree electrical burns . . . scrotal and upper thoracic. . . ." Words that had no meaning for me. I was eleven. Through the glass doors I saw figures with white masks hovering around the oxygen tent and fiddling with tubes and knobs, and the erratic fluorescent flashing graph on the EKG monitor.

I had gone back to the waiting area and sat down next to my mother. "Who is he?" I asked, somewhat sullenly. I was tired and hungry again. It was two in the morning. My sister was comfortably asleep at home, thumb in her mouth.

"He's your cousin."

"How? From where?" My voice was bitterly sulky. I gave the other woman a dark look. She sat as still as ever, her face half veiled.

"Manik is her son," my mother said. "She's your grandfather's cousin's daughter. So she's your father's cousin, and Manik, yours."

One of those numerous unknown relatives of ours, distantly related, like they say, by a chromosome here, a neuron there. My grandfather supported a whole horde of them. "Manik's father teaches in the Kalyani High School," my mother was saying, "and he's disowned Manik ever since he joined the Naxalites."

That was the big Marxist revolution of the day. It had originated in the 1960s in a village called Naxalbari and spread through West Bengal and many parts of India. Thousands of college students now called themselves Naxalites and organized protests and rallies, rarely peaceful. Almost every day there were riots all over Calcutta. Government institutions were bombed, buses set on fire, and many attempted, and some successful, assassinations of people in power. Terrorists, they were called. Many regarded them with awe. There was a lot of talk about Naxalites at school. There were stories: how they eluded the police; how police spies became their supporters and joined them; how they carried cyanide capsules and would swallow them if they were caught; and if arrested and questioned, they never talked. There was a charisma about them that drew followers.

And now, I had a cousin who was a Naxalite. I sat up, my eyes widening.

"Are you feeling all right?" My mother touched my shoulder.

"I want to go home now. It really is past my bedtime."

"Well—" my mother let out an exasperated sigh. "Why did you make such a fuss about coming here with us? We wanted to send you home from your grandfather's."

Lying in bed later, hugging a pillow, I had tried to calm my breathing. Oh, was heaven any sweeter than Naxalites?

Next day at school, I had been surrounded. There are cousins, and there are cousins. As someone said, Calcutta has a new hero every day.

Manik had to spend two weeks in intensive care. Then a month and a half in a recovery clinic. Physical therapy took another six months. My father and his mother were the only people allowed to visit him.

A few weeks before Manik's release from the hospital, we gathered for another conference in my grandfather's house. There would be a trial after he came out, it seemed. Murder charges, assaults on police officers, vandalization of state property, possession of firearms, and a prior conviction. Enough to hang him. No hard evidence, except the raid on the armed vehicle. But he was a terrorist according to the law. My father sat down with the Police Commissioner and made a deal. Manik would leave the country the moment he came out of the clinic. He could never come back. And where would Manik go? Stanford. A friend of my father's was teaching there, and he had clout. So Manik had been driven straight to the airport from the hospital and put on a flight for California. Six years. He finished his masters and got a Ph.D. in physics.

For those six years I had fascinated my friends with stories about him. I re-created him from fantasy alone. "Somewhere between Byron and Shelley in personality," I declared to my school friends. Actually, I had no idea who Byron and Shelley were at that time, except that my other cousins would toss out those names and "romantic" and "radical" in the same breath. What did he look like? "James Dean." I had to imagine it all—what else could I do? He was my shadow warrior, and I had to reinvent him to make him my own special creature. He had given me special status among my friends.

After six years, the government relented and allowed him to reenter India for two weeks, to visit Calcutta, but he was to be kept under constant surveillance.

And so we sat waiting for this shadow from the past to reappear. My father had decided that Manik would stay with us for the two weeks. Manik's father didn't want to see him. His mother would come and visit him here. Besides, Dad at that point was Secretary for Home Affairs, so his word was law. The police wouldn't be able to harass Manik at our house. Dad was committed to protecting Manik, and I couldn't quite understand why. He laughed when I asked him that.

"What if he has done all those things they say he has? I know there wasn't actual evidence for all the charges, but still—"

"I always champion the underdog," Dad said. "That's all. Set up the room upstairs for him. He'll be able to walk around on the terrace since he can't leave the premises."

My friends were wearing me out with their curiosity. When could they meet him? they asked me every day for a month. So while we waited, I prayed desperately that Manik would be transformed into the creature of my stories by the time the plane landed in Calcutta. Some of my other cousins, who had their special grudges against me and my father—having been snubbed brutally somewhere in the unforgettable past—had curled their lips at my excitement. "Stanford—just like that. Fellowships, plane tickets—just like that. For a bloody criminal," yelped one such cousin. My twelve-year-old sister was the only one who remained disdainfully unconcerned, in spite of all of our excitement, or perhaps because of it. "Just another cousin," she rolled her eyes, tossed her pigtails, shrugged her skinny shoulders. "Just another guy." Hers was the ideology of *cool.*

I ran to the balcony as I heard the car pull in, but I could only see the top of his head, and a medium-size blue duffle bag. I ran back inside and sat down next to my mother and sister. We froze in a straight line. "Hello, hello." My father walked in, lazy, languid, a humorous gleam in his eyes, with Manik hesitant behind him. "What's this—rigor mortis? Looks like we'll need wrenches to loosen you people up."

One of the servants took his bag and went upstairs to deposit it.

"Oh, you must be tired, hungry." My mother was overdoing her concern.

I was paralyzed on the couch.

"Come on upstairs." Dad took him up to the terrace.

"Get up," my mother said. "Tell Ram to bring out the kababs and beer, and . . . and . . . a gin and lime for me." She sat down heavily on a footstool.

"You're wringing your hands," I snapped. "Stop it."

"It's . . . it's. . . ." Her voice trailed into a helpless sigh.

"We should have put some flowers in his room."

My mother looked at me. "What does he need flowers for? He's a . . . he's a. . . ."

"Criminal? Say it. That's what everyone's saying. And a criminal is going to stay with us for two weeks. Your reputation at the Bengal Club is shot."

My mother got up and went into the kitchen to find Ram. I looked down at my feet. I was taking it out on her. Why did I ever say James Dean? How would I transform him? And the flowers—we always put flowers in that room when we had guests. This time we had forgotten.

Throughout dinner I kept my eyes on my plate. Mom and Dad talked to him about Stanford. My sister finished her food quietly and disappeared to "work on her summer project." I racked my head for a good enough excuse to leave the table. I had just finished high school. This was my summer between two worlds, my summer of absolute freedom. The future was mine to choose, I felt. So I ate slowly to the white noise of their chatter. I tried not to look at him. Except twice, when he laughed. I'd have to keep my friends away from him somehow. When I was about to slip away from the table, Manik looked up and smiled. "You two didn't say a word. You're awfully quiet kids."

"I'm not a kid. I'm almost eighteen."

"Oh—I'm sorry. I didn't mean—"

"It doesn't matter what you mean."

"Pia!" Dad's voice was sharp. I got up and left.

"You're grounded," my mother called after me. "*Difficult*, you know," she apologized to Manik.

"Just a tad *difficult*—the jargon." Beverley steers me out with a wide smile. "Come on, let's go to the reception. Sometimes these brilliant people can get a bit opaque. Come now, we have to get to know each other *all over again*. We never really had a chance to do that. For so long I could only imagine what it would be like to backtrack and figure out what really went on, and what went on inside your head while he was there, and just to figure out what that *meant*, you know, *that*—"

"Beverley, Beverley, Beverley!" She's surrounded by sighs and gasps and arms. "What a coup! How did you corral all these stars into being here?"

"That Jean V—he doesn't look anything like his jacket photo. Must have air-brushed the nose and chin. But that teal silk suit—I could kill for it."

"Your book, my dear," a voice purrs. "We need a speech."

Amidst the clamor of voices, softer lighting, Beverley's eyes narrow. "It took me fifteen years to do this book," she smiles at the goateed owner of the purring voice. "You all know my former work, the more general one on terrorism in India. But this one," she looks at me for a moment, "is *special*. I have never experienced such conflicting theoretical issues as I did when putting together this book. And as I struggled, wrote, analyzed, revised, I *grew*, I *changed*. It was as if the rain that drowned me out twenty years ago in the muddy streets of Calcutta came back to reclaim me and unite me with *my terrorist*. I became almost one with him, one with the rain." She paused as someone gasped. "The force of it—of the rain—it will strike again once this book hits the stands, next week, and the world will know what it means to fuse with one's subject—the true nature of political experience. The sky splits apart in your head." She looks straight at me again. Her eyes are searching mine for vindication. Is this what we are here for—to vindicate ourselves for what we had done? To free ourselves?

Controlling a sudden urge to throw up, I run to that ladies room again. Potted gardenia sits on the vanity. A dislocated rainsmell trapped in polished stone.

The stone floor of the terrace glistened under the silver glow of gathering rain clouds as I walked toward Manik's room carrying a vase filled with gardenia and tuberose. There was an urgent rumbling all around. Calcutta, limp, sun broken, waited for the monsoon to hit. Any moment, any moment, the weather reports were buzzing.

The door to the terrace room was partially open. I knocked and entered. Manik was doing sit-ups on the floor in a pair of blue shorts and a cream T-shirt. I placed the vase on the table next to the bed. He gasped, "Seventy-five," and lay back on the floor.

"Flowers," he gasped again, surprise bringing laughter into his voice. "No one's ever brought me flowers!"

"We always put flowers in this room when we have guests."

"Ah. There's a definite distinction here."

"Yes. It has nothing to do with you."

"No, of course not," he said rather too timidly, with downcast eyes. Then looking up, "Parents giving you a hard time?" he asked with a quick smile.

"I'm grounded for a month."

"Great," said Manik. "Two of us under house arrest then. No solitary confinement."

"Were you in solitary?" It slipped out before I could think.

"Thanks for the flowers," he said. "They smell great."

"Did you always change the subject when you were questioned?"

"I can't wait for the rains to start. Can you smell it? The only thing I've really missed for the last six years is that first thunderstorm that sets the stage for the next three months." There was a strange excitement in his voice.

"Are you a Naxalite still? Are you going to get involved with all that shit again?"

"I've got frightful jet lag. I'm going to fall asleep again."

"You're really exasperating."

"So are you." I wanted to hit him.

His eyes narrowed. "What's going on here?" He got up and took a turn around the room, circling me. His voice was amused and puzzled. "You've never laid eyes on me. But you're resentful, yet curious. What could be going on?" He sat down on the bed and faced me. "What could it be . . . except perhaps disappointment?"

I was beginning to sweat.

"Oh, no," Manik let out a sigh. "You haven't made up stories about me, have you?"

I squared my shoulders, my face defiant.

"I am so sorry," Manik sighed again. "So sorry that I don't live up to expectations."

I took a deep breath. "Can you live up to my imagination?"

A heart-stopping clap of thunder made us both jump. And then the rain came like a thousand dams crashing.

"That—" Manik stared at the rain pounding on the terrace, "that is beyond imagination. Come outside. I have to feel that rain." He pulled me out onto the terrace. "And tell me what I have to do to live up to your imagination."

I dragged him back into the room. "I need to take a good look at your face."

"Don't worry about my face." Laughing, he propelled me out to the terrace again. We were soaked to the skin in seconds. "My chameleon face," Manik said, "will change and change and change. It's been rearranged so many times. I will be whatever you want, only let me stand in this very first rain of the season."

He had a pointed pixie face, and restless, bright, dark eyes with thick, long lashes. It was a soft face; not the face you would imagine on a man who had been charged with assassinations, bombings, mindless violence. I had imagined a beautiful face, perfect in its lines, invulnerable in its inscrutable intensity. Intense this face was, but due to the transparency of emotions that played across it, everything was laid bare as he flung himself into the rain. And lying on the terrace with his face raised to the thrashing shower, he was vulnerable to this, his own unique marvelous joy. "Just wish however you want me to look, how you want me to be," he shouted through the din of the rain, "and the rain will change me. Look—I'm changing already! The rain knows what you want. The rain never betrays or judges you. Just washes you clean. Of all pain. Of blood, bruises, fear, humiliation."

I kneeled and touched his face. "All that is over."

He closed his eyes and lay still. "Life's not over," he said softly.

I tried to pull him up. "We're soaking."

"Never go away from this rain again," he muttered, "never."

"Come on. Let's go in."

"This incredible smell," he was whispering, "this is what kept me going. This is what I'd hear, smell, feel, no matter what they did. Never go away from this rain again."

Finally I managed to wrench him up and drag him inside. He sat on the floor, hugging his knees, shivering from the blasts of the air conditioner, while I took his clothes off and dried him. Face pressed against his knees, he refused to uncurl from that position. It was difficult to get him into fresh clothes. "Come on, relax your legs," I said, letting escape an exhausted sigh. "Let's get these pants on."

"Go away."

"You can't sit here naked. Servants could walk in."

"Should you be here with some guy you don't know and who doesn't have a stitch on?" The delirium seemed to be vanishing. He sounded almost matter-of-fact.

I looked at his body with interest. He was slim, wiry, well toned, with ridgy surgical scars on his back and chest and middle. I tried to control the spasm that came up my throat painfully. I saw him again hooked to those tubes and wires in that oxygen tent.

He hurried into his clothes, combed his hair. "Well, what have you told your friends? Out with it. I'll need to know all of it if I'm to save you embarrassment."

"Shadow warrior," I said. "Like Kartikeya, the lord of the clouds. You never see him in battle. The clouds hide him. Or Jimmy Dean. You can choose."

"Why not just a plain terrorist: wretched and psychotic."

"Too boring. Besides," I added loftily, "terrorism is a term to denigrate any form of insurgence. It's a label manufactured by the dominant capitalist power to contain political opposition."

"Ah, yes of course. Mustn't forget that one."

"Pia!" My mother's voice came shrilly from downstairs. "Some of your friends are here."

"Don't come downstairs," I said to Manik. "I need to go dry off and change my clothes. I don't want them to find you."

"Found you!" Beverley squeezes my elbow. "Don't slip away again. I have to talk to you."

She must have practiced this smile a million times before her mirror. "One thing I must say to you: quit this capitalist department of yours and join Cultural or Women's Studies, teach about exploitive economics in the Third World, and feminist politics. Anyway, come have a drink and meet my friends. Judy's a performer and a poet. Brilliant reviews."

"I'm creating a performance about a terrorist," says Judy, playing with a dragon mask. "He's a psychotic sex maniac and masturbates into his aquarium while his angel fish swim around."

"Doesn't Judy have some imagination?" Beverly laughs. "She's performing tomorrow."

"I'm seriously thinking about exploitive economics," I say, "and feminist politics."

But no one, alas, is listening to me at this point. So rapt they are in each other's experience of the real thing and the avocado-salmon mousse.

"Tell us, Bev, about your first contact with the terrorist."

Beverley looks at me. "Should I now? It's all in my *book*. Nobody's going to read it if I *tell* everything." She makes a coquettish little moue. "But maybe just a little appetizer before the entrée? Well let's see ... it was quite a challenge to even get through the door, and then to get a peek ... well...." Her eyes roll. "When I first saw him, hmm, I think I almost giggled...."

Eight girls from school stood whispering and giggling in the living room, all waiting to catch the first glimpse. Some were balancing like tightrope walkers on six-inch heels, some in micro-miniskirts, some in saris that looked like cellophane. It took me a few seconds to realize that their faces were not bruised but made up. Eyelids and cheekbones had turned purple, mauve, copper, maroon; lips smeared red, brown, and even black; hair, so teased, tossed, curled, uncurled, let down, piled up, and so lacquered that even a typhoon couldn't have mussed them. They surrounded me, smiling like vampires. "Here," gushed one, fluttering eyelashes that were coming unstuck and handed me a box of Swiss chocolates. A rhinestone pin dropped into my hands next. Green lipstick, stick-on tattoos, the latest edition of *Playgirl,* a cricket ball autographed by Clive Lloyd and Pataudi, a black lace glove, a leather wristband with silver spikes, a crystal ball, and a wickedly studded black leather belt. I arranged the loot in a row on the carpet and rocked on my heels.

"Where is your special cousin?" A chorus.

I must kick these silly things aside and curl my mouth in disdain. Ah, but this wristband, this belt. "Sleeping," I said. "Jet lag."

"You could—" one wrinkled her newly pierced nose, "let us have a peek."

"I don't know." I frowned, looked away from the wristband. "I have to think about it." I walked around the items on the rug. "Well, you guys will have to remove your shoes so you don't sound like typewriters on speed."

Barefooted, giggling and shushing each other, they followed me up the stairs. As we stepped onto the terrace, "You'll have to be quiet," I said loudly. "He's sleeping. Jet lag." The door was closed. I peeped through the keyhole first. Manik got the hint.

"Hmm." The last one straightened up after a good thirty seconds. "Why is he lying on the floor?"

"The prison-cell experience you know. Can't deal with beds after that."

"But he's been in America for six years!"

"True." I offered my best shrug. "But that was exile."

"I couldn't quite see his face," complained another.

I shrugged again.

"Nice legs. Is he an existentialist?"

"Without a doubt. Plays the sitar."

They frowned hard, trying to figure that one out. I turned them around toward the stairs.

"I bet he's had an incredible sex life."

"Good in bed, you think?"

"Where is the sitar? Can't quite see—"

"One peep, remember?" I pushed away a head from the keyhole. "Down the stairs—go on. You gave me only three little chocolates." Enough is enough. And I didn't want to feel like I'd sold myself.

"He wanted to *sell* his image, I could see clearly," Beverley continues to her spellbound audience. "This terrorist of mine. Disturbed, confused, he wanted *me* to be his voice, to tell, indeed *sell,* his story, to see the world through his eyes. And I did, as *you'll* see when you read my book."

"And soon you'll sell the movie rights," cackles someone from the audience, "that is, if it hasn't already been worked into your huge advance."

"My huge advance," Beverley retorts, "has gone toward fund-raising for this conference. Please, a hand for our most generous sponsor, Raindance."

A small, round man waves over the crowded room. The Eurasian waitresses are suddenly everywhere with trays of champagne. The enormous screens all around the room light up and are drenched with computer-generated rain and beautiful people dancing with bottles of Raindance champagne.

"I convinced Mr. Raindance over there (no, his name is not Raindance) to choose Raindance as the name for his products. Did I not transform you, Chuck?" She blows a kiss at the small man who rises from the center of the room and bows dutifully.

"That you have for sure."

The screens fade out and a young man raises his glass of champagne at Beverley. "But there must have been a lot of flak along the way from your readers and editors? What were their opinions, what did they say? You must have met with resistance to your ideas?"

"That's what my book is about—*resistance!* Bourgeois voices of resistance. Unique voices of resistance. My terrorist's resistance, the resistance I met with. And about how we've all *changed,* and will further change, all of us here, over the course of these three days. It's an incredible moment! Let's drink to resistance!" Beverley's eyes glow in green ecstasy. She pulls me aside and hisses in my ear, "I feel it even when I sleep. The way the rain changes India—*operation monsoon*—do you understand now? I've *transformed* your mocking label into political experience. Boy! Do I love the rain in theory! Even when I sleep I feel it.

The secret revolution, the secret undermining of the establishment, the transforming imagination."

It wasn't just my imagination—I could swear that his face was indeed changing. That restlessness was disappearing. Because of the rain? Did it pass through him, fill him up, reclaim him? Was he not the lost god, lost without the shadow of clouds, lost without the silver light of rain? The shadow warrior who had his being in that uncertain glimmer between day and night? His world, a world of secrets, written in the language of rain. He must never again be separated from the rain.

Lying in bed at night, with the desperate thrashing of the rain against the windows, I imagined him walking on the terrace melting, and re-forming in the rain. I would hear the door open upstairs as soon as the rain started. And although I couldn't hear anything but the rain, I knew he was out there receiving all it had to give. This was his special surren-der—to be broken by the rain.

Rain. It did not disappear with the dawn. It carried on with re-newed strength. The lawn flooded, the drive, the streets, and all of Calcutta waded waist-deep in water. My sister and I made paper boats and dropped them out of the window on the swirling brown waters. Venice of the gutters, my father called the city. Makeshift rafts con-tested for traffic space with choking, sputtering buses, trucks, cars, and rickshaws.

After a few days of flooding, the city came to a halt. My father went to work in a police jeep, a vehicle that churned through the water like a turbine. So when a rickshaw arrived at our front door, pulled by a pant-ing man with a well-oiled body to keep away the leeches, I slid down the bannister in excitement. Ram ran to the door and carried my tiny grandmother from the rickshaw to the house, as the front steps were now well under the brown flood. We gasped as she walked in, leaning on her elephant-headed cane, a complete affectation as she enjoyed perfect health, as none of the maladies of old age afflicted her. Her shining white hair floating around her face gave her an elfin aura. She hadn't stepped out of her house in years. She hated what Calcutta had turned into. She clung to her Calcutta before the Bangladesh War, before the refugees, the constant riots.

"What has your husband done?" she asked my mother, one eyebrow raised.

"Tea?" My mother waved frantically at Ram.

"What is he doing?" I snapped back. What had my father done? Was he having an affair? My mother's sister had been hinting for months now that he was indeed, with the wife of our ambassador in Romania.

"If you want to bring down the rain," my grandmother said harshly, "you better know how to stop it."

"She's blown a head gasket this time for sure," my sister snorted.

"Are you talking about what people are saying? We don't care what people outside say or think," I said.

"Outside!" She threw up her hands. "What about the people inside?"

Head gasket is right, I thought. My mother poured the tea and offered her a cup. She waved it aside. "No one understands," she whispered. "Your father wants to float in between. And what about the rain?" She caught my shoulder gently and looked into my eyes. "It changes the order of things, don't you know? When you bring on the rain, *everything changes*. It's not the same place anymore. *The rain takes over*. We yearn for it and then when it comes, we don't know how to stop it, and we curse it. Can't make up our minds, can we, what's right or wrong? And then when something changes, we don't like it, do we? Desire becomes fear. Tell your father I stepped out today, after all these years, and came here."

My mother sighed and picked up a magazine.

"Would you like to meet Manik?" I asked. Manik would like her. She had become stranger than ever. I liked the bit about the rain. "Come," I pulled her along, "meet Manik."

Seeing her, Manik sat up. She stared at him, trance-like, and stretched out her hand as if to bless. "Some trust you," she said to him, her voice like a low chant, "with doors open, trust you not to break their hearts. That's all you can trust someone with—not to break your heart."

I shifted my weight from one foot to the other, cleared my throat.

Manik held her eyes as if she was speaking to him in a secret language.

"Good-bye," she said, and left. She swept through the waters on that creaking, groaning rickshaw like an ancient river nymph on a bad-tempered crab.

My father scowled when informed of her visit and cryptic lecture and shut himself up in his study for the rest of the evening.

"What do you think she was going on about?" I asked Manik.

He bit his lower lip. "Terrible things," he said.

A few days later, a slight blue shadow under a black umbrella walked up the drive. The water level had gone down to knee-deep. I must be seeing things, I thought. Nobody waded voluntarily, except those who didn't mind a brush with leeches, floating sewage, and dead animals. And no one wanted to be battered by the weather (except, of course, our guest upstairs). I heard the front door open and close, heard Malini, my sister's *ayah*, talking to someone, but no one came inside. I waited for a good ten minutes and went down. I found a woman standing outside with a dripping umbrella. Her blue cotton sari was wet and mud splattered. She looked tired and anxious. "Manik is here?" She asked with a weak smile. His mother! Of course, Dad had mentioned that she would visit him here.

I brought her in and took the umbrella from her. "You need to dry off. How did you come?"

"I took the train, and then the bus from Sealdah."

"In this weather! You should have called from Kalyani. We'd have sent the car. . . ." my voice trailed off. They didn't have a phone. Manik would have called her otherwise. "I'm going to get you another sari." I took her to my room. "You need tea, immediately." I smiled, trying to put her at ease.

"Manik?" she asked again.

"Yes, in a minute." I ran out and went to my mother's room. She had left for an afternoon bridge session at the club in a police jeep. Flooded streets did not curtail club activities. Why not take an army helicopter? I had suggested. It could airlift from the terrace, and she and her bridge friends could parachute down to the club roof, designer saris billowing, etc. I had received a pained glare in return. I went through my mother's saris and picked out a silk one.

"Silk," she fingered it hesitantly.

"My mother won't miss it. Don't worry." She looked shocked. "Well, just change into it while yours dries." I didn't know what else to say. "Tea, and Manik, right away."

Malini was in the kitchen washing dishes. "Why didn't you bring her into the living room?" I asked.

She let out a snort.

"What's that supposed to mean?"

Malini turned around from the sink. "People like that have never come into this house, not as long as I've been here, and that's twelve years. We can't just let anybody in. Look at the way she was dressed."

"Make some tea," I ordered.

"What for?"

"For Manik's mother."

"Oh, well." Another shrug. "Why your father picks up people like them. . . ."

I arranged the tray, adding a plate of ginger snaps while Malini poured the water in the teapot. "There," she said. "You think she's seen a teapot before?"

I walked out slowly carrying the tray.

"Hope she doesn't steal any of those things," Malini hissed under her breath.

I closed my eyes, took a deep breath, and turned around. "Malini—" I took another deep breath. "You're fired. Get out."

She clutched her throat with one hand and with the other, the edge of the sink. "You—you can't fire me."

"We'll see about that. Go pack your stuff."

"A good hiding is what you've never got—"

"Out of the house. Right now."

Manik's mother sat on the edge of the bed as if afraid to create even the slightest wrinkle in the heavy silk bedspread. I set the tray down next to her. "I'm going to get Manik now. Will you start on that please?"

Manik ran down the stairs with me, agitated and as anxious.

I halted him in the corridor. "Relax, will you. It's only your mother."

"You don't understand. They took her in for questioning when I—when I—" He crouched down on his knees covering his face with his hands. "I don't want to see her," he mumbled.

"She's come all this way in this weather. Get up." I tried to pull him up. I seemed to have no strength at all. My knees were threatening to buckle, and I wanted to join Manik in that fetal crouch.

"Your grandfather got her out before they could ask her anything at all. But she sat in a holding cell for hours. You've no idea."

"Right. I have no idea. Get up." I sat and held him until he stopped shaking.

His mother almost dropped the cup when he opened the door.

"You shouldn't have come here—" Manik tried to turn away, "shouldn't have—"

I punched him hard between his shoulder blades, pushed him into the room, closed the door.

I went to my mother's bathroom. The light pounded against my eyes. Black and white marble, brass, and black onyx, a large stained-glass window, plants, mirrors in wrought-iron frames, wrought-iron chairs with black velvet seats. She spent hours in here. Her favorite prison, we called it. I leaned over the black marble sink, splashing my face and eyes with water. My eyes continued to burn. A sudden stomach cramp made me double up. Was I going to throw up? I mustn't throw up in this sink. I kneeled before the toilet bowl. Another gut-twisting spasm. I stuck my fingers in my throat, gagged and retched but couldn't throw up. I wanted to kill someone, anyone, the guards, Malini, my friends. . . .

"What's wrong? Get up. What on earth—why are you crying like this?" My sister was shaking me. "Should I call the doctor? Are you sick?" I pushed her aside and staggered out of the bathroom, and back to my room. She followed me in.

"Where's Manik's mother?" I managed to mumble.

"Left about an hour ago. What's wrong with you?"

"Cramps," I said. "Go away."

"What did you say to Malini?" my mother demanded over dinner. "She's terribly upset."

"I want her fired," I said.

Everyone looked at me in surprise, including Manik.

"Don't be ridiculous," my mother said. "What on earth for?"

"Either she goes or I do."

"Malini gave her cramps." My sister sniggered.

"Shut up, idiot."

"What is the matter with you?" My mother brought her hand down on the table with a sharp slap.

"Come, come." My father pacified her, patting her hand. "Overreactions galore. Now, I don't know what the matter is—but—Malini had asked for leave for next month. Let her go to her village for a few weeks now instead. She can go tomorrow. I'm sure Ram and the others can handle things quite well for a while." He raised his eyebrows at my mother, an amused apology in his eyes.

"Aloke, you have spoiled her beyond—beyond—"

"We don't have to subject Manik to this." He patted my mother's hand again.

She flung his hand off and left the table.

Manik bit his lower lip and looked down at his plate.

Something was changing, subtly, but undoubtedly.

I spent all of the next day in my room. Ram brought my food. Curled on the windowseat I watched the rain. It was hard to sleep. I dozed off in between storms. The rain woke me up with its sharp fierce slap against the glass. On the third day, Mom and Dad came to my room.

"All this grounding nonsense," Dad was muttering angrily.

"The stubbornness needs to go," Mom snapped "Are you ill? Should we call a doctor?" Her voice hit falsetto.

"Go and see your friends, go for a movie or something." Dad gave an encouraging smile.

"Movie!" Mom snorted. "Should be on lithium, she should."

"Get lost," I said.

"Hear that? What did I say? You're grounded until you learn to behave."

Dad shook his head and left. Mom followed him out and shut the door with a bang. I turned to the rain and waited for the world to change.

"And I have managed to create a change." Beverley raises a fist. People cheer. The two FBI agents circle around with bored faces. More champagne floods in. I empty my glass into a silk ficus.

There's no escape from this room or this hotel. I want to go see some shows, go for the *Star Trek* ride. I slip out to find out about my room. It is finally available, and it is so bland that I am stunned. Like any decent hotel room, comfortable and nondescript. But lo and behold—the entire ceiling is mirrored! I can lie in bed and think about what really has changed. I get up and go back to Beverley holding center stage.

They are all eating. As I reach the buffet table, Beverley's arm blocks me. "We need to talk and *negotiate*." I blink at her. "Tell me what happened—your part in it. Because in the movie, your character will play a big role. I need to study you as you were then."

"Movie?"

"Don't tell a soul," she hisses, dragging me to a secluded corner. "I haven't signed anything yet. My agent is raising the bid. I'm re-creating some of the details. There has to be an explosion, a big one, before the escape. The hotel next to the house explodes."

"But there was no hotel—"

"And *details* of the escape plan. Your character helps him escape in the middle of a tremendous thunderstorm. At the same time there's a diversionary explosion created by his people. The neighbor's house is rocked to its foundations. The roof flies off in the explosion, the hotel bursts into flames, and—"

Just then, the entire hotel trembles as if an earthquake has struck deep underneath its foundations. We rush to the lobby, spilling champagne. Across the street a building collapses in on itself. A waitress hurries over with more champagne. "Just an old building coming down, ma'am. We are building an extension over there with a bigger casino."

I blink again. "I need to eat something."

Beverley pulls me back to that corner again. "Not until you disclose the real story. You will agree to meet with the director? I will negotiate quarter of a million for your cooperation initially. And then some more."

"You're mad." I try to free my elbow.

"You need to get it out of your system, Pia. Clear your conscience. I've cleared mine with my book. The movie will release us both from the grip of the past. We can be *friends*, allies, work together. We can *trust* each other. Let's *negotiate together* with the producers. We can make more money than we can dream of, kick free of academia, go live in Majorca, Capri, St. Tropez. Buy an old Tuscan villa. Sunbathe on marble terraces—"

"Oh, yes, with a damsel on a dulcimer singing to us." I wrench my arm from her grasp.

"You *do* understand, don't you, finally? Yes! *A damsel on a dulci-*

mer—prophesying war. For he on honey dew hath fed and drunk the milk of paradise—" her voice cracks as I pull free.

Hunger pulled me away from the window. Two o'clock and no lunch. What was Ram doing? I'd been starving since twelve-thirty. I paced the room. Mom must have told Ram not to bring me any food. So I'd come out and beg. If she thought that I was going to come out crawling—I'd rather die. I sat down on the bed heavily. I was beginning to feel weak. Two and a half hours—I couldn't remember going hungry for that long. Did they always bring you food on time in prison? Or did they starve you out of spite, to hear you beg? How did they break you, completely, so that you had nothing left to hold onto? Except the rain. I could feel it drumming inside my stomach. I would not go out and ask for food. What was it like to starve to death? I am going to lie here and wait. The world vanished into the silver screen of rain.

"Here, get up." Manik stood by the bed with a tray. I fell on the food like a famine victim.

"I'm going to have it out with my mother," I said, between mouthfuls.
"Why?"
"Why was she holding up lunch? To starve me out?"
"Not her. I did."
I choked and coughed up rice and chicken all over the bed.

He slapped me on the back. "A person on a hunger strike shouldn't expect meals," he said. "Now, I would really like to go for a walk, with or without the armed escort, I don't care. The water's gone down quite a bit. And you need some fresh air. Ask your father if you can step out with me for about an hour. Just around the house and the park."

"That would really be playing my dad against my mom."

"So what? You've done it before often enough. I'm sure they're used to it by now."

"I didn't realize you were so unfeeling, cold."

"Don't they say I've killed people?" His eyes shone. "Now, please ask your father if we can go for a walk."

I shook my head. "You can't have everything your way."

My mother was going over bills with Ram. I looked down at my feet.

"Can I go for a walk? Can Manik come out with me for a short while?"

"I have to call your father about that." She frowned at me, surprised and suspicious at my sudden meekness.

With two guards following about fifteen yards behind, we waded ankle-deep through the park, which was empty except for a few dogs pawing and digging for scraps. The rain had stopped a few minutes back. It was still stormy, and occasional lightning streaked across the growling clouds. "Not a part of Calcutta I'm familiar with," Manik said. "This is the still colonial Calcutta. Look at these houses. Georgian legacy. While the rest of Calcutta chokes in the gutter."

"Oh, don't stop there. Dish out the whole shit. It's criminal to live like this when two-thirds of the country starve to death . . . and, well, don't forget, it's that hated one-third that pulled the right strings and saved your life. You're out here walking because of that one-third."

"Yes, and may I never be allowed to forget it!"

"And you've lived a very privileged life for the last six years in the most capitalist of countries."

"Ah, yes. Stanford. I worked very hard, you know. It wasn't like I was sitting on my butt all that time. A Ph.D. and post-doc work."

"Did you make friends?"

"Some. My name was always a joke to them, to anyone I met. They always put a 'c' at the end: manic! M-a-n-i-k, I always spelled it out. But it didn't work."

"But 'manik' means gem or precious stone, didn't you tell them? It also means beloved."

"Made no difference to them."

"Any girlfriends?"

"No, not really."

That was odd, I thought, no girlfriends, but I felt curiously relieved. "What about your friends here?"

Manik became very quiet. Had they all been killed? I swallowed. "If there's anyone you want to see, I can call them for you," I said, swallowing again, "from an outside phone."

"Would you now? And what if that got you into more trouble than you bargained for?"

"There wouldn't be any trouble at all."

"And do you think my friends could just walk in through your front door?"

"We could work something out, sneak them in or something. But you must swear not to plot something and not to run away."

Manik shook his head slowly. "My swearing's worth nothing. And you're much too impulsive."

"Do you or don't you want to see your friends?"

"Yes, I do. Two of them. One you could call, but the other's in jail." He gave me an amused look. "Game?"

"And what's my reward?"

"Adventure."

"Can I trust you not to run off?"

"Trust?" He laughed lightly. "That's simply a matter of choice. You will do what you want. And it will have very little to do with me."

Something was getting terribly out of control, I felt, when during dinner my father announced: "A Beverley Newton, from the University of Pittsburgh—freelance journalist and writer—wants to interview you, Manik. Should I say yes or no? She's writing a book on terrorism."

Manik shrugged and said, "I guess that's all right."

Bright yellow mustard flowers spun wildly in my head.

While I tried to shake off the mustard flowers, my aunt decided to come forth with her counseling services. "This is really too much," she said to my mother the next day. "As it is, he's frequently lunching with that woman at the Grand Hotel. And now he plants this criminal in your house, causing gossip and talk all over the place—can't go anywhere and not hear about this—this—character in your upstairs. Then to bring this foreign woman to publicize everything on an even greater scale—how long are you going to take this?"

"He hasn't brought her," my mother said frigidly. "She asked to come here."

"The technicality is irrelevant. This is going to hit the newspapers. And besides, what got him to plant that criminal—murderer, I believe—" She paused, letting out a hissing sigh, "Stick him inside your house with growing daughters—" She turned to give me a quick, malicious glance. "What if he did something to her—why don't you think about consequences?" She sat back, smug. "Well, what I'm saying," she continued, "is that he's a rotten example for growing children. Anarchy, no discipline, no responsibility, a loafer type, a psychotic criminal. Servants are talking, you know, about him upstairs, his odd behavior, lying in the rain or something, some kind of wildness, and Pia always on the terrace with him, and he's not really related, is he? A stranger, really, unknown quantity, lower class as well."

"Don't be silly," my mother protested weakly. "Nothing lower class about him. He's all right."

My aunt sniggered and rolled her eyes. "You'll have trouble under your roof if you don't watch out."

My mother tried her best to appear exasperated, putting down her nail file and examining her immaculately manicured nails. I sat quietly, my fingers curling to fists, tightening, as my aunt turned toward me again with that so-you're-going-to-be-a-slut look, the look that kicks you behind the knees before you've barely learned to walk, so I continued to grip that nothing-in-my-hands feeling harder and harder, until my nails cut into the flesh of my palms.

Manik raised his eyebrows at my bandaged hands. I had wrapped gauze rather generously. "That much padding for digging your nails in?" he asked.

I stared at him, wondering if I should lie. "How do you know?" I yelled. "How do you always know everything?"

"I don't know," he said. "I guessed."

"How?" I grabbed his arm and twisted it backward and up. He drew his breath sharply in pain. "Tell me, how did you guess."

"Go on," he said in a whisper, "just a little harder, and it's sure to break. I'd rather you break my arm than gouge your palms."

I let his arm go and moved back. He stood shaking his head, the hint of a smile flickering about his mouth, but there were tears in his eyes.

"I'm sorry—" I stammered, stopped, then threw myself against him, almost making him lose his balance, and began to cry, striking his chest with my fists.

He pushed me back against the wall. "Never," he said, giving me a shake, "never let anyone humiliate you. Kill them if they do."

We sat quietly for some time listening to the rain thrash on. The order of things had changed. The rain was not just the rain anymore, but a mirror in which the world kept changing.

"I've caused problems. I'm sorry," Manik said.

"The problems were always there. No one wanted to recognize them."

"Sorry," he said again.

"How do you always know?" I asked. "And why won't you tell?"

"I don't know, Pia. I just guess."

"But how?"

He turned and smiled. "That's all I've lived on for a long time now—hints and guesses. And you're so impulsive, you give yourself away."

"Should I change, then?"

"No. Not ever." He reached out and gave me a hug.

"What do you really want to be or do? Tell me!"

"Oh—vanish into a shaft of lightning, become the rain. . . ." his voice trailed to laughter.

"Trying to rewrite yourself for me?" I laughed back at him.

"Why not? I've been rewritten so many times by so many voices, so many hands, what difference will one more rewrite make?"

"If it's yours, uniquely, your version of you, and everyone listens, then it will change everything."

"You're hopeless," he said, boxing my ears. "You're lost. Beyond saving."

"Saving from what?"

"From yourself. You dream too much."

"So do you. Or you wouldn't want to change the government."

"Well—" he let out a sigh. "When your fingers curl around a 9mm, all dreams come to an end."

I took a deep breath. "Have you really—I mean—ever killed anyone?"

Manik let out a whistle. "I see that you are feeling better."

"I guess you called them executions, and necessary."

"Executions, and necessary, hmm. . . ." He sat quietly for few seconds. Then glancing sideways at me, with a crooked half smile, "I'm hungry, you twerp," he said. "Can we go down for a bite?"

"Why don't you ever tell me anything?" I stood up and stamped my feet, furious, my eyes smarting again. "I want to know the truth!"

Manik got up. "Whatever you choose to believe is the truth."

"But what should I think about you? So many people say so many things!"

"I still don't know what to *think*," Beverley says. "But *you* know. You *know*. Why won't you tell me? Twenty years have gone by. What is it that you are guarding so jealously?"

"It's late. I'm tired. I need to sleep."

"You've got to help me." Her nails dig urgently into my arm. "I've promised the publisher a sequel. My book at present deals with his personality—the intensity, the haunted-hunted look, my experience in Calcutta in the rain—God, did I hate that rain—it kept getting in the way!—and his background, a history of the movement, of the leaders, my critique of all that. But what I want to add is other people's impressions—yours—you were close to him. For the movie, the captivity, the escape. A dramatic representation. You adored him, didn't you? And what really brought on that whole weird incident? Was he trying to shock?"

"Do you remember what you asked him?"

"Yes. A simple question. A few simple direct questions. I expected honest answers."

"Your tiny black Sony tape recorder looked amazing, like a high-tech grenade. Did you know that? You held it above your head as you waded through the waterlogged drive, remember? And your umbrella!" I begin to laugh at the surprise in her eyes.

Her umbrella had been blown out the other way by the storm. She clutched it like a life jacket with one hand. The other hand, raised over her head, gripped a tiny tape recorder. She was mud splattered from head to foot—splashed by a bus, she said. Even her round Lennon glasses had a mud smear on them. She was so wet I couldn't quite figure out what she looked like! More composed after a shower and dry clothes—she always carried a change of clothes with her in Calcutta, she said—she sat down with Manik. "Will you tell me everything—*the goods?*" Her eyes narrowed, one eye closing, as if she was squinting at the crosshairs before pulling the trigger. "I am interested in what you have to say. I can help you. Perhaps I can be your voice. I think you're *so* courageous. You must have suffered *terribly.*"

I squirmed in the corner. Gag me, my cool little sis would have said. I had been allowed to sit in the room and "Be a good girl." How could I let anyone leave me out of anything concerning Manik? Besides, I had a feeling she was actually afraid to be alone in a room with him. After all, he's supposed to have killed people.

She bit her nails from time to time making them jagged and ugly. The first thing my mother had noticed about Ms. Newton was her nails. "Good God," she said to my aunt, "I thought Americans were very particular about nails and hair and teeth. She even has split ends."

"Maybe she's afraid to go to a hair salon in India," my sister said. "Maybe she thinks she'll pick up lice."

"Well, she's busy picking that up anyway, right in your living room!" My aunt couldn't help herself.

"What do you see around you?" Beverley Newton asked Manik.

He began to laugh softly. "Nothing," he said, "nothing." And then he turned to the window to look at the rain coming down so thick and hard that it wiped out the world.

"Nothing, he said he saw *nothing!* And I was supposed to buy that?" Beverley gives my arm a shake. "I was, and am committed to causes like his. There was a reason for his silence, and such silences have to be translated, interpreted. He was begging for that through his silence. But I also sensed a dangerousness about him, a dangerous tormented silence, dangerous and perverse, and a madness in his eyes. Because he had relocated, no, dislocated parts of him. I need Judy's input. It's all about remapping the body."

And Judy remapped her body that evening, to the metallic grating of the Time Band. First she crooned, "I get a kick from Jean V" to the tune of "I Get a Kick Out of You." Then she danced, a strange spastic dance, chanting the explanations to her movements. With a yellow-gloved hand she claimed she removed her clitoris, then began to stroke the dislocated part high above her head. Falling to her knees, as the music pulsed, "This is something you can do anywhere," she said in the tone of an army sergeant. "We have to assume our own salvation, play with our own reality. If you can rearrange your body at will, then you transcend the body, erase shame and humiliation. Nobody can disseminate you except yourself. This is what empowers the terrorist. Are you listening to me? Answer me, you pricks!"

"Isn't she something? Isn't that something! *He* had done it! Erased his body. No wonder! Questions bounced off him. There was nothing to *interface* with!"

"Do you remember what you asked him?"

"How many people have you killed? How do you position yourself ideologically? What colors do you like? Any women in your life? What do you believe, what do you want us to believe? How do you regard yourself? What is the truth?" She rapped them out as if reading from index cards.

He looked at her, his mouth tightening. Slowly, he began to take off his clothes. First, the belt. Then his shirt, jeans, underwear. He stood calmly looking down at his toes. "This is the first step after they arrest you," he said quietly. "Five or six pairs of eyes—all want to know the truth. And all you want is for the cold hard cement floor under your feet to open up and swallow you, cover you up, hide you, because you have nothing to tell, and they are not interested in listening, but only want to see you squirm and scream. That is also part of some vague truth."

He picked up his clothes and got dressed. I felt dizzy, sick, and angry. Beverley Newton, who had crouched on the edge of a sofa with her mouth open, gave a strangled scream and ran out.

He hid his face in his hands. "Sorry," he muttered, "sometimes I get so very mad. Shouldn't have done that. I don't give a damn about her, but I didn't mean to make you uneasy."

"What are you trying to do?" My anger and unease faded as I stared at his slouched-over form and listened to his shallow and rapid breathing. "Why don't you explain to her anyway? Perhaps she could give you a voice, at least it might be positive publicity, I don't know. Tell her to leave you alone or talk to her."

"What's there to say?" he snapped, his voice muffled by his hands.

"Then ask her to leave you alone!" No more Beverleys. Must talk to Dad and put a stop to it. I wanted to help him straighten out his life; help him be at peace with the world, I suppose, if that were possible—for someone who related only to thunderstorms to be at peace with the world! What was he? Could one call him tormented? Would that be romanticizing him? Or was he to be left to linger in that shadow space between those two well-defined territories of "hero" and "villain"? No one wants to know him as he *is*. As if no one dares. No one wants to look at the world through his eyes. Some fragile membrane might collapse, and his crudely constructed world of dreams and ours of cautious delicate reality might collide and dislocate our steady feet from our firm dependable ground.

I always champion the underdog, Dad had said. And *she* wanted to be *his* voice. Servants whispering; my aunt and club members pouring into my mother's ears constantly how all this would appear socially—a criminal staying at your house, where governors, ministers, diplomats gather at your terribly important parties. . . . Are you doing the right thing? And then there was curiosity: go bring your cousin, what is he like, let's have a look. What should we believe about you, how do you feel about women, what kind of food do you like, what do you feel just when you're about to pull the trigger against someone's head, what's your favorite color, what is the truth? And he, doubled over, wanting only the rain—

I touched his head. "What do you want? If you don't want to go back to America, tell my father, and maybe he can negotiate something."

Manik raised his head slowly. "No. No more trouble for anyone else."

"Just get married to someone then. That's the perfect Indian solution to everything." Manik's eyes widened. "I'll marry you, if you like," I added, "for a few months, until you find some place to live and a job." Manik blinked. Something *I* said had taken him by surprise.

"You want to marry me?"

"No. Not at all."

He blinked again.

"Otherwise," I smiled, "what do you want to do about the rest of your life?"

Manik began to laugh. "I don't know," he said. "But I'd like to get in touch with a friend."

I made a face and touched my forehead in mock salute.

"Mock me all you want, sweetie." Beverley hands me her book, "*My terrorist.*"

"Congratulations," I say.

"Why are you being so difficult?" She tries to grab my shoulder. I step away quickly.

"Let's share in good faith. Come on, tell me the real story. You did help him escape, didn't you? I know you did. You were mad about him. Anyone could tell. You were ready to do anything for him, weren't you? You wouldn't leave him alone with me. Protective! In a way I'm almost glad about that now. But now I must know everything about *my terrorist*—and yours." A mild concession there.

I bite off a smile. "Tomorrow, Beverley. Sweet dreams."

"Pia, we have to come to terms with this thing that's been between us for twenty years! We have to come to terms with each other."

Her eyes are pleading. All of a sudden her "image" seems to have slipped off like a mask. Her eyes are earnest, though still the new green, but earnest. "You've done well in your field. I have, too. But we can do so much better, together. Even if we can't be good friends, we could be great collaborators. That's what academics can be."

"You said you wanted to be free of academia." I am genuinely curious.

"Yes, free of it, not escape it. The only relationship one should have with academia is one of absolute power and the power to wield over its head."

"You will have that now, with your book and your movie."

"But I'll have nothing if I can't get my hands on the truth about what happened. I won't get the satisfaction of knowing the truth."

"The truth. . . ." I shake my head. For the first time we stand face to face without hostility. It's a strange feeling. I, too, would like to escape, from this conference.

But there's no escape from this place. The mirrors on the ceiling of my room reflect the bed back at me. Looking out of the window, I see the runway glimmering. Planes landing, taking off. But until that shuttle arrives tomorrow to take me back to the airport, there's no getting out. A sequel to her precious book! A movie! And this book, lying on the bed, its glossy jacket glowing darkly. I have no desire to read it. I flip through it though. Critiques, profiles: historical, ideological, cultural, psychological. . . . Two hundred and sixty-three pages. Not one word had she got out of *her* terrorist, but she had written him down in two hundred and sixty-three pages! Her terrorist!

I take out the folded piece of paper from my wallet and spread it out on the bed. It is so faded that the image on it is barely discernible. I gently trace the shadowy lines that run across it. Her terrorist. You would do anything for him. Anyone could tell.

Bid me to die and I will die a thousand deaths for thee. With that echoing in my head, I phoned a cafe called Paragon near College Street and asked for a waiter called Siddhu. Ask Binoy to be at a certain bus stop at one sharp, Thursday, was the message I delivered. I was curiously relieved that the friend was male. There had been a lurking fear that I might be asked to phone an old girlfriend. Next I had to call Beverley Newton. She sounded relieved about rescheduling her second visit.

"Rain check," she said. "The streets here look like a muddy river. This damn rain has left me *marooned.*"

Rain check, Ms. Newton, I repeated after I hung up. And hope you dissolve.

I now had to figure out the complications of this plan. I was to wait at the bus stop and bring Binoy back with me, pretending he was a friend of mine, since Manik was not supposed to communicate with any former acquaintances. Only family, and within the walls of this secured area—our house. It seemed only fair to me that Manik should be able to meet a few friends after being away for so long. But I also fervently hoped I wasn't unknowingly becoming part of some plan. Manik wasn't using me to escape—was he? All these intense deliriums about and in the rain, the shocking hard honesty in his eyes when he spoke, that half-playful, half-sad smile—could all of this be an act? I liked him. I wanted to trust him. *You trust someone not to break your heart,* said my grandmother. *Trust was a matter of choice,* said Manik. But had he not made me trust him? Or had I decided, from the moment I became aware of his existence, looking at his shadow form in that intensive care unit, decided with that unique spine-thrill, that this creature was going to be mine, mine to show off, to re-create according to my imagination, that I would trust him, naturally? Because in essence, he was that part of me that would always remain suspended in borderlands. Was that not one of the truths?

But still—how would I pass Binoy off as a friend of mine? Twenty-seven, said Manik, but looks eighteen. I had never brought any male friends home, indeed I had no male friends who were important to bring home anyway. And bringing this guy home, out of the blue, would only confirm my aunt's message to my mother. How would I explain any of it?

"No guts!" Manik gave me a shake. "No one's around then. The guards go to the backyard for lunch and play cards all afternoon. The servants disappear after lunch. Your sister is at a friend's house these days since the water's gone down again. Your mother is at the club, and your father's at work. So, what's the problem?" He had it all figured out. "You're wondering if I've been hatching something."

He could read my mind. I was thinking the obvious.

"I've nothing much to do, so I quietly observe what goes on around me, that's all. I can't wander through the city streets, so I imagine the city as I watch the rain."

"I'll do as you say," I said. "But if I get into any kind of trouble, you'll have to come clean."

"Lay down my life for you." He smiled a wicked one-sided smile.

My head will be served up on a platter tonight, I thought while I waited at the bus stop. How I would recognize Binoy, I couldn't fathom. People stared at me. My skirt felt too short and too tight. Girls like me didn't stand at bus stops. We never even took the school bus. We were driven to school. I groaned as it started to drizzle, and then in seconds, pour. There was no overhead shelter. A bus screeched and skidded to a stop. Everyone sprang back as the front end of the bus gently crushed the two poles that held up the Bus Stop sign. Rain obliterated vision. I couldn't distinguish one face from the other. People poured out of the bus struggling viciously with the people trying to get in. A man with an open sack of coconuts fell against me, making me trip and fall. Muddy water in my eyes and mouth. Spitting, I tried to scramble to my feet but slipped and fell again. Two hands grabbed me above my elbows, pulled me up, and practically dragged me across the street.

"Calm down. It's all right."

I was hyperventilating, unable to stop.

A hand stroked my back and shoulders very gently. "It's all right, all right, all right. Manik can be such a bastard at times. I'll beat him up for you." His voice was magically soft. He walked me down the street toward the crossing. "What does he want me to do this time?" he asked. "Wait another seven years?"

I turned and looked at him. Binoy. He had curly black hair and a very smooth face. He was strikingly attractive and did look very young. He was a trifle shorter than Manik and quite thin. "You have to come home with me," I stammered. "You have to pretend to be my—someone I know," I finished hurriedly.

He walked quietly looking at the traffic.

"Are you a Naxalite?" I asked, and bit my tongue the next instant.

"No, I'm not and have never been arrested for anything either." He closed his eyes, his face taut with anger.

No guards at the gates or on the porch. I took him upstairs, both of us dripping water and mud along the way. Manik looked up from the bed and began to laugh. "Drowned rats!" That left us shuffling uncomfortably for a few seconds. What gratitude! Binoy went toward Manik slowly, then with a sudden backhand blow sent Manik flying across the room. Manik's head struck the wall and he slipped to the floor. Binoy watched him silently as Manik rolled over groaning. "I won't wait any longer," Binoy said. "You're on your own now."

Manik got up and stumbled to the bed, clutching the side of his head. "I'm sorry," he said.

"Your sorrys don't mean anything anymore."

The world was changing again before my eyes, uncovering a private arena where I didn't belong, where I had no right to be. Yet I couldn't move, stunned by the pain in two pairs of eyes that watched each other like two fatally wounded animals.

Somehow I cleared my throat and moved my feet. "I'll be outside, on the terrace." As I turned to step out into the rain, Binoy kneeled before Manik, held him, pressing his face against his hair. They were whispering, touching each other's face, hair, hands, shoulders.

Under the pounding rain, I crouched and hugged my knees. I felt a slow ripping inside, as if something very fragile had been stretched to its limit. A question was answered, a mystery solved, and a world disintegrated.

The rain stopped that night. The clouds were still there, pulsing with lightning. A stormy wind started, breaking off branches, dragging down electric lines. At breakfast, we realized that Manik was scheduled to leave the next day. Manik's mother came to see him again, this time driven over by my father. Beverley Newton arrived as well.

"He's not available," I said, fists at my waist. "His mother's here, and she's far more important than you."

"I don't understand—" she stammered. "Why are you so hostile? I must speak with him. This work I'm doing is extremely important."

"It's not important to him."

"Oh, but it is! He'll realize that once the book is done. The Third World is going to be a very important academic area very soon, and my book is going to be a landmark."

"Sorry," I said and closed the door.

That afternoon, when the guards disappeared for lunch, I stood out on the porch. The rain had held off, and it was still windy. I knew it would rain again by the evening. The clouds were almost black. The front steps had emerged from the water and a piece of wet paper lay stuck against the side of the steps. I picked it up, but before I could look at it, it was taken out of my hands. Manik stood behind me. I hadn't heard him creep up behind me. "Incredible," he murmured.

"What?"

He pointed at the paper. It was a chart of some sort, a faded maplike print, with dates and other numbers and arrows I couldn't understand. "It's a meteorological chart," Manik said, sounding surprised.

"So?" I couldn't keep the sullenness out of my voice.

"What do you mean *so?* This is part of a weather watch. Look at these images. It's a record of the path of the monsoons, where they're coming from, where they're going."

"But the dates," I pointed out, "those are today's and the next two days' dates. Isn't that odd? It also looks a bit like a road map." I traced a faintly winding faded black line that ran diagonally across the sheet.

"Hmm." Manik pursed his lips and looked at the soggy paper intently. Then he folded it carefully and put it in his pocket. "Isn't it surprising what the rain brings?" He smiled and made a face.

"Why are you keeping that?"

"Something to remember you by, kid. Something we found together."

"We?"

"We." He nodded. "Yes, we."

"And what about Binoy? Isn't he part of any special *we?*"

"But this rain map is ours. Forget everything else." He took it out of his pocket and put it in my hand. "Hold onto it."

"No—you keep it." I put it back in his. "You'll need your rain map where you're going."

"Do you see me getting lost in the rain?"

"Yeah, maybe." I forced myself to smile.

"This is meant to be yours." He tucked it back into my palm again.

That night the rain struck the city like a tidal wave. The pent-up fury of a wronged god, my grandmother would have said.

I awoke to the sound of heavy boots running all over the house, up the stairs, splashing through the submerged front lawn and backyard. My sister burst into my room. "Manik has disappeared!" Breathless, excited, even a bit scared, her cool had peeled off. "Come downstairs. They want to talk to you." She ran out.

My clock showed nine-thirty. But was it morning or night? The landscape outside was a water wall shot by blinding waves of lightning.

The Police Commissioner—a short squat man with a mean smile, my mother, my sister, my aunt, the servants stood in a half-circle like a review panel. Where was my father? "Someone was seen at the door yesterday afternoon," my aunt said. "I believe you spoke with him."

"Yes," I said, suppressing my need to swallow. "Some guy trying to sell something—hair oil."

"And he didn't ask to meet with anyone, or did he meet with Manik, perhaps?" The Commissioner squinted hard at me.

"Nope."

"Now, sit down," my aunt patted a footstool. "Manik must have mentioned friends or his future plans to you, right? After all, you were spending twenty-four hours with him."

"I'm afraid we only talked about the rain." I took a deep breath.

"The rain." My aunt raised an eyebrow and looked around at everyone. "I think the girl needs to see a therapist."

"Look," the Commissioner circled around me, "just tell us everything he said to you. I know you're scared. He did get you to help him escape, didn't he? Just tell the truth. We understand you're only a child. You didn't know what you were doing. I can see you're frightened. You wouldn't want to be taken down to the station, now, would you? Nasty place. A very nasty place indeed. Come, now, just tell me."

I closed my eyes. And they ask you and they ask you, what is the truth, the truth, the truth, and all you want is for the hard cement floor. . . .

"Where is Dad?" I asked my mother. My throat hurt.

"Important meeting," she muttered.

"You've no right to question me this way. My father would have never allowed it." Where was he? What meeting on a Sunday?

"Ah, but I did ask your father if I could talk to you, dear," the Commissioner smiled, reaching to pat me on the head. "He said I could."

"I don't believe you."

"Tch-tch, come, come."

"Oh Pia! Just tell him—"

"What did he ask you to do? Don't be difficult. You're already nose-deep." Another pat on the head. "I know you're scared, very, very frightened. I can see it in your eyes." Fingers lifted my chin. "The way you're clenching your fists, hmm, come now, just tell me what did he ask you to do?" And another pat on the head.

Don't ever let anyone. . . .

I knew it then, like the relentless assault of the rain, forcing that inevitable, unconditional surrender, shattering your fear, making you find a trigger somewhere and look them straight in the eye and pull.

"The young man I mentioned, the one seen at your front door yesterday, he was killed, by the way. One of my men got a clean shot to the head while they were trying to get away last night. He was involved in the escape. Binoy Sarkar. Name ring a bell?"

I tried not to swallow. Where? Why? I wanted to scream. Binoy, Binoy! That so young face. Blood splattered, lying in the mud. I couldn't stop the tears. *Don't ever let anyone. . . .*

"What's going on here?" My father entered, scattering their aimed eyes. An arm around my shoulder. "Go to your room. It's okay."

A police cordon had made the terrace and the room upstairs off limits. They were busy turning the room inside out, letting the dogs sniff around. The blue duffle bag had been left behind with most of the clothes. Sitting in my room, I took out the map Manik and I had found and spread it out gingerly. A washed-out blue shadow as if someone had retraced the black line that made it look like a road map. I opened up my volume of Romantic Poets, placed the paper on "Kubla Khan" and closed the book. I felt a halfhearted relief.

My father got rid of everyone within an hour. My aunt helped escalate the level of agitation as usual. But my father was undisturbed, flipping through work files in his study, smiling to himself as he came out to ask for tea or coffee, even humming snatches of songs from old Hindi films.

Cool had returned to my sister, who got extremely busy cataloguing her stamp collection. I sat in my room and played solitaire, a game I hated.

Ram knocked on my door around five and ushered in Beverley Newton. "I know you had something to do with it," she yelped in a high hysterical voice, "and I will definitely urge the police to question you thoroughly. You've been party to something very dangerous and wrong simply because—" she paused, drew in her breath sharply, "you wanted to keep him away from me! You couldn't deal with anyone getting near him, you didn't want him to tell me everything that he hadn't disclosed to you. You couldn't stomach that. *That's what's at the bottom of it all.*"

"Get out of my room. Get out of our house. If you want your Third World dirt, you'll have to find yourself another trash can."

"How dare you speak to me that way, you vicious brat. You've ruined my work. Ruined my Fulbright. I had everything planned out so carefully—"

"Oh, yeah—like a secret mission. Operation Monsoon!"

"Shut up, you little—" she choked and spluttered. "I'll get a book out of this in spite of you." She shook her fist and left.

I fell on the bed and laughed till I cried. God, they were all just absolutely ludicrous. The only person who could have given Manik safe passage was—not me, not poor Binoy, not anyone, except my beloved—I didn't want to think it. *I always champion the underdog.* I covered my ears. The ringing was relentless. Where was it? Not inside my head anymore. That was my father's personal line, the hot line. It was the only one that had that odd buzzing ring. It never rang for this long. Either he answered it, or it stopped after three or four rings. I went to his study and knocked. No answer. The phone buzzed on. I opened the door and walked in. The little red light flashed with each buzz. What the hell—I picked up the receiver.

"Aloke?" asked a woman's voice.

"He's not here," I mumbled.

"Who are you?" she asked. "No one else is supposed to answer this line."

"Who are you?" I asked back. I knew this voice, and it didn't belong to anyone who was supposed to call this number.

"Never mind," she said. "I just wanted to know if he was going to Geneva next week for the World Bank business."

I was stunned. "He doesn't have anything to do with the World Bank."

"He's got a new position—oh, never mind." She hung up. I replaced the receiver, my hand shaking. Did I have a spot of hard ground to stand on?

My father joined us for dinner singing, "A mad wind on a stormy day. . . ."

"I need to decide about which college I want to go to," I said to him, for lack of anything else to say, for fear I might blurt out something that I'd regret instantly. "Loreto looks good."

"What a good idea." My mother laughed nervously. "We'll go tomorrow and pick up the forms."

Drumming the table with his fingers to the beat of the song, he smiled at us. "You'll go to college in Delhi. We have to leave in about a month. I'm in the Ministry of Finance as of this morning. I also have to go to Geneva next week."

"Delhi!" my mother gasped. "Oh, I've always wanted to live in Delhi."

"Mrs. Bose called on your personal line," I said. "Don't you think Mother ought to know if you're having an affair with her? What else gives an ambassador's wife such special privileges as your personal line?"

A glass crashed, then a chair. I was spun around, slapped across my face. I had no idea my mother's hands were so hard. My sister ran from the dining room. Servants disappeared into the woodwork.

"You're not supposed to answer my personal line." He sat there calm, undisturbed as ever. I could not understand.

"So—is it true?" My mother turned to face my father.

"Don't be silly." He got up humming, went to his study, closed the door.

"You have ruined our lives, you, with your stubbornness and willfulness. You have destroyed everything. Just chaos now." So low, my mother's voice, as if from a great distance, a whisper.

The whisper of Binoy's voice, next to my ear, at the bus stop, "Calm down. It's all right . . . it's all right. . . ." So magically soft. And to Manik: "Your sorrys don't mean anything anymore." Binoy, oh—my heart broke for Binoy. If only I hadn't offered—if only I hadn't called. I couldn't get him out of my head, the sight of him bleeding to death in a mud pool, blood pouring across that beautiful face. *A clean shot to the head.* Oh God. Did Manik see him get shot, see him fall? Was he even there? What about Binoy's parents? I saw Manik's mother's face again, so painfully anxious, with only one question in her eyes: was Manik all right? Was he all right? Was he? No one mentioned him at dinner tonight. No one remembers Manik or the day's events. He vanished into a roaring monsoon night. He has become the rain.

He has become the rain. . . . I blink hard to refocus, but my eyes blur. Could I say that to Beverley? He entered our house like a ghost and disappeared much the same way, leaving no trace. But our lives changed completely. The atmosphere inside our house lost its ozone layer forever. It would be impossible to explain that to anyone, to Beverley—I don't even want to explain to Beverley. Who cares?

Beverley? Here she is, in a smartly tailored black dress, rising to give her talk. Eyes all around me are misting in anticipation of Beverley's grand finalé. "I have been all over the world for these silenced voices," she says, a heroic ring in her voice, "and in Sulimaniya in Iraq, I found this scraped into the wall of a solitary confinement cell in the basement of the Internal Security building where the Kurds were detained for questioning. Here is a translation:

> *My dear love, you, Leila,*
> *I hope you know now*
> *How many poems I have made for the beauty*
> *Of your face.*
> *I hope you know now*
> *That when I am tortured*
> *At that time,*
> *Even those times,*
> *The fascists are afraid of me.*
> *My dear love,*
> *I have cut to pieces so many chains*
> *And so many of the killers I have repelled.*
> *Now I am standing*
> *Silent*
> *Because I kept silent*
> *And kept silent.*

"My work, and all our work, is not limited to issues of terrorism, but reaches to explicate these silences and transform them to voices." Her voice breaks theatrically, breaking *voices* in two. They stand up to clap and cheer and toast the success of their whole show with Raindance champagne.

Beverley runs over to me with a bubbling over glass. "You *have* forgiven me, haven't you? I felt my life's work had been—been washed away in the rain! Oh, how I hated that rain." She waves as if to drive it off her face. "We *have* come to an understanding, haven't we? Help me now, no more grudges. Don't keep the rest of the story from me, please."

With a sigh I remove the folded paper from my wallet and hand it to her. "This is all I have, Beverley. I don't really know what it is, but he gave it to me before he disappeared. It may have been the map he used to escape, but I had nothing to do with it. I honestly can't help with the sequel or the movie, but I can supply minor details. However," I pause and look at her and try not to smile at the reaction I will get when I drop the next piece of information, "you might want to research his Stanford years."

"*Stanford?*"

"Oh, yes. He was at Stanford for six years."

Beverley's eyes widen. "Unbelievable!" she breathes. "He had been in America. My God! He must have planned his escape from America. Perhaps he's still at large—perhaps he's *here!* At the conference! Out of curiosity!" Her eyes zoom out, across and around the room. "I'll seek him out," she whispers, "the Scarlet Pimpernel!"

"Damned elusive, though, Bev," I say.

"In heaven or hell, but of course he *must be in America.* Where else would anyone run away and hide?" Breathless, she pours over the faded piece of paper. "The possibilities for the movie, oh! I knew you'd come round, my sweet." She flings her arms around me and kisses me on both cheeks. "A terrorist in Stanford. *Unbelievable. And oh my God!*" Beverley lunges forward and grabs me again. "*It has just hit me,* like a lightning bolt. *What that meant!* Taking all his clothes off in the middle of your living room—what else could that mean, except that he was going *to tell me all, all!* It was a physical symbol, a *signified* of the signifier to be articulated, his silent scream of revelation. He was going to tell all to me." She releases one of my shoulders and raises a fist high above her head. "*Yes, I am Lazarus, come back to tell you all* . . . I know exactly what it meant."

I take a quick look around to make sure we are no longer the central spectacle. No, thank God, everyone is milling around the table now laden with delicious hors d'oeuvres. Beverley gives me a shake. "My dear, dear Pia, I love you. If I hadn't seen your face here, if we hadn't talked, made peace—we have, haven't we? I wouldn't have cracked the code of that striptease. And you have known all along what that meant. Why else did you hate me so much? Jealousy. I, too, was jealous of you, my dear. Simply *green*." She kisses me again, this time very lightly on the mouth. "But we are where we are now, ma petite. On the verge of a deeper understanding."

I swallow and move back, forcing myself to smile, because I must smile. I owe her that much. And I have my paper to deliver in fifteen minutes. *It is impossible to say just what I mean—*

I hear Binoy's soft voice again, *it'll be all right.* Blood and mud caked over that so young, so beautiful face. And I hear Manik, laughing with the rain.

"I'll be in touch, ma cherie," Beverley waves, "half million, Capri, St. Tropez. . . ." She claps everyone to attention and announces her movie deal and her new investigative sequel.

Kick academia off, retire in Capri, sunbathe on marble terraces, if that's what she wants—but can she give up the glory she's bathing in right now? What we dream of, what we want, what we get, what we seize. . . . That faded map in her grip, a ticket to freedom, a release from the past, tracing back to the past. Now you'll go searching America with your new green eyes and Chanel suit, backed by Hollywood money, for your terrorist. You'll have your sequel, your movie, a tiny bit of my help. And the labyrinth I've now thrown you in. No Minotaurs, alas!

As I face my audience of eight fidgeting academics in another room, I see Jean V again, holding forth on "terrorism," amid the din of the casino, giving that classic shrug.

Beverley catches me again after my session. "Sorry I missed your paper. Do e-mail it to me." She drains her glass of champagne. "What did you think of that poem from Sulimaniya? When I read it first—I can't tell you what it *did* to me. It just broke my heart. I cried for a full hour. I had to put a cold pack on my eyes for the rest of the day."

"Terrible thing for your eyes," I say.

She waves aside my words. "Amazing—you—amazing—you look like him—you do! You've changed."

"*Changed?* You mean, not *transformed?*"

As soon as that shuttle drops me off at the airport, together with the two FBI agents, who look sleepy and as bored as ever, I toss Beverley's book in a trash can. Because this is her story, not mine, and definitely not his. The *real* story, Beverley, will never get written in this your black-and-white language. He escapes your pages. Only the rain captured and absorbed him. For there is no other place for him to be.

THE MATCHMAKERS

Watching the boy from her windows, Bela absently switched on her computer. The Internet connection took its own Calcutta time in spite of the fast connection she subscribed to. The boy caught her gaze and smiled up briefly, holding up the wire holder of spiced tea and masala omelet as his usual early morning salute. Bela's eyes watered and she blinked. These windows brought in too much light. Father Reid always scolded her about the bare windows. How can you work on that screen facing such bright light? You'll ruin your eyes, your special eyes that regard the world with such candor and fantasy!

Of all the absurdities. She was perfectly placed, the screen in front glowing saffron, and the large double windows to the left, framed in dark polished wood, offering the street. The focal point was the *dhaba*, steaming, crowded, noisy, from which the boy slipped out, and into which he disappeared. Around that nerve center, mornings, afternoons, evenings clamored with vendors, servants, children, dogs, neighbors, cars, rickshaws, bicycles, passing cows and goats.

Reid wouldn't understand why she sat here, just so, glancing occasionally. She drew her shawl tightly around her thin shoulders. It wasn't that sunny bright this morning. The sky was glazed grey by filmy clouds that signaled a Calcutta December. The boy was almost at the gates, giving that one-sided smile he kept only for security guards. How swiftly he moved, with almost a dancer's grace, all those cups perfectly balanced. Her eyes teared again. Was the screen too bright as well? She quickly reduced the brightness. The e-mail signal was blinking furiously: mail, mail, mail. That Ahuja again.

From: ahuja@hotmail.com
Subject: pls. reconsider

Dear CEO, COO, Senior Exec.VP,
Can I not have even one person's name so I can write dear Mr or *Ms*?

Pls. reconsider. I understand fully your line of work completely diff. But bodyshopping equally if not more money-making and you have established credentials. If you would search according to my specs. consultants: Java architects, C/C++, broadvision, some financial exp. then I can give you 3% of rate. Specs will change month 2 month. Germany also looking for similar specs.

Bela sighed and hit delete. Before going on to the next one, she exited from her e-mail and went to her favorite shopping sites. She placed orders for her office supplies, even a new mouse pad with an antique map of the world design. Belgian chocolates, Kona coffee, the best Darjeeling tea, Demerara sugar cubes, jams, jellies, and biscuits got tossed into the next shopping cart, followed by two boxes of Edward Gorey notecards, a table runner with William Morris patterns, and two Gypsy Kings CDs. She went to another site and placed an order for a dozen yellow roses and a Black Forest cake to be delivered to her parents' house a few days later, when her brother would arrive from America. Letting out a satisfied sigh, she exited again, checked her stocks, cursed the market, and returned to her e-mails.

The next one came up on the screen automatically.

From: swali@aol.com
Subject: marriage convention

Dear CEO,
I am inviting you again, and again, to please come and be on the panel for "Marriage and Family in the South Asian Community Abroad" in our Community Convention 2001, February 24 and 25. We will fly you first class on Air India (proud sponsors) and you

can stay with a family, or at the Sheraton. You will like Syracuse. Lots to see nearby. Biggest mall this side of the country. So many people are so eager to meet you. Must you remain faceless for the world? I'm also arranging an interview in SiliconIndia. We must have photo. Please send as gif ASAP.

Yours truly, and in admiration,
Suresh Wali.
Dewitt, NY
cell phone: (917) 220-0670

P.S. My sister-in-law's cousin can't stop singing praises. Her son's marriage went off very well. They were amazed to find that their in-laws' great-grandparents came from the same town in Karnataka as their own great-grandparents. How did you manage to trace the connection?

Something flashed at the corner of her eye. The wire carrier in the boy's hand. The boy was looking up again, his face shining.

Olive, Victorian writers would call his skin, with that sheen you saw on old paintings of boys at temple altars, with lustrous eyes reflecting the painter's fascination; by an ancient brook or lying on flower-splashed sunlit meadows, surrounded by sheep and nymphs, the long, elegant throat, the adolescent shoulders and waist and hips draped in muslin. Bela shook her head sternly. It was the light. The screen buzzed again. So many messages, so many connections to be dealt with and settled. The fax came alive with its high-pitched whine. Her cell phone chimed from the corner of her desk. Bela squared her shoulders. Why was the boy lingering downstairs?

As if sensing her impatience, the boy nodded at the doorman, handed him his mug of tea, and made his way to the elevators. A whistle made him turn around and squint toward the tea stall.

Bela lifted her head sharply at the sound. Two men waved at the boy from the benches and sat down. She had seen those two men many times. They were regular customers at the tea stall. The place drew all kinds. They, too, regarded the new boy with curiosity. But then, who wouldn't? There was something different about this boy. One couldn't help wondering where he came from. She had a keen eye and nose for sensing these things, doing what she did all day—researching the candidates biologically, socially, financially, genetically, astrologically. But it was impossible to get the specs on this boy in the normal sort of way. Casual conversation, where are you from, who are your parents, would be problematic for someone in her position with the tea-stall boy. Or to ask, however innocently, how did you land up here where I can see you looking up at my window frequently? Are you planning a burglary? You certainly have an odd hungry look about the eyes, a look of some uncanny purpose. There was no pull-down menu from the eyes or mouth to click and open.

Bela had left the door open, so the boy came in and put her breakfast down just as she liked it by her computer, on the pull-out tray of her table. She signed on her account sheet and handed it back to him. He paused again, mesmerized by the screen, every blink of the eyes like a click to download and save. She let him stare with that dark, disturbing stare. He was in his frayed denim shirt as usual, over dirty khaki pants, the sharp bones of his shoulders and hips faintly outlined under the thick fabric. Barefoot. "What is it?" she asked gently.

He scratched his head, his mouth twisting. "Something I might want to learn if I could. Everyone's into computers these days."

"Have you been to school?" She swiveled around in her chair.

"Completed my eleventh."

"What are you doing at this *dhaba*? Why didn't you finish high school?" She bit her tongue as soon as the words were out. She knew very well why boys and girls like him never finished their schooling, never got the chance. They hung forever on the periphery of making a living. "Why don't you come study with me?" she asked slowly. "I have tutored students in the past for free. The security fellow's nephew studied English with me before taking his high school finals. Maybe you can finish your twelfth then, and do much more."

"And where's the money for school?" He turned away scornfully and disappeared, banging the door.

Tight-lipped, Bela concentrated on the screen. He had some nerve, banging the door. Why did she have to ask touchy questions even if she only wanted to help? He had a self-sufficient air. He had potential. She had sensed that right away. With the right education, and all class problems erased, he could be reformatted into something divinely marketable. He could go places. But he wasn't interested. Why did she have to—oh, the screen again, beeping insistently for her immediate attention! Mukesh Gupta, here he was, ecstatic, exclaiming on Yahoo's Instant Messenger, so very definitely interested in Sushma Parmar.

The astrological charts have matched, and Sushma looks like a dream in the attachment I've received. Should we not meet now, or at least e-mail? My parents, too, are very eager. And how on earth did you find Mrs. Aluwalia, who knows my own parents *and* the Parmars? A true miracle! But I knew, from the most reliable sources, that you would find me special connections such as this. When living so far from one's home country and looking to find one's own kind to marry, it is so comforting to find that even per-fect strangers are connected in the strangest of ways. Mrs. Aluwalia *zindabad!* We can proceed with relief and joy. Please, please, can I not book a flight to California next week? Ottawa is unbearably cold at present for my parents.

A little thrill went up Bela's spine, but was short lived. "He is not at-tractive according to my specifications," Sushma Parmar had e-mailed back.

I don't like mustaches, and his hair seems to be thinning at thirty. He doesn't seem to know what colors suit him either. Or perhaps your scanner doesn't work well? And do his parents live with him permanently or what? Mrs. Aluwalia seems to think they visit often, for long stretches. I'm not saying I'm not interested. Perhaps you could drop a few hints?

"It is not always possible to match charts and all specifications to the perfection of Vishnu," Bela replied back calmly. "If his hair looked better and he shaved his mustache would that work for you? He is going to be very rich, very soon, as soon as he sells his B2B, which is extremely hot right now, and already has offers of over fifty million. Why don't you exchange a few e-mails and see how your communications go?"

She swiftly e-mailed Mukesh Gupta:

Yes, you may e-mail Ms. Parmar. However, remember it is your first contact. Strongly recommend you explain that your parents only visit once in two years, during the summer. That this year is an exception because your father needed a bypass. And, by the way, although we don't like bringing up these things except to offer suggestions, please go to a doctor. Get Rogaine for your hair. There's no need to go bald at an early age these days. Also, you have such a nice face. Why hide it under a mustache?

Her mouth tightened in distaste as she sent that off. Always these minor physical issues. Not fair skinned, hair too little or too much! Eyebrows too thick, ears sticking out, nose a little flat. . . . Why insist on the background checks and the astrology then? In-law and financial issues were far more important—didn't these people understand? She always researched the parents and families first, and oh, so thoroughly. There were dangers, situations ripe for exploitation of the worst kind. There were people ready to sell women to the Middle East, to harems, and even to America, as mail-order brides. She investigated her clients down to their chromosomes. Questionnaires, doctors, private detectives (terrific for finding such invaluable connections like great-grandparents in remote towns, and the above-mentioned Mrs. Aluwalia in West Boylston, Massachusetts), and especially her cousin, Nimki, who had done so much prying and poking into so many families in her own deviously ingenious ways.

Without Nimki, Bela couldn't have started this business, *couldn't have survived*, she sometimes felt. Dear, *sweet* Nimki, a contradiction in terms—as "Nimki" meant salty snacks—but dear, *sweet* woman that she was at times, having so casually divorced her husband, now running a beauty salon on Park Street much to the shock of the entire family. Bengali women from north Calcutta didn't do things like that—own salons, that is, or even divorce docile and boring husbands.

Darling Nimki, how she had stood up to Bela's parents. You should be ashamed of yourselves! Nimki had shouted at them. Having sent your *son* to America, you now want to marry your *daughter* to a doddering old invalid simply because you consider her undesirable and too old at thirty-one?

And Bela *was* undesirable, crippled by polio, the left leg thinner than the right, she walked with a considerable limp. Her face, whenever it stared back at her from mirrors, seemed nondescript. Although not light-skinned enough, she had good skin, even if she must say so herself. Glowing, and yes, olive! Perhaps not with that wondrous dewy sheen the boy possessed. But that was youth. Her features were regular, nothing that drew attention. A small nose, a humorous mouth, an obstinate chin with a little cleft, and eyes that Father Reid had called special, filled with, what was that? Candor and fantasy. Bah! Lately, when she looked at her face, she saw only her eyes. As if the rest of her slight self was out of focus, blurred. Only her eyes shone back at her, brightening, dimming, like her computer screen.

Rubbish. That's what Nimki would say. Head filling with nonsense as she sat tapping at the keyboard, tap, tap, tap, letters, numbers, symbols, control, shift, alt, control, shift, delete, control, alt, esc, return—what was she doing?

Nimki would give her a shaking if she were here. Tall and full-bodied like temple sculptures, she had spread out her muscled arms for Bela five years ago. Her vivid, imperious face hot with her flame red lipstick, she had yelled Bela's parents and meddling aunts into quivering submission. Unnerved, and willing to be rid of their unmarriageable daughter, Bela's parents contributed toward buying this large, one-bedroom apartment in Ballygunge (a south Calcutta address is a must, Nimki had insisted) with the money that had been set aside for her wedding. It was a good location, and in the high-rise where her corner apartment was set, people were friendly. Bela had insisted on getting this third-floor apartment in spite of Nimki's protests. During power outages she'd have a hard time climbing to the third floor, she knew. But first or second floor was too open to close contact.

It was tricky for a single woman, well under fifty, to live by herself without a hint of gossip. But her deformity saved her, and her reputation as a successful businesswoman. Nimki had ordered a close male friend—a web designer—to help set up Bela's web site. The business idea was Nimki's.

Her parents had given up on her after the polio attack at the age of five. But Nimki swept her up in her arms, sitting with her as she diligently did her homework, prepared for exams, all through the school years, massaging her wasted left leg at night after its whole day in the uncomfortable brace. Bela had studied history and English and completed her masters in English. Teaching for a few years in Loreto House had been hellish. Although the nuns were tolerable, the students were mean. Half the class limping around the playgrounds mimicking her made her devise various forms of torture specially suited for nine- to twelve-year-olds. But the day she designed a mechanically viable guillotine, on paper, for severing legs, she decided to quit.

She had saved up some money with which she bought her computer and floated the web site. Nimki got her set up with credit-card access and foreign-exchange permits. The business had taken off like information flying through fiber-optic cables, just as Nimki had predicted and liked to point out. People want to mate with their own kind at the end of the day, she decreed. If they haven't met the person of their dreams by accident or guile, they'll welcome an intensive search. Most Indians are conservative about marriage and family. You will provide authentic, reliable, well-researched, first-class service. You will be a global connection.

Global! The very word transported her. How she imagined all the places she read about and received e-mails from. Granada, Salamanca, Avignon, Lisbon, Milan, Istanbul, New York, Toronto, Moscow, Athens, Beijing, Vientiane, Bangkok, Manila. . . . All the places she had seen so vividly in the historical novels she devoured. She visited web sites hungrily, feasting on the pictures, memorizing architectural details, lingering in street scenes, shopping arcades, paved courtyards luxuriant with unknown flowers. She pressed her fingers against images of old stone walls and traced marble friezes.

She had traveled a little around Calcutta with her parents, some of the neigboring districts, as well as Puri, Darjeeling, Shillong, the usual places Bengali families went to vacation. But to look up at Mediterranean skies! Just look at this villa in Zakynthos!—where two of her clients would honeymoon, at her suggestion. With the very image this Calcutta sky, too, brightened, shed its grey haze and burst blue after the rains, moving into the freshness of December, blowing away the choking in her lungs that threatened from time to time. The screen beeped. New entries were coming in. She clicked on the *Personal Details* icon on her home page. Five new applicants, two men and three women, had filled in the questionnaires in the last ten minutes. Bela went over the preliminary forms her prospective clients had to fill online if they were interested in using her services. The forms collected basic information and asked for their thoughts on what kind of person they were looking for. After this first step, Bela conducted an online personal interview to decide if she and the client would be able to work together. From the five, she disqualified two right away from the initial screening.

Subject: Ideal Husband

Personal Statement: Hi! My name is Radhika Chawla. I was born in Lucknow and moved with my parents to Detroit when I was two. My father's a neurosurgeon. I've just finished my law degree from Harvard and have passed the New York bar. I'll be working in Alaska for a year and a half—a federal job. I am sick and tired of American men and their assinine treatment of me as a dark exotic beauty. I want to meet a great looking Indian guy (age: 27-32). He must be smart, sophisticated, should know how to cook (as I can't to save my life), educated from a good school. A bit of European exposure would be a plus. Career: he's got to be able to find respectable work in Alaska. I mean, Pizza Hut or McDonald's is NOT an option. Something funky, creative, and lucrative. And obviously, he has to be highly marketable, because I don't want him sitting and moping at home in Alaska, or wherever it is I move to afterwards . . .

Bela didn't bother reading the rest. Ms. Chawla was looking for a dating service, it would appear. Marriage was serious business.

To: Radhika@spectra.net
Subject: Re: Ideal Husband

Dear Ms. Chawla,
Thank you for thinking of us. We would love to help you in your search. But we are a little swamped at present to help you right away. We will, however, save your file, and if you are still in need of assistance in three months' time, we'll be happy to be of service. We understand if you can't wait, and we don't expect you to. So we wish you all the best in your search. We will contact you in three months' time just to make sure.
Sincerely,
B

Alaska! Perhaps she would meet a seal and get a gorgeous jacket out of it. Bloody footprints on the snow—that's what this client would mean. Her fingers flew over the keys again in response to the next three. They looked hopeful: serious, committed. And here was the other that needed to be dragged to the trash right away.

Subject: lovely wife.

Personal Statement: I am 33 and a mechanical engineer and a management consultant. My name is A. Srinivas Velu. I have lived in America for ten years. I came as a graduate student. I want someone who will be very devoted to me and my home. She can have a career, no problem, but part-time and must respect my parents who live with me here in Toledo. I have a very nice house with a pool. I have good friends who are doctors and lawyers. My wife should have a nice nature so she makes friends with their wives. I am interested in dowry as I have a lot to offer. I am fair skinned as you will see on my photograph, and play tennis all year round. My wife should have good figure and be tall. Thank you.

No, she could not possibly foist him on some unsuspecting gentle creature, and it didn't pay to be nasty in her line of work.

Back to work. Click, click, click. She was everywhere. Connecting someone in Stockholm with someone in Cleveland, Berlin to Toronto, Madras to Poughkeepsie. Doctors, engineers, currency-options traders, CEOs of e-commerce companies.... The world that she traversed in minutes, the men and women she communicated with second by second.... The world at your fingertips, my sweet, Nimki had said, and doing well, my dear, doing fabulously in this trying culture.

Nimki had certainly done fabulously. NRIs went to her salon, or day spa as it was called, as well as many foreign tourists. They got aromatherapy, massages, mud soaks, sandalwood body masks, skin revitalizations together with whatever they wanted with their hair and nails and feet. She, too, had her web site, and sold so many products—her Devi line—to clients in Hong Kong, South Korea, Thailand, the Philippines, all the lotions and potions she had started boiling and bubbling on her kitchen stove a few years ago. Now one of her boyfriends manufactured all the products in his "reusable natural waste" factory. Bela tried not to think about it. After all, she herself had used the "Ganges Silt" as a face pack a few times and hadn't yet changed into a newt or root vegetable. Nimki got a great deal of information and a lot of leads at her salon. She passed it along to Bela while she chopped her coal black, pike straight hair into a stylish pageboy every eight weeks. There, she'd say with her heart-stopping vermilion smile, is Bela-rani hot or not? She hated to be called that. Bela-rani. But it's sweet, Nimki laughed, and so archaic and quaint. Belarani was almost a household name these days.

Belarani.com, her web site. NRIs swore by it.

The boy looked over his shoulder at Bela's window before making his way back to the tea stall. Bela ignored the glance. She could see Gauri, the tea-stall owner, gesturing violently at the large aluminium kettle whistling out clouds of steam. She even caught the boy's grimace at the dishes already piled high under the tube-well to the side, and the laden plates of *kachuris* and omelets lining the worn wood of the makeshift counter that had remained makeshift for twelve years now. The two men continued to stare at the boy. It was a skin-crawling kind of stare, a greedy, lip-licking kind, like someone looking at a plump little lamb. The boy ran into the stall and rescued the kettle, poured the tea, picked up the plates and mugs, and served the crowded benches. "Oh, my boy," Bela heard Gauri sigh loudly, rolling his age-crinkled eyes, "hurry, hurry." He pointed at the two men at the far end.

Bela squinted against the glare. Was the boy looking upset? He was biting his lower lip as he walked over and set the food down on the long trestle table. The younger of the two men tossed him a few rupees.

The boy wasn't turning around. They were talking, it seemed. Something was going on down there, something not quite right. The man made a strange, exaggerated gesture then motioned with his head at his older, fat, *dhoti*-clad companion. The fat man grinned at the boy, his tiny eyes disappearing into the folds of his cheeks, his expansive middle bouncing with silent laughter. The companion, who sat much taller, trimmer, of a beaten-steel body and a terrifyingly pitted face, coiled his long, plaited hair around his fist. They were up to some *dhanda*, Bela could swear. The fat man's scalp, through his thinning hair, glistened with oil. She could almost smell it, so familiar that shine looked, the musty smell, like woodrot, of a particular hair oil used by people up to no good. That's what Nimki used to say.

The mean-looking younger man waved at the boy dismissively. The boy moved away, his face a mask.

"Oh, Bela-*ma*," Bela heard from the door. "What is this madness for the last few days? Breakfast from the *dhaba?*" Her maid walked in, one hand at her waist, the other swinging a striped plastic bag of vegetables and fish.

"Sparing you the trouble, Lata's mother," Bela smiled from the computer.

"How will I be spared when you get cholera-typhoid-jaundice? Who will be taking care of you? I could drop dead any day. Here—" she swung the bag up to Bela's nose. "See? The freshest fish in the city. From *my* man at the bazaar. Just a little more expensive, that's all. Don't complain. You make a lot of money. I'll go start in the kitchen."

Although bent from hard work and old age, the woman went about her business like a tightly braided, singed, coir rope: dusting, sweeping, mopping with vengeance, then getting ready to start the day's cooking. She chattered throughout, her shrill voice setting Bela's teeth on edge. Who needed to subscribe to a scandal sheet when the local dirt spewed with such zest morning and evening? She knew everyone's business in this building and in the next three down the road. Who might kill whom, who might go to jail pretty soon, whose son might be a drug smuggler, whose daughter the next big movie star. About affairs and adultery, the narration came in code: joint secretary's wife closed the door and drew shut all the curtains after so-and-so arrived at two in the afternoon. Left disguised as a woman. So-and-so's wife disappears every day at eleven and returns at two-thirty. Black Maruti picks up and drops off at the post office corner. Eleventh floor you-know-who comes home late every Tuesday. Changes shirt and sprays cologne before getting out of car. Travel agent lady, in 8A/A, weekly increase in jewelry, foreign clothes, and perfumes.

"I'm leaving the good teapot out with the cups for the padre," Bela heard the woman call from the door hours later. "Your lunch is on the table." Every Thursday, Father Reid at four-thirty. Bela stretched with pleasure. Subhash in Brussels and Romila in Quebec City had set a date for their wedding in New Delhi.

Bela stretched again a little after four and rolled out of bed. The book was hard to put down. Her head was full of the fifteenth-century air of

Trebizond. But she must turn the kettle on. Father Reid would never touch the *dhaba* tea. Always the best Darjeeling with one cube of Demerara sugar, and toast points with butter and black currant preserves. She unlocked the front door, then went to the kitchen. Remodeled last year by a contractor who did kitchens and bathrooms for NRIs, it gleamed with red granite counters. She switched on the bright electric kettle presented by one of her clients, shooed off the crows perched on the window ledge with a rolling pin, and returned to her living room-cum-office.

Sunlight was streaming in at a slant, burnishing her teak desk and the tan leather chair. She loved this late afternoon light, how it covered everything with a lazy golden warmth. The boy was waving from the gates of the building complex. She waved back, motioning him to come up.

He stood at the door breathless, a glitter in his eyes. "Can you get me some hot *jalebis?*" she asked, handing him money. "I'm expecting a guest."

"My dear," she heard and started. "If ever I saw the eyes of a hunter when he sighted his quarry." Father Reid ushered her back to her living room and dropped a book on her table.

Bela curled up on the chaise as was her custom every Thursday afternoon, while Father Reid brought in the tea tray, poured, and settled down on the fawn velvet sofa with his cup. "Where's the toast?" Father Reid raised a finely marked eyebrow.

"I've ordered a treat for you."

"Oh, no." Reid struck his forehead.

With a light knock the boy entered, bearing a dried palm leaf steaming with sugary vapor.

Father Reid bent over the pale gold coils translucent with syrup. "They look like pretzels." A frown deepened over his rimless glasses.

Bela waved at the boy to leave. "Just bite into one."

"Oh, my!" Reid breathed after two *jalebis*. "A little *too* sweet perhaps, but not bad at all. What will I die of?"

"Indulgence, obviously. Now what did you mean by eyes and hunters?"

"Oh, nothing, nothing." Reid poured himself a second cup. "How do you like my new shirt?"

Bela's eyes narrowed. Brian Reid was a vain creature, she had learned quickly. Unhappy about his five feet eight inches, he had made the most of his softly angled face with the two days' growth he always wore and his longish silver-gold hair. He tanned marvelously and kept himself fit by jogging, playing squash, and swimming, and at forty-six had the stamina of a twenty-year-old, or so he said. She had been stunned by his flamboyant clothes the first time she had seen him on the playgrounds of St. Xavier's while visiting a friend who taught there. In a flowing white silk shirt over violet trousers, he was herding a large group of boys back to class. And then she had seen him again, walking out of the chapel of Loreto House with the Mother Superior, only this time in black clothes and white collar.

They had spoken to each other for the first time at a school picnic six years ago, and she had taken an immediate liking to his understanding blue eyes, which never carried a hint of pity, never acknowledged her severe limp. She had been surprised by him, at the ease with which they had become friends. Differences of culture and race had crumbled under the onslaught of his flippant wit. After she left the school, he paid her weekly visits, to have a civilized tea, he said, and to have his clothes admired.

"Where did you get that kind of silk?" she asked.

"The mother of one of the boys has an export business. Sand-washed silk. I had to tutor him to pass trig. Aquamarine, wouldn't you say?"

"*I* say, don't fake astonishment when certain young men follow you around with spaniel eyes."

Reid shook his head and sighed. "It's your sexuality that should be called into question, not mine. What's that boy all about?"

"He's the new boy at the tea stall."

"Why that odd look in his eyes?"

"What odd look?"

"Like he's on the scent of something. Not you, I hope."

"Don't be silly. I find him most interesting. Go look out the window and you'll see what I mean."

Father Reid settled back against quilted, black silk pillows. "You tell me. Your fantasy is far more engaging than my reality."

"He seems about seventeen, but very androgynous. Voice musical, not harsh like the street urchins. I just wonder where he comes from and what he's doing here."

"You are not developing a crush?" Reid leaned forward.

"Oh, please."

"Intrigue? What do you want *me* to do—with regard to him?"

Bela's eyes widened.

"Oh, come on! You wouldn't have ordered him here with those things if you didn't want me to take a good look at him."

Bela smiled sweetly. "Well, he seems to have potential. To be more than just a tea-stall boy. Could you get him into one of your lower tuition schools? I could pay. He's finished his eleventh, you see."

Father Reid closed his eyes for a few moments. "Does he speak any English?"

"I don't know."

"He can't go into *any* school, you know that. The class issues would be overwhelming. And the only way he can get a *free* education in one of 'our' schools is to convert. I could get him into a school in Kerala, though, without much trouble."

"Kerala!"

"That's the best I can do. My advice: you tutor him privately so he can take the exams next year. Then he goes into a polytechnic institute of some kind. He could even learn computer stuff if he's smart enough. That would be a realistic approach." He looked at her with a dense blue intensity she had seen a few times, a look so remote, yet surprisingly intimate, glimpsed only when he stood at the altar with the cup and host, when he watched cricket matches, and when he spoke of Scotland. "Or you could just leave him be."

"I think he wants me to help him," Bela said, her voice dropping.

"He wants to see what he can get out of you. And he already has your sympathy." Reid frowned. "He doesn't strike me as helpless. He seems very self-possessed."

"He's struggling to make a living," Bela said sharply.

"He's struggling to package and repackage himself for the likes of you, and—" Reid raised a hand to block Bela's spilling protest, "and I know about packaging, let me tell you that. Haven't been in the Catholic church for twenty-odd years without—" Reid waved off the rest. "Before I forget, on the subject of packaging—the same dear boy's mother of the glorious shirt has begged an audience. To present her darling nephew all properly gift wrapped, I'm sure. I told her it is quite impossible—to see your face, that is. She wants help to locate a suitable wife in America for the nephew, currently a police officer. I gave her your e-mail address. Not a problem, I hope?"

Bela popped a sugar cube into her mouth and sucked for a few seconds. "How did she connect you with the web site, Brian?"

Reid shrugged. "She didn't. While collecting her offspring one afternoon, she asked me if I knew about the web site, and if it would work for her nephew. She said she had heard a great deal about it, and wondered if I knew anything more. I said I didn't."

"Are you sure?"

"Are you accusing *me* of betrayal?"

"Of course not, *Father*. But that shirt is rather unusual."

"Yes, isn't it, rather?" Reid murmured, touching the fabric lightly. "More might be coming my way."

"You slime! What about that vow of poverty?"

"There's no ban on receiving presents."

"You did not tell—"

"Bela, you know I didn't. I simply gave your site a rave review." He stood up and smiled brightly. "I have something to tell you. I'm going on a trip soon." He walked around the large room like a satisfied leopard. "New York! I'll be at Fordham for a week. A conference on Ecumenical Theology. Then the next two weeks at a novitiate in Syracuse. A seminar. February." He paused and looked out of the windows. "It's been a long time."

Bela pursed her lips. Reid had loved his years at Harvard even more than his time at Oxford. He had spent many years in America. His sister lived in New York. Reid turned around. "I asked if I could sail. A cruise, starting from Portugal. It's a lovely ship. Dutch."

His eyes sparkling, he dropped a light kiss on top of her head and left.

Bela was about to smash the teapot, but the phone stopped her hand.

Nimki's voice was playfully urgent. "Hey! I've a new client for you. VIP. Come tomorrow. You *must* meet them."

"Are you crazy? Have them e-mail me."

"One favor. Make an exception. Please, just this once. I'll treat you to a fabulous lunch afterward."

"No one must connect me—"

"I've sworn them to secrecy, don't worry."

With a worried frown Bela put down the phone. Even here, in this very building, no one had yet connected Belarani with Bela Mitra who lived in apartment #3C/3. They knew she had some type of Internet business. And since she led a quiet existence without too many visitors—her maid guaranteed that to all around—people didn't bother prying. Perhaps she was worrying too much. Nimki had never asked her for anything. She would always protect her. Bela picked up the book Reid had left. He brought her books and videos every week. No video today, just this very attractive, glossy book called *Winter Cruises.*

Bela threw it as hard as she could against the wall at the other end, then recoiled as her doorbell shrieked in response. Her maid was back to clean up again, set dinner, and give her an earful about everybody's misdeeds in the neighborhood.

She let her in, then sank back with the dented book full of gorgeous pictures. Nimki had been on a cruise last winter. Nimki had been to Bangkok, Kuala Lumpur, Manila, Singapore, Tokyo, Bali. Each time with a different man. She sighed angrily. How does one live with such contradictions?

Nimki, who had agreed to an arranged marriage with complete indifference; who had left her husband because she was bored; who had reckless affairs before, during, and after her marriage; who had forcefully rescued Bela from a similar marriage, then set her up to go into business arranging marriages.

But it wasn't the same thing, Bela knew, and as Nimki had argued: You are not forcing people to marry. You are providing a service for men and women abroad that helps them make up their own minds. You are offering intensive research. Arranged marriages are not arranged the same way they were fifty years back. Young people make their own decisions nowadays; they simply want to make those decisions from a certain kind of data. You are providing that data, and if they want, an analysis as well. $350 to start with and $650 more for full service to find the right match.

And to Bela's open-mouthed amazement, they paid. With credit cards, NRI rupee accounts, wire transfers. . . .

She knew she inhabited a strange place, one that didn't have hard, solid ground underfoot. A world of buzzing sounds and images moving before her eyes at 750 megahertz. A world you could not smell or taste; touch only by clicking on a mouse or tapping on a keyboard. But it was swarming with people and their words, their demands, dreams, desires, discontentments. It brought a perverse satisfaction, and the hard real money she needed to survive. To survive in her tough, day-to-day world that she was loath to face. The world that had rejected her, called her a cripple. She had left that world, risen far above it, simply floated away.

And how did she get here? She, who hardly went anywhere. From an old north Calcutta house that generations had lived in, from limping around with her shriveled leg and sucking tamarind pods on the terrace to this? To this computer screen. She *had* traveled for sure, oh, yes, she had traveled, an immense distance, light-years, like those space voyagers, sought out new worlds, worlds with infinite possibilities, and boldly gone . . . much, much farther than Reid or Nimki. Not over oceans or mountains, not across the deserts of Africa or the snows of Siberia or the rain forests of the Amazon, but she had crossed the mythic seven seas, the thirteen rivers, and the vast, vast wilderness to arrive, in a flash of a flame red smile, to a truly magic kingdom: Belarani.com!

"Arre, what is this dotcom-dotcom I keep hearing? Is it some kind of fairyland?" Bela heard Gauri rasp at a customer. The man paid for his order and laughed. She leaned over her balcony with a cup of tea.

"Now I know why I've been stopping here on my way home these eight years." The man smiled at Gauri and then up at her. "How are you, Miss Mitra? This old man keeps us grounded, doesn't he?"

"Ah, not possible anymore," Gauri sighed. "You're all floating, feet quite off the ground, in computer-heaven nowadays. Everyone is in dotcom. I'd like to see this dotcom place."

"Easy," said the man, taking a sip of the hot spiced tea. "Just go down the road past the bazaar to Broad Street, and you'll see quite a few doors that read 'Cyberworld,' 'Netcon,' and the like. Walk in and you'll enter this brave new dotcom world of ours."

"And what will I find there?" Gauri rasped again.

"People just like you and me—"

"You and me not alike, mister—"

"To a computer, we are, old man, when we sit in front of glowing screens and swallow the world."

Bela saw the boy sit down, cupping his face in his hands. The man carried on. "They are all rushing to America—on demand. Germany, too. Just sent off two fellows to Hamburg. Visas? Just have to be a computer consultant or have a dotcom address. People from the slums around the tanneries are doing business with designers in Italy and America," he said. "They should rewire their brains in the schools. I tell my daughter, geography has changed. No need for world maps, just world wide web. Continents, oceans, India, America, all one territory, all Internet space. The dotcom colonization!" People laughed with him. "We may have missed the industrial revolution, but I tell you, we're running over America with our IT consultants."

The *dhaba* was filling up swiftly as the workday drew to a close. Gauri was yelling out orders at his cook for hot fritters and chicken cutlets. People came to the counter and picked up their food themselves when the rush set in. They liked chatting and joking with Gauri. "I don't understand this dotcom business," he kept grumbling to all. Bus drivers, rickshawallas, teachers, lawyers, college students, CEOs, the whole neighborhood came to Gauri's.

Recently, Gauri had started supplying cold beer along with Coke, Pepsi, Marlboros, snacks, and tea. That had definitely increased his popularity. A few rich *Marwari* boys, under eighteen without a doubt, had become regular customers of late. They gathered around a table with several bottles of Taj Mahal and made a great deal of noise. This evening, they got too loud, swore at everyone, overturned tables and benches. A wiry little man got up suddenly, cuffed two of them hard, then whacked them out to the street with a walking stick to the cheers of the rest of the customers.

Bela almost clapped along with the crowd. She felt so much a part of the *dhaba* when she sat on her balcony. Her window was good in the mornings. An occasional glance to relieve her eyes from the screen. But after five, the balcony, gilded by the dropping sun, shone irresistibly. The street below, or lane rather, was narrow, voices carried distinctly, and Gauri always acknowledged her presence on the balcony with a nod and a smile. She liked that old man.

Her back stiffened involuntarily. The mean-looking man was standing behind the boy, gripping his shoulder. The boy got up and followed silently. At a distance from the crowd, they sat around a table, talking. The man caught the boy's hand. He was being given something. Drugs? Was Gauri aware that the boy was getting into bad company?

"I'll be on my way," she heard the maid call and was forced to turn away from the unfolding drama.

"Lata's mother," she called quickly. "Come here a moment."

The old woman came to the balcony, squinting. Bela motioned her to come closer. "Do you see those two men with the boy?" she asked. "Do you know who they are?"

The maid rolled her eyes. "The fat one is Shankar-*babu*, used to be a matchmaker. And the other is Ghoton. Up to no good usually. Hmph." She snorted and removed the empty cup from Bela's hand. "That boy's a nice sort, I think. But that face, that face is troubling."

"What do you mean?"

She scratched her head with a gnarled finger. "It's a pretty face, if you know what I mean, with too ready a smile."

Bela frowned after her hunched back as she returned to the kitchen.

"May I come in?"

Bela sat up with such a start that the book leaped to the floor.

The old woman was long gone. She could smell the dinner on the table in the next room. The boy looked at her shyly from the door. How did he get in? A mild worry pricking her spine, "What is it?" she asked. The boy came forward, picked up the book, and put it on the coffee table.

"I'm in a bit of a fix," he said in a whisper. "I need some help."

"Are you looking for new work? You don't like the work at Gauri's?"

The boy smiled and shook his head. "Oh, no, nothing like that. I like Gauri. I like working there." He shuffled from one foot to the other, then removed a ball of paper from his pocket. "I wanted to learn to do some stuff on the computer. I believe horoscopes and natal charts can be done very fast by these machines. Is that true?"

Bela's spine tingled again. "Why do you want to do horoscopes?"

"I don't want to learn it as a trade." He scratched his head. "If I go to an astrologer to get charts prepared, it costs a lot. I've been told it doesn't cost anything on the computer."

"Why do you need to have natal charts prepared?"

"I need to get my sisters' charts prepared—for marriage purposes."

Bela felt her hands sweat. Had someone sent him to spy on her? "Why come to me?" she asked. "How am I connected to horoscopes?"

The boy looked flustered. "I thought you wanted to help me. You . . . you said you could teach me . . . I'm sorry." He turned to go.

"Wait." Bela stood up. She went to her computer slowly, controlling the limp as much as possible, then sat down on her chair. "What's your name?"

"Shomu."

"The truth—why have you come to me with this nonsense about natal charts and your sisters?" she asked sternly. "What is this really about?"

Shomu handed her the crumpled piece of paper. "These are my four sisters' dates of birth. I need to get their charts for the matchmaker so he can find suitable husbands for them."

"Shouldn't your father—"

"He disappeared a long time ago. My mother died last year."

"Who's going to help you marry off your sisters?"

"Someone I met recently. A matchmaker."

"Are you sure he isn't a crook?"

"I'm sure."

Bela looked at the piece of paper closely. "Your sisters are barely a year apart, and thirteen and fourteen are too young for marriage. Fifteen and sixteen are also very young. You can't legally marry before sixteen, anyway. What do they do at present? Where do they live?"

"Bishnupur." Shomu looked at her anxiously. "They work in rich folks' houses. If I can't help them, who will?" His eyes filled up with a sudden bright wetness. "I came to you because you are kind to me. Gauri speaks highly of you. Everyone says you do computer business. Market astrologers can take advantage of me. Sometimes they tell you bad things are in the stars and you need to buy special rubies and diamonds from them. I have very little money."

"Now, now." Bela reached down and patted his shoulder. A likely story, she said to herself. You need an excuse to talk to me. But no need for such a harebrained tale. But what to do with the harebrained tale? She ought to send it packing together with the rascal, for he was a rascal, wasn't he? The eyes, filling up on command, no doubt, knowing exactly how to win the confidences of lonely older women. Waiting to burgle, scoping out the apartment. What else? She must be wary.

Shomu sniffed and wiped his nose on his sleeve. "It's been difficult," he said with almost a sob.

Bela touched his shoulder again. Somehow the eyes and mouth seemed marked by real pain. "I think I should get you out of the clutches of this matchmaker quickly," she said. "Maybe I could find you a different job—"

"No!" Shomu sprang up. "They're helping me. Can't you please help me with this? My sisters are not going to get married right away. Finding husbands takes time, especially ones that don't expect any dowry."

"You need special programs to do natal charts," Bela said. "Machines can't do things by themselves."

"Do you have those programs?" Shomu leaned over to peer into her screen, which was swimming with the colorful fishes of her screensaver.

"Those programs are expensive."

"I've heard there's some way to get them for free. *Download*—that's the word a lot of people use. They all talk about *downloading* things."

"Why don't you sit down and learn a little more."

Bela touched the keyboard to clear the screensaver, opened the program, entered all the dates and times, pulled down a few menus and clicked a few times. Shomu watched closely.

"You have such a program? Now the machine will do everything? Do you prepare charts for people?"

"No," Bela lied. "I have a few of these programs to play with, for fun. Now, I'm going to go down to get my mail." Bela went to the door and waited for him. "These charts will be ready by the time we come back."

He took her elbow as they stepped off the elevator. She was surprised by his gentleness. The guard downstairs touched his forehead. "He's a good boy," he told her with a nod. "He's been helping old Mrs. Choudhury with her shopping, twice a week."

"You've been busy." Bela smiled up at him. He was quite a few inches taller than her. But then everybody was taller than her. She was barely five foot two and thin as a reed.

"She calls me every Monday and Thursday from her balcony, what can I do? She's a sweet old lady. Gauri told me to help her."

"She pays you, I hope."

"Twenty rupees each time."

"That's a relief. She hasn't settled her account with Gauri for four years!"

Shomu laughed. "But Gauri continues to send her daily breakfast of *kachuris* and *halwa*. I think he's hoping to make it into her will."

Bela freed her elbow. "I don't need assistance," she said primly. "I can walk on my own."

"Sorry." Shomu made a face. "I'm used to taking care of people, cooking and cleaning."

"You can do a lot better. I'll help you make a better life for yourself—"

"I'm doing just fine."

His face shocked her, it changed so swiftly. Reid's words flashed in her head: hunter, quarry. Ruthless determination, or was it deep, deep damage?

"I know private detectives," Bela stammered. "If you give me adequate information I could help you find your father."

"I'll get him," he said in the same chilling tone, "one of these days."

"What was his line of work?"

The boy gave no response. They went quietly back to her apartment.

"Come and sit," Bela said. "Let me get you something to eat." She hobbled to the table, poured a glass of water, and served some of the food on a plate. He ate quickly, holding the plate on his lap. "Were you hungry?"

"No. But this is like my mother's cooking."

He finished the food and took the dishes to the kitchen. She heard him wash up. He came back wiping his hands on his threadbare trousers and sat down.

"Well," she shrugged and turned on the printer. "Here are the charts. I hope things work out."

He took the crisp white sheets and nodded his thanks. "I've only a hundred rupees," he said. She waved off his hand.

"What I'd like," she said gently, "is to tutor you so you can take the high-school final exam next year."

"I'd like to do that." He came forward eagerly. "I've learned a lot just watching you work on your machine." He gave a nod and slipped out into the dimly lit hallway.

Bela paced on her balcony, waiting for the taxi. Eleven o'clock. She could hear the rattle and hum of Calcutta traffic, which never eased off. What possessed Nimki to fix this appointment? Has to be a rich, important client she wants to keep happy. Nimki had never asked any favors of her. Nimki had protected Bela all her life.

Where was the taxi? She wanted to get it over with fast. She didn't want to be late. And she wanted to shake off this mild headache that nagged at her temples. Why did the boy really want those charts? That suspicious-looking fat man, a matchmaker? Forget it, she said to herself firmly. A likely story. He wanted to form a connection and his sisters' marriages were a convenient excuse. Her taxi finally arrived at the gates and drove last evening out of her head.

The driver weaved through traffic, avoiding cows and people occasionally, then went over the tram tracks until they were perfectly aligned for a head-on collision with the oncoming juggernaut that bore down on the taxi with relentless indifference. With barely half a yard of clearance, the driver swerved the taxi back into the stream of traffic. Bela heaved a sigh and dialed a number on her cell phone. "Mr. Dutt? I have a job for you," she said to the responding voice. "I want some people followed." She sank back against the seat.

Shomu had appeared cheerful when he had brought her tea this morning. "Thank you," he had said, his voice warm with gratitude. Four astrological charts. What paper had she printed them on? Bela shook her head dismissively. She had fed in blank sheets, she was sure. She had *not* handed the boy natal charts printed on Belarani stationery. The taxi pulled up in front of Nimki's salon.

One of the Chinese girls ushered her through the crowded, buzzing space to Nimki's office. Two women were waiting there, one in her late forties, the other in her early twenties. Nimki flew in and dazzled them all with her fiery smile. "Mrs. Poddar and her daughter, Chaitali. And this, of course, is my very dear cousin, Bela. They wanted to meet you very badly. I'll leave you in peace with excellent coffee."

Mother and daughter looked her up and down with mild astonishment. Bela smiled politely. "This is rather an exception," she said. "People contact us on the web site, via e-mail. We never meet clients face to face."

"We understand," stammered Mrs. Poddar. "I didn't realize you had a . . . I mean, we would have come to you if I had known—" she stopped, breathless. "I mean, what a lovely sari," she said quickly. "Ikat is so elegant. Mauve and white—two of my favorite colors. We will not disclose anything, you can be sure. Thank you for meeting with us. It's an honor." Her breathing grew rapid. "Your web site is so highly regarded. My husband and I would really like to find someone settled in America, preferably on the East Coast, Connecticut if possible. She wants to do her Ph.D. at Yale—"

"Mummy," Chaitali interrupted, "let me." She was tall, slender, with soft, wavy hair down to her waist. She wore a little too much makeup, but was undeniably gorgeous in her hip-hugging jeans and short silk-knit T-shirt. "I don't want the typical arranged marriage," she said. "That's why I wanted to connect with you. I'd like to see the photographs, go over their backgrounds myself. Mid-to-late twenties, smart, with hopes of financial success. I'll want to meet each one of them—the ones that appeal to me, that is. They can come here, or I can go there—"

"Chaiti!"

"Wait, Mummy." She made a little *tch* of impatience. "The ones that want me to go there will have to fly out both me and my mother. Also, I would like to maintain the same standard of living. I can't give up things I like," she paused, fingering her long gold earrings glittering with diamonds. "I don't want 'him' to have unrealistic expectations. I can't really give you very specific details, but I'm sure you can make an educated guess about what kind of prospect I would like, the kind of men who would suit me. I read a lot, love European films, play the piano, like Sting, Tina Turner, Elton John, light classical music, antiques, Max Azria clothes. It has to be someone *I* can fall in love with. He must be *romantic*." Chaitali raised an eyebrow and waited.

Bela cleared her throat. "I will, of course, give you whatever information I can. I will need your photograph. It's not exactly a one-way street, you understand?"

"But I'd like to pick first. And I don't want my photograph and personal details all over the Internet!"

"There's no danger of that," Bela assured. "Once your specs are entered, only candidates who match the criteria, or whose criteria you match, will be sent your file. It is an extremely exclusive and selective process, and completely confidential. No one will have your name until you feel ready to give it out. It's an interactive site, too, as you will find once you register and log on."

"I still want to pick first."

"You would want to 'pick' from an interested group, no?"

Chaitali's eyes flashed confused scorn. "Of course they would be *interested*."

"Yes, of course." Bela nodded vigorously. She handed Mrs. Poddar her card. "Please call me in a few days and I should have worthwhile information. I do have to go through all the candidates and find the ones suitable for *you*. And I will need your complete background." She smiled as engagingly as she could.

"No *home* address, Miss Bela?" Mrs. Poddar stammered for the second time, scrutinizing her card.

"As I said, we do everything on the Internet."

Nimki opened the door as if she had had her ear to it. Over lunch at Peter Cat, "So I am to arrange a *swayamvar*," Bela said, throwing up her hands. "A princess to be won! What feats should the candidates be performing? Can't do the arrow-through-the-eye-of-the-fish-on-the-ceiling-while-looking-at-its-reflection-in-the-pool-below. An online hunting game of some sort? Shoot the princess?"

"Just do it the way you do things. Some of the girls here are too spoiled."

"Why did you force me to meet with them?" Bela shook her fist.

Nimki's magnificent eyes gleamed with guilty mischief. "Sorry." She wrinkled her nose. "Very, very selfish. Mrs. Poddar has a distant cousin in Hollywood who owns a salon and beauty-products store. Rich and famous clients. Mrs. Poddar is talking to her about carrying my Devi line. So you must get Miss Impossible married ASAP."

"Nimki! You sold me out for—"

"I didn't. Sworn to silence on pain of death and dismemberment and curse of vile skin over next three generations. Does she know she'll have to cook and clean over there?" Nimki's eyes gleamed again. "Better find her a very rich guy. For sure, currency-options trader or dotcom owner or specialist surgeon. She'll be going for her manicure and pedicure and massages every week without fail. She comes here to get her hair washed every three days, conditioned every two weeks. She says it's too much for her to handle. I'll make sure she gets a real good trim before she boards the plane."

"You're a number." Bela broke down and laughed.

"And you, my little one," Nimki leaned across and patted her cheek. "Your flowers were greeted with ecstasy, by the way. They got in last night. Anupam looks great and the little boy's got a temper, mind you. Your mom and dad's chests have expanded a few inches at the sight of their fair-skinned grandson."

"Does he look like Anupam?"

"Thank God." Nimki touched her forehead and chest. "You'll see them all in a few days, I'm sure, when Jenny's got over her jet lag. I can't stand the way your mother mollycoddles her. Ready to prostrate herself before white skin. Jenny's so earnest, she makes me gag."

"Nimki." Bela felt a surge of anger. Her sister-in-law Jenny, with her reddish brown hair and nervous hazel eyes, was a sweet, timid creature who fell apart in seconds under Nimki's withering scorn.

"She's working-class, damn it! What goes wrong with our men once they go over there? Don't they recognize class over there? They are blinded by white skin and blue eyes. And girls like Jenny are looking to catch rich doctors. Thank God you're here to consult, otherwise we'd lose all our good men to working-class American women."

"She's a sweet woman," Bela said sharply. "She means well. She dotes on Anupam. "

"She's an idiot. And she's a nervous wreck whenever she comes here."

"Well, don't keep looking down your critical nose at her all the time."

"Don't you go defending her after the stupid things she says!" Nimki's eyes flashed warningly. "She tells me, when I stopped by this morning, 'Oh, it must be hard for Bela.' I wanted to slap her silly. She brought scented soaps for you. Anyway, forget it. How is that delicious Reid doing?"

"He's going to America soon."

Nimki smiled mischievously. "I wish I could seduce him. Undress him slowly."

Bela rolled her eyes. She remembered Nimki flirting outrageously with Reid when they first met. She remembered with an equally mischievous smile Reid's comment. "I don't think I have the emotional stamina for that woman. Don't ever put me in the same room with her again."

"Hey," Nimki slapped her hand. "What are you smiling about?"

"You." Bela made a face.

"Me? You're the hot number, Belarani, your famous web site! You deliver America!"

Bela felt her head spin. Did she indeed? All the young men and women clamoring from India, what did they want, what did they ask for? She told them everything about living in America. She had scoured all relevant web sites. Where to shop, what to buy, what to ask for, what cars, what kind of houses or apartments. She told them about Neutrogena and Clinique, about JCPenney, about The Limited and Express, The Body Shop, Esprit, Ann Taylor, Nordstrom; she told them about wines and cheeses she had never tasted; about Victoria's Secret that she would never discover.

They hung on Belarani's every word. They couldn't believe their luck.

To the ones living abroad, looking to find their future mates from India, Belarani opened all the designer doors in Calcutta, Jaipur, Madras, Bombay, Hyderabad, Bangalore, and Delhi. From saris in fashion and styles of jewelry to music, art, antiques. The Indians abroad seemed to live in a time warp. Quite a few of them were still obsessed with the heavy, unwieldy saris, and huge chunks of gold. She gently persuaded them toward the elegance of Baluchari, Bomkai, and Ikat saris, stylishly light jewelry, and connected them with the new, young art dealers.

"I look at you in wonder," Nimki said with a shake of her head.

Bela felt a sudden overwhelming urge to cry. "Nimki, you're crazy," she said with a catch in her voice. Why did you ever get married or divorced? she wanted to ask her for the millionth time. "Are you happy?" she asked instead.

Nimki gave a quick smile. "I don't think of my life in those terms, happy or unhappy, my sweet. You know that. I live for excitement, for pure pleasure. I'll die from it I'm sure." She lit a dark, gold-tipped cigarette and sighed. "All this bustle about marriage. Marriage, it's serious business. One must take it very seriously. I say, marry often, and well."

Bela started to laugh in spite of herself. "Is that what you want me to tell my clients?"

"Wouldn't it be just grand for business? Constantly negotiating, constantly searching for the next best loot!" Nimki smiled again.

I got married because I couldn't get out of my parents' clutches. I got my two beautiful girls out of it. And I got divorced because my mother-in-law was on the verge of flinging herself from the rooftop driven to distraction by me—Bela could hear Nimki's words echo in her head whenever she smiled that way.

Bela tapped the taxi driver on the shoulder and made him stop in front of the old cemetery on Park Street.

Biting her lip, she walked in through the rusted gates. Her leg had begun to hurt in the brace in spite of its newer, softer padding. But she wanted to go somewhere this afternoon. Somewhere quiet, abandoned, overgrown, fragrant with wild blossoms, away from the din of Calcutta, away from her demanding screen, somewhere she could sift through the nagging thoughts. Had she become involved in something evil? Evil! Absurd that the word should invade from nowhere. Involved? No, she never got involved. She had managed to disengage from this harsh world roaring around her. She blinked twice fiercely.

Tumbled stones and obelisks, some large and curiously carved, surrounded her. The paths running among the ancient graves were all shrouded with creepers and shrubbery. Had she wandered in by accident, in search of colonial names, drawn by the scent of honeysuckle, gardenia, jasmine?

She shouldn't have come here. Was it not an unforgivable invasion of privacy to walk up to him as he knelt by the headstone of one tended grave, as he lay down a bouquet of roses so gently? Her cell phone startled them both brutally. Bela dropped her bag in shock, her knees almost buckling.

Reid picked up her bag, fished out the shrilling phone, and turned off the ringer. "My grandmother," he said, motioning at the moss-covered headstone.

"I know."

Reid's eyes narrowed.

"Mother Superior told me. She said you were connected to India. Your grandfather had served here." She answered the next unasked question. "Mother Superior told me you come here Friday afternoons."

"Is something wrong? You could have called me." Reid's face changed instantly. He reached for her elbow. She shook her head.

"I've been feeling a bit odd. Nothing really. Just wanted to go somewhere, I don't know." She shrugged. "I better find myself a taxi."

Reid dusted his trousers and picked up his cloth bag. "Come," he said, and took her elbow firmly. He led her along the tangled paths to a stone bench and made her sit. Removing a metal flask from his bag, he poured tea into two steel mugs. "Look around you," he said. "So many English buried here. See there. Rose Aylmer's grave with 'Ah what avails the sceptred race' inscribed on the tomb. Fascinating place. Wonder what another poet twenty years from now might write? 'Ah, what virus nailed the Internet age?'" He laughed lightly. "Don't be embarrassed about coming in here. I was startled, and yes, a bit upset. But not anymore."

"Why not?" She looked at him, unsure.

"Because it's you, and it isn't that great an intrusion into my private life. I never met my grandmother, you know. I come here, I suppose, to breathe in some kind of romance, strange, distant, yet curiously intimate. In my head, only in my head, of course."

They sat and drank their tea and nibbled on the chocolate cookies Reid fished out from his bag. "Does it feel like Calcutta has disappeared?" he asked.

Bela shook her head. "I can still hear Calcutta and smell it." Even in this deep green wildness, the city air filled their senses, warm with sunshine and roasting peanuts. Hot caramel gusts came with the strong breeze, straight from the swinging doors of bakeries along Park Street. The city throbbed under their feet, with the renewed energy of the winter months.

"Tea in a cemetery," Reid said and laughed. "With all our ghosts."

Bela felt a sustained humming in her ears, deep and unceasing. It seemed to grow louder very, very gently, as if advancing softly, but surely. Was it the city? She looked into the mug of half-drunk tea. The dark rounds of her eyes stared back at her.

"What's upset you?" Reid asked, taking the mug from her and refilling it.

"Nimki."

"Ah." Reid raised his mug in salute. "May heaven keep me from her. The way that woman looks at me—ready to rip out my entrails in a private disemboweling. So what did she do?"

"Nothing." Bela looked down. "You're looking forward to New York, aren't you?" she asked. "You'll get to see your sister."

Reid smiled and winked. "Good old sport, you know."

Bela looked into her mug again. She did know. Reid's sister, older by a few years, had indulged her little brother all her life. She had done well. She worked for an international advertising firm in New York and traveled a great deal. Reid was proud of her achievements. They had grown up outside of Edinburgh, helping their father run a small hardware store. Reid had run into his first Jesuit one summer morning at the same store. He was sixteen then. The tall American priest had come to the store to get a key made, and while he waited, had spoken with Reid about America and his life in the church. Later, Reid wrote to him, asking to meet with him. He spent the next summer at a novitiate doing odd jobs. Two months later, he joined it. The Jesuits sent him to Fordham for a year, then transferred him to Oxford. After that, along with his accent, everything changed. In three years, he reentered the world, reinvented himself, and got on a plane to Harvard.

His parents were both dead, the hardware store now a large automotive store. All tangible shadows of his past were irretrievably deleted. Now he was simply the brilliant Father Reid, and his sister, a senior executive vice president. Money? Had he not taken a vow of poverty? His sister had shipped an eighteenth-century Turkish divan to him last month, for him to lie on and read her next present: a beautiful leather-bound, first edition of Fitzgerald's *Rubaiyat*.

He could have had anything, Bela thought, couldn't he? He had no defects, no deficiencies, no trammels. Yet he had he chosen to remain in a life of strange commitments. It afforded him an infinite freedom, she knew. She had tasted it vicariously. But had he given up the world? Or had he let his world shatter to bits only to remold it closer to his heart's desire? Heart's desire, what was that? Some kind of passion, some riveting intensity, however short-lived, but *lived, claimed,* gripped so tightly in your hands that the whole body burned.

"I need to get back. My maid will be waiting," she said. She, too, had entered a cloister, no, a web—of infinite possibilities. File, edit, save, cut, paste, forward, delete, escape, format, return, search. . . .

Reid gave her that long, deep blue look. "Something has happened. Aren't you going to tell me? You came looking for me."

She kept her eyes on the ground. "Last night I did something without thinking. Without thinking of the consequences. I'm not quite sure what I've participated in. I keep brushing it off as nonsense. This morning I woke up with a sense of evil. I've never thought about that word really. I don't think I've ever seriously considered that word." With a little sigh she looked up. "I thought I was gaining the boy's confidence. But maybe you were right. Maybe he is simply using me, playing my vulnerabilities."

"Which are . . .?" Reid raised an eyebrow.

"I was looking for mystery. I thought it was a little game. There's an air of mystery about that boy that drew me in."

"Mystery is not always clean."

"I know. I don't know what I have done."

"My dear, do you mind spelling it out for me?"

She told him quickly.

"Maybe he's going to sell the charts. Maybe it does concern his sisters and their prospects will improve with computer-generated charts. God knows, you've indulged him enough." Reid rolled his eyes. "You're sweating over this?"

Bela chewed on her lower lip. "I'm not sure, but I may have printed out the stuff on my business stationery."

"Fame comes with its pitfalls." Reid laughed and shook his head. "He won't make the connection. Neither will the parties he rubs shoulders with. Why, they might actually think he got it off the Internet! Maybe he'll even flaunt the illusion." He groaned, half covering his face. "Bela, Bela, why is it you need to tangle with the web of the world when the world wide web swirls around you at the speed of light? We have surrendered our lives to the simulacrum of symbols. We play with symbols to fulfill desires." He laughed out loud again. "By the way, don't forget that IPS officer I mentioned. He'll be e-mailing you for the American connection. I told his aunt, the streets are *mean* over there."

"Are they not mean enough here?"

"You need a vacation, my dear. You need to get out of your apartment. I'm going to drop by after dinner with a bottle of the best single malt you've ever had, and," he paused, his mouth twisting, "lead you into temptation."

"I've never had single malt."

"All the better. You did say you've developed a thing for mystery. Now go home and banish that ragamuffin from your head."

He had a dirty cotton scarf wrapped around half his face this afternoon. She saw him running back and forth passing plates, picking up dirty dishes as she stepped off the taxi. She stopped at Gauri's stall after a great deal of hesitation and placed an order for chicken cutlets to be delivered later. Thankfully, the place was practically empty at this hour. Gauri smiled at her with his nicotine-stained teeth. "Bela-*di* at my door for the first time. Welcome, *didi-moni*. You, too, do computer work, I've heard. I tell everyone, she's my special dotcom-*didi*." He tapped his chest twice. "I hope my new boy's not been rude or anything?"

Bela shook her head. "He's a good kid. Make sure he doesn't fall into bad company."

"They all fall into bad company sooner or later. It's in the air we breathe." Gauri forced out coughs, slapping his chest. "But he's all right, I'd say. He's working to get his sisters married." Gauri wiped his face with the red cloth hanging on his shoulder. "A good marriage can save us, though. Gives one's life balance, goals, wouldn't you say?" He carried on without waiting for her response. "But the old ways are dying fast, *didi-moni*. When I got married, the village matchmaker came around with all his information and I sat down to marry whoever he and my parents chose. Never laid eyes on her until the day we married. These days, the young people are arranging their own fates."

"Well," Bela cleared her throat. "People like to feel in charge."

"I know, I know," Gauri sighed. "But one shouldn't interfere with fate, I tell my children. It's all fated who you marry. And the gods play tricks with us. They make us feel we know best. But our elders know better. So I called the same village matchmaker to get my children married. He found good prospects for them. They have better lives."

"You're mad, old man," an incoming customer said from the side. "What's wrong with your life? You keep us all happy. Isn't that something? What's this fate stuff? Your fate depends on how you present yourself, how you act. Life's a daily transaction. Then it's gone, old hat, like Visual Basic. Got to keep moving. Java, Broadvision. So just keep those cutlets coming, and the tea. It's all illusion. Our entire system crashed at work today. Virus arrived in an attachment called 'open sesame.' Tomorrow, we'll refine it and send it back as 'love you too!' Is that their fate or ours? Or are we part of a larger network, eh?" He laughed gleefully at his own wit.

Bela moved away quietly. She must not get drawn into idle conversations with strangers. Strangers—were they? She knew their faces from her balcony. She knew who they were from her maid. This gentleman had a software company and had recently negotiated an offshore contract with Aetna. He knew her face and her name. They both lived in the same building. It was not possible to be faceless, was it? Except in her business transactions. The Internet provided anonymity. That, too, had collapsed for her today. She had been manipulated into meeting a client by a woman she loved and trusted.

There was a strange trick like dice tossed in the air, and it was imperative she toss it back the right way. The gods play tricks with us, said Gauri.

But her dealings were not with the gods. They were with clients and their desires, in an element that was neither earth, air, water, or fire. She was defined by parameters, not by politics; her decisions, by data provided. She did not play, she *performed*.

She lifted her chin and looked around for the two men. There they were, at the far end, looking as suspicious as ever, and in deep discussion with a third fellow who had the muscled frame of a construction worker. What tricks were they up to? The boy glanced at her briefly as he came to the counter to pick up orders. His eyes were dark and blank over the scarf, which he adjusted tightly before carrying the plates over to the three men. Was that the same boy? Was his hair a lot longer and curlier? Nonsense.

Bela found her maid sitting on the steps smoking a *biri* and grumbling to herself. Apologizing profusely, she let her in and went to the balcony to get out of her way. All the children were at the park, their *ayahs* busy with gossip. Gauri's stall was filling up densely as the sun neared the horizon and disappeared in a red-gold haze over the burnished treetops rustling with bird wings. She tried to catch the boy's eye in vain. The three men were coming toward him. He joined them and they walked away to the main road.

Bela sat down on a chair slowly.

Her maid, Lata's mother, as she was called, came out to the balcony, frowning. "I've finished. It's getting dark. Mosquitoes will be coming. Come in. Let me close the doors and windows."

Meekly, Bela followed her indoors. "About the fish," she started hesitantly. "I'm not sure if I should be paying so much—"

"It's the best in the city!" Lata's mother snapped. "It's only ten rupees more."

"Ten rupees!"

"His fish is the best, Bela-*ma!* Don't you understand? And his son is helping my sister's son-in-law get a job, and it is her son-in-law who comes running whenever your kitchen sink blocks up."

Bela raised her eyebrows. "I will pay two rupees over the price. That's it."

The woman's forehead scrunched with deep furrows. "Five," she said after a few seconds.

"Three-fifty."

"I'll have a talk. Now," she knelt and reached for Bela's left leg, "let me remove the brace and massage your leg."

"Now," Bela smiled, "about that boy and the two men. Have you any idea what is going on? Why does he keep disappearing with them?"

The old woman got up, her mouth twisting grimly. "I believe they are helping him find husbands for his sisters," she said. "That's what they say."

"You don't believe it?"

Lata's mother sighed heavily. "I'm only a silly old woman. I don't know all that much. Sometimes knowing too much can be troublesome. People might consider you a liability."

Bela laughed. "But you know everyone's business this side of town."

The woman cocked her head to the side. "I think there's someone at the door."

Bela heard her open and close the door, her footsteps shuffle out, and high heels come clicking in.

Chaitali held out tuberoses. Their scent filled the room. She wore the same clothes Bela had met her in. The earrings had been changed for simple gold hoops. She smiled a very different smile, apprehensive, almost guilty. Bela controlled her facial muscles.

"May I?" Chaitali picked up the nearest tall vase and went to the kitchen. She came back in a few minutes and placed the arrangement on her coffee table.

"How did you know where I live?" Bela unclenched her jaw.

"It wasn't very difficult. I had my driver follow you. He told me you lived in this building. I have friends who live in this building. I haven't given you away. I swear. I described you, saying I had seen you at Nimki's, that's all."

Bela's facial muscles threatened to spasm. "I really must ask you to leave immediately."

"After I've explained myself. May I sit down?"

Bela shrugged. Chaitali remained standing.

"I'm sorry," she said, "for my atrocious behavior earlier. I *meant* to be impossible. I don't want to marry someone in America. I'd rather meet someone here and live in India. My parents are hopeless. They are so into money and prestige."

"And you are not?"

"Not as much, no. I mean, I don't want to marry a pauper."

"But—?"

"But I don't want an *arranged* marriage. I'll find the person myself." Her chin went up. "I don't want you to find me anyone. Just give my mother extremely inappropriate candidates."

"That will be very bad for my reputation."

"How can you go around arranging marriages! It's medieval!"

Bela frowned for a moment. "How little you know about my work. I provide information. I don't arrange marriages. But I don't need to explain myself to you. I wasn't going to work with you anyway."

"Why not?"

"I have my reasons. I suggest you leave."

"But what are you going to do? About my mother?" Her eyes were desperate, an expression Bela found at odds on this arrogant, beautiful girl. There was something annoyingly heartbreaking about her face.

"Go home."

"Not until you tell me."

"I won't do a thing," Bela said calmly. "Now, please leave."

"I'm going to meet the man I dream about. Don't you screw up anything."

"And how do you intend to make this person materialize?"

"He won't be bloody computer generated!"

"You'll work with a lump of clay."

Chaitali put up her hands. "I guess I deserved that."

"Think about this: how does one meet the person one marries in any culture? And then go buy your chunk of marble or bronze."

"Copper brings out my skin tone best." Chaitali tossed back her hair. "I simply intend to bump into him." She gave a little shrug and swept out. Bela rubbed her eyes. She must have been dreaming.

Reid entered sniffing and holding a bottle up in salute. The cutlets steamed on the coffee table. "From my grandmother's own town." He poured carefully into two glasses. "Now let me tell you about—" he stopped, catching her eye. "What disaster now?"

"I was right!" she yelled. "He's involved in something very bad. He's involved with very *evil*-looking characters!"

Reid burst out laughing. "The devil he is, the bastard!"

"It's not a laughing matter," she shook her glass at him. "And just a few hours ago a client, who I intended to blow off, marched in here and threw an outrageous fit."

"What? The sacrosanct portals invaded? The face unveiled?" Reid clutched his throat and fell on the couch. "I'm sure you sent her packing. Now sit down and don't spill, you silly woman. You've been had. That boy's used you for some petty fraud. Thank God, you're crushingly disillusioned. I want to talk to you about traveling."

Bela buried her face in her hands.

"Dear ostrich," Reid patted her shoulder. "I hear you're being repeatedly invited to some conference on marriage and family in Syracuse, New York."

Bela looked up slowly. "Close your mouth," said Reid. "The IPS boy's aunt told me. No, no, she doesn't know you as *you*," Reid waved impatiently. "She doesn't know you are Belarani.com. She thinks you're a group of people. The gentleman who keeps sending you the e-mails regarding the conference is a business associate of hers. Everyone thinks your dotcom is the guest of honor at this conference."

"Why won't these wretches leave me alone?" Bela punched the couch.

"Leave you alone? You've woven yourself into the very matrix of interconnectedness. You won't play by the rules of your business?"

"Play? Play?"

"Well, interact, then. At least be willing to engage, Bela. I'm afraid, everyone has an investment in the transaction of human relations. How long can you remain outside the web (pardon the pun) you've created?"

"Leave me alone. Just this evening. Leave me alone."

"I can do that, but what about the rest? Stop treating yourself like a cripple, physically and emotionally. Face yourself in a real sense. You're not merely a bloody hot web site. Why must you cripple yourself far more than the world ever has?"

Bela looked up, and taking a deep breath, slapped Reid so suddenly that he almost fell off the couch. Her eyes blazed. "You like wounded animals—is that it?"

Reid stood up rubbing his cheek, his face white. "Wounded animals—not you, surely?"

"Why then? Why then have you been my friend?"

"Oh, why else? Why else indeed!" Reid wrenched open the front door.

"Brian! Don't go. I'm so sorry," Bela struggled to reach the door. "Don't know what's come over me," she said brokenly. "I'm so sorry. Please don't leave."

"I do understand what you've been through," Reid slammed the door so hard that the entire apartment shook. "But I find it extremely difficult to pity you. You're a successful businesswoman. You've faced life with a great deal of courage. You have money, you have time. Enjoy it. Don't hide in your apartment. Go to this conference. *Meet* people, don't avoid them. Let the world know what you've achieved, who you are, who you have *become*."

"It's all very well for you to say," she whispered bitterly.

Reid's voice softened. "I've known you for almost six years, Bela. You devour the books and videos I bring you. They all deal with adventures in foreign lands. Complex romances. You reached out to this boy because you sensed, as you call it, mystery, a certain *cri de coeur*. But whose *cri de coeur* is it really? What more do you want me to say?"

"I see in that boy rage and damage and the rising potential for ruin. And something bad that I have helped along without forethought."

"You won't do it again. It was an error in judgment. Not a crime." He refreshed their drinks and put the glass back in her hands. "You're the one with a sudden penchant for imaginary wounded animals. Now—can we enjoy this scotch?"

The phone cut off her response. It was her private investigator. She heard what he had to say, then put down the receiver.

"What's the matter?" Reid asked. "Who was that? You look a bit stumped."

Bela sank down on the couch quietly. "He wasn't lying," she said. "He went to a wedding. A very small affair. My private investigator—"

"You did not!"

"I had to find out if I had got myself into any kind of trouble."

Reid snorted.

"My PI didn't enter the place. But he is quite sure a wedding took place. Maybe the boy did manage to get one sister married. He didn't mention anything to me, though."

"A rush job."

"Perhaps things were underway, and he came to me for extra validation."

"Let's not waste time and energy over this any longer."

"But I still have this nagging—"

"Oh, have another drink. Even if it's the fucking end of the Internet. The way the dotcom stocks are doing."

Bela gave in. After a few sips she felt her taut back muscles relax. She closed her eyes in wonder at the smoky aftertaste on her tongue. Reid was talking about sixteenth-century England. About all the proposals for Elizabeth's hand and how she juggled and played with them. It was impossible to think anymore, her mind felt numb, and her body. . . . She felt her head come down on the arm rest, felt Reid slip the empty glass out of her loosening fingers, cover her with a shawl, and the slight rush of wind as the front door opened and closed.

The grey wash of dawn woke her and she sat up on the couch to the early sounds of people coughing, sweepers swishing at street corners, voices chanting prayers, and the acrid whiff of wood smoke and burning incense. Outside, the sky turned milky rose.

The phone made her straighten up sharply. Her mother's voice was ecstatic. Jenny had brought so many presents, including a spice grinder. They would all visit her soon, in a few days. Bela got ready quickly. The dull headache lingered. Damn single malt. Damn Reid. Shomu was at the door, knocking impatiently.

He didn't come in, but handed her the breakfast at the door. He seemed in a hurry. Why didn't he tell her about the wedding? He rushed off before she could ask. But there was no time to worry. Her computer was beeping like a security alarm. Mukesh Gupta again. Oh! All was well. Sushma Parmar sounded very positive. She would like to have a phone conversation with Mukesh, she said in her e-mail, and then definitely meet. Bela sat in front of her machine all day, trying to catch up with yesterday's messages. Lata's mother finished her chores in grim silence. Bela ignored her. She rose from her desk in the early evening. She didn't bother going out to the balcony. From her windows, she had seen the boy leave in the late morning. He hadn't returned.

As the sun dropped, Lata's mother marched in with a fierce scowl on her forehead.

"Had a talk," she said. "Will charge a little less." Oh, the fish. Bela smiled tiredly. Her back and shoulders ached and her eyes burned.

After the cooking was over, "Would you like me to give you a massage?" the old woman asked to Bela's surprise. "You look very tired." She had gone about her evening duties looking ready to blow a hole through somebody.

Accepting the offer like a blessing, Bela went and lay down on her bed. Lata's mother's deft though rough hands moved over her back and shoulders with just the right amount of pressure for Bela's thin frame. "I used to do this regularly when I was younger," Lata's mother said. "These days, I only offer if I really like the lady."

"Thank you." Bela smiled sleepily.

After the door closed with a click behind Lata's mother and the room darkened around her, Bela dreamed the most bizarre dream. She fell into a sleep like a stupor to the smell of something sickly sweet floating above her face. A shadow hovered around her for a moment, then drifted away. She was aware of vague sounds, tapping on the keyboard, whirring of the printer spewing paper. After that she remembered no more. She had never slept so deeply. Loud knocking forced her to open her eyes. Her head felt heavy, as if she was smothered under one of Nimki's mud packs. Lata's mother was calling her name.

Bela stumbled out of bed. Her legs felt wobbly. "It's past nine o'clock!" Lata's mother wailed. "This is the third time I've come knocking. Are you feeling all right?"

Bela rubbed her eyes. "I must have been really tired and your massage must have released every ounce of tension. I overslept."

"Move, move, let me finish quickly. I'll be late."

Bela stood under her shower until the hot water ran out, which it usually did in ten minutes, due to the size of the heater.

Shomu must have come and gone with her breakfast. She went out to the balcony. Work had slowed down at Gauri's. It was almost ten in the morning, and everyone was at work. Where was the boy? The security guard threw her a salaam, catching her eye. "I'm done," Lata's mother yelled, as she slammed the front door. Bela sat down at her desk and stared at her computer. The keyboard seemed a little angled. She straightened it and turned on the computer. She had told the woman not to touch her desk. Was that a tiny smudge on the printer? She wiped it off with the dusting cloth she kept at hand. Ah, here was the e-mail from the IPS person.

From: tarunP@rediffmail.com
Subject: intro

I'm 27. Would you please draw up my natal chart? My information is given below. I will call to introduce myself properly. Thank you so much for agreeing to help.

Sincerely,
Tarun Palit

Bela cut and pasted the information and opened the natal charts program to create the new file. Casually, she ran her eye over the list of existing files. The files she had created for Shomu were missing. She searched for the files all over her several drives. All returned the same message: "No files found." She must have deleted them, but couldn't remember when. As Tarun Palit's chart came out of the printer, she noticed the paper tray was low on paper. Bela tapped her head. She was getting absentminded and distracted. Turning to her e-mails and queries, she intently read over and responded to the fifty-two personal statements that had come in during the last twenty-four hours.

She worked through the afternoon, abstaining from her afternoon nap. She had slept more than enough. Her web site had to be updated with all the recent success stories, with all the "thank you" letters and comments of adulation that were waiting to be downloaded. So many new requests to post ads on her site. Pottery Barn wanted to advertise, and Williams and Sonoma as well. Terrific stores for bridal registries, she knew. She already had Bed, Bath and Beyond, Linens 'n' Things and Pimpernel advertising on her site among various others. But why was Northface asking to post ads? Well, let them come in. It only meant more money. Bela blew out noisily. So many decisions to be made, so many issues to be resolved competently.

As the *dhaba* stirred into activity in the late afternoon, Bela rose from her chair, stretching, yawning, and strapped on her leg brace. The doorbell made her groan. Lata's mother was not coming this evening. Not that obnoxious girl again!

A tall, young man smiled at her. "I said I would call," he said in a warm, rich voice. "I hope you are free? Tarun Palit." He did a quick *namaste*.

"You were to call—"

"Here I am."

"No, no—" Bela put up a hand. "How did you find me? I don't meet with clients. I work entirely on the Internet."

"Oh, I'm so sorry. I had no idea." He half turned to leave. "But since I'm here, can't you make a one-time exception? Please?"

Bela hated smiles such as his. Nimki could produce them on command. His smile had a genuine, guilt-laden, imploring droop. With a helpless gesture she let him enter.

"Oh, how nice!" He beamed. "What a nice place. Such light. And so tastefully decorated." Tarun Palit poked his head into the kitchen and exclaimed in pleasure.

"How did you find me?" Bela asked again.

"I am a police officer—a detective." Tarun Palit wrinkled his nose. Then he threw open the French doors to the balcony and stepped out. "Wonderful! You must love to sit here. May I sit here for a while? How many cups of tea you must have enjoyed here."

"I was about to make some."

Her head buzzing, Bela plugged on the kettle. Things were getting out of hand. Palit came into the kitchen to carry out the tray. "I cannot allow you to wait on me, Miss Mitra. Please sit down and let me do the honors."

"I must ask you not to tell anyone that I—"

Palit placed his right hand on his chest, "Please don't worry. My aunt doesn't have a clue. I often let curiosity get the better of me, but I don't leak professional information."

Bela watched Palit smile at the *dhaba*. His face glowed in the setting light. It was an intelligent face. Animated and full of purpose. It was a face that would achieve. A face that dreamed. "Does the *dhaba* supply good snacks?" he asked, turning. "It's very crowded. That old man is obviously doing good business. Seems a little short handed."

Shomu had appeared again, and was running around busily to whistles, finger snappings, and shouts. The two unsavory figures were sitting apart as usual.

"I live in a very large house," Tarun Palit said. "My grandfather's mansion. It's like a giant square, looking into a large courtyard. The balconies all face the courtyard. And the outer balconies open to the lawns. There's a wall around the property. It is so wonderful to sit here. Almost a part of the street, yet quite removed from it."

"I grew up in an old house like yours. It wasn't as large as yours, or with that much land. I used to run—" Bela caught her breath, "spend a lot of time on the terrace."

"There were great old houses right here, years ago. Did you know that? Old Victorian mansions, built by the British and rich Bengalis. Then developers came along in the last thirty years, bought them up, razed them to the ground, and up came these towering monoliths."

"Why don't you give me some details while you're here." Bela picked up a notebook and pen from the tea table.

"Details?" Tarun frowned at her.

"About yourself, and about the kind of person you might want to marry."

"Yes, of course. Um—" he tapped his lips. "Attractive. Perhaps even a little arrogant. Romantic. Ready for adventure."

"Adventure?"

"Trekking, hiking, white-water rafting. I even go skiing in Switzerland and Austria."

"Which part of America did you have in mind?"

"America? Oh, no, no, no. My aunt wants America, not me."

"Your aunt wants to be married as well?"

"She wants *me* to be married to someone in America. Her own son is too young for her plans. I'm quite happy here, with my job at present. I have a challenging case on my hands."

"I'm not sure if I can help you then."

"All it needs is research," Palit smiled. "And you have an excellent PI."

Bela's eyes narrowed.

"As I said, I am a police officer." He looked apologetic. "Couldn't help checking out a few things. I think I should leave now. I've taken up enough of your time."

At the door, "Would you mind very much if I came by tomorrow? Just want to bring you my photograph and some other details you may need." Before she could shriek out "absolutely not," he had leaped down the first flight of stairs. From her balcony she saw him walk out swiftly. Where was his police car? All government officials flew around in their flagged vehicles. This one had come incognito. But invasive, all the same.

Twice, in so short a space, like dangerous attachments breaking through firewalls. And that boy, she had opened her door to him. One could always turn off a computer, initialize the hard drive. Once you open a door . . . but people come and people go. People connect. People move on. She was on her balcony, not down there.

Hushed giggles made her look up. Three girls leaned out from the balcony two floors up and waved at her.

The next few days passed in a haze of intense work for Bela. She continued deflecting the repeated invitations to Syracuse, but pacified them with, "I'll think about it," to her own surprise.

Her brother visited with Jenny and the toddler. Some of her ex-colleagues from Loreto came to visit. She gritted her teeth through all of the calls and canceled her Thursday tea with Reid. She saw Shomu disappear with the two men three more times during the week. When he dropped off her breakfast, he was withdrawn and in a hurry. Bela tried not to worry in spite of the tiny muscle twitching furiously on her left temple.

The next morning, he didn't show up. She looked out at Gauri's stall from her window. Shomu was nowhere to be seen. When her maid arrived, she casually mentioned his disappearance. The woman shrugged. "He wasn't there when I went for my tea. He had to go somewhere, Gauri said." The two men were not around either. Panic throbbed in Bela's heart, but she held steady in front of her screen.

Tarun Palit turned up during lunch and smiled that self-reproaching smile again. "My particulars." He handed her a large envelope. "May I step out to your wonderful balcony?"

"Busy time again at the *dhaba*." Palit rubbed his hands together. "That poor boy running ragged."

Bela drew in her breath sharply. Shomu was back.

"Multitasking, wouldn't you say?" Palit's eyes narrowed as he watched the boy collecting plates, pocketing tips from a table, taking orders. The two characters were there as well, together with a third man, not that muscled guy, but a small, hunched person, all wrapped up in a brown shawl. Palit turned around. "I must leave. I promise not to barge in like this again. I will e-mail or phone."

"Where is your jeep?" Bela asked.

"Oh, I don't want to disturb the neighborhood by arriving in a police vehicle. I wouldn't want people wondering why the police were paying you a visit. You know how people talk. My Maruti's down there."

A hammering on her door prevented her from craning over the balcony. Palit ran to open it. Chaitali practically walked through him. "You've been talking to my mother!" she shouted at Bela, fists at her waist. "What is this thing about some guy in Boston? I told you to stay out of it!"

Palit raised his eyebrows.

"You're very much mistaken," Bela said calmly. "I've done nothing."

"But Nimki passed on the info to my mother. What other source could it have come from?"

"Not from me." Bela glared at her. "Leave."

"Like hell!" Chaitali stamped. "Ask someone to get me a taxi."

"May I offer you a ride?" Palit stepped up. "Where would you like to go?"

"Mount Everest."

"The base camp is next on my list." Palit took her elbow firmly. "Good-bye for now, Miss Mitra. I think I can handle this."

Grinding her teeth, Bela called Nimki. "Madam is in conference with a new client," said the receptionist.

"Get her," snarled Bela.

"Oh, what's up now?" came Nimki's annoyed voice over the hum of dryers and running water. "I'm in the middle—"

"How dare you interfere like this?"

"What are you talking about?"

"The Poddars!"

"I'm trying to take the girl off your hands. I got a lead—"

"Off my hands! Off my hands! You drove her straight into my living room! It's as if you've sent me a virus—my door keeps popping open on its own and people walking in. Open sesame! That must be it!"

"I don't understand why she—"

"Don't do anything more." Bela banged down the receiver.

The Poddars, a computer virus. Bela turned around to look at her computer. The screen beeped in response. As she read over new e-mails, she got the distinct feeling that something funny had happened to her computer. She ran a Norton Utilities check, but came up with nothing. Someone had touched things, she was sure. Lata's mother must have dusted the computer and her desk. She picked up the mouse and looked at it. Was that a grease smudge? The old woman's fingers. She was imagining things. Could it have been Tarun Palit, while she was in the kitchen? He had gone straight to the balcony. She picked up her cell phone and called Reid. "I will not speak to you for a week," he said petulantly. "I missed my tea. I also had something interesting to tell you. I won't now."

"Don't be an idiot," she said. "Brian, did you play with my computer that evening?"

"My dear, I wouldn't dare."

"You can come for tea next week."

An exasperated sigh blew into her right ear.

Bela continued to stare at her computer all afternoon. You're being an idiot, she scolded herself. The machine is fine, everything is as it was. She ran the antivirus twice. No contamination. No infected disks. She had a firewall; nothing harmful would ever get through. New e-mails were automatically scanned. As e-mails came through, she watched the antivirus go into action.

"*Scan attachment?*" it inquired. She clicked on "*Scan and download.*" It was a file from a friend. The attachment was blank. The file hadn't come through. The message indicated some hot new shopping site. Her screen went blank suddenly. Bela froze in her chair. Before she could reach for the mouse, the screen filled with floating teacups.

"How do you like your tea?" appeared in golden letters, followed by "Enjoy all the teas of the world" and "Best Brews." To the music of tinkling bells, a little dance started, the colorful teacups bobbing and twirling, the tea in them bouncing like waves. Globes, with maps of the world, entered the screen from all sides. They circled around the teacups in rhythm with their movements, and gently dropped into the cups, the tea splashing a little. "Drink me!" ran across the bottom of her screen. "Sink me!" "Swallow me whole!" Then they all disappeared, blanking the screen again. Within seconds her screen reorganized to its familiar face.

Bela grabbed the mouse and rolled it, clicking furiously on the "back" icon. The screen reverted back to her e-mails. There was no sign of the e-mail that had brought forth the teacup medley.

"What the hell?" Bela slapped the side of the computer lightly, did a search, checked everything she could think of. At a loss, she played with the brightness controls, then paused, sniffing. What was that? A scent. Aromatic—a smell of something wild, herbal, yet vaguely familiar. Bela leaned forward and smelled the screen. How could a computer give off smells? Spice, oil, smoke, no, yes—that was it. Cooking. From other kitchens. Smells from the *dhaba*. Of diesel-fumed streets. Of the tube-roses on her table. Rotting garbage. Incense. Mud and flowers mingling on temple steps. The boy's greasy clothes.

Calcutta, Reid would say.

The boy was absent from his post again. She took a fleeting look at Gauri's stall and the benches before answering the door. Lata's mother shuffled in, muttering. She seemed excited. Bela asked her to bring her a cup of tea to the balcony. She must sit and watch. "So what's up?" she asked her maid as she took down the dry clothes from the line and folded them carefully, putting aside the ones to be ironed.

"Lot of talk going round," she said with an impatient sniff. "Newspaper people asking questions."

"What about?"

"Asking Gauri all sorts of things."

Bela waited. "About the people who come to his *dhaba*. People getting anxious. No one wants certain things coming out, you know. I don't think madam-two-floors-above-you would want her whereabouts between eleven and two discovered. And that man—look, that one." The woman pointed to a young man of about twenty on Gauri's benches, smoking with two others. "Twelfth floor, on that side," Lata's mother cocked her head. "Packets of white powder in his closet. I was putting the polished shoes back. Fifteen years with hard labor. That's what it would be."

Bela stared at the old woman in awe.

"I think the police have been sniffing around. I'm not sure," the woman's mouth tightened. "But I'm sure I smelled something."

"Could it be the milk you left on the stove?" Bela's eyes widened innocently.

"Oh, my goodness! And here I am carrying on." Lata's mother rushed off with the clothes.

After dinner, Bela settled down on her couch with the book on winter cruises, turned on the TV, then sank into sleep unawares. A sharp click woke her. It was dark, except for the light cast by the TV. A shadow moved in front of the TV screen. Bela reached for the book on the coffee table.

"Sorry," the shadow said. "Don't be scared."

"How did you get in?" Bela managed to choke out.

"You need to put a better lock on the door. Don't turn on the lights." Tarun Palit turned off the TV.

"What are you—"

"I'll explain fully. I just want to run this program on your computer."

"It was you!"

"I beg your pardon?"

"You tampered with my computer."

Palit gave a low whistle.

"What did you do to my computer?"

Palit placed a finger against his lips. "I'm here to find out who did, and what."

Bela staggered up from the couch. "I am going to turn on one light."

"I'll turn on the hallway light." Palit reached the switch before she could take a step.

She looked him up and down in the faint light that came into the living room. He was dressed in crumpled *kurta*-pajamas.

"Sorry," he said with that regretful smile. "I was working late with a friend. Getting this ready." He held up a disk.

"This is outrageous. Why didn't you call me?"

"I wanted to check out your front door."

"Are you suggesting someone—"

"I'm confirming it. Now please allow me."

"You wait a minute." Bela planted herself squarely in front of her desk. "Sit down."

She picked up her cell phone and punched in Reid's number.

To Reid's groaning "hello" she yelled, "Come over at once."

"Surely it's not my soul you want at this hour?" he asked full of sleepy irritation. "Shouldn't you call the police if you've been burgled by that kid?"

"Everything's still here," Reid grumbled, walking in tousle-haired half an hour later. "Where's the gypsy?"

"Sit down." Bela handed him a cup of coffee. "Meet Tarun Palit."

For the first time Brian Reid seemed at a loss for words. He took a sip of the coffee and rubbed his eyes. "Someone *does* have designs on me. Did *he* ask for this date? Or am I here as a chaperone?"

"Listen carefully, and wake up!" She smacked him on the head. "He thinks someone has been tampering with my computer. You can explain now," she said to Palit, who, all this time had been ordered to keep his mouth shut. He had sat quietly on the couch while Bela stood guard over her precious machine, tapping her foot, waiting for Reid.

Tarun Palit cleared his throat.

"I'm surprised you let him in at this hour." Reid patted the cushions in place.

"She didn't."

Reid fell back on the couch and covered his eyes.

"Miss Mitra," Palit said gently. "Please sit down. I must run this on your computer first."

They watched him turn on the computer and slip in the disk. They saw a cylindrical object spin on the screen. It became apparent that some kind of data was being retrieved. "Come here," Palit said finally. "These are the files."

Bela's jaw dropped. Seventy-two natal charts had been drawn up, printed, and deleted. Palit had used sophisticated "rescue" software to retrieve the deleted files. "These are being used, Miss Mitra," he said, "for quite a scam. I've had two men working undercover for a few weeks. Our crooks have been using that *dhaba* of yours as a meeting place."

"That boy—they are using him—"

"I don't know for sure how that boy is involved."

"What kind of scam?"

"I can't tell you right now. But I will, once I've wrapped up the case."

"You can't *not* tell me!" Bela gasped. "This is *my* computer. That boy has been delivering *my* breakfast every morning. He's *not* a bad sort. He might be in danger!"

"Miss Mitra—"

"You barged in here. Invaded my privacy. Broke in here tonight. *You even had tea on my balcony!*"

"Oh, my word! *Le balcon!*" Reid slapped his forehead. "*Le balcon* indeed!"

"How can you—"

"I am—" Reid placed a hand on his chest, "I am truly amazed. You, sir, are not looking for a bride, but a scoundrel."

Palit laughed. "I may end up with both if my luck lasts."

"Am I in any kind of trouble?" Bela asked angrily.

Palit put up a pacifying hand. "The charts being used lately have the blessings of Belarani.com. After I checked you out, I realized you couldn't have been participating in the scam. But there will be some talk afterward. I mean, I can't keep the reporters at bay."

Bela covered her face. Palit knelt before her.

"Please, Miss Mitra, don't worry. I'll make sure your name is kept out of it. I'll try my best." He touched her hands gingerly. "But I can't keep the web site out of it. You do understand? Seventy odd sheets of paper. I wouldn't even have come to your doorstep if some of the charts hadn't come into my possession."

"But you came to me because your aunt—"

"Not exactly. I needed to investigate you."

"What? But your aunt asked Brian—"

"I told her to ask him. My men saw the boy come to your apartment frequently. They also saw him." Palit glanced at Reid. "It was pure luck that he was tutoring my cousin, my aunt's son, that is. One of my undercover men got hold of some of the charts. I had to investigate the connections."

"You thought all *three* of us were involved?"

"I wanted to make sure your web site was doing legitimate business. Can't you understand my position?"

"All I understand," said Bela furiously, "is that you lied to me, used me, used Brian—"

"I came to your place *after* some of the Belarani charts were retrieved by my men," he offered defensively. "We were simply watching everyone's movements before that."

Bela looked around wildly for something to hurl.

"I've been tracking the villains for over a year," Palit continued, removing the book on winter cruises from her grip. "All over Nepal, Bihar, Orissa, and West Bengal. I didn't think I would be getting this opportunity to catch them red-handed without these Belarani charts. They became a little too smart when they set about using you. And," he gave that unforgivable smile, "maybe it was fate. My aunt, your charts, chance encounters."

"Do they know who I am?"

"No." He shook his head. "They saw you as easy means. Single woman, living alone, with a computer. But I think they do know about Belarani.com."

"Then they know—they've made the connection—"

Palit frowned, biting his lower lip. "Not necessarily. They probably couldn't believe their luck when they saw the Belarani logo on the charts. They may now consider you to be connected somehow. But do they think *you* are Belarani.com?" Palit's forehead creased again. "They probably don't."

"What do they know about computers?"

"That boy does, a great deal. My men have followed him into many a cyber hole tucked away in the unlikeliest of neighborhoods."

Bela stared at the floor. In the flooding moonlight the mosaic glistened with a heartstopping dewy sheen.

She stood up with some effort and went to the kitchen. Reid snored softly on the couch. She made the young man some eggs and more coffee. The sky had started to pale. "I should get going," Tarun Palit stood up, rubbing his eyes. Reid yawned and stretched. "Where's *my* coffee?" he inquired, cocking an eyebrow.

"You'll have some explaining to do to your superior, won't you?" Bela smiled sweetly.

"For my all-night romp in the hay? Hmm, there *is* hay in my hair." Squinting into the hallway mirror, Reid drew out a dry yellow stalk from his sleep-ruffled hair. "The real explaining, Bela, will be yours." He grinned wickedly. "How will you explain to this part of south Calcutta *two men* leaving *your* apartment at the wee hours of the morning looking *as disheveled* as us? Why, Tarun looks practically mauled!"

Before she could throw the coffeepot, they were out of the door doubling over with laughter.

Bela couldn't move from her balcony. Lata's mother grumbled about the dust blowing in with the light breeze. The strong afternoon sun burned

Bela's face. Shomu had vanished again. Were they all vanishing? Reid soon to be off on his cruise to America. Nimki with her new man off on some exotic vacation. Her brother and Jenny set to fly away in a few weeks, back to America.

The light blazed white into her eyes, then shone gold and melted to an orange-mauve.

"A cruise for your thoughts." Reid stood there, dressed in a black T-shirt and black jeans, a black pashmina scarf wrapped loosely around his throat.

"Have you learned to work my very secure door lock as well?" she asked. "Where are you cat-burgling?"

"At a designated hellhole." His eyes were almost indigo in their depths as he redirected her gaze to the *dhaba*. The boy had materialized out of this rose-gold ether. He was making his way toward the main road, and a short, thin man, clumsily adjusting his shawl, followed at a distance, at a leisurely pace.

"You better find Tarun a suitable wife," Reid said. "Look what he gave me. A present to keep." Reid held a gun in front of her face. "A Les Baer, model 1911, with a stainless-steel barrel."

"Are you allowed to possess guns?" she asked, a little taken aback.

"I'm very much allowed to receive presents."

"What on earth are you going to do with it?"

"Gaze at it in wonder."

"Why would he give you a gun?" Bela blinked a few times to adjust her eyes.

"Someone has to have the adventure on your behalf. I'm going with Tarun tonight. He said everything's in place to grab the whole gang. I'll come back with the entire story."

"I don't believe you."

He touched her shoulder. "That's a very good idea."

She sat still and watched him disappear into the fading copper light. He was fond of teasing her. That gun could have been a toy. He held it out for barely a second. Black clothes, all for effect.

What really had happened and how? How had she opened herself up for such invasions, such tricks? A subtle but deadly infiltration, like a virus, throwing the entire system into unimaginable chaos. The world spun around her. If she could only log out.

"Bela-*ma*," she heard. "Come inside. Let me close the doors. Mosquitoes."

But the dark buzzing clouds had already formed all around her. She swatted wildly while Lata's mother, watching her flailing arms, laughed an ancient cackling laugh.

Who are these people? Bela scrutinized the seventy-two charts one by one. They were not that different from one another in spite of the differences in dates and times. The age of the candidates ranged from seventeen to nineteen. Except for two, all the subjects were male. The common thing about the charts was that they all presented attractive prospects, as if the dates and times had been researched so that the moon was always located in the most beneficial houses, Saturn always kept at bay, Jupiter shining bright in the house of career prospects and luck. Venus ascendant where it should be, Mars energized appropriately. Could we all remodel our original coordinates thus! Could we all be born after the best stars and planets had been clicked into position with the help of a mouse and keyboard! What a wonderful life it would be.

The Moving finger writes; and, having writ, Moves on. . . .

Fingers had indeed been at play. Written, printed, deleted, disappeared.

Was there a real difference between that mystical, mysterious finger and the very real, slightly greasy one? All illusion, that joking customer had said to Gauri. Web of the world, and the world wide web, Reid had laughed. Why tangle? Mortal coil. Did she not click away as well, juggling stars and traits and skin tone, annual income, in-law issues, lifestyles, desires, demands, packaging imperfections to meet with delighted approvals, delivering seeming glory?

She, too, had been packaged and used. It was unreal, bizarre. She sat on her couch in the dark and rocked. If only she could click open that boy and read the hidden files.

A light knock made her hobble fast to the door. Reid stood there, his face white.

"The traffic was something unbelievable." Reid sat down heavily. Bela crouched down next to him.

"We drove. Three hours or so. Roads choked. Sluggish traffic jams." He spoke in an odd halting way. "Getting out of Calcutta—a nightmare." She saw the lines of loaded trucks blocking the roads. Cows, goats, buses, cars, cyclists, with a few ducks and chickens scampering through, choking the junction. He laughed, half covering his mouth. "A tornado. That's what I thought. Would have cleared the space. Could it have found a way in."

"Where were you going?"

"North of the city. Tarun had organized a car to pick me up with one of his men. We were following a taxi." He threw up his hands.

"Who was in the other taxi?"

"Your little protégé, I believe. Palit's man said they had been clever enough to choose different locations every time."

"To do what?"

"To arrange marriages, of course."

"Arrange marriages?"

Reid pushed his fingers through his hair and gripped his head. "I asked him why the families of these girls never did a thorough check. The man said these were poor people. That daughters are a big responsibility. Marrying them off costs money. If a matchmaker comes along and finds them a groom who wants no dowry at all, it's a godsend. Plus, these last ones had your stamp."

Bela felt a damp chill creep up from her feet.

"What about the boy?"

"I need a drink. Where's that bottle of scotch I left behind?"

Bela watched him drain four shots in thirty seconds.

She had no idea how long they sat in silence in the dark. The only sounds, the gurgle of scotch poured out at short intervals, the glass coming down on the table with a gentle clatter, and a low murmuring. Reid, his knuckles white with pressure, muttering something to his tightly held silver crucifix.

The sky paled, the sun rose with a sharp suddenness, making her start. Loud, agitated voices burst in through her window. The *dhaba* sounded like Howrah station all of a sudden. The screech of police sirens cut through the commotion. Lata's mother was pounding on her front door.

The woman stood there breathless. "Scoundrels!" she shook her fists. "That boy! Posing as a groom from heaven! Over and over again. Sometimes, posing as the bride!"

Bela caught the side of a bookshelf.

"Using fake astrological charts! Telling the poorest of families they had found the best match for their daughters—arranging false ceremonies with that boy as the prize groom—then shipping the girls off to brothels. To Nepal, I believe." Lata's mother stopped to take in a deep breath. "And Shankar-*babu*? A longtime pimp, that's what he is! That Ghoton, the same." She inhaled noisily again. "No dowry necessary, they told the poor mothers and fathers. Only give few items of jewelry!" She spat on the floor. "No need to have a big wedding, they said. No need to feed so many people. Have you any idea how many girls? And boys, too!"

"Boys?" Bela asked weakly.

"In high demand in the Middle East, I hear."

"Where did you hear all this?"

"Just coming from Gauri's stall. Everyone's talking. They were telling the families, the groom's got a job in Dubai, and he would leave with the bride right after the wedding. That's how they got away quickly."

"But boys?" Bela rubbed her eyes.

"I told you that boy had too pretty a face. Just wrap a sari around him and—" the woman snapped her fingers. "Bride to match!"

It was as if her firewall had dissolved and viruses shot in. She could only stare with her light-stunned eyes. Image after horrifying image, sending shockwaves through her entire system, her fingers numb with the crackling static of their swift and furious entry.

Palit arrived at ten o' clock, his face grim. "I see you've heard."

There were two screens in front of her suddenly. One, intensely blue, the other, shiny black. From one to the other, signals flashed, and before her eyes, a semiotic drama downloaded itself, at 800 megahertz, in response to the pressure of her fingers.

Attachment 1: The Perfect Match.

A boy with a heartbreaking face. No dowry required.

Attachment 2: The Wedding.

The breathtaking scent of flowers and incense. A young girl, swathed in red-gold silk, hesitant at the altar, her face veiled. The groom, his face covered by a screen of woven flowers, his foot-steps, equally apprehensive. The flames leap as the priest chants, hands meet, the red powder touches the bride's forehead.

Attachment 3: The Vanishing.

There's bit of a rush at the door, as the just-married couple is bundled into a taxi. The taxi drives to a rented room you needn't know where. Before the girl can lift her veil, a chloroform pad goes over her face. Whatever jewelry she wears is removed, and the inert body taken to Bihar, then sent straight to a brothel near Kathmandu. The brothel owner pays well. He is buying—he claims—for his international clients.

(But that is the next investigation, after the negotiations go through with the Nepalese government, Palit adds).

A sickly sweet scent surfaced in Bela's head as she saw the girl fall to the floor under the cotton pad. A smell that had hung over her face that night when she fell into a stupor, the night of strange sounds, of the printer and her computer buzzing.

Bela rubbed her eyes.

"No one saw his face," Palit said. "All this time, for over a year, that boy played the fake bridegroom. Recently, they used charts off your computer to seduce the families. The parents were only too eager to get the girls off their hands. No dowry. A free groom. The Belarani connection. What luck. Mothers and fathers, bundling off their daughters like excess food about to go bad."

Tarun Palit paced her living room. "I joined the service with such romantic ideas and then found myself utterly bored, sitting at a desk and reading files. Last year, this case fell into my lap."

"You'll be in the papers tomorrow, Tarun," Bela said huskily. "You are a hero."

"I still have to track down that Ghoton."

"Track down?"

"He got away, I'm afraid. We got the fat guy. I'll get the other one, don't you worry, and the girls. The station is filling up with villagers: parents who happily 'married off' their daughters."

Bela felt her heart stop. "The boy?"

Palit looked down. "Vanished."

"Vanished?"

"I'll find him. We caught a third fellow, did I mention? That boy's father! Been in the scam with the other two for years. Sold off his own daughter a few months back. We've tracked down the girl."

I'll get him, Bela heard, in blood-chilling tones. *One of these days.*

"Funny," said Palit. "It was such an old-fashioned crime, committed in an old-fashioned way. Selling women. Your web site and your computer were merely tools. It was an age-old hustle, using age-old tricks. Latest technology, a mask, creating an illusion, nothing more."

"What's to happen now?" she asked, her voice breaking.

"Some of the charts have reached the press. But I have most of them. They can't connect Bela Mitra to Belarani, not really."

Bela couldn't stop the choking sound that came from her throat.

"I've something to say to you." Palit came forward and caught her hands. "The timing is awkward, but I need to tell you. I think I've met my destiny."

Bela staggered backward. Reid gave a hoot of laughter.

Palit went down on his knees still holding her hands, his eyes bright with triumph and adoration. Bela tried to swallow. It couldn't be. Impossible.

"Fate. You. Magic." His fingers tightened over hers as he breathed out another word. "Chaitali."

"So be it." Reid clapped his back. "Allow me to take you out for a double scotch. By that expression on Bela's face I can swear you'll need it."

The next day, she dodged e-mails from hundreds of reporters and clients. The papers had no answers, just one enormous question: "Dotcom Matchmaker and Petty Pimps?" Bela wanted the ground to part and take her in.

Under her very nose, it had happened. Here she sat, in her solitary apartment, helping men and women from all over the world arrange their marriages; down there, in the middle of the crowd and smoke of the *dhaba,* a macabre matchmaking carried on undetected, a hideous parody of her own business.

Just as she had ripped the papers into confetti, Palit phoned. "Turn on the TV in fifteen minutes. Watch the Calcutta station."

In a daze, Bela did so. Lata's mother buzzed around in excitement with the duster, relaying the latest from Gauri's. The Calcutta station's anchor announced a press conference. Bela saw Tarun Palit on the crowded steps of the Lal Bazaar police station, his face shining in the sunlight, his eyes determined. Tarun Palit, with the approval of the commissioner, faced a battery line of microphones. She read the names of the leading news channels on the microphone stands. BBC and CNN bobbed up and down on the screen.

Lata's mother hovered over her shoulder. "That young man was seen coming into our building," she gushed. "He was watching the scoundrels all the time. Gauri's certain that plain-clothes officers were stationed at his *dhaba* for weeks. They had their sights on that boy. I knew he was up to no good."

"I want to set you straight about Belarani.com," came Palit's voice from the TV. "Stop slandering Belarani.com," Palit's face went white from flashing cameras. "Without the assistance of that famous dotcom's team we wouldn't have succeeded in busting this gang. Belarani's team was working with me. It was a sting operation."

Within half an hour, she saw her web site on every news carrier, TV and Internet. The next few days, the papers went crazy. "Belarani.com Not-Com-menting," screamed one daily. "Dotcom Matchmaker Snares Pimp's Bridal Network in World Wide Web," whistled another absurd headline.

Her parents, her brother and Jenny, and Nimki showed up, all together, at the same time, six in the evening, as if they had coordinated their arrival. "What are you going to do now?" her mother howled. "How did you get involved with all this? Why haven't you called Naren-*da,* our family attorney? Are we to watch dumbly as they drag you in handcuffs to jail? What is to become of our family name?"

"Why don't you come to America with us for a few months?" her sister-in-law Jenny suggested with a half sob, her hazel eyes anxiously moving from face to face. Her brother raised an eyebrow encouragingly. The little boy in his arms scowled at her, thumb in his mouth.

"Oh, shut up, all of you!" shouted Nimki. "She's sitting here cool as a cucumber. So everything must be under control. Isn't it?" She whirled around to face Bela.

"Yes," Bela said, biting her cheeks to keep the tremor out of her voice.

"But the papers are slandering your web site," her father said in his clipped lawyer's voice. "Maybe I should give Justice Banerji a call."

"There's really no need," Bela said as firmly as she could. "They are not making any accusations anymore and they haven't connected *me* with the web site. No one really knows who the owner of the web site is or where he or she or they live—in this half of the world or in the other."

"That's it then. Come along, everyone." Nimki flung everyone out of the apartment. "She's fine, the Mitra family's name unblemished, all secrets safe."

"Are you really all right, my sweet?" Nimki threw her arms around her after closing the door.

"Yes, yes." Bela twisted free. "I'm fine. There are people protecting me. Don't worry."

"I'll always worry."

"Why?"

"Because I helped you shut yourself in this ivory tower." Nimki pointed dramatically at the computer. "Should I stay the night?"

"Don't be silly. I've had too many people crashing on my couch lately." Bela pushed Nimki out the door gently, relishing the mystified look on her glorious face.

She stepped out on her balcony cautiously as the *dhaba* sizzled into its breakfast preparations. It seemed as if Gauri was hosting a press conference of his own. Reporters milled around the counter and filled the benches. Lata's mother joined her, wiping her hands. "How is Gauri managing?" Bela asked.

"Better than ever, as you can see."

A tall, thin girl of about sixteen, dressed in a grease-stained *salwar-kameez*, hurried out of the dark interior of the *dhaba* with a wire rack of clay cups steaming with tea. Her untidy, curly hair swung in the breeze, veiling her face.

"Gauri's niece, a few times removed," Lata's mother informed. "Turned up last night, just like that, from Bishnupur. Her father died a month ago, her mother, a year after she was born. Gauri was happy to take her in, what with the scandal and that boy vanishing. He says he didn't know of her existence until last night. Fate, he says, swooping in just when he needed help. Hmph. He's going to have her learn computers, he's telling us. Old men like pretty faces, pretty faces in different wrappings."

Bela turned around sharply.

Lata's mother's eyes glazed over. "Old women like me ramble so."

Bela stared at the girl running about, lithe, quick, her skin radiant in the morning sun.

"That boy stole a whole heap of money from Mrs. Choudhury," Lata's mother said, her voice taking on its subject-changing, news-delivering tone. "Used to do her shopping twice a week. Never gave her straight accounts. Pocketed half the money. The old bag thinks it's her punishment for not settling Gauri's account for four years." She rolled her eyes. "So she's giving Gauri a computer. Her son in America wants her to e-mail."

Bela looked at the woman in shock. "You know about e-mail?"

The old woman's mouth, nose, eyes spasmed and twisted. "No, no! But everyone does it! On the computer. You do, too, I know. Mrs. Choudhury's son sent her a computer for e-mail only two days ago. But Mrs. Choudhury's frightened of the machine. So she decided to settle her account with Gauri by giving it to him."

"But the computer's worth—"

"She didn't pay for it so she doesn't care."

"She's going to be my dotcom girl," Gauri's voice sailed up. "And boss here—" Gauri slapped an omelet-devouring young man on the shoulder, "is going to put me on-the-line!"

"He'll be dancing like a peacock by the time the sun goes down," cackled Lata's mother. "E-mail, hmph, e-mail." She said it like a slightly foreign word, and with exquisite contempt.

"I get this dotcom thing finally," Gauri laughed, throwing Bela a morning salute. "Super powerful. Like the hand of fate. Swooped down on the crooks and felled them. Vaporized that rascally boy. Pouf!" He snapped his fingers. "Brought forth my unknown niece from thin air. Inevitable. We are all dotcom sooner or later. Oy, Keshto," he yelled at his cook. "Bring out those special 'dotcom cutlets.'"

There was "net tea" on his chalkboard menu now, and "web omelets," killing hot with extra chilies.

Watching them from the balcony, Bela swallowed.

"Do you want me to tell Gauri to keep delivering your breakfast?" the old woman asked. "That girl—"

"No—" Bela caught the railing. "You bring it—you pick it up from Gauri's on your way here every morning."

"And how are you?" Reid stood at the door, much later than his usual four-thirty. Bela let him bring the tea tray in as usual. "Palit took a huge risk at the press conference," Reid said.

Bela sighed. "Does this put what I do in a new perspective?"

"Don't be bloody ridiculous."

"How do you feel about this city now?"

Reid poured and handed her a cup. "How I've always felt. It's wonderful, messy, tastes fabulous, and anything is possible. Here, anything is possible." He sat down. "Evil things happen everywhere. You don't expect me to condemn a whole culture, do you? India is ancient and eternal, has survived much more. You have survived." His eyes glowed like blue flames in the creeping darkness.

Survived. The very word set her trembling. Had she not escaped? What had she wanted? To be safe, to protect herself from the world that had rejected her, called her cripple? The world in a cup of tea, brought to her doorstep by a beautiful mask. How could you protect yourself against that?

"If you've lost something, then you must try to win something. If something has shattered, then it must be rebuilt."

"Right. Whatever did you do with that gun?"

"Gazed at it in wonder. I'm repeating myself. It's in the hands of my superior, who got a tremendous charge out of it. Everyone in the house is taking turns sleeping with it under their pillow. I'm impatiently waiting my turn."

"You need a good knock on the head."

"I'm sure." Reid pushed his cheek out with his tongue. "Humpty-Dumpty. Remodeling can be very effective. Even if we can't put together the broken pieces, we can always reinvent ourselves a million times. Perhaps it is time to restructure and claim the world."

"This is an evening for cliches and cryptic statements?"

"This is an evening too late for tea."

Bela stared at her computer screen. Hundreds of messages. Her story was all over the Internet. She returned to her home page and stared at it. It was vibrant with colors like a wedding sari. The first page carried a large mandala, a circle of intricate designs, paisleys, twisting vines, flowers in vivid hues of saffron, red, indigo, white, deep green. Shehnai music came on with it. As a visitor stepped in and clicked on the highlighted flowers and paisleys to browse, the site sprang to life like a wedding itself, its general information opening up like floral displays and hennaed hands spreading out. It was a visual marvel. The imaginative web designer had used a special tool (created by someone in Hamburg) that allowed triple the speed of anything currently on the market. He had taken her well beyond the ordinary, he said. To a completely new realm. And left her there.

She had mastered its strange currents alone and reached her dream kingdom.

Her kingdom. She had taken the world and turned it inside out. She had contained it and controlled it. But had it, in fact, waited in the wings, laughing silently, only to trap her with a cup of tea? What was it saying now? *Claim me.* And if she did—it only took daring—*the awful daring of a moment's surrender*—what would she weave herself into? Another grand illusion?

Tarun and Chaitali. A boy and a cup of tea. Gauri with his new computer and his new menu. Grand illusion? Connecting Shaila in Kandy with Rohit in Tucson. A perfect match, stars and class. Telling Mukesh Gupta, *get Rogaine.* Pacifying Sushma Parmar, *his parents visit once in two years.* Negotiating with Lata's mother, how much for the fish? Juggling the fundamentals, reformatting the peripherals. Touching a keyboard, transforming lives. Arranging the futures of others, glued to her screen, glancing at the windows. Loath to step beyond her balcony. For six long years.

Bela felt a white flash rip through her head. Escape? Transcendence? Even gods didn't have that luxury. Vishnu, reincarnated in every age, to struggle, triumph, die. In each new age, a new persona to tackle the new demands.

If they call you cripple, dance.

Believe nothing, believe everything.

The world revolving inside Krishna's mouth. Sitting before a saffron screen, swallowing the world. Play me, the game says. What then?

Hit that return and, bloody hell, *engage.*

She didn't hear Reid slip in as her maid left for the evening. She started as his hand touched her shoulder gently. "I've booked you a deluxe cabin," he whispered in her ear. "Here are tickets to Oporto, for the ship, and from New York to Syracuse." He dropped a large white envelope on her desk. "You will have constant Internet access. You can write me a check when you've made up your mind, by the end of next week. I'm sure the conference organizers will reimburse you."

"You've presumed a lot."

"I have a goal."

She turned to look at him.

"To get you married, of course."

They laughed until tears ran down their faces.

"You will come?"

"To do what?"

"Why, to go to the conference, to shimmy across the Milky Way, and above all, to have a little fun."

She played with the mouse.

"Well?" Reid gave her a little shake.

Bela swiveled on her chair, a faint smile playing about her mouth.

"You did say, Father, I had developed a thing for mystery. You'll have to wait on the deck and see."

Outside, as a gauzy mist gathered over a mild Calcutta night, the glitter of city lights seemed to fade away like land moving away from a ship leaving the harbor.

RE: MOHIT

Date: Mon, Dec 4, 2000, 21: 21: 32 -0200 IST
From: Ranjit Dutt <ranjit@hotmail.com>
To: Mohit Dutt <mohit@yahoo.com>
Subject: re: for mother

Dear *Dada,*

How was San Jose and our American cousins? How's your new job? You didn't give any details about your trip!@#$%^&*!

I can't believe you're actually there and traveling coast to coast already! *Fare forward H1 voyager*! I'm traveling with you, e-mail by e-mail.

Ma, constantly worrying, has entered into a different set of negotiations with her Krishna. He is on notice, I'd say, to deliver: protect and save you from harm. I told her it was pointless admonishing the poor guy, so preoccupied with his flute. *Dada* has disappeared into the www! I got my ears boxed promptly. Babli gave me one her looks as well. I'm under constant tyranny.

By the way, you're missing a marathon blackout. It's been seven hours now. Thank God it's winter. I'm typing by candlelight, flame flickering, throwing long, dancing shadows. Biltu's laptop (borrowed for the evening as your PC lies in a coma for the duration) is running steady on battery power. (I would really like a similar laptop as a birthday present. And a pair of Nike sneakers.) This is a numinous moment, with faint moonlight, a light, cold breeze and this violet screen. And it moves me to say things you would consider gibberish.

*If I thought that my words would be to someone who would ever return . . .
this flame would remain without further movement.*

I know you think your brother is a freak.

Have you contacted Vishnu-*da?*

E-mail ASAP.

Love,
Ranju

Date: Mon, Dec 11, 2000, 1:33: 04 -0500 EDT
From: Mohit Dutt <mohit@yahoo.com>
To: Ranjit Dutt <ranjit@hotmail.com>
Subject: Re: re: for mother
Attachments: mohit.doc <word file>
                    pictures.gif

---

mohit.doc

Dear Ranju,

I hope you're studying hard for your finals. Don't spend too much time
with that loafer Biltu. Do you have to write your e-mail during a blackout? You could have waited. The computer I left at home is far more
powerful. If anything happens to that loafer Biltu's laptop, his dad will
carve out pounds of flesh from all of us. Concentrate on studying and
doing well. I know you'll do well and be on your way to college next year.
St. Xavier's would be a good college for you. Better you stay in Cal while
I'm in America.

Is Babli bossing you around too much? She's just being overprotective,
now that I'm not there to watch over you. She has only you to order
around now! Tell her she'll be getting married in two years' time. I'll have
saved enough by then.

I envy you sitting by the open window. Cold breezes! Fooh! Don't call
Calcutta winters winter. You should see the winter here. There's two feet
of snow all over and it's cold like I've never experienced before! Gets dark
by four. Bought winter jackets and shoes and gloves.

The situation re: work is pretty fantastic. Sun systems admin *zindabad.*
Tell *ma* not to worry. She need not mutter angrily in front of her altar.
Tell her, Krishna is definitely obeying her commands this time. I'm fine.

H1 in pocket. Green card in process. I'm working on a big project—eleven months at least.

Living arrangements are good. These Avalon Arbor apartments are not bad at all. Heat, electricity, parking, gym, cable all included. Cable connection for the Internet as well. Laundry across the courtyard. We could have installed washer and dryer in the apartment, but we're using the tiny laundry room as an extended pantry since laundry facilities are so close by. Actually, the laundry room is great! Two comfortable couches, TV, and Internet hookup, even two computers online twenty-four hours. I tend to hook up my laptop when I'm in here doing my laundry and write my personal e-mails.

The apartment is expensive: twenty-two hundred a month, splitting with Pradeep (Oracle apps. developer), my roommate. He's a decent sort, neat and tidy. A little shy, but cheerful. We're in a third-floor loft apartment, meaning, I'm in the loft part of it. (See attachment) Downstairs, two bedrooms and two bathrooms. His wife (Ritu) will be here soon, and after that we'll decide if this arrangement works or if I should move out. At present, it's better this way. Pradeep's been here for four months, hired by the same company. He's just bought a BMW 330. We commute to Cambridge together. Tell *ma,* everything was all organized here from the moment I landed at Logan. Although my boss (the guy who hired me at ISolutions, not my project manager at AllAmerica) can be short-tempered, he encourages parties every evening. The marketing people go out and have a good time. Us consultants go when we have free evenings. We have to be a little bit in the background. Nature of our work.

Let me explain the scene here: the company that's hired me, ISolutions, is a small IT solutions company. It was started by my boss, Rayal, five years ago. His brother also runs a similar company, but he does application development. Rayal's company does staffing. He has ten marketers, and about hundred and fifty consultants on his payroll. His marketers call other staffing agencies (third parties—as they call them—to get requirements for IT consultants. Who needs what—Java architects, UNIX administrators, VB/ASP guys, whatever. Then they find the consultants who suit the requirements, customize their resumes, set up their interviews, and send them to the companies. The marketers make good commissions on their successful placements. Rayal gets the consultants (like me!) from India (most of their guys are from Andhra Pradesh—I'm the Bengali exception), processes their H-1 visas, and then starts processing their green cards. He recruits consultants here as well. There is quite a large pool of

Indian consultants in the U.S. There are hundreds of companies, run by Indians, just like ISolutions, in the U.S.

Re: San Jose. Chinu uncle—the great Saurav Gupta, the golden boy—is not very cooperative. I spent Thanksgiving with them, but I'm not sure if I want to spend Christmas with them. It was a bit boring. The kids are nice. You'll like them. Aunty Jill isn't the greatest cook, but has a "greater transcultural understanding" of things, or so she said, due to her three years with the Peace Corps. She has a huge collection of brass statues of all the Hindu gods and goddesses all over the house and Buddhas of different shapes and sizes in her rock garden. She calls them her "energizers." I don't think I'll be seeing them very often. They are too far away in San Jose. They have a huge house and all, but I think I prefer the East Coast. I'm about forty-five minutes from Boston. Went to Quincy Market last weekend.

Oh, before I forget, tell Ramji at the *dhaba* I'll settle my account soon. I will call home on the 25th and on the 1st, early morning IST. After that, strictly e-mail. No point wasting money on phone calls.

We shall float around in virtual reality, information at our fingertips, communicate without shouting at each other. When you type *ma's* e-mails, she'll be forced to present her imaginary worries in a coherent fashion. And when I respond, I won't be interrupted every two seconds with, "you're not listening." Last time I called, I felt we were having a serious language problem.

Love,
Your big brother

P.S. I'll send Vishnu an e-mail soon. Haven't had much time.

Date: Tue, Jan 9, 2001, 7:42: 33 -0200 IST
From: Ranjit Dutt <ranjit@hotmail.com>
To: Saurav Gupta <sgupta@msn.com>
Subject: Re: Mohit, From your sister

Dear Chinu,

Happy New year. Hope you received my card.

Please look after my son. As you know, he's only twenty-one and impulsive. He ought to have finished his college degree instead of taking up all this computer stuff. But such is the craze over the last few years, everyone wants to be in computers. Please keep an eye on him. After mother died, I took care of you. Can't you just phone him once a week to make sure he is all right? If you had offered to help with his graduate studies, he may not have got into this consulting line and could have pursued a medical degree. He called twice only to say that you are not at all friendly. Couldn't you have invited him over for Christmas?

I don't know what to say to you. It seems you have turned your back on us. It's not as if we want anything from you. But you could have been a strong father figure. He—they did lose their father at a young age, and it is because of my late husband that you managed to go to the States.

God bless you.

—*Didi*

Date: Wed, Jan 17, 2001, 18:32:40 -0700 PDT
From: Saurav Gupta <sgupta@msn.com>
To: Ranjit Dutt <ranjit@hotmail.com>
Subject: Re: Mohit, To *Didi*

Didi,

I would have replied earlier, except that I was out of town on work.

I have kept my mouth shut out of respect and love for you. In case you don't remember, I have a wife (whom you like to ignore) and two children of my own whom I have to provide for. Jill quit her job two years ago due to her knee problem. I won't finance your son's future when he is quite capable of doing so himself. He had no interest in medical science or any science for that matter, except for the science, no, the alchemy of making money. From what you've told me over the last three years, your son has determinedly trained himself to be a Sun System Administrator at your neighbor's company's expense. He's achieved the first part of his goal, and now he's embarking on the second, which is to make his dollars.

We had him over for Thanksgiving, and all he did was complain how bland the food tasted. Shaila and Robi tried to engage him to play computer games with them, but he opted to lie in front of the TV. They were excited to meet him and spend time with him, but I guess he felt they were too young for him. Jill and I did invite him for Christmas and New Year's, but he said he had plans with his friends. He wanted a loan to buy a BMW and I turned him down. Now I don't consider that a tremendous deprivation. Do you?

Your son needs a walloping reality check. I have worked very hard for fifteen years to be where I am. My late brother-in-law's money did not get me where I am. It bought me a plane ticket, that's all. Yes, you did take care of me. But pray do not hold that over my head anymore. Your late husband left you a comfortable bank account, and now that your son claims to be making eighty thousand a year, he can support himself adequately, I hope, BMW or not.

With love and regards from Jill, Shaila, Robi, and me,
Your brother,
Chinu

Date: Wed, Feb 14, 2001, 23:47: 05 -0500 EDT
From: Mohit Dutt <mohit@yahoo.com>
To: Vishnu Laha <vishnu@lido.com>
Subject: update
cc: Ranjit Dutt <ranjit@hotmail.com>

(Ranju, are you studying hard? You haven't sent any e-mails for some time, although I've sent off a few short ones. Are you wasting time with Biltu?)

Hey Vishnu!

Happy Valentine's Day! Ha, ha! No Valentine at this end! But bought four colognes on sale! Wanted to e-mail you long time ago but wasn't getting a good enough chunk of time. Now that we're both in the same part of the world we should meet soon.

How's your project coming along? I'm putting in weekends lately. Which city are you in or near? You left Calcutta almost three years ago and I still don't know exactly where you're living. I know, I know, you say you keep moving.

At my end, I'm overloaded with work. But I work fast, and my boss at AllAmerica is thrilled with me. Some of my Indian colleagues who are working on the same project are not very good, I'm sorry to say. I'm not sure how they got hired. They are not from ISolutions. There's only one other guy from ISolutions here with me. Sri. In some ways, an impossible character. More on him later.

My roommate's wife (Ritu) has arrived. She spent the first week sleeping. Jet lag. Then one evening we come home and the whole place was filled with the unbelievable aroma of chicken curry and Basmati rice! We fell on the food like famine victims. I haven't had good dal for almost two months. Ritu's the first vegetarian I know who makes a good chicken curry! The next day our apartment and all our clothes smelled of curry. I opened all the windows in spite of the snow and cold air. Ritu screamed.

I asked both of them if I should move out. They wouldn't hear of it. Ritu said it wasn't a problem at all for the time being. She's quite an interesting character. I'd say she's in her late twenties. She's not overtly bossy, but she manages everything with a subtle control. In some ways she reminds me of my older sister, Babli. Of course, Babli is tall and beautiful and has a temper like a thunderstorm. But they both have a similar managerial attitude. If you meet Ritu, you'd understand. There's a calmness all about her, her face, her walk, her voice. It's soothing. You want to be around her at the end of a tough day. And of course she's a fantastic cook.

She writes, by the way. The second bedroom is her study. I'm not sure what she writes. Poetry, perhaps? (You know, Ranju has taken to poetry. He reads Robert Browning and Shelley and T. S. Eliot, and wants to make movies. Seventeen and a half is what it is.)

I'm glad Ritu's here. This place feels more like home every day. There are Indian paintings on the walls, curtains on all the windows and plants (hibiscus and gardenia, and flowering!) in front of windows. I'm relieved they didn't ask me to move out.

I wish I saw more sunlight though. When I leave the house, the sun's barely up. Then I'm inside the office. Drab fluorescent lighting. I catch half an hour's sun during lunch. I come home in the dark. Pradeep says the days will get longer soon and we can play tennis on the courts here.

Oh, news of the day! I've found a club nearby that has squash courts! Pradeep plays squash too, but not very well. The membership fees are quite high. So I gave them a demo. After that I signed on as the weekend pro. I told them I'd do it for free if they waived the membership charges. They couldn't believe their luck. I'm ten times better than their regular pro—I could read it in their faces. Pradeep is going to have to pay the fees.

But I talked them into giving him a huge discount. Evenings are fun these days. I've bought myself a superb racket. Dunlop. Titanium. Top of the line. Ritu comes along once in a while. She sits and observes everything. She wants to work, she said. She has an advertising and PR background from Bombay. She also wants do an MBA. A determined woman, like Babli.

Give me some company gossip from your end.

Your best pal,
Mohit

Date: Fri, Feb 16, 2001, 22: 26: 54 -0700 PDT
From: Vishnu Laha <vishnu@lido.com>
To: Mohit Dutt mohit@yahoo.com
Subject: Re: update
cc: Ranjit Dutt <ranjit@hotmail.com>

Mohit! (And hello to Ranju)

You're here! I've been wondering why I hadn't heard from you. I knew you had arrived sometime before Thanksgiving.

Happy to hear you're comfortable and getting lots of good home-cooked Indian food, and squash to work it all off. Make sure you follow the squash news on the Internet and go and watch Trinity College play Harvard. You know, you would get a full scholarship to Harvard if you gave their coach a demo!

Continue sending long e-mails. It's like getting an old-fashioned letter. We tend to shoot out abbreviated messages and try to stay connected with a few words now and then. I'm fine, how are you, very busy, pls send x info ASAP, so on and so forth. Try piecing together anyone's day-to-day existence from e-mails. Perhaps our lives are turning into a sequence of short sharp hits on various web sites. A motley existence. Oh, well, I tend to digress darkly at times as you well know.

About Ranju—poetry? Last I remember, he wanted to be an archaeologist and search for Atlantis. He must be preparing for his final exams, no? How is Babli, and your mother? What wonderful meals I've had at your house. And the kite-flying and all the scrapes we got ourselves into. Those are my best memories.

There's not much to tell at my end. I don't get involved in company politics or pay heed to any gossip. Working hard, basically. My company (the company that hires me out) is not much different from yours, I suppose. My boss is a bit of an ass. He's fat, thirty-fivish, always fretting. From what I hear occasionally, consultants pull disappearing acts every few months. Which means, he loses one or two consultants every three months or so. Everyone's looking for better opportunities. A lot of things have changed in the market. The UNIX guy who spent four months by my side disappeared two days ago. My project manager yelled at my boss, who, I'm sure, yelled at his marketing fellows in turn. Supply chain, I call it.

Cheers, and welcome to America.

—Vishnu

Date: Wed, Feb 28, 2001, 1:17: 07 -0500 EDT
From: Mohit Dutt <mohit@yahoo.com>
To: Vishnu Laha <vishnu@lido.com>
Subject: Re: re: update
cc: Ranjit Dutt <ranjit@hotmail.com

(Ranju, don't show this e-mail to *ma*. She'll worry needlessly. And why aren't you e-mailing? I've tried calling quite a few times but couldn't get through. Is the phone working?)

Vishnu—what to say, man, changes at the homefront. Dinners dwindling. Ritu wasn't content sitting at home. She's now working at ISolutions as a marketer. It seems she's learning quickly how to prepare consultant resumes and get requirements. She has to make three placements a month. That's the quota per marketer. I didn't know that. Doesn't sound like too much work. She's already made two in her second week. Rayal (boss) was happy. Threw a big party at his house last night. His wife has doubled in size since I saw her last. All the marketers went out and bought Chinese food and bottles of wine and took it to Rayal's house. I got there late. But there was still plenty of food. They have a lot of parties, it seems. I mean, the marketers.

It was interesting, at the party at Rayal's house. The marketers—they've never worked anywhere else before. I mean, they've no experience of working in an American company. At least, us consultants get pushed into the American scene. The marketers were almost boorish in their manners. This is an odd group of Indians. I mean, you're sure to find one of these types in a group, but to have a whole group of them under one roof is peculiar. I wonder how they interact with clients?

(Hold on. Need to put my clothes in the dryer. Wonder what my mother would think of Bounce!)

The marketers, as I was saying, didn't seem to possess any people skills. Ritu, on the other hand, is well spoken, sophisticated. It was clear the other marketers do not like her. Two of the marketers are young women in their early twenties. They've been hired very recently. They were not very friendly toward Ritu either. Ritu was unperturbed, though. She never loses her composure. But such obvious dislike—obvious from the snide remarks flying around—is not healthy. I mentioned it to Pradeep. He had noticed it too, but he was confident Ritu would be able to handle it. I hope so. Ritu's not a confrontational person from what I've gathered. If those snide remarks had been directed at Babli, she would have incinerated the lot of them within seconds with her scorching tongue.

I'm beginning to be wary of the strange culture.

Okay, my laundry's done. It's started snowing outside. Ranju, you'd find this fascinating: the flurries, they give a neon glow to the darkness.

Closing laptop.

Cheers,
Mohit

Date: Sat, Mar 3, 2001, 19: 18: 53 -0200 IST
From: Ranjit Dutt <ranjit@hotmail.com>
To: Mohit Dutt <mohit@yahoo.com>
Subject: Happy Holi!
cc: Vishnu Laha <vishnu@lido.com>

Dear *Dada* and Vishnu-*da,*

Glow is the order of the day! Happy Holi! My face is completely purple from the special color Biltu prepared. We doused everyone in the neighborhood with it! Threw same dye-filled balloons at almost everyone! Babli and her friends stuck to colored powders, and after the look she gave me, we didn't dare throw any liquid color on her and her friends. Wish you were here.

Sorry no e-mails for some time. Phone lines were down, and you told me not to borrow Biltu's laptop. It's getting hotter and hotter and the sun is merciless. Exams start next week.

By the way, Babli got a promotion. She's now third in charge at the Grand Hotel. She took us to lunch at the coffee shop to celebrate. *Ma*'s getting quite worried. Babli's turning twenty-four tomorrow and still snarls at the mention of marriage. (She thanks you for the b'day card.)

Ma had quite a fight at the altar today. She has now started calling Krishna "Mohan." It's a more comfortable name to berate him by. "Now listen to me, Mohan—if you don't do this—" or "Mohan, don't you dare—" or "Mohan, I'm telling you—" or perhaps it's closer in sound to your name! It's a lucky thing that Krishna has a hundred and eight names to choose from. She has also replaced the sandalwood statue of the elegant Krishna with the flute to a framed picture of child Krishna, crawling around stealing sweets and looking guilty. Now this little Krishna, sorry, "Mohan," gets quite a yelling. I tried telling her that replacing an adult god with a child god may not be a smart idea. An adult Krishna is more likely to be reasonable. A two-year-old Krishna didn't have the best reputation in mythology.

I've downloaded all my latest favorites from Napster, off Biltu's CD burner.

Please remember to buy my Nike sneakers.

It's terrific that you've found a squash club. Show 'em what real squash looks like.

By the way, have you met any gorgeous blonds?

Just looked at my face again in the mirror. It was me in the dark. A strange meeting: *I knew you in the dark.* Where are we now?

Love,
Ranju

Date: Fri, Mar 9, 2001, 23:21:08 -0500 EDT
From: Mohit Dutt <mohit@yahoo.com>
To: Vishnu Laha <vishnu@lido.com>
Subject: Re: re: re: update
cc: Ranjit Dutt <ranjit@hotmail.com>

(Ranju, you little!@#$%*! *Where are we now!?! Strange meeting?!* Did
you drink *bhang* with that loafer Biltu? If you don't watch it, he'll turn
you into a drug addict. You need your ears boxed. And, yes, I wish I *was*
there to box 'em thoroughly too.)

(Ranju, edit this e-mail below before you show it to *ma*.)

Hey, Vishnu,

How's it going? You got a full taste of Ranju from that e-mail he sent! I'm
suspecting he drank *bhang* that evening with that loafer, Biltu.

Sometimes his little poetic one-liners make me feel weird. Combined with
the lack of sunlight—well . . . Do you feel strange sometimes? I mean,
about the nature of our situation? I've been having some odd dreams—
Ranju's purple face looming up now and then from my computer.

I've been noticing some things in my office. We consultants aren't a very
noticed crowd, are we? I mean, we sit in these closed offices in front of
our screens and work away all day, late into the evening. Others outside
these rooms don't really talk to us. We don't talk to them either. I was
starting to get depressed. I was wondering what is our purpose? What are
we doing really, so far from home? What is our status? But then a flash
of light went through my head just as the system at work crashed due to
some virus called Shiva.

I know what we are! We are the secret machinery. We are the secret
machinery—divine in our potential and knowledge—in the enormous,
never-ending epic of the Internet. The H1B visa is like a mantra that
invokes us, brings us here. We are the hundreds of deities making life
(or should I say money-making?) smoother, quicker, better. My mother
quarrels with her god on a daily basis. She's got him, a sitting duck on
her altar. My boss here grumbles at me few times a week when I point
out what miracles are not possible. Here, I am orchestrating part of this
company's internal network, almost unseen by the world.

My world, our special world, is an in-between sort of world, isn't it?
Neither earth nor air nor fire or water. Talk about ethernet! The word
has special meaning. Our physical presence is not really acknowledged. I
sometimes feel people literally look through us. I'm not a frozen idol on
my mother's altar, prayed to, blamed, berated according to her moods and
levels of frustration. Right now, I'm the holy of holies to my boss here.
(He'd prostrate himself if given the hint.) Flitting from system to system,
station to station. Aren't we the fingers of fate?

Ha, ha!
Mohit

Date: Fri, Mar 9, 2001, 23:52 :08 -0500 EDT
From: Mohit Dutt <mohit@yahoo.com>
To: Vishnu Laha <vishnu@lido.com
Subject: Re: re: re: update contd.

(I didn't want to send the rest of what I have to say to Ranju. He and *ma*
would worry.)

On another front, a different set of lesser fingers are interfering with happiness. I have to move from ether to earth in the click of a mouse. (I think
some of Ranju's poetry has downloaded to my system.)

Trouble brewing. Ritu is doing pretty well since she started off, making
quick placements. So I wasn't sure why Pradeep and she were looking
upset all last week. I asked them finally, unable to stand the tension. I was
afraid they wanted me to move out.

Remember I mentioned the parties? The marketers are forced to throw
quite a few of these parties. I mean, practically every single evening during the week. Anytime any one of them makes a placement or gets some
paperwork processed toward their green card, or buys a car, or even a
stereo, some of the more aggressive marketers, and Rayal's older brother,
who runs the other company, force the party issue. Ritu was forced to
throw a party at one of the Indian restaurants here. Her bill was $997.

This weekend, they were going to return the stereo they bought. I felt
really terrible. I bought the stereo from them. So it's still in the house.
And I won't be taking it with me either, if I move from here.

There are two really aggressive marketers, who eat like twenty pigs each, never throw any parties themselves, but force others to spend huge amounts of money almost every evening. Ritu says this is part of the culture in the company. She wants to quit. But that might affect Pradeep's job. There's a lot of politicking that goes on, she says. She discovered something recently. Every employee in the company is either a relative of Rayal or a friend of a relative or a friend or relative of another employee, marketer or consultant. If Rayal wants to harass someone, he will often put vindictive pressure on the relative or friend who is also employed at ISolutions.

Thank God, I'm a Sun System Administrator, completely unrelated and above all this.

But to make a confession: the guy who placed me, one of the pig marketers, let me call him Pig 1—he e-mails me twice a week and tries to harass me about my rate. Says my boss at AllAmerica doesn't want to pay as much and would like to cut my rate by ten dollars. I told Ritu about this. At first she kept quiet. Then she made a face. She said, that Pig 1, Pig 2, and Rayal are all assholes, and they try to rip off the consultants. They just want to increase their commission margins by paying the consultants less. The Americans who hire us for the projects don't mind paying the rates. (Although rates are coming down, I know.) Rayal is always ripping off the marketers and the consultants. He never tells the marketers what he actually pays the consultants. For instance, he may hire me out for seventy-five dollars an hour, but he will pay me forty dollars an hour, and he will tell the marketer who placed me that he is paying me sixty-five an hour. So he pays 20% commission on ten dollars instead of on the actual margin of thirty-five. Rayal's wife cooks the books on a daily basis. Four consultants have vanished this last month (as in your company.) Phone disconnected, no forwarding address. Rayal's taking it out on the marketers who were in charge of them. Apparently, this sort of disappearing act has happened before.

The other really harassing thing is that my pay gets held up by almost two weeks. I have to keep calling Rayal asking for my paycheck. I'm not alone in this: both Ritu and Pradeep have to do the same. I don't know why we don't get our paychecks in time. It's a constant headache every two weeks.

Ritu has a new look on her face. I would like to call it steely determination. It's as if she's on a mission of some kind. She said to me last night after dinner, "It'll be all right. We've survived a great deal. Fate has its own incomprehensible logic. In the end, it all makes sense."

Your best pal,
Mohit

Date: Mon, Mar 12 2001, 16:28:09 -0700 PDT
From: Vishnu Laha <vishnu@lido.com>
To: Mohit Dutt<mohit@yahoo.com>
Subject: politics

My advice to you: move out of that apartment. Either live with other single consultants or alone. Don't get involved with company politics. What you're hearing is no different from what goes on in any of these small IT companies. You're a consultant, stay focused on your work and pick up the new stuff quickly so that you build a good repertoire of skills. Take classes in the evenings if you have to.

Try to involve yourself with life in this country. There's lots to do besides weekend trips to malls, grocery stores, and relatives' houses. Start thinking about your long-term goals. Don't get too wrapped up in distractions, and if I may say, abstractions. How's the squash going? Make new friends.

—Vishnu

P.S. It's a good thing you didn't cc the last e-mail to Ranju. Your mother would have had quite a scene with Krishna over that one.

Date: Wed, Mar 14, 2001, 23:21:08 -0500 EDT
From: Ranjit Dutt <ranjit@hotmail.com>
To: Mohit Dutt <mohit@yahoo.com>
Subject: Re: re: re: re: re: update-edited

Dada,

This is the edited version of your March 9th e-mail that I showed *ma:*

Sometimes his little poetic one-liners make me feel weird. I've been having some odd dreams—Ranju's purple face looming up now and then from my computer.

I've been noticing some things in my office. We consultants sit in these closed offices in front of our screens and work away late into the evening. I was wondering so far from home. Then a flash of light went through my head.

I know what we are! We are the secret machinery—divine in our potential and knowledge—in the enormous, never-ending epic of the Internet. We are like the hundreds of deities making life smoother, quicker, better. I point out what miracles are not possible. I am orchestrating this company's internal network, unseen by the world.

My world is neither earth nor air nor fire or water. I'm the holy of holies to my boss, flitting from system to system, station to station. Aren't we the fingers of fate?"

Ha, ha!
Mohit

I gather this was the gist of your e-mail. *Ma* was quite stunned. Babli felt sure you had consumed a very large quantity of some substance similar to *bhang.*

About gods and deities, and your sense of power—there is a Greek word that would *"show you fear in a handful of dust."*

Your little brother,
Ranju

Date: Tue, Mar 20, 2001, 1: 14: 02 -0500 EDT
From: Mohit Dutt <mohit@yahoo.com>
To: Ranjit Dutt <ranjit@hotmail.com>
Subject: Re: re: re: re: re: update-edited

You can't play around with my words like that, Ranju! Your editing made me look like some kind of a hallucinating-on-drugs character. I could skin you alive.

But I'm going to spare you this time—please straighten things out re: edited e-mail with *ma.* I going to spare you because I have a very exciting thing to tell you. You're not going to believe this. I went skiing! One of the people I coach in the evenings and weekends at the squash club, Jon Lilly, has a cottage in Vermont. Really nice guy. To my surprise, I found out we are both working at AllAmerica. He's on the management side, in business development. Went out for a few beers with him. He invited me to go skiing with him for the weekend. It was COLD! I spent most of the time rolling down slopes. Jon gave me all the clothes and shoes and skis I needed. After sunset, Jon did some night skiing, while I sat in the ski lodge next door and drank hot toddies. This was an experience I'll never forget. You would have spouted some poetry if you had been here. The stretch of snowy slopes in the fading light had a fluorescent look, like a computer screen. I felt I had walked through it.

Love,
Dada

P.S. I'm 100% sure you did drink *bhang* with Biltu after Holi.

Date: Sat, Mar 24, 2001, 23:17:34 -0500 EDT
From: Mohit Dutt <mohit@yahoo.com>
To: Vishu Laha <vishnu@lido.com>
Subject: re: politics

I took your advice and now I'm facing the fallout. Made friends with one of the Americans in my company. My Indian colleagues are not talking to me any longer. They don't socialize with the Americans. I don't understand this. Rayal (my boss) doesn't have any Americans in his company, except for the receptionist and the HR person. Both are women. My uncle in San Jose has many American friends. Of course, his wife is American.

I asked Jon if he knew other Indians. He said he has many Indian friends, from college. He was surprised by what I told him about the strange culture in our company. He said most of the Indians he knows, academic, corporate, or whatever, all mixed with Americans. So is it only these Indian consultants and the small IT companies that have this strange stick-together culture? Jon did say, though, that he is aware that there are large groups of Indians who don't mix with Americans. Same with some other ethnic groups. Why is that? Is it class, money, culture?

I've been thinking about this lately. Why I'm unable to socialize with the people at ISolutions, but am quite comfortable with Jon and Pradeep and Ritu. You and I are from upper middle-class families. Pradeep and Ritu are pretty urban—Bombay, you know. Ritu's father retired as senior vice president of an advertising company. Pradeep's father is still in the Indian

Railways, a general manager. He was not too happy about Pradeep becoming a computer consultant. Wanted him to do an MBA. Well, my mother's dream is that I'll become a neurosurgeon. To this day she refuses to acknowledge that I can't bear the sight of blood. Can you see me drilling through someone's skull or doing a nerve graft on someone's spine? They'll have to slap the defibrillator on my chest as I drop with the scalpel to the floor!

However, most of the consultants at ISolutions are from small towns and villages, and definitely from a lower income background. The thing is, I've come to America to make money and have fun. I think they've just come to make some money and go back. Or perhaps to stay and bring their families over. My family, my mother, that is, would definitely not want to relocate to America; she has it too comfortable at home. Servants, relatives, friends. If she had to do all the housework and groceries and laundry—she would have a nervous breakdown! And if she couldn't spend every single morning shouting at the servants, she would suffer severe emotional trauma.

Anyway, I'm not going to stop being friends with Jon. We get along well. And what's the point of living in America and staying away from Americans? Jon's going to take me out on his boat this summer. I met his girlfriend. She's Italian. Not exactly Sophia Loren, but pretty hot all the same. She will introduce me to her friend, Karen. I hope she's blond!

Do I keep talking about women?

I didn't realize this until I left Calcutta—that all my life I've been taken care of by women. It's frightening to admit that to myself. But also amazing. As if I've had goddesses circling around me, goddesses more powerful than any of our gods. I can say this to you because we grew up together and you've spent so much time with my family. You know my sister and mother. When I told Jon about my family (not what I'm telling you now—just regular details), he gave me an odd smile and said, "You're a lucky man. You didn't grow up hating strong women." He says things like that sometimes. I laughed.

I understand what you mean by getting to know America, and I take your advice in good faith and seriously. But I know America, more or less. Have seen it on TV, in movies, in magazines, read about it in books. And what I'm finding here, now, isn't all that different from the images they presented. Except that they are not all Bold and Beautiful (my mother's devoted to that soap). There are all sorts of people here, okay, so what?

Some I will like, some I won't. There are very few secrets about America. Everything is huge, highways and houses and streets and theme parks and cars. I don't know yet if I want to settle here. Just make lots of money. For me, America is a drive-through right now: pick up my burger and drive on. Do I really need to negotiate (Jon's word) through all the cultural attitudes and hang-ups that come and go? I know what I need to know: have to get my sister married, have to make sure my kid brother gets to come here for his graduate studies, and have to support my mother. May be I'll get married some day. Family is top priority. And squash, for sure!

Yours,
Mohit

--------------------Forwarded mail--------------------

Date: Wed, Apr 4, 2001, 15:39:23 -0200 PDT
From: Ranjit Dutt <ranjit@hotmail.com>
Fwd: Jill Taylor-Gupta <jill@home.com>
To: Mohit Dutt <mohit@yahoo.com>
Subject: Re: For Reba, hello!

(*Dada,* below is an e-mail sent to *ma* by Aunt Jill. *Ma* didn't react to it very positively. She spent a long time at the altar praying to be rid of evil influences and bad manners.)

Dear Reba,

Just wanted to drop you a line. We had Mohit over for Thanksgiving, I'm sure Saurav has told you. What an attractive young man he has turned out to be. I think he looks very much like you. Has the same jet black wavy hair. I must say there's a family resemblance between him and our children. They too inherited the hair and the mysterious dark eyes of your temple gods.

I know you and I have never been on the best of terms, but for the sake of our children why not put aside our differences? Now that your son is here, wouldn't you like to visit? I believe your younger son has just finished his high school exams. Perhaps both of you would like to come here for a holiday? Shaila and Robi would love to meet Ranjit. Please think about it.

Take care,
Jill

————————Forwarded mail————————

Date: Tue, Apr 10, 2001, 23: 07: 04 0500 EDT
From: Mohit Dutt <mohit@yahoo.com>
To: Saurav Gupta <sgupta@msn.com>
Fwd: Jill Taylor-Gupta <jill@home.com>
Subject: Re: re: For Reba, hello

Dear Chinu-*mamu,*

E-mailing you to say hello. I've been very busy. How are Shaila and Robi?

Just wanted to mention something briefly. Ranjit forwarded an e-mail to me, and I have fwd. to you. It was to my mother from Jill-aunty. I understand that she meant well when she invited them over for a vacation. But I guess she didn't realize that round-trip tickets from Calcutta to California are pretty expensive, and neither I nor they have the money to finance such a vacation at present. I hope to be able to bring them over here after a year or so.

Also, as you know, my mother is somewhat traditional. Do you think aunty would mind addressing her as *bowdi?* Or at least as *didi?* Since my mother is quite a few years older than aunty, the first name thing didn't go over that well. I'm not saying all this to piss you off, or even to complain. But like aunty said in her e-mail, to put differences aside, some allowances will have to made from her side. She is, after all, a liberated woman, with a "greater transcultural understanding," as she said at Thanksgiving.

Regards,
your nephew,
Mohit

Date: Sat, Apr 14, 2001, 17: 12: 13 -0200 IST
From: Ranjit Dutt <ranjit@hotmail.com>
To: Mohit Dutt <mohit@yahoo.com>
Subject: FIREWORKS!!

Dear *Dada,*

(Happy *Poyla Boishakh.* Hope you haven't forgotten it's the Bengali New Year.)

YOU MUST MAKE SURE YOU DON'T START FIREWORKS!! Chinu-*mamu* forwarded your e-mail to him to me, and then he called last night and—I would like to say, all hell broke loose, but that would be understating it. *Ma* and he had an Olympic-level shouting contest over the phone. After half an hour, the operator who was listening in, said she had gone deaf, and cursed them both. She got an even louder earful! Anyway, why do you have to forward what *ma* says to you to them? You're turning into a troublemaker like our late great aunt. Have you any idea how often *ma* cries about you and Chinu-*mamu*. She had quite a row with Krishna after her fight ("Mohan, you wretched little up-to-no-good . . ."). He better think of pretty inventive ways to pacify her now. Be careful what you e-mail and to whom. Don't want to sound like my older brother now.

I'm dying to meet Jill aunty. I believe she visited when I was two. I can't quite remember. Apparently she made a great big fuss about not staying with us so *mamu* booked a room at the Taj Bengal for two weeks.

But anyway, back to the fireworks: all sorts of accusations were flung. You have been packaged as the overindulged, spoiled rotten, impractical prodigal son. (I added brilliant strategist and genius Sun God to the list bravely.) *Ma* called Jill aunty a lice-ridden hippie. But from what I know, she came well after the hippie movement. What did you think of her? She was working for the Peace Corps though, when *mamu* met her. And in the early photographs, she did have long straight hair and a bandana across her forehead.

Oh, Shaila e-mailed me and invited me to visit. For a twelve-year-old, her taste in music is pretty mature. She plays violin and piano and likes classical stuff, especially Chopin and Bach (dead musicians!). I was relieved to hear she also likes Nirvana (Cobain's dead as well, though).

I'm trying to piece together your life over there. But I can't quite see it like a movie. I try to picture your apartment from the pictures you e-mailed, but I'm not able to see it as a whole. But what you said about walking through a computer screen, that I could picture. Everything getting smaller and smaller, and then opening up, like space. *Dada*, you're everywhere when you're on the Internet. Then again, you are nowhere at all. You are simply @

"Dream kingdom, in the violet hour."

Although you deal with sophisticated language systems, the above is plain gobbledygook to you!

By the way, I showed your entire e-mail (March 9th) to *ma* and that had an even more intense effect. She sat dumbly in front of the altar for a half a day.

Love,
Ranju

re: your P.S. about *bhang: Flower o' the rose, If I've been merry, what matter who knows?*

Date: Tue, Apr 17, 2001, 1:13:18 -0500 EDT
From: Mohit Dutt <mohit@yahoo.com>
To: Vishnu Laha <vishnu@lido.com>
Subject: Re: re: politics

The constant babble I have to put up with. My mother doesn't get along with my American aunt and I get caught in the middle. I actually tried to suggest some helpful interactional methods. I give up. To top it all, Ranju is giving me advice. He's happily undermining my character and authority with all kinds of tricks. I'd trounce him if I were at home right now. He keeps throwing poetry or something like that at me. And he definitely got high on *bhang.* He practically admitted it.

On another subject: my roommates are terribly anxious again. Apparently Rayal has threatened to cut Ritu's pay in half if she doesn't make three placements by end of May. Pradeep will be coming off his project soon and is worried. A lot of consultants have come off projects of late. Ritu said there are nine people on the bench right now. Saw an alarming piece of news on the Internet: about 50,000 consultants are going back to India. There was also some news about several hundred cars left in parking lots with keys in the ignition. They belonged to computer consultants who had left the country. Just left their new cars at the airport parking lots and went back. I'm having nightmares about masses of shadowy figures crossing the Atlantic.

My God, I hope I haven't come to America at the wrong time. As it is, my mother considers this country a place where people get lost, I mean swallowed up, seduced from their near and dear back home. She's always been paranoid. People choose to come here, seduced or not. Life *is* better here. I can't complain, not yet. And I'm not some wide-eyed village boy. Indeed there aren't any more of those wide-eyed village boys left in this world.

Everyone knows how cutthroat the world is and tries to survive whichever way they can.

Man, this is turning out to be a dark e-mail. I'm hung over. Went out with Jon last night and talked till two about the capitalist, imperialist monster America is. I mean, *he* talked, I listened. The guy's a fucking Marxist! Can you believe that? I thought the breed thrived only on the sidewalks of Calcutta. Remember all the Lenin-talk Shontu-*da* used to feed us years ago? Jon kept telling me how exploited I am. Like the sweatshop workers. So much discrimination and all. The guy's mad. (Of late, he's grown a pointed goatee. He twirls the ends as he lectures!) Does he have any idea how much money I've saved in these four and a half months? I think I make more than he does. Has he any idea that if I walked out with the other Indian consultants his company would fall on its face?

How did *he* become a Marxist anyway? His parents live in Maine, in a grand old house with white columns in front, with stairs that go down to a private beach. (Showed me some pictures.) Where does Marxism come in? Must be these bars he takes me to—sports bars. Smoke-filled, awful music and TV screens with football players hurling themselves at each other like demons in mortal combat. I can't stand the lighting, I mean, the light is smothered by the smoke. My eyes sting and water constantly. Jon adds to it by smoking *biris,* if you can believe a management consultant smoking foul-smelling *biris.*

Oh, I've got to tell you this: some of my Indian colleagues smell foul. I don't know which hellhole they've come from. They don't do their laundry. And they definitely do not use deodorants. I had a long talk with Sri (remember? I mentioned him once. Sits right next to me converting VB stuff to C/C++) about this. Some of these guys are giving the whole lot of us Indians a very bad reputation. Between you and me, they are mostly South Indians. I admit some Bengalis stink pretty bad, too. But not as many. I also told Sri to get some Altoids or something. I mean, we ought to exude the perfumed smoke of sandalwood incense and burning camphor! Deities! Deities! Not foul-smelling demons mucking about in reeking caverns. This lighting here, though, sometimes fudges the distinction.

Have to close. Clothes are done.

Ciao.
Mohit

Date: Tue, Apr 24, 2001, 20: 42: 43 -0700 PDT
From: Vishnu Laha <vishnu@lido.com>
To: Mohit Dutt <mohit@yahoo.com>
Subject: Re: re: re: politics

Your Jon sounds like a character. A little bit pâpier-mâché, I think, the Marxist persona.

They all think the Americans are exploiting and abusing everyone. So what's new? H1-B visa category was created to bring in mass skilled labor (not your magical conduit for heavenly spirits). And we poor little Indians are so naive and ignorant . . . Right. Why do they all think the Third World inhabitants are weak, misguided, mistreated . . .? Most of us are proper rogues like the rest of them.

Put all the cards on the table: the high-tech needs of the American corporations are being serviced by Indian consultants. (We Indians have an advantage—we speak English, even if some of us have terrible accents.) Are we underpaid? Actually, no. How else would these body-shoppers rake in their profits if they were hiring us out cheap? Let's drop that awful term—body-shoppers—because are these IT service-provider companies any different from any other staffing agencies in their practices? The difference between you and me and the American consultant is this: the American gets his job, either permanent or contract work, directly with a company, or through an employment agency. If it's through an agency, then the consultant gets a percentage of the rate. Example: say the rate quoted to a company is 75 dollars an hour. The agency will take 15 dollars and the consultant will get 60. For an Indian consultant, whose H1 was processed by a company like ours, the rate quoted is still 75 dollars. And the consultant may sometimes get 58 or 59 dollars per hour. Why a few dollars less sometimes? Because ISolutions may have got you your position at AllAmerica through another employment agency. So the 15 dollars (or sixteen or seventeen) is split between the two agencies and the consultant may or may not lose a dollar or two depending on how many intermediaries there were. It's business. The American company is not paying any of us any less because we're Indian.

What are the activists saying? We pay social security, but won't benefit from it. Well, if you get your green card processed, become a citizen, and stay in this country until you retire, you probably will receive social security (if the Republicans haven't got rid of it by then).

Discrimination? Didn't you tell me your boss at AllAmerica is ready to prostrate himself at your glowing golden (actually light brown) feet? My dear fellow, don't *you* dare tell me South Indians smell! Discrimination is a global attitude.

As you said, we haven't come here all wide-eyed innocents abroad. (You think we are super beings—perhaps we are, I will give myself the benefit of the doubt.) We've come knowingly and willingly to make our dollars. Some of us will go back, some of us will stay. There was an article about Chinese consultants living all squeezed into some hellhole. How much like a packed sardine do you feel at present? I'm not part of a Chinese IT consulting company. I don't know what goes on there. *I only know what I am experiencing.* The bad things are not always on the outside—as you are well aware. Fingers of fate, eh?

Listen, Mohit, work hard, make new friends. This is a country where one can achieve a great deal in spite of all the sociological problems. Go to a mirror and ask yourself: who am I, where am I, and what do I want? I'm two years older than you, but believe me, I still get a different answer each time.

—Vishnu

Date: Wed, May 2, 2001, 15: 43: 56 -0200 IST
From: Ranjit Dutt <ranjit@hotmail.com>
To: Mohit Dutt <mohit@yahoo.com>
Subject: Happy Birthday!

Click on the address below to pick up your greeting card.

http.www.bluemountain-cards/cgibin1356psbimn/bluemountaincards.com

"By the pricking of my thumbs . . ."

Date: May 3, 2001, 23: 47: 08 -0500 EDT
From: Mohit Dutt <mohit@yahoo.com>
To: Ranjit Dutt <ranjit@hotmail.com>
Subject: Re: Happy Birthday!

You little turd!

That card froze my hard drive! If this is what that loafer Biltu is teaching you then you are not to associate with him anymore starting the moment you read this e-mail. I will tell Babli to get rid of the computer and you will have no more access to all the junk games and poetry chat groups. Don't think that just because your big brother is away he doesn't have any control over you. You still want your Nike sneakers, don't you?

Date: Fri, May 4, 2001, 9: 24: 02 -0200 IST
From: Ranjit Dutt <ranjit@hotmail.com>
To: Mohit Dutt <mohit@yahoo.com>
Subject: Re: re: Happy Birthday!

You must have got quite a shock, you, great Sungod of an IT consultant that you are!

"That loafer Biltu" is going to Chicago with his parents next month. They will also go to Disneyworld. I'm dying of jealousy. When can you take me to America? Save money for my ticket, please.

Life is full of wonders.

The heat is so intense that your feet would blister instantly if you stepped out barefoot on the veranda in the afternoon.

Last night the first storm of the season hit. *Dada,* I lay awake all night, watching. My window went blazing white every two or three minutes. The lightning didn't come in streaks. It broke like a flood of white fire across the Calcutta sky. I heard from someone that in the Universal Studios at Disneyworld, they can simulate storms. But last night wasn't just a sound and light show with smoke and mirrors.

In the morning, Calcutta lay wrecked all around. Corrugated tin roofs and pieces of slum sheds were strewn along roads and parks. There were branches everywhere as if forests had exploded.

Then spoke the thunder.

To you.

As always,
Ranju

Date: Wed, May 23, 2001, 1: 21: 09 -0500 EDT
From: Mohit Dutt <mohit@yahoo.com>
To: Vishnu Laha <vishnu@lido.com>
Subject: news

My project got terminated due to some financial cuts. I was half afraid I'd be on the bench like a lot of others. But they found me another position in two days. Luck. This was scary, Vishnu. I thought there'd be a warning, I mean, my project manager would let me know a week or two in advance. But that jerk got fired first and then the project got canceled. Sri told me these things happen. Sri—the smelly guy I mentioned earlier, is on the bench. He's been on the bench before, and is very nervous. Apparently, last year, he was on the bench for almost three months.

Anyway, my new position's in Boston. Pradeep drops me off at the train station in Cambridge and I take the T from there. This is a tiny office, and I sit in a tinier cubicle. We're in a basement. No windows. I can't wait to get out for lunch. I have two Chinese colleagues (mainland) who never even return a smile. Now tell me, why can't they be a little friendly? We're both foreigners in this country. I tried to talk to them about Tibet and the Dalai Lama. They looked at me blankly. There is definitely a language problem here and it's not Basic.

The systems analyst I'm working with (a German guy) always makes me communicate everything to the Chinese duo. I'm not even sure if they are listening to me—they keep their eyes glued to the screen. But they do the work, so I guess they get the messages. What is wrong with them? Sometimes I catch them staring. A flat stare from stone eyes of jade statues.

I know you're going to tell me I'm being discriminating and all that. But I'm having to deal with these two weirdos every single day. The wait-ers at the Chinese restaurant across the street are completely different. They now call me by my name and chat with me about India. So I'm not generalizing about the Chinese. All this political correctness! I tell you, some of these politically correct people need to spend some time in the Third World. They won't know whether they are coming or going in their political correctness after a good three days in a coffee house on College Street. Jon the Marxist will go in Leftist and come out north by northwest.

Maybe I sound like a jerk, but given the "categories" (Jon's word) we are surrounded by in India, and the diseases and corruption and social hypocrisies we wade through, and of course my mother's ever-failing, promise-breaking gods, it's a little difficult for us—for me—to join the word political to the word correct. It is easier to forgive the little Krishna for not living up to expectations. As for all the exploitations worldwide—what should I do? Go out on the street and wave banners and shout slogans? Haven't we done enough of that with Shontu-*da* in Calcutta? Man, do you remember that tear-gas attack we got caught in on Chowringhee? And then bundled into that police van, you with your head cracked by a billy club? And then slapped around at the police station? And then slapped around by my mother and sister! We were only trying to cross the street.

Jon dragged me to a talk a few days ago at the University of Massachusetts campus in Boston. An Indian guy talking about the ills of capitalism and how we should be out protesting on the streets. I felt like I was back on the front steps of Shontu-*da*'s house. Except that Shontu-*da* actually organized rallies and helped labor unions and got arrested once a month. This guy at the university—what a joke, man. In a wool *kurta* and jeans, with a shawl around his shoulders, all comfortably protected by his cushy job at some school, living comfortably in this very capitalist country, benefiting from every perk capitalism offers, and spouting forth about how complacent *we* the audience were! Would he give up his TIAA-CREF? Aren't retirement benefits a huge perk of this capitalist monster? And what makes these "intellectuals" assume that the downtrodden don't have the capacity to think? I know I'm not an intellectual. But I'm not an idiot.

He got plenty of clapping and cheering. In Calcutta, he'd be wiping rotten eggs and tomatoes off his face.

I think the lack of windows and fluorescent lighting is affecting my mood. This laundry room is the same. Sometimes I wonder if I'll ever get out from the shadow of this non-light.

How's your life, pal?

M.

Date: Mon, Jun 4, 2001, 17: 21: 23 -0200 IST
From: Ranjit Dutt <ranjit@hotmail.com>
To: Mohit Dutt <mohit@yahoo.com>
Subject: ???

Dada,

What's going on? Haven't heard from you for a month. Have you been very busy? Why haven't you called? *Ma* is very worried. Poor Krishna is getting the scoldings of all his reincarnated lives. And the quality of food is suffering. *Ma* is not paying much attention to what is being cooked for lunch or dinner. My Sunday potato fritters and prawn cutlets were completely forgotten! I told *ma,* your older son has been reconfigured and uploaded and is now a bloody virus that is screwing up my daily life and every meal!

Please call or e-mail ASAP or you will *walk in darkness, torn on the horn between . . . hour and hour, word and word, power and power . . .*

Simply,
Ranju

Date: Tue, Jun 5, 2001, 19: 27: 24 -0500 EDT
From: Mohit Dutt <mohit@yahoo.com>
To: Ranjit Dutt <ranjit@hotmail.com>
Subject: Re: ???

Stop cursing me in code! Don't worry. I'm fine. Have been very busy. New project. Plus squash almost every evening and weekends. Have your exam results come out?

Date: June 12, 2001, 13: 37: 31 -0200 IST
From: Ranjit Dutt <ranjit@hotmail.com>
To: Saurav Gupta <sgupta@msn.com>
Subject: Re: Mohit, From *didi.*

(I am writing this against my better judgment, under protest, and on behalf of my mother.—Ranju)

Dear Chinu,

I hope you and your family are well. I was extremely upset by the unpleasantness last time we spoke. My heartbeat was erratic for two whole days, and our family doctor was quite concerned about my blood pressure. I feel like I'm losing my family one by one. First, our parents, then my husband, and now my brother, and my son. My daughter declared her so-called "independence" many years ago. What is happening to us?

I am sick with worry. Something is very wrong. Mohit hasn't been sending e-mails or calling. He has also said some very strange things in one of his e-mails. I am sure something bad has happened to him and he is not telling us. Could you please phone him and check? Who else can I turn to in this situation? Please try to reach him and then either call or e-mail me. I haven't slept in three weeks.

With love,
Didi

Date: Fri, July 6, 2001, 15: 46: 47 -0700 PDT
From: Jill Taylor-Gupta <jill@home.com>
To: Mohit Dutt <mohit@yahoo.com>
Subject: Hi there!
cc: Ranjit Dutt <ranjit@hotmail.com>

Dear Mohit,

This is your aunt Jill, as you'll see from the e-mail. How are you? How did you enjoy the Fourth of July fireworks in your neighborhood?

I'm not sure if you're aware that your mother is a bit anxious about you. Saurav has called you a few times. Have you moved? Parents living in India don't understand how busy we are in our day-to-day lives over here. You must be very busy with your projects. Make sure you're getting your veggies, and take vitamins. Now I'm beginning to sound like your mom.

Do call us. Come visit when you a get a few days off. Labor Day weekend would be a good time.

Shaila is giving a recital this evening. Robi is getting better at tennis every day. I'm organizing "India week" at Shaila's school. I'm helping them decorate with saris and we have some dance performances and an Indian fashion show organized by the South Asian students. I'm trying to replicate the atmosphere of color and sound and smell (spice and rice!) in the school gym for a whole week. We'll have videos running, music, folk dances, all at the same time. I'm also giving a talk and slide show on the various gods and goddesses of India and what they mean. You would enjoy the show. (It's all of next week. You could come for the weekend. Southwest Airlines has a special right now: $265 round trip from Boston.)

I've always been mad about India. There were invisible spirits all around. I could sense them energizing me. I don't know if I mentioned that.

If you've moved please let us know your new address and phone number. I know that you wonderful computer-wiz folks have to move every few months.

Hope to see you soon,
Jill

Date: Mon, Jul 9, 2001, 21: 38: 36 -0700 PDT
From: Vishnu Laha <vishnu@lido.com>
To: Mohit Dutt <mohit@yahoo.com>
Subject: Re: news
cc: ranjit @hotmail.com

Wanted to let you know that I'm jumping ship. My project boss offered me a permanent position in the company. They'll transfer my H1. My Indian company will throw a fit. But H1s are transferable, and permanent positions are better than these project-hopping, city-hopping positions. As you know, I've moved six times in the last two years. But I've come to like Seattle, and I think I'd like to stay put for a few years. I've moved out of my apartment into an efficiency. If anyone calls you asking about me, say you know nothing. I've had no vacations in the last two years, except for the few long weekends and the official holidays. I negotiated a four-week vacation with my new boss. I'm going to Calcutta during Christmas.

−Vishnu

Date: Wed, Jul 11, 2001, 18: 17: 24 -0500 EDT
From: Mohit Dutt <mohit@yahoo.com>
To: Vishnu Laha <vishnu@lido.com>
Subject: Re: re: news
Attachment: mohit1.doc <Word file>

Good luck with your new job. It sounds like a good situation.

I've time on my hands, and this update is going to be a long one, so I'm sending it as an attachment.

mohit1.doc

My American aunt is trying to spy on me. What a moronic e-mail she sent me, with cc to Ranju! How are you, etc. How busy we are in this country. Eat your veggies. I'm organizing India week. You'd think my uncle would have married someone halfway intelligent. My young cousins are pretty bright in spite of their mother's genes. Takes after our side of the family. Hopefully there are intelligent American women around. I haven't met any yet. I did meet that Karen, Jon's girlfriend's best friend. Last weekend. Face like a horse, wild hair, and talked nonstop for two hours about I've no idea what. Good night to that one forever. Do you think attractive women like having ugly women as close friends?

To the crisis at hand: I've been on the bench for a week now, and the idiot marketers haven't been able to line up a single interview. The second assignment—I barely had time to breathe in that project—ended two weeks ago. Now I'm sitting in the ISolutions office everyday, learning some new stuff on my own, and finding out too many things I don't really want to know. I thought I'd go on a little sight-seeing vacation. But I'm not being allowed to do that. I have to stay here in case interviews come up. I have company, though. Eleven consultants are on the bench with me, and quite a few of them have been without a project for over two months.

We spend our days inside a room in the office. It's the only room that doesn't have windows, because it's flanked by the main office on three sides and a closed corridor on the other. The lighting has an odd grey-violet tint like the ten computer screens that hum around me. I sit around learning some Veritas tools on my own. The other consultants fiddle around looking sulky. An atmosphere of all-pervasive gloom.

It's our strange little underworld, completely ignored by the rest of the world.

The marketers ignore us, as if we aren't really here, as if this room isn't here. Rayal pokes his head in a few times a day to bark out someone's name, take the poor bastard out and harass him.

You know, we don't really have names. We are identified by our skill sets: VB/ASP, Java, C/C++, Sun System Admin, Oracle DBA. When calls come with requirements, they say, "Get me a Java with such and such." Did I ever have a name here? Where am I now?

You wouldn't know you were in America, if you were here. I can see the HR person and the receptionist through the glass doors. They move around like shadows. This office of ours could have been an office in India, full of the smell of Indian food they order for lunch everyday. The voices, the gossip, the backbiting, the curses—little India around me, dislocated, misplaced, somewhat lost.

We sit like sullen idols, waiting for missions. Sometimes I wonder if we're really here, or am I dreaming.

I can't tell my family about my situation. They would panic. I know I'll get a position soon. I just don't know how soon.

Most of the guys on the bench, seven of them, have not been paid for six weeks. I've been spending a lot of time with Sri. Remember Sri? The smelly C/C++ guy I had mentioned? Thank God, no more smell, thanks to me and Arrid and Altoids. He's been twiddling his toes for over two months. Poor guy, he's very depressed. Rayal hasn't paid him a cent for seven weeks. Sri was made to sign a leave letter. Rayal told him that way he gets to keep his H1 status. Sri wanted to go to Hyderabad to see his family. But that wasn't allowed. I don't understand why they don't let him go if they are unable to find him a position. Rayal's rude to him all the time and harasses him on a daily basis. Sri's failed three interviews. The real reason: marketer Pig 2 lied through his teeth when redoing Sri's re-sume. Sri doesn't speak English too well either. I told him to learn some of the new tools. But he's lazy and doesn't want to do that either. Sometimes I don't know who to blame in this business. He sulks in a corner and flips through *SiliconIndia*. He could quit and go look for jobs on his own. But he won't do that either. All of these guys could quit and go out and find something. I would, if I'd been on the bench for over two months and not getting paid. (But there's the H1 catch. Can't hang around without a job. Would lose H1 status and get sent back.)

By the way, I don't do my personal e-mails from work. All Internet activity is monitored by Rayal's computer. The guy's suspicious to the point of paranoia. He wants loyalty from his employers, while he wants to exercise an FBI-type surveillance over everyone. And the methodology of this surveillance? Gossip, backbiting, favoritism, constant harassment. Rayal wants the parties (going out to eat and to drink gallons of wine and scotch) every evening so he can keep his eye on them even after work. He even tries to get all of them to get together over the weekends. Some of these marketers are married with kids. But they are so insecure about their jobs they do whatever Rayal wants.

Let me explain the nature of the harassment: Rayal's tactics to maintain control over a marketer: he makes them feel they are not doing a good job. They are not working hard. Their skills are no good. Bring down their self-confidence and sense of self-worth, basically. Master-slave relationship, as Jon would put it (I meet him at the club three times a week).

That's for the marketer. Now the consultant. Take Sri again. Pig 2 finally gets a requirement that matches Sri's skills. But Sri really has seven out of the ten items required. Some of these Project Managers, who send in the requirements, are also a little too smart. They want so many skills and with three years' experience only. Realistically, someone with seven to ten years' experience would fit exactly. But they'd have to pay a great deal more. Therefore, three years. Okay. Pig 2 customizes Sri's resume, lies, in short. Tells Sri, study hard and learn these three other things. Sri tries to pick up all the stuff. But then he's asked something about some financial shit at the interview. Now who's at fault?

Rayal hauls Sri into his office. Tells Sri he is wasting Rayal's time and money, he can't keep him here with full pay. Take two weeks' vacation, Rayal tells him, and cashes his vacation. Then he asks Sri to give him a leave letter, saying, that way he can maintain an H1 status. Poor Sri's at a loss. Rayal stops paying him after two weeks on the bench.

Ritu told me this is wrong. Why should Sri be made to cash out his vacation? Rayal should pay him on the bench for another two weeks. Rayal won't terminate a consultant easily either. He wants the resources at hand, but doesn't want to pay for them.

I can't figure him out. Is he stupid or too cunning? I overheard him ask a guy who came to interview for a marketing position if the guy would work without pay (only on commission) for the first two months? The guy made a few odd noises and left.

From what I see, the employees here have no self-respect to speak of. They pay homage to Rayal from five-thirty in the evening. They provide entertainment in the form of parties, eating out, even going to his house and cooking dinner for him and his wife. Pradeep and Ritu show up for these evening *shosha-giri* sessions reluctantly. They are desperately trying to find a way out of this company. But Pradeep's green card is being processed and he can't leave until it's done. Ritu's pay has been cut in half. Rayal yells at Ritu throughout the day about how inept and worthless she is. (Irony, my little brother would have said.) What a bad judge of character Rayal is—hope he finds that out for himself the hard way.

I've been cooking dinner lately, trying my best to be cheerful. The two of them are very quiet around the apartment. Ritu spends most of the evenings in her study. She's constantly on the Internet. Says she's doing some research. That look of steely determination has become even more acute on her face. She had no idea that they would be in this kind of a situation when Pradeep came to the U.S. recruited by Rayal. Thank God, Pradeep is not on the bench yet. I wonder what Ritu is really doing. She's still calm and composed in spite of the harassment. She reminds me of Babli after father died. Babli took charge of us all, running the house, handling money matters, everything. I like to call myself the man of the family, but it is Babli who has always taken care of us.

Watching Ritu at her computer, so very focused, working intently, makes me focused in turn. I'm concentrating on learning some new backup tools. Although worried sick, Pradeep relaxes once we are all home, and we've all had a good dinner. (I've become a pretty good cook.) I've promised myself if Pradeep comes off his project and is on the bench, I'll pay the rent. Pig 1 promises me everyday that he's getting me an interview soon. There is a good chance that we may all end up in different cities with our new positions.

I think I'm going to feel somewhat lost without Ritu. I wish I could get her out of this situation. She really doesn't have anyone to count on. In some ways, Pradeep and I cling to her emotionally.

Have I always clung to women?

Why is it in my life women have been stronger and more reliable than men?

I'm afraid to look into mirrors.

Date: Fri, Jul 13 2001, 21: 48: 05 -0700 PDT
From: Vishnu Laha <vishnu@lido.com>
To: Mohit Dutt <mohit@yahoo.com>
Subject: Re: re: re: news

Your skills are in high demand. You'll get a position. The market's not so good anymore. You ought to know that. There are too many Indian consultants floating around. Planeloads are going back.

So why are some of the consultants hanging around moping in your company? There's security in just being in that office of yours with others of one's kind. The sheer horror of being out there on one's own!

A bit of gossip: just before I left my last company, one of the consultants (who was on the bench for three months) got fired. His wife (married about a year) went back to India with some excuse, and then her family asked for a divorce and for the dowry money to be returned!

Do you see how much better your situation is compared to that poor fellow's? Think positive. Stop looking into mirrors. And e-mail Ranju about your situation. Don't keep them worrying in the dark.

—Vishnu

Date: Sun, Jul 15 2001, 17: 56: 52 -0200 IST
From: Ranjit Dutt <ranjit@hotmail.com>
To: Mohit Dutt <mohit@yahoo.com>
Subject: *Dada!?!*

Will you please let us know what you've been up to? *Mamu* called to say he's left four messages for you already but you haven't called back. And I saw Aunty Jill's e-mail to you as well. You're turning into quite the Cheshire Cat. Now all we have is the smile. *Or do we?*

My exam results are out. First Division, and among the top five! *Didi* threw a party for me at the hotel. I also sat for the I.I.T admissions test. I've got admission to I.I.T Delhi. All this happened two months ago. But since you haven't bothered to e-mail us, I decided not to share the good news. We're all off to Delhi next week and will be staying at the Oberoi , courtesy *Didi*. I've never stayed in a five-star deluxe hotel before! We'll get ten-star service because of *Didi*.

To Carthage then I came, burning . . .

Your brilliant brother,
Ranju

Date: Fri, Jul 20 2001, 22:29: 07 -0500 EDT
From: Mohit Dutt <mohit@yahoo.com>
To: Vishu Laha <vishnu@lido.com>
Subject: Re:re: re: re: news
Attachment: mohit2.doc <Word file>

Hey, Ranju did damn well in his exams and has got into I.I.T Delhi. Smart kid. I'm proud of him. My mood brightened up the moment I got his e-mail. –M.

---

mohit2.doc

I know you want me to tell them about my situation, but I can't. I'm still on the bench. I don't want my mother to feel disappointed. Actually, she'll go out of her mind with worry. I don't want them to feel I've failed somehow.

Rayal's cut my pay in half. Is it legal?

I'm now witnessing day-to-day turmoil.

The office atmosphere is tense. One of the marketers has disappeared. Rayal's foaming at the mouth. The vanished creature was a young woman from Rayal's hometown. Rich family. She was here for two months, then one morning, no show. Phone disconnected, apartment keys turned in. Another marketer, a nineteen-year-old girl, has quit. Too much pressure, she said. It's something, the way these young women have thumbed their noses and simply vanished. The men are crawling around, bowing and scraping, held hostage by their H1s or green cards in process.

There will be more consultants coming off projects soon. The marketers haven't made very many placements. Rayal's fired three consultants finally. His new war song is "make end-client" placements. He's got hold of a new Chief Operating Officer, a smart, corporate guy. Rayal wants the new COO to turn his bumpkins into high-powered sales executives.

You should have seen the agitation in the office with the entry of the new COO. (I'm not sure how Rayal got hold of this guy. He's Indian, but was working at an American multinational company.) The day he sat down at his desk, the marketers, Pig 1 and Pig 2, to be precise, went out to lunch with Rayal's younger brother (I think I forgot to mention this guy—the younger brother. An absolute nincompoop and more or less invisible. He's employed here because he can't get a job anywhere else. He does odd jobs). I went along out of curiosity.

Lunch was full of questions re: COO: who is he? why is he here? how can we get rid of him?

Why the need to get rid of him? you want to know. The new COO doesn't seem to be kowtowing to Rayal. Rayal seems to be a little in awe of him. Oh, my God! What if the new COO finds out within a day or two how useless most of the people in the office are and gets rid of them? And little brother will be out on the street first, won't he? So they brainwash little brother. You should be the COO, Pig 1 and Pig 2 tell him.

I almost buried my face in the fried rice to smother my laugh. This type of plotting and scheming went on for a week. The COO had meetings with each of the marketers, observed for a week, and quit! His parting words were "fire the lot of them and hire real account executives." The "party, party" rallying every evening must have made him puke. Actually, the so-called partying has died down. Lately, Pig 2 and another guy go to Rayal's house in the evenings and fix dinner.

In the middle of all this, to impress the new COO, Rayal hired two new consultants. Straight from Andhra Pradesh. They arrived last week. What attitudes, Vishnu! These two guys called from the company guest house. They need rides to the office. Rayal calls me to his office. Says, "Here are the keys to the office car. Since you're not doing anything worthwhile, go pick them up."

The company guest house, a studio apartment, is literally across the street, across Route 9, to be precise, about a ten-minute walk.

When they opened the door, my jaw dropped. I've never seen such a pigsty in my life. Even slum shacks are cleaner. The whole place reeked of rotting garbage and unwashed clothes. The first thing they tell me is

that I'm late, and they need to go food shopping. So I call Rayal on my
cell phone. He says to take them to the store. But first, they ask me to take
out their garbage. I simply pointed at the chute down the hall. Next stop:
Wal-Mart, where they pick up a DVD player, jeans and shirts, CDs, DVDs
and then we go to the grocery store. They bought Coke, chips, Doritos, all
other kinds of snack foods. I asked them if they needed any real food. No,
of course not. Their breakfast (coffee and doughnuts) is delivered to their
doorstep by one of marketers, lunch by another, and dinner is at Rayal's
house, they tell me proudly. This is how life should be, they imply. After
all, they are hard-to-get IT consultants, and should be waited on hand
and foot.

Hate to tell you, Sri had the same attitude before he found his rear end
on the bench second time round. I feel bad for Sri. He has a wife and
daughter in Hyderabad. I don't really have anyone depending on me. I'm
not sure if it's completely legal to not pay an H1 employee. But who's
going to the INS? Everyone's got their own insecurities. The marketers
have to hang on to their jobs (and their H1). The consultants don't want
to lose their H1 status. And Rayal uses all of this to keep them licking his
shit. Anyway, the new consultants were fired promptly as soon as the COO
walked out. Apparently, they weren't as hot profit as they thought they
were, and one had lied beyond belief about his skills.

It's all profit and loss to Rayal, everything and every one of us. I am big
profit for sure if Pigs 1 and 2 would place me quickly.

What he doesn't know yet (or perhaps vaguely suspects) is that Pig 1 is
doing business with a California staffing company. He is giving them
business by placing their consultants or by getting them requirements.
How do I know this? While walking over to Ritu's desk the other day, I
caught a glimpse of Pig 1's screen. He was checking his Hotmail account.
He turned off the screen as soon as he saw me. So I went back to my
computer and broke into his account. Pig 1 has been receiving e-mails
from this other company and the nature of the e-mails made it crystal
clear what he's been up to. Now if Rayal was to find out about this he
we would be having a pig roast tonight! Pig 1 is the one who forced Ritu
to throw that expensive party. Pig 1 used to harass me about cutting my
rate. I could do some damage now.

But Rayal can't really get rid of Pig 1. Ritu told me (I shared the above
info. with her) that Pig 1 brings in 40% of the company's business. He's
not been doing that well lately, though.

Rayal, Pig 1, Sri, all of us—we're all strung from the same rope—yanking, dangling, necks twisting, choking—H1, green card, profit, loss . . .

A pig's breakfast—that's what this is.

Best,
Mohit

Date: Sat, Jul 21 2001, 15: 36: 48 -0700 PDT
From: Jill Taylor-Gupta <jill@home.com>
To: Mohit Dutt <mohit@yahoo.com>
Subject: dinner/visit
cc: Ranjit Dutt <ranjit@hotmail.com>

Hello Mohit,

I hope everything is well with you. How interconnected we can be! E-mail to you, cc to your little brother. Families should stay woven together.

We'll be in Boston day after tomorrow. Saurav has some meetings. Since the children have holidays, we're all coming together. We're staying at the Sheraton. I'll call you as soon as we get in. We hope you will come and spend some time with us. How about the 24th? Come and join us for dinner.

See you soon. Shaila and Robi are excited about seeing you again.

Take care,
Jill

Date: Thu, Jul 26 2001, 23: 12: 15 -0500 EDT
From: Mohit Dutt <mohit@yahoo.com>
To: Vishnu Laha <vishnu@lido.com>
Subject: sushi
Attachment: mohit3.doc <Word file>

---

mohit3.doc

Out of the blue my uncle and his family land up in Boston. Had to go and have dinner with them. Obviously had to be pretty careful so they don't find out I'm on the bench and at once go and throw my mother into a frenzy. They weren't as curious as I thought they might be. Although part of the meeting was a type of surveillance to find out what was going on with me. But my aunt Jill had too much to say about some India week she organized at her daughter's school, and the two kids were excited about the aquarium. So I didn't have to do too much talking.

My uncle has a disturbing way of looking at a person. He kept staring at me with a frown. Anyway, I got to leave after a couple of hours.

At the ISolutions office today, all the consultants on the bench seemed like the little pieces of fish I had for dinner, all chopped up and waiting to be eaten by Rayal.

Am I going to get another position or what? I need to get out of here, but how?

At the office, they are planning a weekend trip to New York. Corralled tightly, everyone's going with Rayal and his wife. I, definitely, am not. Neither are my roommates, but we are not telling him.

Ritu is up to something. She sat me down this evening like my sister does at times. She said, "You're just about twenty-two. Why didn't you finish college? You should consider going back to school. "

I was a bit taken aback. "Is something wrong?" I asked. Stupid question. Yesterday was Pradeep's last day at his project.

Ritu's eyes narrowed and she said to me, "Everything is wrong. We're being held hostage by Rayal. The man is not very enlightened. What makes him think he can treat employees this way and get away with it?"

"He's been doing it for the last five years," I said. "He doesn't seem to possess any human emotions."

"Well, there has to be an end to it."

Believe me, my eyes widened. I had an intense visual flash through my head much like the scene at the royal dinner table in Kathmandu.

"No," she said. "I'm not going to do anything to him. He'll meet his own nasty end through his own actions. I'm going to get us out."

"If you quit, you'll have to go back to India."

She gave me that steely look again.

For some bizarre reason, I feel Babli is here. Or at least she has somehow sent some of her own fiery energy to Ritu. Through the Internet?!? Or is it Krishna, driven to distraction by my mother?

Ritu asked me for my resume. She said she needed it as an example.

"Very well presented," she said, reviewing it.

I saw pieces of fish again, wrapped in seaweed, on a shiny black lacquer tray. So shiny, it reflected the food.

Yours,
Mohit

Date: Mon, Jul 30 2001, 21: 46: 02–0200 IDT
From: Ranjit Dutt <ranjit@hotmail.com>
To: Mohit Dutt <mohit@yahoo.com.
Subject: food for thought
cc: Vishnu Laha <vishnu@lido.com>

How was dinner with our American cousins? Yes, we are all interconnected and can see through the murky air your deep dark doings.

Mamu called last night and said they had dinner with you in Boston. He, too, is sure that something is not quite right.

Younger brother or not, *Dada,* I think I'm right about this. Are you on the bench (I believe that's the term used for consultants who are in between projects)? You said your project was to run for eleven months. But then you mentioned "new project," and then you fell silent.

I understand that projects get canceled quite often. Why don't you just tell us? What do you think *ma* and *didi* will do? Yell at you? Aren't you be-having like a guilty child although none of whatever is happening is your fault? Why don't you just come back? We miss you. Or if you don't want to come back then keep us informed. You're not letting anyone down. No one has ever expected anything from you—I mean, of course we all want you to succeed in life, but I know there are all sorts of problems in life and bad things happen.

Who said you can't kick and scream and throw a fit? Please throw one in your next e-mail.

Part your hair behind, eat a peach, wear white flannel pants and walk upon the beach.

Force the moment to its crisis.

All our love,
Ranju

Date: Fri, Aug 10 2001, 22: 06: 23 -0500 EDT
From: Mohit Dutt <mohit@yahoo.com>
To: Ranjit Dutt <ranjit@hotmail.com>
Subject: Re: food for thought

Ranju,

How dare you cc your e-mail to Vishnu! I'll slap a rotten tomato instead of a peach on your face.

I AM FINE.

I've moved. I'm in Philadelphia. My address is: Apt 24B, Lyndon Place, 201 Rye Street, Philadelphia, PA. Cell phone: (267) 864-4488 Home phone: (267) 330-0900.

I know this will come as a big surprise. But I was given a golden opportunity, a godsend, *ma* would say. A goddess to the rescue, to be precise. No need to worry. Will call over the weekend.

Love to all of you,
Mohit

Date: Fri, Aug 10, 2001, 22: 38: 45 -0500 EDT
From: Mohit Dutt <mohit@yahoo.com>
To: Vishnu Laha <vishnu@lido.com>
Subject: Re: re: re: news
Attachment: mohit4.doc <Word file>

---

mohit4.doc

Ignore my brother's e-mail. You know what a pest he is. I've tried to put their minds at rest.

So much has happened here. I'm still processing it all. I'm in complete awe of Ritu.

Ritu, the quiet, composed, calm, determined Ritu.

Here it is—for your eyes only:
The situation at the office got worse every day—every day that I witnessed. Sri had started to break down, I mean, he would cry silently. It
was terrible to watch. Sometimes I'm not sure who suffered more. Sri, his
face buried in his hands, or me, feeling my nerves slowly snap one by one
watching him in the corner. I felt like I was in an underground train that
would never stop, never surface.

Last week, Sri disappeared. No trace. Two days later I got an e-mail from
him. From Hamburg! Some German software products company recruited
him. I asked him how he managed that. He wouldn't tell.

Then six other consultants on the bench disappeared the very next day.
Had they gone to Germany as well?

Rayal was foaming at the mouth again. He marched up to me and told me
I wasn't going to get paid until I got a project. He had to take it out on
somebody and I was standing right outside his office when the news of
the six disappearances broke. Pig 1 received a paycheck with all kinds of
deductions. His face was black for the rest of the week. Pig 2 spent every
single night of the week cooking curries and washing dishes (dishwasher
broke down as well) at Rayal's house. Two other marketers went along to
cut and chop and clean. Thirty years ago they would have all got their
Masters in Home Economics in no time!

Ritu had called in sick for the whole week. Rayal tried to interrogate me
about her. Was she really sick? "Well, she was in bed and coughing when I
left this morning," I said. This was true. I hadn't seen her much lately. Ritu
had been shut up in her study making a lot of phone calls. That's all I
knew. And I did hear her cough.

"Lies!" shouted Rayal, frothing at the mouth, and called her at home. "I'm
going to fire Pradeep! Where's that bastard?" he kept yelling while the
phone rang into our voice mail. "Where is she? She's not at home. She's
not sick!"

He looked at me like he was going to rip my head off. I really wasn't sure
what to say at that moment, but at that very imminent head-ripping moment, Ritu walked in. Before Rayal could bellow out another word, Ritu
handed him some papers.

"Your company has engaged in too many INS violations," she said softly. "I don't think you want your company to close down in a week."

Rayal was staring at the papers. I don't know what they were. His face was turning a funny color.

"We're leaving." Ritu took me by my elbow and marched out. "Where's Pradeep?" I whispered.

"Downstairs."

"Are we getting on the next plane to—"

"Freedom."

In the car, she explained. After the first week of working at ISolutions she knew she had to get out of there. Not only did she not fit in, she wasn't going to be held hostage, harassed by a sociopath because of a technicality: H1.

She knew she and Pradeep were stuck, but there had to be a way out. So she watched carefully all the goings on in the company. She kept a record of all the dealings with the consultants. When she found out about the pay cuts, and no-salary situation after two weeks on the bench, she started making discreet inquiries. She researched the H-1B category and spoke with two immigration lawyers. Rayal is supposed to pay the consultants as long as they are working for ISolutions. He could have terminated their positions. But then he would lose manpower. So he bullied them into signing leave letters so he could get away with not paying them. Example: Sri.

The consultants were afraid to leave for fear of losing their visas. They would have to find another position in another company and that company would have to agree to transfer their visas. And think about all the hopes they have, their families, back in India, have—how many people would be heartbroken in the fallout. As for the marketers, they knew it would be very difficult for them to get another job with their limited experience. Besides, most of the employees are having their green cards processed by ISolutions. All technicalities. But nooses, all.

So Ritu started to look for permanent positions for Pradeep on her own. She also started to look for a similar position for me. She helped Sri get his job in Germany. Ritu did intensive web searches and found a company in Hamburg that was looking for consultants—foreign consultants. Where do you think the other six went? She's made a good commission, too!

Then she gathered evidence against Rayal regarding INS violations.

She knew—and this is where I'm left speechless—bullies need only to be confronted. Our quiet, nonconfrontational Ritu!

Like a magician (or should I say patron goddess?) she has found both Pradeep and me permanent positions. She's going to go to school.

"Now, you will have your own life, dear Mohit," she said to me, "but you will find yourself an apartment. You can cook your own dinners, and visit us when you have time off."

I am in Philadelphia and settled, more or less, at least for the next year. Of course there are no guarantees. My new company is a start-up that's still in business and doing well. The ghost of Rayal or ISolutions hasn't been quite deleted from my memory although I was mostly a witness.

Secret machinery, I had imagined myself. But whose deft fingers took charge of fate?

Your best pal,
Mohit

Date: Wed, Aug 15, 2001, 22: 43: 02—0700 PDT
From: Vishnu Laha <vishnu@lido.com>
To: Mohit Dutt <mohit@yahoo.com>
Subject: you, Mohit
cc: Ranjit Dutt <ranjit@hotmail.com>
Attachments: Fwd. mohit1.doc, mohit2.doc, mohit3.doc, mohit4.doc

---

Mohit, don't blow your lid when you see this e-mail. I felt it only right to fwd. some of your e-mails to your brother. I couldn't bear the picture of your mother railing at poor little Krishna any longer. How much can the Lord of the Universe bear, really?

Ranju—I understand how full of gaps communication can be on the Internet and I hope these e-mails convey some semblance of continuity regarding Mohit. I have a feeling he may have left out some of the details in his e-mails to you, but how much can one convey, over e-mail, about one's day-to-day life in another country? Besides, who wants to create

anxiety in the hearts of loved ones? You will now understand in retro-
spect some of the issues that motivated your brother's silence.

Mohit—you're out of ISolutions, in a different city. Good luck. There are
certain risks in our line of work. These things happen. Even to deities.
Sometimes held hostage on altars, sometimes flying through a murky
ether. Disembodied beings, creating, uncreating languages that are babble
to outsiders.

You said something about secret machinery in one of your e-mails. I'm
trying to live up to your imagination. Perhaps you are caught, in medias
res, in someone else's epic.

Am I making sense? If not, convert me to html!

Your best friend,
Vishnu

Date: Thu, Aug 16, 2001, 21: 37: 08 -0500 EDT
From: Mohit Dutt <mohit@yahoo.com>
To: Ranjit Dutt <ranjit@hotmail.com>,
    Vishnu Laha <vishnu@lido.com>
Subject: Re: you, Mohit

This is no way to treat me!

I've tried to spare my family my mental agony and all I get is humiliation
from my best friend.

Date: Fri, Aug 17, 2001, 20: 49: 32 -0200 IST
From: Ranjit Dutt <ranjit@hotmail.com>
To: Mohit Dutt <mohit@yahoo.com>
Subject: Re: re: you, Mohit (I, Ranjit)
cc: Vishnu Laha <vishnu@lido.com>

Dada,

Humility is endless.

H1 will be H1. You will still be a magical deity, the fingers of fate. Just
make sure you touch the ground once in a while. Emerge from your valley
of mists *to see—once more—the stars.*

(Send my Nike sneakers through Babli.*)

Ma placed a bowl of sweets at the altar this morning, but only after a good scolding. I ate them all. I don't think "Mohan" minded very much.

I fwd. the copies of all your e-mails (plus the ones that Vishnu-*da* fwd. to me) to Biltu. He has put them on several web magazines and Internet newsletters. He says he will make sure justice is done; blow ISolutions and other companies like it out of their cesspools; and he will redeem himself in your eyes. The loafer that he is—what to say! You are truly everywhere now, *dada,* and rewritten—converted to html as well.

*Babli will be in New York early next month, and she said to tell you, with that look in her eye, that she will visit you in Philly. (Sneakers, remember.)

There is another tremendous storm raging as I strike away at the keys.

Do you think all hell will break lose over the world next month? And we will completely rethink our lives and the nature of the world that we live in?

Da, said the thunder.

Love,
Ranju

DESTINY

A tidal rush of high-pitched voices made Nisha Paul drop the notebook in her hand and run outside toward Lachmi's house. "Why? Why this, oh, lord?" she heard Lachmi scream as she ran up the red dirt road leading to Lachmi's polished teak door. The entire village was at her door, watching Lachmi beat the red dust, tear her sari, scream and sob.

"Where's that husband anyway?" an old woman asked. "She'll scream herself to death. Did she dream something?"

"Saw her open that window," the *dhobi* said, turning to Nisha, "as I was passing by. The look on her face almost gave me another heart attack. Distorted—" he pulled and twisted his cheeks with his gnarled hands to explain, "in pain."

"We heard the window slam all the way from the bazaar," the flower boy said excitedly. "Bang!"

"That door burst open with such violence that I," the *dhobi* touched his chest, cleared his throat, "thought I was going to have another one. One should treat teak doors with more respect."

The old woman shuffled forward with her basket of eggs. "If you had seen how Lachmi flung herself on the ground," she drew her breath in sharply and touched her forehead. "And then the scream, the scream of a wounded animal."

"Could something have happened to Kanu?" Nisha asked in a low voice.

"He'll turn up all right," said the barber, spitting on the ground.

"Must have passed out on the way home. Send those brothers of yours to find him," he said to Lachmi, raising his voice.

"But he always comes home at night, however late, always." Lachmi struck the ground with her fist, "Always. He always sleeps in his own bed at night."

Someone tittered in the crowd.

"Perhaps my brother has seen the light at last." The sneering, high-pitched voice made Nisha turn her head sharply. Nirmala—who could never miss such an opportunity. Too bad, Nisha had left her tape recorder and notebook behind. What a fabulous crossfire of voices—and at the point of their intersection lay Lachmi.

"Get up, Lachmi," said some of the older women. "Get up, bathe, go to the Shiv temple with flowers, light a lamp, ring the bell." But Lachmi continued to tear her sari, cry, strike the ground with her fists. "Did you dream something?" the old woman with the basket of eggs asked again.

Nisha looked at the crowd gathered around Lachmi. What could this dream be that the old woman seemed concerned about—yet another superstition? The people here didn't appear terribly concerned; they gave casual advice, but made no attempt to console this hysterical woman. Nisha had learned in the past two weeks that Lachmi, although regarded with awe because of her money and her house (the only two-storied house in the village), her thuggish brothers, and a flourishing dairy—forty cows and a contract with the government dairy—was not liked. They considered her arrogant and unfeeling. She had refused to help out during the plowing; three families had pleaded with her to lend them four oxen for three weeks, but she had shaken her head the wrong way and closed the door. Her late father had been the same. And her brothers, somewhat slow witted but built like their well-fed bulls, did whatever their younger sister said. Lachmi's husband, Kanu, was popular, however, pitied now that he had turned to the locally produced *tadi* to drown his frustrations—his curtailed freedom. He had to work in the cow stalls during the day. His days of wandering along the riverbank with his flute stopped the day he put the garland round Lachmi's neck. So people watched, shrugged, made concerned noises, but did not go toward Lachmi to help her to her feet and wipe her tears.

Jealousy, Nisha had entered in her notebook a week back. *Rich, own-*

ing house, property, independent inspite of being a woman. Orders the husband around. Silent, aloof.

The first thing since her arrival to disturb the lazy calm of Binjhar, Nisha noted mentally. Must enter, inquiry about a dream, missing husband, fate oriented possibly. Use in project. She squared her shoulders and pushed her way through the crowd to Lachmi who was now striking her head against the hard red mud.

Nisha had developed more than a fondness for this tall, statuesque woman who always walked with her head a little flung back. Lachmi, she had noticed, never looked up with her eyes. She would raise her head, but keep her eyelids lowered halfway, giving her eyes a partly languid, partly scornful look. Lachmi brought Nisha her dinner twice a week; she would enter slowly, holding out a plate made of bell metal on which the food had been neatly arranged. A hibiscus or a spray of basil was Lachmi's special touch on the side of the rice. "This is how it will be," Lachmi had told her, placing that very first plate of food before her. "Twice a week from my house, since Ramu will take two nights off and will not be able to make you dinner." A slight lowering of the head, a flicker of a smile, and then that slow withdrawal as if she were leading a retinue out of a palace.

Nisha Paul looked at herself in the mirror after Lachmi's first visit. She saw bamboo groves sway as the wind moved through them; she saw banyan trees with their dark leaves and long hanging roots shade and cool the cracked earth below them on scorching afternoons of June. The fading gold of the twilight played tricks in the mirror. Peacocks fanned out their dazzling tails against a lightning-splashed sky. A forgotten world swept in and out in Lachmi's wake. Nisha had closed her eyes and swallowed. Colonial eyes would have dreamed up such visions. She must not. But in the hazy shine of the mirror, she saw Lachmi walk on, through her own slender boyish form, a swaying, mythic dark gold wave. She felt a rushing in her head as if the River Dakhin had swept in unawares. Unbelievable—she shook her head.

Unbelievable for Lachmi to make such a public display of herself unless she had sensed something terrible, beyond her control. Nisha felt strangely unnerved by the sound of Lachmi's uncontrolled sobbing. Not choking, hiccupping bursts, but a sustained moaning like the river out there, a movement of sound dragging everything along toward some unknown destination. Lachmi's fists echoed each tumbling word,

"My . . . husband . . . always . . . comes . . . home . . . at . . . night," with a dull fatality.

"Stop," Nisha said, kneeling beside Lachmi. The village population stood and watched the student in her blue jeans and white cotton shirt smooth Lachmi's hair and put a few Kleenex tissues in Lachmi's hand. Then they nodded, shrugged, made a few tch-tchs, laughed, concluded such was Lachmi's fate, and slowly dispersed to take care of their cattle and crops and stores and children. The *dhobi* lingered for a bit, shaking his grey head, murmuring, "Fate, fate, how can you force, really, what was not meant to be, shouldn't have forced, well, tricked the man to marry you, tch-tch." All went away except for one young man who sat down under the mango tree a few yards away from the two women and lit a *biri* with a shaking hand.

"He'll never come home again," wept Lachmi on Nisha's shoulder, "never."

"Why do you say so?" Nisha asked, mixing a few Oriya words with Bengali. "What do you think has happened? Did you say something to him, did you fight, is there, perhaps—" she cleared her throat, "you know what I mean, another—"

"No, no," Lachmi groaned, "but there was, and maybe I should suffer."

"Don't be silly," Nisha said with a laugh, "go inside, bathe, and, well, why not go to the temple with flowers? You'll feel better, and I'm sure Kanu will be back before the cows come home." She pulled Lachmi up with her, and helped adjust her ripped silk sari. "This one's ruined, Lachmi."

"Who cares?" Lachmi dropped the tissues on the ground and wiped her face with one end of her sari. "I'll get another one tomorrow. But—" she blew her nose into its crumpled wet corner, "but—"

"He'll be home, I'm sure, and soon. You go in now." As Nisha walked away she saw the young man under the mango tree for the first time. He stubbed his *biri* and ran toward Lachmi.

"Lachmi!" he called, his voice half excited, half frightened, and stopped her by grabbing her arm.

"Ramu!" Nisha called after him, surprised. "What are you doing here? You were supposed to fix my bicycle!"

"I will, Nisha-*didi*," he said, scratching his head and looking down at his feet. "I will, in half an hour." She showed him a fist, shook her head, and left for the bazaar. Missing husbands and village life, she thought with a wry smile. Husbands were still hideously important. The letter from her mother yesterday certainly affirmed that. "We've found the right boy for you. He has a decent job, is dedicated to his work, just like you are. We like his face, and the person who made his existence known to us is thrilled after seeing your photograph. His parents are both dead—a good thing in some ways, considering all the dowry deaths in the past few years. No in-law hassles for you. He's stuck in some village right now, but not for long. Will make good money soon. You can decide whether you want to live here in New Delhi or not after the wedding. Your father could help relocate him here. After all, you do want to live in a city you're familiar with. We would like you to get married this summer, so you'd better come home. It really is time for you to get married. We don't want you to go back to America—and if you do, you will take a husband back with you. Otherwise we will consider ourselves so ill fated as to lose all hope." What could they do, really? Could they tie her up and throw her downstream? That was how arranged marriages had always struck her; a ritual offering, a petrified form swathed in yards of red and gold silk tossed into unfamiliar currents. Mothers! Husbands! What would they say if they knew about Drew and the year she spent in his studio apart-ment. She quelled her laughter as she walked into the bazaar in case they might think her mad and proceeded to buy soap and fruit.

Apples and pears looked good, the bananas were pure sugar, the man swore, and the flower boy pressed tuberoses against her legs begging, "Only ten rupees for a bunch, please *didi,* rice is expensive these days, just ten rupees."

"I have kept the leg for you—" said the man in the meat stall, "send Ramu when you get home."

The flower boy wrapped up all her purchases in a newspaper, in-cluding the flowers. "Special for you," he said in English, smiling as she laughed.

They had all treated her as "special" ever since she arrived and moved into the half-constructed school at one end of the village. Ramu, the bangle seller, in a pair of oversized khaki shorts and a dirty white T-shirt, had turned up at the station the moment she stepped off the train in the next village west. "Who are you?" she had asked, a little apprehensive about surrendering herself to this skinny sprite's mercy.

"Ramu, *didi*," he had smiled, touching his head with his right hand. "Dishtri magitray say you train come Shailen-doctor jeep I am." Nisha Paul had blinked twice, taking a few seconds to decipher.

"Slow down! Oh, my God!" she had gasped as Ramu swung around a corner of the uneven dirt road almost overturning the jeep.

"No worry," he had assured her, grinning widely, fingering the copper amulet round his throat. "Charmed life mine." What about mine? she wondered, closing her eyes.

Ramu brought her to the school and helped her settle in, turning an intended classroom into her living space. No school, he had informed her. The contractors had stolen all the money, so the school was never completed. The local children went to the school in the next village, which was bigger, with many more people, a post office, a police station, a small hospital, and the train station. Here in the village of Binjhar, there were none of those brick buildings one could run to for survival when the floods and cyclones hit every year, when the river swelled, broke its banks, and swept away huts, cattle, disobedient children, and rice fields. But this unfinished brick schoolhouse was here, and the dispensary, a quarter mile away, where the doctor worked and lived.

Ramu worked there for the doctor—"Shailen-doctor" as he called him—taking care of the household chores and helping with the patients. "*Sui lagai*," he told Nisha, poking his forefinger into her arm, "do injections." The doctor had taught him how. He had also taught Ramu to drive the government-loaned jeep and was now teaching him to read and write English.

Nisha hadn't met the doctor yet, but knew a great deal about him. He got out of bed at six, liked shrimp and fish, had delivered eighty-seven babies in the two years he'd been here, and possessed a television. Every Saturday and Sunday evening the village trooped to the doctor's quarters to watch movies, to learn about the latest riots in the cities, a civil-war-torn Kashmir, predicted drought in the East, and to relish the cricket highlights.

Although invited by Ramu, Nisha had refrained from walking over to the dispensary to join the ritual TV watching. Ramu urged her constantly to meet the doctor. "You must, *didi*," he said, "you must," while sweeping the floor of her room, cooking her dinner, bringing her tea in the mornings. He handed her malaria pills and told her the doctor's instructions—one tablet a week, for prevention. Dettol had appeared, too, from the dispensary, a first-aid kit, and diarrhea and dysentery pills. *Wants to move into my territory,* she had jotted in her notebook, adding, *with discomfitting ease, hate to admit, bottle by little bottle, just as he has taken over this village. They like him and respect him, trust him too much. He's usurped the place.* It would be difficult now to have free rein: to question their faith in lore, make them doubt their beliefs, try out the ex-periment she had carefully planned with Professor Lennox. If the people of Binjhar didn't like what she said or asked, they could always run to their beloved doctor for reassurance. Perhaps they already had.

Nisha felt a little uncomfortable while eating dinner—was the doctor eating the same stuff? Does Ramu narrate her daily routine to Shailen-doctor? Had Ramu turned her into a joke for the doctor just as he had turned the doctor into a myth for her? Did he tell that doctor all the little things she had asked Ramu: why do you think you have a charmed life? Do you think there's really something that shapes your life? Ramu had laughed and giggled. Yes, yes, yes. Why? Just because they say so? Are you sure things happen this way because things are meant to be? Test them, Sylvia Lennox had told her, question their beliefs, be detached about it. Don't coax, force, or pressure, just be matter-of-fact, detached, give them explanations, see how they react.

There can be quite logical explanations, Nisha had said to Ramu, for everything. Let me give you an example. . . . The doctor be damned. She knew how to do this. Otherwise Professor Lennox wouldn't have chosen her or gasped when she outlined her project. For your book, she had suggested to Lennox. At least three chapters out of six, don't you think? A systematic introduction of chaos: first, the questions, then the doubts, and then the confusion. Can you leave right away? Lennox had asked. Go now? What about Drew? Okay, get me the money, Nisha said, and I'll do it. Let's put the spirit back into anthropology. Like you say, let me make the most of a humanities dissertation. Just a little bit of psychological devilry, that's all. The Third World exists for exploitation—what else? Startled by her tone, Sylvia Lennox had forgotten to ease back against her chair and languidly cross her elegant legs. She had cleared her throat and leaned forward instead. Within the week Nisha held a grant package in her hand. For a moment, a river had swelled and churned in her head, a river she had heard stories of as a child. She had dammed that river up for years. And all of a sudden, in less than a month, she stood face to face with that mad river.

Let me give you an example. . . . Nisha would blink away the swirling waters, lean forward, and tap Ramu's shoulder. But Ramu continued to laugh at her questions and suggestions. The barber's wife, who had turned up to take care of her laundry, much to the *dhobi*'s chagrin, was more receptive. She'd cock her head to the side and listen intently to Nisha devalue destiny. Partly shocked, partly fascinated, "You're different," the barber's wife said. Nisha smiled, inclined her head. She was special, as alien is special, but special as she was quite approachable. What is it like over there? What's your family like? How many brothers and sisters? When will you marry? Why do you cut your hair so short? Nisha happily answered all their questions, some openly, some evasively. She wanted them to like her because she liked being here.

During the half-hour ride to Binjhar from the station two weeks ago, Nisha had surveyed the territory with clenched fists as if expecting something to happen, something inexplicable. After all, her coming here was inexplicable—a just-like-that snap of the fingers, when she was not quite prepared to make this journey, right then, leaving Drew just when she felt the relationship was out of control, animal attraction, call it what you will. And Sylvia Lennox was asking, What's happening to your dissertation? Are you here in my office or in that obsessed artist's bed? So Nisha flew twelve thousand miles away, from neat Syracuse in upstate New York to this tiny straggly village that wasn't even marked on the latest map of Orissa.

As soon as they had left the station—one long platform with a tin shed at one end and a forest of banana trees and bamboo groves at the other—with its stale urine and coal-dust smell, the red dust came wind borne to your nose and eyes, an eerie sweet mixture of rain and blood and mud. This angry red belt—that was the perfect soil for rice, when the rains moved in on time. Fine dark dust from drying dung cakes on hut walls touched you now and then when a strong gust of wind swept in, a pungent but grassy odor. And then you looked up, startled by this mingling of smells, and found an undulating landscape—a jade and turquoise horizon, blazing copper with the setting sun, the ground, rushing by red, sometimes a coppery brown, dissolving in the distance into gold and green mustard fields. And the River Dakhin, with its warm red silt-laden waves, filled with treacherous crosscurrents, infested with crocodiles, and harboring the secret island of the goddess Manasha, swept around south of the village. "Island of No Return," Lachmi's sister-in-law, Nirmala, had said, nodding her head slowly. "Nisha-*didi*, Ramu's mother is there." And Nisha had scrambled for her notebook and tape recorder.

"When Ramu was three, *didi*," Nirmala had said, wiping her son's runny nose with the corner of her sari, "his mother—and the less said about her character the better—brought Ramu to my mother one morning. Burning with fever, Ramu was almost dead. His mother put him in my mother's arms and said, 'I've made a raft, and I'm going to Manasha to bring back my son.' My mother clapped her hand over her mouth in shock. 'Don't say these things, Ramu's mother, you don't know what curse you'll bring down on all of us!' Ramu's mother vowed that from that day on nothing would harm Ramu, that he would have a charmed life. She hung a copper amulet round his neck, for Manasha's protection. 'You can't take away death from him,' my mother told her. 'You have to leave a condition—you can't say that nothing can kill him.' 'Only another man,' Ramu's mother said, 'No illness or calamity will strike my son down.' We watched in horror as the river pulled her away among its rocks and crocodiles. We never try to go there, you know, never pray to Manasha for anything. For if you ask for something, be prepared to lose something similar. Manasha takes when she gives, sometimes life for life. A few days later Ramu's fever left him, and the *dhobi* found his mother's blood-stained sari caught on the rocks near the bank. Wrapped in its folds—oh—" Nirmala had drawn in one horrified breath, "one bloody toe."

"Ever since that day," Nirmala had carried on, "Ramu grew up with us, and Kanu and I treated him like our younger brother. Ramu does have a charmed life because of his mother's sacrifice. He swims in the river, comes back alive. Crocodiles never go near him. Once Kanu tried to drown him—well, boys, you know. Then another time, Ramu was bitten by a cobra, and the cobra died. And Ramu was always jealous of the bigger, stronger, more popular Kanu, and I think he thought Lachmi was going to marry him, but—" Nirmala made a face and rolled her eyes. "Well, Ramu was always at Lachmi's beck and call, running around bringing her flowers, calling her Radha, himself Krishna, saying that they were meant to be, not Lachmi and Kanu. Yes, well, who knows what fate—destiny is such a trick—you never can tell."

"Destiny a trick? Really?" Nisha had raised an eyebrow. "But what you really mean is that Lachmi married the man she wanted to. Ramu was merely deluding himself, fantasizing all along. Right?"

Nirmala had looked at her puzzled. "Well—yes—well, I'm not saying anything about Lachmi, that she's manipulative or anything like that—" Nirmala shook her head vigorously. "Just that she always gets what she wants. Rich people, you know, fate favors them."

"I think you should think hard, Nirmala," Nisha said. "Perhaps it has nothing to do with fate. Perhaps some people are good at getting what they want. Maybe through money or cleverness, or maybe they know how to create favorable circumstances for themselves. Think about that. Start putting two and two together."

"Yes," Nirmala nodded slowly. "Two and two, I see what you mean. Three villages south, you know, a man became very wealthy after his wife drowned while bathing at night. He said he found a chest full of jewelry under a banyan tree. He said a god came to him in a dream and led him to the tree just as his wife was drowning. The god was compensating him for the loss of his wife, he said. That man was hanged, *didi,* by the district magistrate there. When the district magistrate started asking all kinds of questions, it all came out. You see, he had lost all his money gambling, so he asked his wife for her jewelry. She wouldn't give him any of it. Late at night, she went and buried it under a banyan tree. He had followed her and watched her bury the chest. Then he knocked her out and threw her in a pond and went back to dig up the chest." Nirmala rocked on her heels. "The district magistrate wasn't too bothered about gods in dreams. I guess he put two and two together. But Ramu says so many things, *didi,* about fate, about who's meant to be with who, what's meant to be and what's not. Well, so much for believing and not believing, but as for people—who can tell why he's this way and she that way. Those brothers of Lachmi—" Nirmala touched her forehead, her voice rising to a higher pitch, "seen them?"

"No."

"They are always in the cow shed, and in the evenings at the liquor store. Of course, you don't go there, why should you or I ever go that way? They and the father—the father died, you know, six months back—made plans, and well, there was my brother, bewildered, puzzled, putting the garland round Lachmi's neck. Those brothers are hotheaded, you know, very strong, and they do have, well, some say, a nasty, vindictive streak. Ah, well, the less said the better, I'm not one to bad-mouth anyone, I mind my own business, yes. But what Lachmi wants she always gets, yes. Except for a child. Been married for three years now, and seen many doctors, including Shailen-doctor here." Nirmala had adjusted the sari over her shoulder and tucked its end in firmly at her waist.

This was the right spot, Nisha decided, the perfect subject for her dissertation—the ideology of destiny, what makes you believe, what makes you doubt, a survey of belief, how belief functions now in the Third World. In spite of television and injections and malaria pills, the island of Manasha haunted Binjhar, and the general ruling this morning was that such was Lachmi's fate—what was not meant to be can't be.

She had taken photographs, taped their songs and stories, entered their rituals into her notebook. She went to the river in the evenings when the women floated clay lamps downstream praying for the wellbeing of their husbands and children. When Nirmala suggested the winter ritual of oil massages, she frowned for a second and then surrendered. They wouldn't trust her if she didn't accept some of their offers, she knew. However, oil massages were a special luxury. Nisha's grandmother used to insist on oil massages for the children. Hot mustard oil and the afternoon sun. An ecstasy lost since the age of seven when her grandmother died of a stroke. Nisha's *ayah* had been trained by nuns in Goa, and she did not believe in exposing the bare bodies of children to ultraviolet radiation. But here, under Nirmala's deft fingers, that old warmth resurfaced. Nisha saw again her grandmother's eyes misting as she spoke of a river called Dakhin with its secret island.

Tell me more, Nisha urged the men, women, and children. They had surprised her by telling her of their admiration for the doctor who, in their opinion, was "special." Special, though, in a different way. "He is one of us," Ramu had said to her, and Nisha had entered his discourse on "special" in her journal. "He listens, really listens, ear to the ground," Ramu said. "He makes us find the solutions. Doesn't tell us what to do, like the district magistrate." The *dhobi* and his wife had said the same. He was special because he understood them. "You are special, too," Ramu had assured her, catching her frown. But as an alien, Nisha knew. And that made her uneasy. *A doctor who sometimes allows nature cures,* she entered. *How very interesting.*

Thinking about this ideology of "special," and listening to comments about Lachmi's virtues—or the lack of them—over bananas, rice, spices, she counted her change, paid the flower boy. Instead of snatching the money with glee and touching his forehead, the flower boy jumped up and pulled her back.

A long moaning scream assaulted the bazaar. "My brother—oh, my brother!" Nirmala, her hair dishevelled, stumbled in past Nisha and the flower boy.

"That witch . . . she's killed him!" Nirmala staggered to the middle of the crowded bazaar holding up a tattered portion of a wool *kurta* stained with blood. "Look!" she screamed. "This is Kanu's—the *dhobi* found it floating near the bank. Men, women, children touched the bloody fabric with wonder-filled eyes. "I'll not be quiet," she screamed at them. "On my brother's blood, I swear, I'll get even." And with that, Nirmala whirled around and raced out in the direction of Lachmi's house. The bazaar seemed to lift off the ground and follow her. Mouth open, Nisha watched the whole village run to Lachmi's door again.

"Let's go, *didi,*" the flower boy tugged at her sleeve, and she followed.

Standing in a circle, the villagers of Binjhar watched Kanu's sister, Nirmala, drag Lachmi out by her hair. Lachmi swung out and struck Nirmala on the side of her head and freed herself. Nirmala moved back, gasping, clutching her right temple. "You whore!" she shrieked. "Are you satisfied now? You weren't happy taking my brother away from me, you had to kill him, too? Just like you killed the woman he was supposed to marry. Rich father, powerful brothers, and Lachmi, to whom no one can say no. No—a word forbidden, yes? I'll tell it all today—what have I got to lose now?"

All eyes glistened with excitement, and though Nisha tried to intervene, the *dhobi* asked her to just listen to the poor sister's story.

Nirmala screamed out her accusations. "You tell me, if Kanu didn't want to sell his land, why should he? Yes, yes, when rich people want, they must have—so all the wiles began. Lachmi had set her sights on him, and on that piece of land that's now that cow shed. How to rope a man in—she knows how, quite well, can teach you and me a thing or two, I can tell you."

"Get off my land," Lachmi hissed.

"Stop this," Nisha raised her voice and tried to force her way in. "Nirmala . . . this is not right."

Nirmala turned and faced Nisha. "I'm merely putting two and two together."

Nisha blinked and stepped back hurriedly as Nirmala took a step toward her. The men and women around Nisha insisted it was important to listen to both sides of the matter. "But this is only one twisted account—" Again, shh, listen. Two women fighting—why get in the middle? It could turn out to be fatal to get between two women such as these.

"Kanu had never wanted to marry Lachmi," Nirmala yelled. "His marriage had been arranged to someone else the day after he was born."

"Liar, jealous bitch. Get off my land or I'll have you kicked out."

How dare Nirmala carry on like this? Nisha fumed inside. She would never ask Nirmala for a massage again, she decided, never.

"This is how it happened—" Nirmala tore out a tuft of her own hair. "My brother sits drinking with her two brothers—" Nirmala struck her forehead, "my brother was lost, ever since that night! And the next thing I know, screams and yells from this house here. Angry father, murderous brothers, my poor Kanu's nose bleeding, and that whore shrieking about her *izzat*."

Lachmi stood with her chin raised, her mouth curled in a sneer.

"I know for a fact," Nirmala shouted, "that Kanu was led into her room that night and locked in. Drunk and helpless, drunk for the first time, mind you, he didn't know what was going on. And I'll bet she even got Ramu to help her, Ramu, our own adopted brother. What did she promise Ramu? What in return? He was in love with her, so what else?" Nirmala pulled the old *dhobi* forward from the crowd and slapped his chest, making him cough and buckle. "What else? You tell me."

"Careful," the barber said, pulling the *dhobi* back and massaging his back. "Don't kill the old man, his heart's not the same anymore."

"Get off my land," Lachmi said softly, "before I call my brothers from the cow shed and have you thrown out."

"Go ahead throw me out. Go call your brothers. Who knows—perhaps you called them last night and gave special orders. Why are his blood-stained clothes all that's left?

"Get off my land."

"My brother, the good man that he was, believed what he was told and married the empress here. The woman he was sworn to drowned herself in shock. And then he started to drink, night after night. Because of you and your doings with those city contractors!" Nirmala paused, turned, and looked at her audience, whose eyes had widened considerably.

Nisha remembered Ramu once mumbling on about Kanu smashing the windows of the schoolhouse after hearing some talk at the bazaar about Lachmi. One of the junior engineers had bought a pair of silver anklets for Lachmi and had made no secret of it. Silly talk, Ramu had said. I heard Lachmi tell Shailen-doctor that. *Lachmi tells Shailen-doctor everything.* Nisha had scribbled that down. *Why?*

Nirmala didn't give her time to worry over that. Her penetrating voice hit a high note again. "Why did my brother disappear a few nights after he beat you up? All that's left of him is a piece of this wool *kurta*—that I made for him—all red with his blood." Nirmala rolled on the ground, tearing her sari, pulling at her hair, crying and cursing Lachmi who stood surveying the horizon with half-closed eyes. "My brother, oh, my brother—"

"Yes, your brother," Lachmi said with a laugh that sounded like a snarl. "Don't we know what went on between brother and sister. Don't we know why you didn't want him to marry me or any other woman for that matter. Brother, indeed!" Lachmi ran her fingers through her hair, twisted it, and coiled it on top of her head.

Nirmala's wailing stopped. The second worst insult in the country had been flung at her. Nisha heard the crowd loudly suck in breath. Nirmala slapped the ground. "She's going to tear Lachmi's head off," someone whispered.

"You . . . had him killed," said Nirmala and started a fresh bout of sobbing.

"Who killed who, and who is dead?"

Everyone turned at the sound of the voice. Nisha saw the crowd move aside swiftly for a slender man in a black T-shirt and khaki pants who walked, with a very sure stride, up to the two women.

"Shailen-doctor," cried Nirmala, reaching for the doctor's sandal-clad feet. "My brother's dead."

"Really? Where is the body?" he asked, cocking an eyebrow, avoiding her hands.

The *dhobi* stepped forward. "No body. Crocodiles must have eaten him. Only a piece of his *kurta* left behind."

Who saw him last night? Half the male population, at the liquor store where Kanu lay on a bench and emptied a bottle of *tadi*. Drunk, lying on the bench, singing of his garland of thorns, Kanu had entertained them as usual. Then he had staggered to his feet, muttered something about a deal or a meeting or setting something straight and wandered off, taking his usual route home by the river. "Did you find anything, any object?"

"A broken branch on the bank, a large one, from the *neem* tree there," the *dhobi* said. "The wind was strong last night, and the branch was old and cracked. It's very possible," he added, "that Kanu wandered too close to the river, slipped on the mud, and fell in. After that . . . well, who can escape the crocodiles? Especially this time of the year, so close to the goat sacrifice, the crocodiles swim close to the bank now, waiting. Last year, at this time Raji's mother got eaten. We warned her not to wash clothes in the river. The water pump has been installed—" The doctor raised a hand and cut him short.

"Was anyone near the bank last night?"

"Ramu," said many of them. "Ramu's always there in the evenings, at night."

"Search the riverbank," he said firmly. "I'll speak to Ramu."

Nisha regarded the intruder closely. So this was Shailen-doctor. Amazing how he just walked in and took over. Perhaps it was the air of calm determination about him that made them pay attention. So unlike the delicate and fragile desperation that defined Drew's face.

The crowd broke up and went away. Nirmala got up, straightened her sari, tidied herself up, muttered something about hell being here in this life itself, and walked off. Lachmi stood there, her face expressionless, one hand at her waist. The doctor, with his hands in his pockets, his face lowered, intently studied the red dust around his feet. Very slowly, Lachmi moved a few steps closer to him. The doctor raised his face and looked at her.

Nisha waited under the *neem* tree. She waited for the doctor to say something to Lachmi, for Lachmi to say something to him. The look in Lachmi's eyes puzzled Nisha. It was as if Lachmi desperately wanted to ask the doctor something. But she didn't utter a word. Nisha shifted from one foot to the other. *Lachmi tells Shailen-doctor everything.* Ramu's words rang in her head. She took a step forward hesitantly. "Excuse me," she said to the doctor in English, feeling as if she was stepping into a cordoned-off space between two figures who held each other's gaze without blinking, in spite of the blowing red dust and the dazzling light. "Excuse me, you don't know me, but—"

"Nisha Paul," the doctor turned, almost breaking a spell. He smiled and stretched out his hand. "Indeed I hear of you night and day!"

"Well, the thing is," Nisha said, taken aback, "shouldn't you inform the district magistrate and have him send a team over to search the river?"

"Will the Binjhar people, Nirmala, Lachmi, be satisfied if a torn-up body is found, even a skeleton? Will the district magistrate explain why fate worked this way, feel inclined to hypothesize? Like you do—as I understand from Ramu—hypothesize, analyze, quite regularly."

Embarrassed, Nisha frowned. Ramu had no doubt built upon the little things she had asked him now and then. Why do you think Manasha will always protect you? Do you think your mother redesigned your fate? Ramu, solemn faced, had said, "But my grandfather used to say, *didi,* and so it's said in the *Mahabharat,* destiny cannot fulfill itself without timely effort. You work with it, you pay attention to it, to its call, you don't resist it, you learn how to protect yourself with its guidance. I wonder if it is. . . . She had probably said something then to Ramu, yes, like Shailen-doctor said, hypothesized.

And now this man was smiling at her, his dark eyes crinkled in the bright late-morning sun. "Well, what do *you* think?" she asked him a little fiercely.

Gently touching her elbow, "May I," he said, "invite you to come have some *chai* at my pathetic clinic? I have to take care of Chandra's brat's leg so he can go climb another tree. This time he'll break his head."

Nisha listened to his voice carefully. Just a faint trace of a Bengali accent. A voice almost musical with its deep gentle tone. "Well?" He tilted his head and looked at her. Why is he accepted as one of them? she wondered. Why does he know Lachmi's secrets? Did his voice have something to do with it? Or was it the way he spoke, very fast, words tumbling out, just like Ramu and Nirmala, and the rest of the people out here? Like the rush of the river.

"But what about Lachmi?" she asked, walking a few steps with him.

"Someone's always there to take care of her," he said, with an odd coughing laugh that sounded almost bitter, just as Ramu came running up to Lachmi.

Ramu touched his forehead, seeing them, but he turned to Lachmi without pausing to say anything to them. "Lachmi," he said, "listen," and gently pushed her back to the steps of her house. "Sit." They sat down together, Ramu stroking Lachmi's hand as if consoling a child. "Listen," he said, "he won't beat you anymore. It's all taken care of. You and he were not meant to be. I had always known he wasn't for you. So God has taken him from you. He heard your cries and took pity, don't you see?"

The doctor frowned on catching Ramu's words. "What are you saying, Ramu? What have you been up to? Tell me right now, before you get into trouble with the District Magistrate."

"Shailen-doctor," Ramu said softly, "do I look like the kind of person who would dare to kill a bully like Kanu? He used to beat me when we were kids. I would cry and hide, and Lachmi would hug me and make me feel better. I've never hurt anyone in my life. You know that, everyone in the village knows that."

"But where were you last night? They said you're always near the river at night."

"Yes, I was there."

"Well?"

"I was there."

"Don't play the fool with me, Ramu. How come I didn't see you then?"

"I was sleeping . . . you were there, too?" Ramu looked up at the doctor in surprise, and so did Nisha. "But you never go for a walk that late, and I didn't see you, or anyone."

"Are you sure you didn't see—" the doctor caught Ramu's shoulder, "didn't hear anything, a noise, maybe a cry, a shout, someone falling into the water, someone slipping—"

"No. The river was so loud. I didn't hear a thing. I slept. That's all I remember."

The doctor shook his head and went back to Nisha, standing a few yards away.

"I don't think Ramu did anything," Nisha said to the doctor. "It really is possible for someone to fall into the river if he was very drunk."

"Yes, that's true," the doctor nodded, "but sometimes I don't know what to believe . . . the muddle that surrounds us."

Nisha stopped and looked at the young doctor's face. The sun glancing off his sharply defined cheekbones and jawline highlighted the anxiety tightening his face.

"Something wrong?" she asked.

He shook his head.

"Odd you and Ramu didn't see each other or Kanu last night."

"Hardly," the doctor said sharply. "It was very dark, and like Ramu said, the river drowns all other sounds at night." He stopped and shook his head. "Let's not talk about that anymore." His mouth twisted to a smile. "How are you coming along here?"

"Why did you send me those medicines and first-aid stuff?" she asked, as they walked toward his dispensary.

"I wasn't sure if you had anything with you in case something happened," he said. "Ramu said you seemed most disinclined to meet the doctor." His eyes shone when he said that, almost twinkled, Nisha could swear. "The water's not the safest—" he continued.

"I make Ramu boil the water," she snapped.

"Of course, a very wise thing. You can't boil the river though, you know." The doctor's eyes narrowed. "And the river is very, very dangerous. It steals your mind away, enslaves your spirit."

"I'm sure you'll send me an antidote for that soon enough, won't you? What else can save me but your arsenal of pills?"

"I've figured out what you're doing here," he said as they went up the cement steps and into the dispensary. "But why did you choose to come here? Where are you from?" he asked, putting the kettle on the kerosene stove in his consulting room. The room contained a large table, a medium-sized refrigerator, three chairs, shelves of bottles and medical supplies, wall to wall. There was a black telephone on the table, Nisha noticed, surprised. The only phone in Binjhar.

"Well," Nisha said, "I don't know if it matters where I'm from. My family, parents and two brothers, live in Delhi, and I've been in the States for five years. I'm here now because my grandmother used to tell me about a village near hers, a village on the River Dakhin, about the island of Manasha, and that the people of the village were always trying to keep that goddess happy."

He handed her a cup of tea. "So—" he looked at her, his sharp eyes narrowing again, "your grandmother told you of a mythic island on a river called Dakhin. It's a little hard for me to believe that someone would come all the way from the States to find a river and an island on a whim. You've been asking a lot of questions, I hear."

Nisha put her cup down on the table. "Although it's none of your business," she said, "I'm here to do some research for my dissertation."

"Ah. So I thought. Not a sociologist, I hope?"

"A doctoral student trying to put together an interdisciplinary humanities dissertation."

"Little bit of this, little bit of that. Must be interesting." The doctor inclined his head slightly.

Nisha decided to ignore the condescension. Was he trying to provoke her? She wasn't sure. But she was not going to waste time or energy by getting into an argument that would put her on the defensive. "Where is your patient with the broken leg?" she asked, raising her eyebrows.

The doctor opened a door on the right. "Please," he said, "welcome to my surgery."

The surgery was a small room with a long table in the center, raised with bricks, wall-to-wall shelves, and some cupboards containing more supplies. A boy lay curled up on the table. The doctor turned on the light above the table. The boy groaned and rubbed his eyes. "Let's see, now, Tulu." He straightened the boy's right leg.

"Why is he sleeping here?" Nisha asked. "All by himself? Where are his—"

"Shh. His father works in the city, his mother has to mind her store at the bazaar, and he was very tired when she brought him in." She watched him give the boy a lollipop from a candy jar on a shelf to distract him, then feel his ankle carefully and bandage it. "Just a bad sprain," he said. He removed a pillow and a blanket from a cupboard, put the pillow under the boy's head and covered him. "Sleep."

He ushered her back into his consulting room.

"No patients."

"No, no patients right now." he said. "They must have forgotten their ailments listening to Nirmala."

"How do you do anything here?" she asked, a little shocked. "There's nothing here. What if someone has a heart attack or needs surgery or—"

"Ah!" he said. "See that?" pointing at a hammer on a shelf. "One knock on the head and then the ax follows. That I keep outside . . . do it outside, under that *neem* tree, no need to clean the blood, you know, the ground soaks it. Why do you think it's so red?" He laughed and poured himself a cup of tea. "Last month I had to run to the old *dhobi*'s house. Gasping, choking, he was blue in the face when I got there. Pumped in some morphine, Lasix, hooked him to an IV, stuck nitroglycerin under his tongue and an oxygen mask on his face, threw him in the jeep with Ramu holding the oxygen tank and the *dhobi*'s son hanging onto the IV bottle, and drove to the village west of here, to the hospital. Checking the blood-pressure gauge every few minutes, you know, changing gears, turning a bend as gently as possible, turning and looking, phew," he pushed his fingers through his hair. "My own heart ready to stop with every jolt, let me tell you, while the old man went on muttering about living till a hundred and two, it was written in his palm. He's walking around now and thrashing dirty laundry on the stone beneath the water pump."

"Where do you live?" she asked him, accepting a refill of the strong black tea.

"Oh, I sleep in there." He opened the door on the left and showed her a room with a bed and a table and more shelves. The windows in all the three rooms were large, barred, and brought in stunning light. "What else interests you?" he asked, closing the door.

"Right now," she said, picking up her teacup, "that island is very interesting to me. Especially the power it seems to have over everyone here. And Lachmi interests me. How all these people reinvent her everyday—" she broke off laughing, then stopped, catching his frown. "Well, the island has always fascinated me. So you could say I'm acting out an old imaginary script; but now I'll call it research."

He smiled faintly. "No one really knows if there is such an island, you know. I mean, there is some kind of a tiny land mass somewhere downstream just before the river plunges toward the sea, but if there is a temple there, who knows?"

"But surrounded by television, cars, trains, they continue to believe in the whims of Manasha?"

"Very much. The cyclone last year was due to a rather frightful incident, you know," he said, maintaining a straight face. "There was this wretched young man, rude, crude, unbelieving. He kicked a lit lamp from Tulu's mother's hand as she was about to float it on the river after sunset. He said that was all nonsense, superstition. Well," the doctor refilled his cup and spooned in sugar, "within a month the cyclone hit, and after the waters went down and people returned to their homes—what was left of them—from the next village you know, we have to rush to the school in the next village in case of floods and cyclones. It's the only building that's on raised ground. And after a week or so, that particular young man was found dead in the bamboo groves out there. I examined the body . . . his left leg had turned black from the bite as usual . . . a cobra. Manasha's pet animal had struck out in revenge."

"If you wander into bamboo groves, you can very easily die of snakebites." Nisha put her teacup down.

"That is correct."

"I heard Ramu got bitten and the snake died."

"Oh, yes, of course. Now that was a sure miracle. Would you like some of these?" He offered her gingerbread cookies from an orange and black tin marked AMPICILLIN. She picked up two. Quite entertaining, she thought, now that the anxiety had left his face. But there was an air of restlessness about him, the way he moved his hands while he talked, the way he flicked back his hair. "I get them from Cuttack, occasionally, when I have to go there for supplies," he said, rattling the cookies in the tin. "Yes, about that snakebite. Ramu, too, wandered into the bamboo groves, flute in hand, *tadi* in his stomach, hours after sunset. He crawled in through this door after midnight, his leg swollen under a tourniquet. He was having fainting fits, shivering, sweating, all the right symptoms. From what he said, he'd been bitten almost two hours before. I'd give King Kong fifteen minutes if a cobra sank his fangs into his thigh. But there was Ramu, groaning and cursing after two full hours or more. Since he hadn't left this world for the next by that time, I figured he'd make it. When I asked him why he didn't come to me right away, he said it took him some time to kill the snake. He applied the tourniquet himself, slashed open the bitten flesh, and set about his snake hunt. If I die, it dies too, he said to himself. Ramu, filled with antivenin, was hopping around the very next day! But then, he has a charmed life, you know that."

"Why don't you have them clean out the bamboo groves, cut the bamboo? You're the doctor, they listen to you—"

"What!" The doctor slapped his hands together and touched his forehead. "I gave up asking them to boil their water after being here for three weeks. I've only succeeded in forcing them to feed their children eggs and milk at least three times a week, so now fewer kids run around with enlarged spleens. But to ask them to remove the precious lovers' grove with all its secret passions and fatal consequences? Star-crossed lovers would lose their status."

"Star-crossed, hmm, I wonder, what stars are crossing over my head?" Nisha said with a laugh. "My mother has fixed my marriage, chosen the husband, and informed me of my future status."

"Can they drag you kicking and screaming? I don't think—"

"Shailen-doctor, *eije,* Shailen-doctor," from the door cut him off and made him shrug and turn to his agitated patient.

On the way back to the schoolhouse, Nisha went by the riverbank where some of the children were mud wrestling while their mothers oiled their hair and occasionally screamed warnings at them. Nisha stood near the slippery black rocks and looked at the waters. Was Lachmi's husband somewhere in there, full fathom five? Neither Ramu nor the doctor had seen anything or anyone. They had heard nothing, yet both admitted to being here last night. Wasn't anyone going to look for him? Couldn't the doctor use that phone on his desk and—the river was so loud before her, raging, sweeping her head clean.

Dakhin was never calm. Tossing, whirling currents dragged everything down the river's journey to the Bay of Bengal. Fishing or ferry boats did not go farther east from this point. You had to depend on more than man to navigate these waters eastward. Two or three times a month steamers and launches carried city people to see the swamps and the forests. Sometimes speedboats were seen to skim the surface, glimpsed for a few seconds like birds swooping down to lift a fish off the waves before disappearing. These days, with the warm spring-summer breeze on the waters, small, motor-powered fishing boats whirred by often, and the people of Binjhar said that they were trying to intercept the Hilsa on their way in from the sea. Some would be swollen with eggs already. The crocodiles, Nisha heard, were swimming close to the shores, waiting for the goats to be thrown in. Don't step into the river, don't try to row downstream. Only if you wanted to make that journey to Manasha's island would you make yourself a raft and turn yourself over to the river's whim.

Dakhin—when you said it with that sound—Da-khine, like a whisper, it was Dakhin, like the south wind that brought the first rainstorms and cyclones. She recalled a song her grandmother used to sing. My heart touched by the south wind—*dakhin hawa*. Some kind of madness. What was meant to be will be, what was not will not. And what of Ramu's words that *without timely effort destiny cannot fulfill itself*? Was her mother's determination to get her married a hideous timely effort? Or was timely effort in Nisha's own court right now? What about her Ph.D.? What about the rest of her life? What about this moment in time on the banks of Dakhin? "Time for you to get married"—who decides that? Marriage and death are determined by something else, her grandmother used to laugh and say. Your life in your own hands—look! she said, tracing the lines on Nisha's palm. Free, and not free, to do what you want. But then, how do you know when you should do what?

Timely effort—but how do you know the right time or the appropriate effort? A sense of destiny, her grandmother would say, laughing, a sense of reconnecting with that something intimate, ultimate. Nisha ran her fingers through her hair. She was allowing her mind to ramble, her own mind, which she alone controlled. She had come here to do research for her dissertation and provide Lennox some interesting stuff for her book. This stormy noise all around—the waters, the wind—was confusing her, that's all. Must stop this feeling somehow. What she had decided to give up, she must give up. She had already crossed over to that other world. Left this maddening confusion—political, social, mythical—behind five years back. Chosen that other clearer, neater world where one could define with ease this space that surrounded her now as an area of research, of experiment, nothing more.

The next day, the district magistrate arrived in his jeep with a truckload of policemen behind him. They questioned everybody, searched the riverbank, and when the launch arrived, got aboard and searched as much of the river as they could. Nothing was found.

The district magistrate, a little porker of a man with thinning hair, paced the short grassy strip before the dispensary, fists at his back, head bowed. He nodded twice at Nisha sitting on the steps. The doctor stepped out after taking care of someone's bleeding knee and smiled tightly. The D.M. shook hands with the doctor, thanked him for reporting the "nasty business." "Why don't you, you know, make out the, I mean, death certificate," he said, "and we can get on, what do you say?"

"I can hardly make out a certificate of death without a body." Shailen-doctor put his hands in his pockets and looked the D.M. straight in the eye.

"Now, now," said the D.M., trying to pull his khaki pants over his pot belly, "there's no sign . . . nothing left of the man. I need that certified. I mean, how can I write a report, no body, I mean the report must have some certainty, validity, I mean, closure. Otherwise, this'll go on and on . . . no, no, no. A missing person means more searching, launches, helicopters for days, weeks. Who's going to send the necessary—?" he rubbed fingers and thumb together. "You're a doctor. All I'm saying is I need a certification."

"Then you certify it." Shailen-doctor turned on his heel and went inside.

"Phew," let out the District Magistrate. "What a doctor! Your replacement will arrive soon. I've received a telegram, will be here soon, I hope," he said to the doctor's back.

"Eaten completely, possibly," was the D.M.'s report, which he signed with an adequate flourish and put a purple stamp on it to make it valid. Then he collected his men, got into his jeep, and left.

"So you did report to the D.M. after all," Nisha said to the doctor.

"Of course," he said. "After all, I work for the government, you know. And you," he said, touching her shoulder, "are getting far too involved."

"No, I'm not. I like Ramu, I like Lachmi, and I throughly dislike Nirmala for behaving like a harpy and insulting Lachmi that way. I wanted to thrash Nirmala. The nerve!"

"You'll need a tranquilizer one of these days," said the doctor, his dark eyes growing darker.

"Well, you like Lachmi, too."

"She has a way about her." He lowered his eyes.

"Well?" she asked, tilting her head as if to look under his lowered glance.

"Well what?" he asked looking up.

"What way, er, does she have about her, or about you?"

"Are my thoughts necessary for your dissertation, too?"

"Sorry, none of my business."

As they walked along the bank, she asked him if he was going to leave soon, and he said that he'd been hearing that for a year and a half now. "I was supposed to be here for only six months."

"Why don't you ask the D.M. to get some funding for a hospital here? How can you provide adequate medical attention with only first-aid equipment and malaria and dysentery medication?" she asked.

"Ask that oaf? It's all right now. We get around, like I said before. I drive people over to the hospital in the next village in cases of emergency. The doctors there understand the situation. There were two heart attacks, and eleven necessary C-sections over the last two years. That's what I call an emergency, and if anyone splits open his skull—that happened once. Kanu hit someone on the head with a hammer."

"Was he violent, then? I thought he was really popular."

"The two go hand in hand sometimes. But life is not violent in that sense here. No murders, no violent fights, no robberies. But Dakhin can strike you down, or Manasha's curse. The bamboo groves lure you. And look," the doctor pointed at the waters, "my God, look!" Two slow-moving tree trunks seemed to float close to the bank and then float away again toward the dense forests of the other shore. "You never know what it is until you're practically torn in half."

"Where is your family?" she asked him, wanting to move away from this talk of death.

"My family? There isn't anyone anymore. My mother died two years back."

"I don't even know your name," she said, "Shailen-doctor is what they call you."

"That is my name." He smiled and shrugged. "Shailen Roy. I was born in Assam where my father worked on a tea estate. He was killed by the Assamese during the unrest. Well, it's still carrying on. . . . I grew up quite poor, as poor as the middle class in this country can get, but managed to go to medical school in Delhi—yes, I know Delhi." He stopped and laughed. She laughed, too. That world seemed so unreal as they stood on this bank and listened to the growling, snarling Dakhin as the sun went

down and turned the waters copper and vermilion. A salty wind was
coming in from the east that evening, drowning the mud and grass and
cowdung smell. "Well, I came back to Calcutta and started working in
the Medical College. After a year, my mother seemed to be losing weight,
getting dizzy spells. Tests showed cancer." He looked down at his sandals.
"You know, she had come in for more tests, the specialist seemed hopeful. I was in the middle of a difficult myomectomy when she stepped out
to go get some *paan*. She got hit by a bus while crossing the street. You
know how the traffic is on a north Calcutta street, especially that street.
I was told after my surgery was over, successfully over, thank God. The
only other consolation was that the people around had pulled the bus
driver out and beaten him to pulp. He was in intensive care but no hope,
they said, a couple of hours maybe. Now tell me what to believe, you,
who are analyzing destiny."

She told him about Lennox's half-written book, her dissertation.
"Oh, so you're fast turning into a Western Orientalist, too," he laughed.

"I'm not Western anything," she said sharply. She had always sold the
East back there, Eastern, Oriental, together with its mythical mystique.
She had sold the East better than anybody she knew. Exploit what they
exploit, and exploit them as part of the game, she had told an Indian
friend. That's the way to get on here, if you want to make it. Post-
colonial—that's the name of the game now. Academia has discovered
the Third World. "The West doesn't interest me anymore," Sylvia Lennox
would say in that languid drawl of hers. "The interesting stuff is coming
out of the East." Nisha tossed her hair back. Post-colonial—I can be it
then. Appalling, that right now she was so, truly, wasn't she, redefined,
reinvented, colonized utterly to post-colonial, thinking in English,
thinking this river foreign?

This merciless river breeze slapped her face now, hissing out some ir-
revocable curse on her head. What were you selling? it seemed to ask. She
had always known the answer so very well. Shailen had touched the raw-
est nerve. "Just because I was there for a while doesn't make me Western
anything," she said. "Haven't you ever wanted to go there?"

"Where? To the modern Mecca? I should, shouldn't I? But it's only a
drive-through for many people these days. They all go to get a degree or
to shop or to make money."

"Shut up," she said, punching his arm lightly. "Why did you become a doctor, anyway?"

"I'm not sure anymore," he said. "What should I say when someone standing on the banks of this wild river asks me that? Should I sit down on one of those rocks out there, rest my chin on my knuckles, look into the fading light, and say . . . what? Well, maybe, that when I was eight I walked into a room. I don't know how I managed to get into that room where a certain woman was lying, exhausted, weak, barely able to talk. She told me the most fantastic stories and gave me money in secret to buy kites. I thought she was the most beautiful woman in the whole world. What impelled me to sneak into that room and hold her hand as she lost consciousness? It was about three in the morning and I was fast asleep. But I woke up, for no reason at all."

Nisha felt that rushing in her head again. Shailen laughed. "Will that do?" he asked. "Mythical enough?"

"Possible enough."

"Yes, possible only by the banks of Dakhin in the darkness of Binjhar. But how can you believe so easily, you, who are here to question?"

"I believe—" she stopped. "I believe there's more going on here than some people would like to admit."

"Really? Like what?"

"A man disappears without a trace—well, except for a piece of blood-stained cloth. Nobody seems really concerned. They are almost relieved, it seems. And Lachmi, well, I don't know quite what to think about Lachmi."

"What about her?" His voice was cold and flat, the earlier gentle tone vanished.

"I . . . I . . . you seemed—" Nisha scratched her head. "I mean, what did happen to her husband? Ramu was here that night, so were you, on this very riverbank. But even so, no one heard or saw anything, anybody."

"Ah!" Shailen ran his fingers through his hair. "Why don't we examine the bank. Aren't you curious about that broken branch the *dhobi* mentioned? Let's see now." She followed him to the *neem* tree, walking fast to keep pace with him. Under the tree, just like the *dhobi* said, a large branch lay on the hard mud. "Here it is." He picked up the old cracked branch. "It's quite heavy." She took the offered branch, held it for a few seconds, then dropped it on the ground.

"Someone could have hit Kanu on the head with this," she said. "Everyone seemed to have had some kind of a grudge against the man."

"But of course—the motive." Shailen stepped closer. "I think I have a better story. A simpler story. Do you remember what they said? What was it that Kanu said just before he left the liquor store? Something about a deal or a meeting? Perhaps I arranged to meet him here. Then, oh, I could have taken his arm, just like this," he caught her arm just above her elbow, "very friendly, man to man, you know. And before he knew it, or even quite felt the pinprick, I was pumping in some lethal fluid." He let her arm go. "He's limp in my arms within seconds. How many seconds more did it take to drag him over and throw him in?" He moved back a few steps. "You've already figured out my motives in your head, haven't you? It's so easy to fill in the blanks sometimes, isn't it, especially when you feel so adept at analyzing, arriving at conclusions, when you feel so sure that there's always a logical answer—" He broke off and looked at the river. "Well, perhaps we all had our motives concerning Kanu, or Lachmi." Stepping forward, he caught her shoulders and gently pushed her against the tree. "Is that what you think?" Nisha flexed her shoulders. So chillingly calm his face was. "All these questions," he said. "I could do the same to you, couldn't I? It's so dark now, and not a soul around."

"I'm not getting very scared, by the way." Nisha forced a smile.

"No, of course not." He released her. "You drive away all the demons, don't you? But think hard, Nisha, must we question *our* beliefs with *your* questions? Why must you make these people think the way you think? Those are the real questions." He moved away a few steps. "And let me tell you something. Kanu's good riddance for more than one reason, and I don't think there has been a murder or an accident."

"Where is he then? He is now certified dead."

"How can I," he said, interlocking his fingers and cracking his knuckles, "change the D.M.'s report? If he's alive somewhere, anywhere, I can only wish that he'll come back to clear up suspicion and blame. And if he is . . . well, I don't know, life will still go on. Lachmi will still walk the way she does, look at you, me, them the way she does, with her head up and eyes lowered. These things are beyond my control." He shrugged and moved away. "Come," said Shailen, his voice softening, "it's dark, and you should be in your room before Ramu's feast is laid on your table. And I must wait for my replacement to arrive so I can take off for Puri and walk in the sand."

Ramu opened the door as they reached the stone steps of the school. Nisha stood and watched the doctor vanish into the darkness of banyan trees that hid the road leading to the dispensary. She could still hear his deep rhythmic voice, carrying the pulse of the river. And that restlessness was an inseparable part of him. Had he always been this way? Or had the river breeze made him so? She could have asked him that. Maybe invited him in for dinner, made him stay and talk a little longer, maybe sit on these steps in this river-scented darkness. But he had stopped abruptly before the steps, turned, left.

What if . . . what if he had told the truth on the riverbank? Syringe in hand he had waited and . . . no, impossible, not him. But what if it was so? And what if . . . she stopped her thoughts and let out a gasp of laughter. What if Shailen turned out to be—? Some of the details matched: his parents were dead, her mother had written, and he is dedicated to his work, now stuck in some village. Trick of . . . no, just her mother's unique manipulation. A master plan, all right. And then her mother would turn around and say, well, it was fate, destiny, dear. What if it was Shailen . . . good lord, when you let the craziness take over, anything is possible, and why was she even thinking this way? Just a hypothesis, really, and one must always be able to hypothesize. But why should she even *allow* herself to think this way? Madness, madness. It was the river, its sound, its smell. But somehow everything seemed inexplicably connected. No. *She* was doing the connecting. It was in her own mind, confused by this nightsmell, this riversound. *She* was imagining things just like everyone else. Shailen, syringe in hand, waiting under the *neem* tree . . . Nisha shook her head. No, never.

"Looking at him, ah," Ramu murmured, "and why are you looking at him that way—do you know?"

"What on earth are you babbling about, you idiot?"

"Yes, I babble on," he replied, ushering her toward the steaming food. "I babble on, Dakhin dances on, life goes on, fate takes over."

She mixed the rice and dal with her fingers and began to eat while Ramu sat down near the window. He sighed, took a deep breath, and sighed again. "What's wrong?" she asked, taking in his pensive face.

"Lachmi does not understand," he sighed. "She does not understand that we were meant to be together. And now, even now, if we resist what we were meant to be, we'll be destroyed, I know. Happiness will be destroyed if we fight the inevitable. The moment I saw her, when I was four, I knew. She knew, but she denies it. Kanu was a boor. Yes, he was tall and strong and had an enviable face. But he wasn't meant for her. He wasn't meant to live long either. Do you know how many times he beat me up? They all thought he was so entertaining, and funny—yes, funny—when he tried to hang me from a tree, shouting with laughter all the time, saying, Little idiots should be hanged. Perhaps Manasha heard, after all these years, and struck out."

"How do gods strike?" Nisha asked. In the village, they said Ramu was crazy, he was silly, not quite there, a good heart, but something not quite right because of his near death experience. They said he had died and then come back to life. There was something elusive about Ramu, sprite-like. He would appear and disappear as if he sensed what you wanted. She was amazed by the food he prepared every day. It was as if he knew what she wanted to eat, which fish or meat or vegetable. He had also conditioned her palate somewhat. For breakfast, he would bring her tea, but along with it bread and thick, sticky date syrup for dipping. Sometimes he would bring puffed rice mixed with coarse date sugar and bananas. She did not miss toast and eggs and cereal anymore. He would cook cabbage with shrimp and coconut milk, and she would long for it if a week went by without it. He revived for her her grandmother's cooking, a taste she had almost forgotten, a flavor her mother had denounced as too extravagant with spices, salt, and sugar, far too complicated for everyday fare. Nisha cursed herself whenever she imagined Ramu as her reincarnated grandmother.

"Gods strike through instruments," Ramu said, his face changing from pensive to resolute. "They choose instruments who then carry out the will of the gods."

"Like snakes?"

"Sometimes." Ramu reached into his pocket and removed a screwdriver. He studied it intently, turning it slowly, letting the light catch its point, which, Nisha noticed, had been filed and sharpened.

"Instruments like rivers, the weather, wild animals?" she asked, staring at the screwdriver.

"Sometimes."

"You mean something could fall on someone's head? A man could slip and fall . . . he might just be somewhere, er, dangerous, just arrive there due to—"

"Something like that." He held the screwdriver in his fist as if he was holding a knife.

"You ask too many questions," he said. "Yes, gods destroy. But they protect, too."

"I hope so." Nisha swallowed.

"Manasha has protected me three times already—saved me from Kanu twice, and once from the snake. Now I think I'm on my own. She won't step in anymore. They never do more than three times." Ramu put the screwdriver back into his pocket.

"Well, what about Kanu—why didn't any god or goddess help him? What do you think happened to Kanu?"

Ramu looked at her blankly and shrugged. He removed her plate and cleaned up. Nisha washed her hands and took out her notebook and pen. Ramu came back to her room and sat down on the floor. "We saw another part of the Mahabharat, *didi,* on TV. I know this part by heart. Kanu's grandfather used to recite it every evening. But when I saw it on TV—oh!" He clasped his hands. His voice rose in excitement. "Right in the middle of the two armies, bow thrown down, the great warrior kneeling. *I don't know,* he said, *what to do? What is my duty? How can I kill those people out there? They are brothers, cousins, uncles, teachers—*" Nisha recalled the episodes she had seen and squirmed. The production was crude, garish, the metaphor completely lost under a hideous melodramatic literalization. She let out a soft *ugh.*

Ramu continued at the same pitch. "And then he, the other, he dropped the reins and stepped down from the chariot. He touched the warrior's shoulder. *Listen,* he said, *they are already dead. You are not killing anyone. You cannot kill or be killed. No arrow can pierce the life that informs you—*"

Nisha looked at the impish form sitting on the floor hugging his knees. A gleam had entered his half-closed eyes. His voice was like a soft chant. She began to write as fast as she could, yes, Lennox would like this—belief perpetuated, yes, seconded by television.

"*No fire can burn it, no water drench it, no wind can make it dry,*" he recited from memory. *"What you think you are about to do now, next, has already happened, been realized, the action has been originated and completed, what you think you do is the echo, simply the echo. What you see is what you want to see, it is just an illusion. You will think of heaven and of hell and of destiny. Finally you will arrive there; you will wonder, is this it? Then you will sit there and say, I'll go no farther. Then a voice will say, this was the last illusion."*

"Ramu?"

"What you can't see is flying all around, the wind is the beating of its shining wings."

"Ramu?" His eyes were glazed as if in a trance. Nisha wanted to give Ramu a shake, but the cadence of his voice, the rhythm and flow of the words held her to her chair. She was unable to intervene or write any further.

"The lake was shining. The brothers were thirsty. They drank without answering the questions and fell dead. But Yudhishtir said, *I will answer the questions.* And the voice from the lake asked, *Tell me, what is the greatest wonder?* Yudhishtir said, *Every day death strikes and every day we walk as though we were immortal. That is the greatest wonder.* The waters bounced in joy. *What is madness?* His eyes lighting up, Yudhishtir replied, *A forgotten way.* The waves swirled, rose, sparkled. The voice from the lake asked again, *Tell me, for all of us, what is inevitable?* Yudhishtir, without even a moment's hesitation, answered, *Happiness, happiness is inevitable."*

"Ramu?"

"Like it? I learned it by heart." His eyes were sharp again; he was crouching forward in excitement.

"What I'd really like, Ramu, is if you would tell me what you think happened to Kanu?"

"You should ask Manasha," he said.

"I'm asking you, Ramu. Do you think someone killed him? Say, Shailen-doctor?"

Ramu sat up. He removed the screwdriver and held it up near his ear as if he was about to throw it. Nisha sat very still, unable to look away from the screwdriver.

"Don't try this stuff on us," he said softly. "We are your own people. If you have so many questions, ask fate, destiny, that which one can't control."

"I will try my damndest," Nisha said, holding her notebook in front of her like a shield.

She lay in the uncomfortable *charpai* and looked up at the mosquito net so neatly arranged all around her. She saw the screwdriver in Ramu's fist, a syringe in Shailen's hand, Lachmi walking through swaying bamboo groves. And Dakhin seemed to leap up and dance, a sinewy, shining body with a copper and silver wave fanning out like a cobra's head, wiping away all the questions she had prepared and asked. The heaving river glowed beaconlike, urgently beckoning her to an almost forgotten place, to a left-behind otherness. Her research was transmuting to different questions: who, why, how? She hadn't been able to change Ramu's thoughts, but he had changed her eating habits. Her dissertation seemed to be going down this river as well. Perhaps it had been swept away long before. Perhaps her attempt to salvage it, with Lennox's help, perhaps that was an attempt to salvage something else all together. No! She buried her face in her pillow. She was going back. She had come here only to confirm that she must go back there. Life waited there with Drew.

Drew, delicate, high strung, sweeping canvases with his special shade of black. In love, he said, and almost with a vengeance, she felt, against his mother's wishes—to work out his own rebellion through Nisha. Lawyer, doctor, *moi?* he screamed while depositing his weekly two-thousand-dollar check from his mother. She can take a hike, he said. To his mother, calling three times a week from her Beacon Hill apartment: you don't understand. And neither did Nisha understand why the relationship seemed so out of control, frighteningly obsessive, why she couldn't pass the day without. . . . She snatched the grant money and ran. Lennox, a trick of fate? No!

She ran all the way here to find that river she had heard stories of. Why, she couldn't fathom. But the moment Drew pointed at a diamond ring in a store window, her grandmother's voice echoed in her ears, and Dakhin surfaced with its terrible waves and secret island and crocodiles. I must finish my dissertation now with this scholarship, then I'm going to look for a good teaching position, she had convinced Drew. Let's plan, Lennox had said, ecstatically. This is the real thing, you're on to something, you're getting ready to define this thing, to explore and capture this territory of myth and destiny and belief. But she wasn't quite sure why she was trying to define her dissertation then, all of a sudden, after three years of procrastination and avoidance. She could bloody well forget about this shit and just marry Drew. Get a green card, no more immigration hassles, go to Gstaad for skiing trips, to Australian beaches, sip drinks with umbrellas before Hawaiian sunsets. Want to live in New York City or Boston? Drew said. A studio in the Village. We belong there, Nisha. You belong there. Here, with me. And she had felt it, through Drew, the crisp pleasure of being there.

Life moved in two directions in Drew's world, and she was certainly on the up-escalator, smooth and straight. Drew's world didn't spin and lurch cyclone-like. There were always warnings and very few surprises. Cable TV took care of that. And darkness was not this agonizing river scent of tuberose and gardenia trampled against copper mud. Darkness was only the absence of electric lights. No dark goddesses. America had banished them all. No Hecate, no Fata Morgana, no Kali. Just the Statue of Liberty. No destiny to worry about, only opportunity. No karma there, just problems, solvable problems. No dharma, only alternative lifestyles. You have rights in America: the right to vote and the right to buy, and you could even kid yourself that the universe is really like a Sears catalogue or the remote control of a television. It's peaceful and prosperous, with an occasional mass murder to relieve the stasis; and it is the standard of living that the rest of the world envies and covets. Shouldn't that do? Nisha rubbed her eyes. Yes, of course. No island of Manasha to contend with, no mad river to drown all her clear ideas.

Who needs crocodiles and blood and muddy rivers and an epic that is a battlesong of universal destruction?

But instead of seeing studios, Caribbean cruises, chic split-level apartments, or Sylvia Lennox's narrowing eyes, she saw herself, her chin on a window ledge, looking down at the black van that took away her grandmother, a frail body strewn with tuberoses.

That rainsmell of tuberoses hung in the night air all around her now, the night smell of Binjhar.

Everyone used to be terrified of her grandmother, that tiny woman who had cropped her hair at the age of fifty. Silver curls framing a resolute and exquisite face. Her husband, they said, had died of shock. But she carried on like the mad rain wind. She carried on, redecorating her rooms every year, singing while she pickled mangoes, revealing incredible secrets about magic places and people while she cooked. And in the lazy warmth of winter afternoons she created a terrible river and showed Nisha its secret island. A temple, shattered, stones tumbled all around, crawling with cobras, kraits, Manasha's legion, ready to strike any intruders. You float lamps toward the island, say bless me, Manasha, and go back to your homes. Leave a bowl of milk outside for the snake that crosses your yard, and say *string* at night, or *creeper,* never. . . . Take me there, please—I want to float lamps! Only when the wind blows, shh . . . it's talking to you, can you hear?

Dakhin, the mad south wind that swept in like a forest fire and set the earth ablaze with spring. And then it brought the rain, the first rain to this hard red ground. Mud pools like frothing blood.

Cars followed that black van. Ashes were thrown into the river, she heard her father say. But not that river, she knew. They didn't know where that river was. She would find it one day and hear what it had to say to her.

But she had flown over to quite another world and moved that river aside. There was nothing here to hold her, absolutely nothing. What had been here before, anyway? Parents constantly nagging, don't talk so much, don't laugh so loud, what will people say, time for you to get married. . . . She had gritted her teeth for twenty years and then escaped. She had taken charge of her life, given it a definite shape, goals to move toward. But why then had she run away, and why this desperate need *now* to run again? Had she not felt free for five glorious years? But what about now?

Now, through this night pierced with the heady fragrance of gardenia and tuberose, Dakhin was rising, leaping recklessly, to merge with the moonlight, to drown it, rob it of its silver. The night brought no peace or silence to Binjhar. You lay awake and shivered as the river laughed its wicked laugh out there till exhaustion took over and closed your eyes. Laughing, the river was laughing, and whispering, telling you—everything, if only you knew how to listen.

The river rose and rose and rose, and the moonlight kept vanishing into its waves. Then all the waters swirled like a column of light and spread out enormous wings before her. So enormous, you couldn't decide what it was. What is that? she asked the darkness surrounding her. It was blocking everything before her, keeping her in that one dark spot, barring her way.

She tried to move but her feet held her to that dark spot. Suddenly, that shining spinning form swayed to the left, then to the right. A whispery wind wrapped around her. Voices! Whose voice was that? She couldn't make out the words. Whispers blew her hair about her face, stroked her eyes, her throat. A sharp gust slapped her face. The swaying tower of light was swooping down. Nisha ran back, her feet obeying at last. She was running, her feet barely touching the ground, caught in a surging buoyancy.

The river of light raced behind her. Nisha gasped as she felt the light on her back, cold and hot. It was soon all over her, filling her mouth, nose, chilling her lungs, burning her eyes. Then racing ahead, it passed her. She stretched out to catch its flaming tail. So warm, so cool. For a moment, she was wrapped in its blazing spiral heart. Then she was propelled forward, shooting out of it like a stray flame.

The light rose up like a tidal wave behind her. A hushed roar of falling water. Nisha covered her head and fell to her knees. The flooding light swept over her. She saw rice fields, huts, cattle, people float away on shining waves.

Then, through a blinding waterfall of light, she was falling, thrashing around wildly, feeling for something to hold, to brake this descent. But there was nothing to hold on to. Her fingers slipped through shadow forms. The silver torrent passed through her flesh as if she were all glass, like water through fine gauze, and she, too, filtered through its dazzling mass the very same way. What a strange sensation—the mind had ceased to think, oh, what a marvel, had become still, in the midst of this blazing cascade. What a strange sensation, this lighting up like a match almost, yes, illuminated, what a trick, indeed what an illusion!

Silly girl, growled the light, and lifted suddenly. Grandmother! That voice! She knew at last.

Look! Look carefully. Nisha shaded her eyes and searched for the source of that whisper. A river of twisting snakes and the dark shadow of a shattered temple. Are you there? she asked. Grandmother? Only a torrent of silver snakes circling around her, shooting up with a wicked hiss, then swooping down to resume spinning again. Grandmother? Nisha reached out to touch the coils of light. She felt something sharp scratch her forehead.

Where was the river of snakes? Thundering wings beat around her. A million feathers of flashing light flew about. It was flying away, this cloud of light. The tip of its spread wing had grazed her face.

There. A fading thunder. *Remember that. And remember that for everything there is always an explanation, logical, illogical, and that is why you choose—to believe, and not to believe. To every why, there is always an answer but you may not know it.*

Another scratch. Grandmother—? Her voice cracked.

You were there, and I.

"Ouch." Nisha touched her forehead, which burned slightly as if scraped. She was in bed, the sheets pulled up to her chin. She jumped up, nearly ripping off the mosquito net, and ran across to the square mirror on the wall. The sunlight reflecting off the mirror made her blink. She moved her hair back and saw two tiny red scratch marks on her forehead. She must have scratched the mosquito bites in her sleep.

After breakfast, she reorganized her notes and arranged her papers neatly in folders, labeling them, and stacking them alphabetically. She wrote a letter to her mother, telling her she was not going to marry their selected specimen. They should give up these idiotic notions. She tore a fresh sheet from her notebook and wrote, Dear Drew, then scratched it out, tore up the sheet, and threw it away. Ramu took the letter for her mother and solemnly promised to mail it that very day, that he would run to the next village, "But later, not now, because now we must all go to the river—the goats, *didi*, come!"

Shailen was standing some distance away from the bank. He turned, hearing Ramu's excited voice. "Here for the slaughter? You too? Ah, but of course—your dissertation. Had a good night's sleep, I hope?" Nisha looked at him surprised. "Just wondering," Shailen added with a grin. "I find it difficult to sleep sometimes. So much excitement all around, so many questions to keep you awake."

"Really?" Nisha raised her eyebrows. "Why don't you just pop in a sleeping pill or two on such nights?"

"Ah, but then all my torments would cease. I'd have nothing to live for."

"What a pity." Nisha turned away to watch the people gathered at the water's edge.

"Go on closer," he said, "if you want to. I don't have the stomach for these things."

"I can deal with it. After all I must . . . remember all these little details for future reference." She looked at the three goats being dragged to the river, the chanting crowd moving as if drunk. She closed her eyes tightly when the sharp curved blade flashed upward. The arm was swinging down. Faint bleating sounds, three thuds.

"It's over." She opened her eyes. Shailen was looking at her, one eyebrow raised. She flushed and turned to the river. What looked like three black sacks floated away trailing red froth. The river began to churn all of a sudden, as if a flood was coming. The black forms were being tossed around, pulled, tugged, the waters thrashing, foaming white and red. People were running away from the river now. Their faces were wet shining red, their hands, their clothes. *"Ashirbad,"* someone whispered almost on her face. "The blessing." A finger touched her with its red stain.

"Are you—" Shailen caught her shoulders and sat her down under the tree. "Put your head between your knees, down, lower your head." He wiped her forehead with his handkerchief. "Tch, you've been scratching your mosquito bites."

"One husband and three goats," someone yelled. "Manasha should be happy this year." Laughter on red faces.

Sitting with a cup of tea in the dispensary, Nisha watched Shailen inspect tonsils, palpate abdomens, listen to heartbeats, give a few shots. "You were looking a bit peaked when you got there," he said to her over the heads of bawling children, scolding mothers, and groans of pain and discomfort. "Sure you slept well? Or did you dream something frightful—the Binjhar dream?"

She looked at him, stunned. "You did . . . aha!" The doctor smiled and winked. "Ramu gets carried away with the cooking sometimes. A handful of poppy seeds now and then, you know. What was it? Monstrous creatures or falling from the sky?" The grin was malicious.

"I have to go."

"But of course, and write your dissertation, give destiny a talking to, tell the world nothing is inevitable."

He's a jerk, Nisha thought, walking toward the schoolhouse. An annoying jerk betraying his education, a man of science. Damn him. How could he be a doctor and condone such things? A handful of poppy seeds now and then! Did Ramu tell him about dinner last night—her dinner—if he had thrown in . . . the nerve! To tell her now. To laugh. He should have come running and given her something to control the effects. So that's what it was. She felt relieved. It was all Ramu's fault. First the nonsensical talk during dinner and then the adulterated dinner itself. Adulterated . . . doctored, more like. How could she not have suspected anything till Shailen brought it up? How could she have allowed herself to be so manipulated? Was Shailen in on it all along? Perhaps it was his idea. He wanted to scare her. You ask too many questions, he said. Maybe he has reason to be wary. Maybe, just maybe, he was telling the truth on the riverbank last evening. Then it was he . . . no! That's why he told Ramu to put poppy seeds in her food . . . to confuse her . . . to drug her. No wonder he looked surprised when she turned up for the goat sacrifice. She was supposed to be fast asleep, or . . . she closed her eyes for a few seconds and rubbed her temples. This was getting out of control. *There is always an explanation.* Her ears were ringing suddenly. She was imagining scenarios, even accusing, just like Nirmala, like all of them. Her purpose was to reverse their ways of thinking, confuse *them*, not herself. She shook her head. A massage, that's it, that's what I need. Ramu must fetch Nirmala—oh, but! She had told Ramu to tell Nirmala not to come for the massages in the afternoons.

Lachmi was sitting on the school steps. "Where's Ramu?" Nisha asked, a little taken aback. Lachmi shrugged. "Asleep under a tree, probably."

Nisha hadn't seen Lachmi since that day. Lachmi hadn't made her usual appearance, plate in hand. How could she, Nisha had bitten her lips and thought, after such incidents . . . and now what to say to her? What does one say to a woman whose husband has vanished? If she were in America she could say—but then husbands, even wives vanished casually, frequently back there. But here, in the tiny village of Binjhar?

"I heard you told Nirmala not to come in the afternoons," Lachmi said. I thought I'd come and give you a massage. Haven't seen you for a few days."

She heated mustard oil in an aluminium bowl and brought it to Nisha's room. Nisha lay down on the mat on the floor and closed her eyes. Lachmi's hands were softer than Nirmala's. Her fingers pressing in and circling smoothly over her back and shoulders got rid of the ringing in her ears. "How are things?" she asked Lachmi.

"Nothing new," Lachmi said softly, "managing the dairy, as usual."

"Ramu talks about you."

"Mad," she said. "Doesn't understand. Keeps on saying, You and me, not Kanu, taken care of by fate. Mad. I do like him. But he can be difficult, you know. And there's no telling what he might do and when. No sense in his head. He used to sell bangles. Ever since Shailen-doctor arrived, he worked for him. Forgot about the bangles. I was happy he was working for the doctor. He was learning things. Shailen-doctor was teaching him . . . a good man, the doctor—" Lachmi stopped and massaged Nisha's back quietly.

"What about the doctor?" Nisha asked. She saw them again, standing silently face to face.

"He's not like the last one," she said. "That one didn't care who lived, who died, who ate what. I asked Shailen-doctor, how will you leave when you have to go? He just smiled and looked down. I used to take him dinner, too. But now I don't."

"Why not?"

Lachmi shook her head. "He asked me not to. Sometimes things are best this way. I'm glad Ramu works for him."

"Doesn't he sell bangles anymore, at all?"

"If he has any more after that night! Mad, I said, let me tell you how mad. Three weeks ago he saw my husband buy bangles from the bazaar for me. That night—if you only heard the noise! Broke all his old bangles, one by one, against my door. What can I say? Kanu could only put up with so much. 'Come down, Lachmi,' Ramu was screaming. 'If you don't wear my bangles, I'll break them.' I stopped Kanu—God!—from rushing out of the house with a stick. I caught his feet. He had to hit someone he was so angry. And Ramu was going on and on and on, 'I'm breaking my bangles.' What to say, *didi*, I can still hear the glass cracking and tinkling and shattering. The next morning I stepped out and cut my feet on the broken glass. What a mess."

"I can't imagine Ramu doing something like that. He's so quiet, except when he chatters, but I've never seen him violent."

"Quiet, yes. But there's an odd streak in him. Oh, I don't know! He and Kanu never liked each other, and Nirmala would play one against the other. She's another one. Kanu would say, Ramu's a monster that should be destroyed. You see, many believe he died and then came back. You've heard, I'm sure. Kanu would say, Ramu was supposed to be dead. It wasn't right for him to live. People say all kinds of things. And now Kanu is . . . nowhere to be found. Nirmala hasn't stopped screaming yet. She's there at the bazaar even today."

"Nobody's going to believe her, Lachmi."

"Ah, but then people like to believe the worst of me, except Shailen-doctor. I am the rich man's daughter whose brothers terrorize the village. And Nirmala is now a sister without a beloved brother who was trapped into marriage. Well." Lachmi let out a short fierce sigh. "Do they remember anymore Nirmala throwing her only son into the river—a child of three? He called another woman '*Ma*' because he wanted the candy she had in her hand. 'What?' Nirmala shrieked, 'called her your mother? Let the river take you, the crocodiles eat you, you ungrateful, unloving son of a pig!' And one swing and then the child screaming, choking, gasping, swallowing water, till the *dhobi* left the dirty clothes and jumped in and saved the child." Lachmi eased Nisha's tight neck muscles. "Such a mother will they believe."

Nisha sat up, wrapping a sheet around herself. "Maybe they won't believe. But tell me, didn't you say anything to Ramu after he broke the bangles?"

"Yes, I did. I caught him at the bazaar. '*Sala,*' I said, 'what do you think you were doing last night, smashing your bangles?' He looked at me like I was mad. He didn't remember. Maybe he was drunk, who knows? What goes on inside Ramu's head, only Ramu knows. Manasha will take care of me—that's his line. Anyone who hurts me, Manasha will hurt. Such ideas!"

"Do you have any ideas? What do you think happened to Kanu?"

"I don't know what to believe. No body was found, not even a finger or a tooth or a hair. What should I believe? They say all kinds of things about me, *didi*. I don't know what you think. Maybe I shouldn't have married him, I don't know. What's done is done. It was necessary. But to lay blame, without knowing exactly what has happened? Who to blame? Yes, my brothers were angry. Kanu had hit me. Yes, my brothers are thugs like they say. So what? Do you think any brother would make his sister a widow? Too many people hated Kanu. Some, who had lost their cattle to him gambling. Others, whose wives and sisters he had had affairs with. What about them? Ah, Kanu, everyone always smiled when he appeared. But what did they feel inside? Who was going to say anything to his face? He was stronger than everyone. Who to believe, what to believe . . . are they all what they say they are? Sometimes I think our hearts are like those bamboo groves . . . who knows what lurks in there?"

Nisha watched Lachmi rearrange her sari. In the mirror on the wall, Nisha could see her own reflection. With every move, every twist and turn and sway, Lachmi eclipsed Nisha's small-boned self. A whole forest of ancient banyan trees walked with Lachmi. Bamboo groves swayed in her wake. The darkest of rain clouds were shadows of her long thick hair. Nisha's thin, pale shoulders shivered in the mirror. This woman who walked the way she did, looked the way she did, who hardly spoke when she used to bring in those plates of food, was now talking to Nisha, the completely alien being in Binjhar, who had none of Lachmi's awe-inspiring stature or bearing. There was something truly stunning about Lachmi when she looked at you with those veiled eyes and half smile, something marvelous and fatal. Lachmi loosened her long hair, let it down, twisted it and coiled it on top of her head again.

"Nirmala," she said, "has been like a mother to Ramu. But Ramu always followed me around. Nirmala used to tell Kanu, oh, Ramu did this and Ramu did that, and had Kanu thrash Ramu every time she caught him chatting with me. She thought Kanu was her property. Kanu married *me*."

"Look, don't jump to conclusions," Nisha said to Lachmi's reflection in the mirror. "We really don't know for sure."

"But somebody must know something, somebody must." Lachmi turned around.

"Do you think—" Nisha stopped and swallowed. "Do you think Shailen-doctor might, er—"

Lachmi placed her hand on Nisha's mouth and cut her short. "Don't say that." Nisha moved back stunned by the look on Lachmi's face. As if her whole world lay in ashes around her.

"Maybe Kanu will turn up," Nisha said, swallowing. "Maybe we're all letting our imaginations run wild."

"Yes. Maybe he'll come back. I'll pay what I have to pay."

"You're being silly." Nisha caught her hand.

"I'll do something, I will, I won't just sit and do nothing and listen to silly talk." Lachmi pulled her hand back. "Fate, they say, fate, I'll drag it back and forward by the hair, if I have to, but I'll do something. I won't live here any longer and listen to their hateful words like I have for so long." Lachmi stood up with the empty bowl, her chin raised, her eyelids partly veiling her eyes.

Nisha closed her notebook, leaving the pen sandwiched between its pages. Her head began to throb, and a faint nausea began to course its way up to her throat. *"Chalo na,"* Ramu pleaded after dinner.

So Nisha followed Ramu to the dispensary for the TV-watching ritual. She didn't want to meet the doctor again that day, but neither did she want to sit in that sparse, dull room all evening.

"My, my, for the first time. Missing civilization, at last?" Shailen had brought the TV out on the steps of the dispensary, and almost the entire village sat outside smoking and munching, hypnotized by the 25-inch color screen. Nirmala was there with her three children, two daughters and one boy, all three of whom were leaning forward toward the movement of color and sound, sucking their thumbs loudly. Nirmala glared at Lachmi from time to time and whispered occasionally to the two women sitting with her. Lachmi stood under the *neem* tree, her face a dark mask. Ramu sat down two feet away from the screen with the children. Most of the women sat around Nirmala on the right. The men grouped on the left and middle.

"Seat of honor." Shailen dragged a chair to Nisha.

"I can sit on the grass."

"She says through gritted teeth. Come, come, I'm getting a chair for myself, too." Nisha refused to sit on the chair. She sat down on the grass. Shailen took one chair, and the other was claimed by the *dhobi* with, "Don't mind, Shailen-doctor, no one else using it, so—"

"The death toll has risen to three hundred and twenty," they heard. "Forty more dead in Hyderabad," ten-hour curfew, riots, tear gas, buses set on fire. "Why not build a temple next to that mosque?" some of the men asked. "Killing each other, and for so many days." "Prime Minister calls a cabinet meeting"; "Chief Minister of West Bengal struck on the head with a rotten tomato during a speech"; "The Nagas have been shooting several rounds again"; "More riots in Kashmir." Dal Lake came on the screen. No tourists on houseboats. Srinagar streets strewn with broken bottles, stones, shoes, torn clothing. "The army seized thirty-two Kalashnikovs today. . . ." A boy, fifteen maybe, raised his black Kalashnikov to the camera. "Those Kashmiri rugs have been rolled away, together with the shawls, the silver jewelry, crates of cherries, apples, pears. The only trade for Kashmiris now is to bargain for Kalashnikovs at the border."

"This government is useless," someone said. "Either really crack down on the problem or forget about Kashmir, let Pakistan have it." "How can you say that?" another voice challenged. "No Kashmir, no tourists, no dollars—why don't you think? And why should we give anything to Pakistan?"

Nisha blinked. They had decapitated three goats that morning and smeared their faces with blood.

The movie that evening, much to everyone's delight, was an old black and white, one of those mythological movies made in the 1940s. After the goat sacrifices earlier that day it seemed an appropriate affirmation. Everyone leaned forward, their eyes growing larger. Nisha glanced a few times at Lachmi resting against the tree. The actress reminded her of Lachmi. That same resolute face. Yes, that could be Lachmi singing as she walked through a dark forest. Before her rode Yama on a black horse carrying her husband's corpse. *Go away,* he said to her, covering his black face. *Do not follow me. Your husband is mine now, his time had been fixed and cannot be altered.* But she followed, singing of a love that death cannot destroy.

The forest, in the yellowed old black-and-white print, glistened eerily, like Dakhin swirling and snarling under a full moon. Nisha closed her eyes for a moment. Not a forest—a shining river, and the woman floating on the waves in search of her lost husband. The rustling trees carried that rushing sound of the river. Nisha looked at Lachmi again. A hand at her throat, Lachmi was leaning forward as well. She was following that woman's footsteps as if that silver screen had vanished, as if that forest had leaped out and engulfed them in its silvery gold light.

Nisha rubbed her eyes. The film was almost over. Finally, Yama gave up, annoyed, irritated, frowning, helpless before the woman's calm face and relentless footsteps. *All right, here's your husband back, all healthy again, his rotting flesh pure again, the light back in his lotus eyes. Go live your lives now, you'll die together at some later date when you decide to seek detachment and enter a forest to sit under a tree and wait for me. I give up, your faith is terrifying, your determination almost invalidating me.*

"See," the people of Binjhar said to one another, to their children, "see how that works. When the heart is pure, anything is possible."

"If the *wife* is pure," said Nirmala, "then such things are possible. If her hands are not stained with blood."

"Come, come," the *dhobi* said sleepily. "Enough purity for one night. You'll die anyway, pure or impure." Yawns started, and arms and legs began to stretch.

"I have to go to Cuttack tomorrow," Shailen told everyone. "Back in two days. Watch for the air show, planes from Cuttack will be zipping overhead, flying over Binjhar."

"Don't run off," he said to Nisha, touching her elbow. "Can't you even take a joke sometimes?"

"A joke! To hear from a *doctor*—a handful of poppy seeds!"

"What on earth can a handful of poppy seeds do, for heaven's sake? A few nightmares. I can't control Ramu. He's done it to me, too. Now come on. I have two bottles of beer. They've kept the vaccines company for three months in the refrigerator."

They sat on the steps each holding a 750-ml bottle of Taj Mahal. Nisha didn't want to chat and laugh. After all he could be a . . . he could have, really. Maybe he was just trying to con her right now. Sit down, relax, have a beer. And when her mind was slack enough, he might go to that refrigerator again, take her arm so very casually, and—"So serious. What on earth are you thinking, plotting, planning?" He gave her arm a shake. "Something wrong with the beer?"

"No. I'd forgotten the size of the bottles," Nisha said, shaking her head as if to shake off her misgivings, "but then, I'd never had beer until I went to the States." She laughed, thinking of her first beer, Coors Light, in a campus bar.

"Good to hear you laugh. I feel queasy about those sort of sacrifices, you know, but it was funny when you rolled your eyes and went limp."

"I didn't think I would—"

"Nobody does."

"I've always believed that I'm a pretty strong . . . emotionally a strong person, that I have a certain intellectual hardness, detachment—"

"Have you ever witnessed heads being chopped off, blood spurting up, the red stain spreading, the headless body shaking uncontrollably—"

"Stop!" Nisha covered her ears.

"Dissecting a cadaver is one thing; operating on a kid hit by a car—torn spleen, broken ribs, punctured lungs, a leg practically torn off at the knee—well, how do you steel yourself for the unexpected?"

"I don't want to hear this."

"And you don't want your mother to nag you about marriage either. Well, come on then, drink up, bottoms up."

"Just amazing," Nisha said, lowering the bottle and wiping her mouth with the back of her hand, "just amazing. They know what's what. Riots, border disputes. Yet something was made clear on a very different level for them by the movie. I don't understand."

"Is it necessary, to understand, always?"

"Yes. I must at least try to understand."

"I think you do understand, but you're denying it, because the understanding is not taking place in an area over which you can exert complete control."

"I control everything about me." She held the bottle tightly. "Except that . . . when that boy, his face taut with hate, pointed that Kalashnikov," she said, "I couldn't move, as if he were right here before me, and that bullet was going to shatter my head. Something terribly uncontrollable, you know, can't quite explain, can't quite understand."

"Yes," he said, "it's that sense of helplessness. But if you were holding that Kalashnikov, you would feel quite different."

"I wonder. I might have just pulled the trigger out of desperation. The look on that boy's face—it wasn't hate, was it?"

"He believes desperately, that's all."

"So does everyone else out here. I'm not going to let that happen. I'm not going to be caught here and get all torn up between media hype and myth. I got out, and I'll stay out."

"You make it sound like a place."

"It is a place—this place," she struck the ground, "and all that it contains, all the crippling ideas."

Shailen shook his head slowly. "Yes, perhaps it is a place. But I don't think it's under our feet. It moves around with you, that's the problem."

"No, it's not a problem. I've kicked it loose."

"What if that restless river twists around you, reclaims you?"

"Is there such a power? I'd like to harness it then, scan it, know its circuits, use it."

"And you would control it if you knew what it was all about?"

"Naturally. Knowledge is—"

"Don't even say it." Shailen cut in. "That's what I used to think fresh out of medical school."

"You *know* that. You can figure out in seconds what's killing a person. Day by day, you learn, know more and more."

"Yes, and day by day, I walk with my head bowing lower and lower, with each new drug, with each unique death."

"Like Kanu's—"

"No." Shailen cut her off. "He may not be dead."

"Did Lachmi tell you that?"

He turned and looked at her. "Lachmi?"

"Ramu said Lachmi tells you everything."

"Ramu imagines many things," he said curtly.

"About you, too?"

Shailen raised his eyebrows.

"All good things, doctor," Nisha said, "don't you worry. How wonderful and noble you are. You are wrapped in the glorious myths of others."

He laughed, his face relaxing. "Is that what we're wrapped in?"

"What else? Myths of others creating us, reinventing us day after day."

"And do we live up to them?"

"I hope not."

"But when you start believing—"

"But that's where you come in," Nisha said quickly. "You should set them right. The goat sacrifices, for instance. Who ever heard of sacrifices to Manasha? Why don't you set them straight?"

"I can't get rid of the crocodiles and the floods, so how can I set anything straight? I've stopped beating my head against a wall. They're happy this way, and I have interfered enough. Now I just want to get to Puri after my replacement arrives."

"Why?"

"Vacation, really. And future work, too. A friend has opened a clinic. I've saved some money, need some more, lots more actually, to buy a partnership, but I'm planning to do so, somehow."

Nisha laughed. "I have almost five thousand dollars."

"Really? But you are not the charitable kind, are you?" He laughed, too. "What would you live on if you gave that to me, now?"

"On nights like these I can allow myself to feel I could give up everything and live on just the sound of that river out there."

"Allow yourself! I thought you had escaped, that you were planning on staying out."

The night roared around them with the restless thrashing of the river. The darkness lit up in spots, fireflies, like bursts of tiny green flames circling the soft trunks of banana trees, the dark tops of hibiscus bushes. And when the wind swirled into Binjhar from Dakhin, it rushed the darkness with that rainsmell of gardenia and tuberose and the tiny, white, starlike *juin*, a smell made particular to Binjhar as that laden wind collected in its path the mud and blood smell of the red earth that lay beneath their feet and under the river. "These nights make me think of Lachmi," Nisha said, "and tempt me to go to the riverbank and ask for something. Kneeling on the red mud, Manasha, I want to whisper, they say you never refuse, grant my wish then, tell me what to believe."

"On nights like these, with the river so loud, I wouldn't tempt anything with words like that," Shailen said. "Would you really allow a god or goddess that much power? I never would. I would rather my gods failed to deliver; then I could wipe away their tears, and forgive them, love them, continue to pray to them, and not expect anything in return except that precious uncertainty, never really knowing why or how, but always believing, in spite of all the horrors, that happiness is perhaps inevitable, if someday we learn to recognize it."

"I can't believe you're a doctor," she said.

"I can't believe you're doing what you're doing out here. Beware, though, because Binjhar has seduced you."

Mosquitoes had formed buzzing clouds over their heads. They clapped their hands to drive away the insects, stood up, and smiled. "You're in way over your head," he said to her, "I hope you know that."

"Am I to believe you don't give a damn?"

"I am just the doctor."

"There's no need to cover a hurt and tired child with a blanket and put him to bed on your operating table because he's sprained his ankle, is there?"

"I'm just doing my job."

"Yes, so you are, Shailen-doctor, and good night."

Nisha turned and looked back at the dispensary from the cluster of banyan trees at the end of the narrow lane that lay between the dispensary steps and the red dirt road. Under the dim light of the veranda, Shailen stood looking down at the empty beer bottle in his hand. He looked up slowly, not toward the banyan trees under which Nisha stood, but to the left of the dispensary. Nisha moved behind one of the banyan trees, drawing in her breath sharply. Lachmi entered the dim circle of light. Shailen was moving back as if startled. Lachmi said something, but from where she stood Nisha couldn't hear. Shailen shook his head. Was he refusing something or denying something? Lachmi moved closer to him and reached out to touch his face. Shailen stepped back. He sat down on the steps heavily, covering his face with his hands. Lachmi kneeled before him. She touched his hair, his hands, his feet. Then she rose, and with that slow, deliberate walk, disappeared around the side of the dispensary. Shailen sat there, face in his hands, his slender body convulsing, bending lower and lower, until his head came down to rest on his knees.

Nisha walked backward slowly. Well, well, Shailen-doctor, wonder if you have anything on your shelves for such fractures?

From her window, Nisha saw the jeep drive off, trailing clouds of rosy dust. What happened—she bit her lips. No, she was not going to think anything at all. What if—no, he certainly was not. But what if it was his photograph that her mother had seen and decided on? Nonsense. Why on earth should she even think something like that? And about him, too? Especially after what she had witnessed last night. But what did Lachmi say? Did she ask him, accuse him? Oh, no. Nisha pressed her fingers against her temples. Why did she ask Lachmi about Shailen? Why did she have to bloody interfere? Her words may have made Lachmi suspect Shailen. Shailen sitting there shaking, face in his hands. Nisha stared at the road with clenched fists. She had actually smiled then, even felt a twinge of glee to see his pain. She unclenched her hands. Won't do this to myself. She tossed her hair out of her eyes.

The bright sunlight had cleared the dawn mist and the morning air was fresh with the odor of dung cakes being slapped on walls, of guavas and cooking rice. Ramu brought the bicycle around, the chain fixed, cleaned, oiled. She rode to the bazaar all the way along the river, following the red path out of the village. She paused before the bamboo groves, hearing a high-pitched whine above. For a fraction of a second, she saw six silver streaks, MIGs, possibly, or Mirages. She looked at the green forest of bamboo before her.

The wind whistling through the groves brought that warm, fresh odor of bamboo with it. On the ground her shadow was split into two by the shadow of a slender bamboo. One half of her shadow appeared larger than the other half, as if someone was standing by her side. Nisha turned to look. Of course there wasn't anyone, although she could swear she felt Lachmi right next to her, almost a part of her. She turned the bicycle around quickly.

On the way back, she slowed down near Lachmi's house. Two men in *lungis*, their muscles straining, sweat pouring down their backs, were carrying Lachmi's teak door down the front steps. Two boys stood ten yards from the house. "What are they doing?" she asked them.

"Lachmi told her brothers to remove the door," they said.

"Why?" They shook their heads, turned the palms of their hands upward. Nisha watched them for a few seconds. So these were Lachmi's brothers. Yes, they were thuggish all right. Strips of red cloth tied around their shaved heads, burly bodies, curling mustaches. Odd for them to remove the door. Maybe they wanted to sell the wood. They would get a good price for that door.

On the steps of the school, Ramu stood arguing with an old man in a *dhoti* and a brown shawl. She could see the holy string across his chest and back. His head was shaved except for a rat's tail of hair that hung from the crown of his head. On his forehead were three vertical sandalwood stripes. The priest from the Shiv temple! "Right now," he said to Ramu, shaking his fist, "right now!"

"Something wrong?" she asked.

"Oh . . . you are the . . . no, no, nothing wrong. Lachmi is being foolish. She came for the *puja* this morning and said some silly things, so I come here to tell Ramu to go and get Lachmi. I want to talk some sense because when I went to her house her brothers threw me out and said they would do as they were told and began to take down the door. What to say. No education, no common sense. *Puja* is one thing, put some

flowers, light a lamp, a few sticks of incense, say a few prayers, some sandalwood paste on your head, few drops of the water in your mouth—and
go home and forget. But then to have idiotic notions of what can happen
if . . . tch-tch, what to say? Nobody listens to me, what can I say? Old man
be quiet, go ring the bell and cook your rice." He shook his head and
tugged at his holy string. "I'll go back. I'm an old man. I'll come and talk
to Shailen-doctor tomorrow."

"What's going on?" she asked Ramu as the priest walked away slowly,
shaking his head, muttering to himself. Ramu shook his head and
shrugged. "I'm going to the bazaar," he said and ran off. Nisha sat down
on the steps and breathed deeply the warm air.

Winter had vanished. A short sharp exhalation. The long deep breath
of this spring-summer, the regular rhythm of the year had settled in,
as regular as the continual unrest of the river that was leaping its way
toward the sea. Even thinking about Dakhin dragged you along with it.
How terrifying, she thought, how marvelous, and how odd, taking down
that gorgeous teak door.

She sat there and ate her lunch, dozed, sat up startled, as parrots,
dazzling green, fought among mango leaves with harsh grating shrieks.
Then that rhythmic chantlike call of those tiny brown birds faded in, up
and down in cadence. They were those birds her grandmother used to
tell her about, who continually urged, wife-talk-to-me, and that's what
they were called, *bow-kotha-kow,* a name formed from the sound of their
call. That call was so insistent suddenly, drowning out the parrots and
crows and sparrows, as if those brown birds wanted to really hear someone talk. *Bow-kotha-kow-kow-kow-kow.* The afternoon was loud with
voices and wings and feet and hooves.

She watched the sun glaze the banyan trees copper and vanish, felt
the night touch her with its cool river breeze and close her eyes with its
heady scent. Smoke of sandalwood incense came from somewhere, together with the smoke of wood fires. Something was happening around
her, she felt. What if Shailen was . . . what lunacy, not again! What did
Lachmi say to Shailen? Had they been . . . were they still—? He must
have done something, something terrible. Or was it Ramu after all? Was
Shailen protecting Ramu? If he knew Kanu was dead, had been killed,
why didn't he make out a death certificate when the D.M. asked for one?
But had Shailen got rid of Kanu in his own careful way, sliding the needle

in gently under Kanu's skin? He had covered that boy in his surgery so gently. Pulled the blanket up to that boy's chin, moved his hair out of his eyes. Yet when he had caught her shoulders, pushed her against the tree, that eerie flicker of a smile moving from his mouth to his eyes—stop. Hypothesize, Lennox would say, analyze. Shailen's body shaking, his face in his hands. Lachmi had reached out to touch his face.

Nisha touched her burning face. Lachmi's hand against her face. The warm smell of bamboo brought by the wind. "Lachmi," Nisha said softly, "Lachmi." She closed her eyes. She saw her reflection in the mirror merging, vanishing into Lachmi's shadow-dark form. For a fraction of a second, her body felt heavier as if she were breathing in another's shadow. If only she knew for sure, but this heady darkness was all around, re-creating, reviving lost, forgotten worlds.

Something marvelous and terrifying, can't explain, don't know how to express, perhaps it's just illogical and not quite within my grasp, but I'm trying to, why that damned door, why that agitated brahmin, why this sandalwood smoke takes you to dark temple altars, to riverbanks where corpses are set aflame, to sandalwood pyres into which desperate women fling themselves, but what exactly, find out tomorrow, definitely, frame it in the necessary language, but now the night compels silence and thought is, really, if you can believe, quite irrelevant as eyes are closing and the mind lapsing. . . .

"Wake up! Wake up!" Ramu was shaking her. Nisha sat up in shock. "I can't stop her!" he said. "I can't stop her, nobody can, maybe you can."

She ran with him to the river. Not only the people of Binjhar, but many people from the next village were gathered on the bank. Many carried plates of marigolds, hibiscus, garlands, burning incense, clay lamps. The old priest was standing under a *neem* tree and shaking his fists at the crowd.

"*Imbeciles! Idiots! Murderers!* Look," he said to Nisha, seeing her, "just imagine. On that door, look, she's insane, and *they are here with flowers,* look." Nisha ran down to the bank.

Lachmi stood there in a white cotton sari with a red border. On her wrists were bangles made from white conch shells. Her long black hair was wet and hung below her hips. "Lachmi," Nisha whispered. Lachmi turned with blank eyes. "My husband will come back," she said. Her two brothers, their eyes red and streaming, carried the heavy door right to the edge of the water. They came back and touched Lachmi's feet, and moved back, crying loudly. Men, women, children, all bowed and touched Lachmi's feet. There was silent awe on their faces. Nirmala stood with her children a few yards away, a sullen, confused look on her face. Ramu clasped Nisha's hand and began to cry into her palm. "Stop," said Nisha, "stop," her voice faltering. "What are you—" They pushed her away, told her to be quiet, not to disturb such a holy moment.

Lachmi walked slowly to the water and stepped on the door. She raised folded hands, looked up, then at the river, and closed her eyes. She sat down in the center of the door, folding her legs under her. Her two brothers, crying, wiping their faces, pushed the door onto the river's surface. The waves lifted the door and pulled it out. *"Jai ma, jai ma, jai ma. . . ."* Flowers were thrown in, lamps floated. People stretched out on the bank and touched the earth and the water with their forehead. *"Jai ma, jai ma, jai ma."*

Nisha's knees touched the soft red mud. Her hand was wet with Ramu's tears. The brahmin under the *neem* tree was shaking his fists still, but now screaming out a string of arcane abuse, *"Scoundrels! Cads! A race of pigs! Children of whores! Diseased offsprings of diseased whores! Ignorant asses with worms in your heads! May Shiv strike you down!"*

Nisha tried to call out but her voice had disappeared. She coughed to clear her throat, but only a gurgling sound came out, much like the gurgling sound wetting her hand. Shailen, she was screaming inside, God, if only he would hold her hand. Shailen, come and stop this. Why aren't you back? Lachmi sitting erect on the bouncing teak door. Nisha couldn't see her anymore. The currents pulled the door around the riverbend, and Lachmi disappeared among the waves and dark rocks of Dakhin. "Phone—" she gasped, "Ramu, must phone D.M."

Dragging Ramu, she ran to the dispensary. It was locked. Ramu, crying hysterically, ran around to the back and brought a hammer. She began to strike at the lock and the bolt. The lock broke. They flung the doors back and rushed in. Nisha picked up the phone and listened to the receiver intently, then replaced it. Dead. There was no jeep either to drive to the next village, to the post office, to the hospital. They could walk or Ramu could take the bicycle. But where was Lachmi now?

Ramu pulled her back to the river. No one was there. Flowers had been washed back, garlands of marigold, hibiscus. The air was still scented with sandalwood and camphor. Nisha sat down and leaned her head against the *neem* tree. That limey bitter smell. Ramu's head was buried against her side, his body convulsing with sobs. The river breeze felt like a slap in the face. Tears rolled down her face. She couldn't stop crying. She bent forward, bringing her head over her knees and covered her face.

She hadn't been able to do a thing. It had happened, just like that. Without even a hint. Where was Shailen, damn it, where was he? Lachmi, proud, beautiful, and, oh God, young, torn to pieces by now. Nisha gasped through her sobs and hugged herself. She felt her own skin tear, rip off. A thrashing river, thrashing with its merciless creatures, Dakhin, a mad wind gone insane with blood and myth. Why did she have to be witness to this?

What was happening? She didn't have a clue. They were arguing about Kashmir, about the government two days back. Today, they had aided and abetted—what was the psychology of riots, Hindus and Muslims killing each other, day after day? A Kalashnikov in the hands of a fifteen-year-old boy. A TV screen red with a bloodstained street, a river red with blood and red silt. And they were standing in between, unable to move.

She had frozen, hadn't been able to stop them or Lachmi. She had taken notes, written everything down diligently, asked her clever questions, to some extent even got them to question what they believed. It'll be an exciting dissertation, Lennox had said. She would write it, and then go back and defend it. She hadn't been able to—she hadn't paid attention, hadn't listened carefully enough, hadn't observed—hadn't learned to—look, the voice in the dream had whispered, look carefully—the door, the brahmin. She had sat and relaxed and let it happen, hadn't, yes, analyzed what was happening before her eyes, on this red earth, hadn't even looked! Failed so utterly that there were no words, no emotion devastating enough—Lachmi had floated away like a feather drops and floats away from a bird's wing in flight.

Two boys and three girls wandered near the bank. They looked at the two huddled forms, tilting their heads, listening to the gasping, choking sounds coming from there. When the sound of a backfiring jeep cut in, they turned their heads.

Running footsteps came to a halt. Nisha moved, only to fall sideways, burying her face in her hands. "Get up, stop this. Pick him up, bring him along." Nisha felt hands lift her up. She was flung over a shoulder. Blue cotton, a faint odor of diesel and dust. "Stop," she heard again, and began to scream, "No, no, no." They were moving. She was lowered and pushed into the back of the jeep. Ramu was pushed in after her. The priest got in and began to smooth her hair, muttering, tch-tch-tch, *shanti shanti shanti*, with each bump on the way, every jolt, every slap of the red dust that rose and obliterated vision. Then she was pulled out, flung over the shoulder again, pushed into a chair.

"Oh, Shailen-doctor, oh, Shailen-doctor—" A woman's worried, anxious voice.

"Ki?" Shailen turned toward the door.

"Tulu ate poisoned berries—now vomiting blood."

He pressed his temples with his fingertips. "Bring him in."

"The phone's dead, dead," Nisha heard herself whisper, her voice hoarse.

"I know. It was that damned air show, the MIGs, flying low to show off and scare the Cuttack crowd, flew into the phone lines and tore them off. I'll drive back and—don't struggle, I don't have time—I'm going to give you both sedatives. Won't hurt much."

"Ouch."

"There. Put her in there, Ramu in the other one. Where's the boy?"

Nisha felt drops of water on her mouth. She opened her eyes and saw a dropper above her face and a hand holding a glass. "Here, drink, you asked for water, and sedatives can make you thirsty." She raised herself and drank from the glass. "The D.M.'s assistant's come and gone. They are going to search the river. Now I'd like you to get up slowly, splash some water on your face, and go to my office and sit there. I have to stitch someone's finger before it falls off."

"Don't you know what's happened—don't you care?"

"I need this room and table for an emergency, now, and there is nothing physically wrong with you, so please."

Ramu was asleep under Shailen's table, one fist under his chin, the other under his head. Outside, people were sitting in rows, groaning, coughing, sneezing, calling on God, destiny, and Shailen-doctor. Nisha stood up, straightened her clothes, and walked out slowly.

The door of the schoolhouse had been left open, but everything was still there. She went to the room that functioned as a kitchen and found Nirmala cutting vegetables. "What—"

"*Didi, didi*—" Nirmala threw herself on the floor and caught Nisha's feet. "*Didi* . . . don't send me away . . . no one wants . . . they turn away . . . turn their faces away . . . Shailen-doctor, assistant D.M., they gave everyone such a talking to . . . now everyone looks at me like—"

"Could you just make me some tea or something?"

"Yes."

Nisha went back to her room. She rearranged and relabelled her files. Nirmala brought tea spiced with cloves and basil. Nisha sat looking at her notes, crossing out words, adding commas, semicolons, dashes. What had she written? Page after page after page filled with what they said about the doctor. She documented his daily routine, his likes and dislikes, what he had said to the *dhobi,* to Ramu, the barber's wife, what they said he had said to them; then she had written Ramu's version of it all; and Nirmala's; everyone's except Lachmi's. Lachmi's words had never entered her journal. Why not?

She stared down at the words. The doctor this, the doctor that, Shailen, Shailen, Shailen. . . . When did she write all this, she couldn't remember. Had someone altered her entries? Did she really write all this? Why? She reached forward and pressed PLAY on the tape recorder. Nirmala's high-pitched voice . . . yes, she remembered that story. The *dhobi*'s voice came on next, then Ramu's, then the barber's wife's. All talking about the doctor! And about Lachmi. Three-quarters of her material was centered on Shailen. What possessed her . . . ?

What would Sylvia Lennox say? My dear, who gets to tell whose story, and why? And was there yet another narrative that she had missed completely, hadn't a clue about, a narrative containing all? Nisha covered her face with her hands.

"Shailen-doctor *aiche.*" Nirmala entered quietly and ushered him in.

"A letter for you. The *dhobi* had gone to the post office in the next village to collect the mail."

"Why?" she asked. "Why did they let . . . how could she—?"

"How should I know?"

"You must know! What did she say to you? What did you do?"

She couldn't understand why Shailen stood there with his fists clenched, his face drained of color. "Just go away," she said, her voice breaking, "I would like to be alone."

"You sent him away like that, *didi*," Nirmala whispered. "Did you not see his eyes? Don't cry, *didi*, don't." She wiped Nisha's face with the corner of her sari. "Not what I wanted, God," Nirmala said. "What could I do, or you, or anyone, don't cry, *didi*, I will have to live with this and tears don't help."

The next morning loud voices, running feet, and whirring engines woke her. She dressed quickly and ran out. Everyone was running toward the river again. A helicopter had landed. Policemen were moving people away from the river. Shailen was knee-deep in the water, examining something. A policeman stopped her with his club. "Please, miss."

"Don't come here," Shailen turned and said, hearing the policeman. A large canvas sheet was thrown over whatever the doctor was bending over and then carried to the helicopter. The corner of a white and red sari leaked out from the bundle. People touched their foreheads and then their chests. "*Shanti ano ma, shanti.*" Shailen was removing blood-smeared latex gloves from his hands. He came up to her. "Come, let's go." Ramu was whimpering under the *neem* tree, rubbing his head against its bark. "It's all over," Shailen said. His eyes were blank.

Within the hour, the temple became the stage. Bells rang constantly, mountains of flowers surrounded not only the Shiv *linga*, but the altar and temple courtyard as well. The smoke from burning incense, oil, wood stung the everyone's eyes as they reached the stone steps. The brahmin's assistants were handing out rice with ghee, together with chopped dates, and sugar candy in banana leaves sprinkled with holy water. And being a Shiv temple, *bhang* was poured generously into every glass, cup, mug, or vessel held out. So for three days, Binjhar swayed, heady with *bhang*, and its usual accompaniment, *ganja*. Even Ramu loudly sucked the clay *chillum* offered and, after draining a glass of the milky, saffron-scented fluid, poured a glass on his head. Nirmala was drinking glass after glass of *bhang*, and even feeding her children the same, saying, "Drink, drink, and hope there is forgiveness."

"Who killed Kanu?" the *dhobi* asked, slurring, hiccupping, stretching out an arm toward the altar. "You up there, tell me."

"Lachmi for certain," another slurring voice assured.

"Manasha called Lachmi," the barber's wife said, rolling from one end of the temple courtyard to the other. "Manasha called her, yes, called her," she chanted as she rolled back and forth across the flagstones, her eyes turning up, showing their whites, white foam dribbling from the corners of her mouth. "She'll call us, too, call us, call us, call us, call us. . . ."

Nisha clutched Shailen's arm. "Have they gone mad?"

"Drink," Shailen said, "drink up," grabbing an offered glass. "What are we resisting anyway? Do we know any more than them, really? Don't we want to forget?" Then she was laughing, like everybody else, crying sometimes, giggling, crying again, as Lennox's voice kept echoing in her head, Analyze, hypothesize. Gift-wrapping reality for Sylvia's three chapters. If only she could have dragged Sylvia to the river when that door had bounced away, made her feel jagged teeth on flesh, water filling her mouth and nose and lungs, made her smell this red silt with blood frothing on it.

They rolled on the temple courtyard, laughing, crying, singing, stumbling to the river, rolled on the mud, crying for Manasha and Shiv, rubbing the mud on themselves as if its redness might cover the other deeper red that now held them captive. Caked with red mud, they fell asleep wherever they were, woke up, went to the temple, ate kilos of rice and fruit, and the *bhang* again, and *ganja.*

On the fourth day the rice ran out, the *bhang,* the fruit, the flowers, except the *ganja,* and their *nasha.* But now they had entered a different stage of intoxication. Every sound was magnified by a hundred decibels, every color turned blinding bright, and every movement, slower, heavier. When out of the hot white sky a silver helicopter descended, the people of Binjhar ran out of the temple courtyard in slow motion, covering their ears and eyes, and with impossibly stiff jaws and lips called out to Manasha to save them from the claws of the bird of death, from destiny.

Nisha and Shailen walked a little swifter than the others, were a little less muddy. The whirr of the engine stopped. The door opened, six men jumped out holding between them what looked to all like—a madman. Trussed up with ropes, bare to the waist, a bloody bandage around his head, the man was screaming hoarsely as if he had been screaming for days. The district magistrate came forward. With him was a woman in a blue sari, her greying hair rolled in a bun behind her head. "Shailen-doctor, my goodness, what on earth, you look . . . here, take mine, clean and starched . . . oh, well, yes, now I can see your face somewhat, but what . . . never mind, look here, missing person, out of the blue."

"What are you doing here?" Shailen asked the woman next to the spluttering D.M.

"Why, you wrote you were waiting for a replacement so that you could leave," she said to him.

"Yes, yes, they informed me that she, Dr. Sanyal here—" the D.M. added, "needed a lift to get here, so I said come along, since I have to—"

"I wasn't expecting you so soon," Shailen said, wiping dry mud off his hair.

"Why, you're . . . you're—" Nisha stammered and stopped. It was Dr. Sanyal, from Delhi, an old friend of her mother's who had left Delhi when Nisha was three or four. What was she doing here? She recalled her mother writing about Dr. Sanyal recently, that she had come back to Delhi, to work there. But here she was, standing two feet away, smiling inquiringly as if expecting Nisha to explain what Nisha was doing here. And why was Shailen talking to Dr. Sanyal as if he had known her all his life?

"I have to show you the place," Shailen said to Dr. Sanyal. "Things are a bit of a mess."

"But . . . but—" cut in the D.M., "you are not looking, I have come to deposit the missing person and make an arrest. The missing person, doctor, look."

The people of Binjhar stood in a semicircle, red clay statues melting slowly as if they had run into a blast furnace, and regarded the madman with mouths hanging open. "Kanu," someone whispered.

"He was hit on the head last night, you see, three villages down west, drunken fight, then went running to the police station with, 'I remember, I remember.' This business with the dead woman—the recent suicide, I've entered it as the Manasha business. But when you called me first, remember? When you wouldn't make out the death certificate? Before that, he says he was hit on the head, so the doctor there said he forgot; second hit, he remembers. Now we must arrest."

Ramu had crept up to Nisha. "Not possible," he gasped.

"Him, him!" The madman stamped his feet and screamed hoarsely.

"Handcuffs," the D.M. ordered. Two policemen stepped forward.

"He was there!" The hoarse scream again. "When the branch hit me on the head."

"Wait a minute," Shailen stepped in between the two policemen and Ramu. "You have no bloody proof except for that oaf's screams. So just wait a minute. You want to say something, Ramu?"

"Shailen-doctor, if Manasha took him, how can he be standing there?"

"What did you do?" Shailen asked.

"We'll question him at the station, come, come."

"No." Shailen pulled a shaking Ramu to the side. "What did you do?"

"For one last time I thought I'd try to kill him!" The madman was struggling with the ropes, tearing at them. "My wife's been eaten by crocodiles because of him."

"I was sleeping under that tree near the water," Ramu said. "It was dark, and suddenly I woke up because somebody was strangling me. Kanu was trying to kill me. I struggled but couldn't free myself, and I was going to die, but then—" Ramu's eyes became glazed.

"A branch fell on my head—" Nisha stared at the madman pulling at the ropes and screaming. His "enviable" face was streaked with mud and blood, and so was his body. He looked strong enough to wrench a bull's head off.

"Yes," Ramu stammered, "fell on his head from above, and he fell down. Then as I looked at Kanu lying at my feet, the river—"

"What?"

"The river swelled up and grew so loud. Manasha was calling, telling me to give Kanu to her, since he had tried to kill me . . . so. . . ." Ramu tugged at his lower lip and moved back toward Nisha.

"He dragged me down the slope and rolled me into the water. Let me get my hands on you. I was stunned by the blow, couldn't move."

"Picked up shortly, you see, by a launch, but they didn't know, he had memory loss, you see, so dropped him off three villages down."

"You little—" Shailen shook Ramu. "Why didn't you tell me?"

"I forgot. I was afraid."

The people of Binjhar opened and closed their mouths. "The husband brought back. The wife goes to Manasha, and the husband comes back." Another whisper like a wave, and thick red mud dripping from bodies with every movement. Nisha closed her eyes for a second. It was the smell of that mud, the same smell as on that red finger that had touched her face with its wetness on an afternoon when everyone had turned shining wet red.

"Here, here, just a minute," the district magistrate tapped Shailen on the shoulder. "I am thoroughly confused. I don't like this business at all. Ruffians, liars. I shall leave. I have important things to take care of." He waved his hands at his men. "Untie the beast. Let's go."

"But you can't leave Kanu here," Shailen said agitatedly. "He'll kill Ramu."

"Oh, really? Untie him." The D.M. clapped his hands. The policemen untied Kanu. Kanu shook himself like a bull shaking off water and mud. With heavy steps, he walked toward Ramu, who was hiding behind Nisha. The D.M. marched swiftly and pulled Ramu out to face Kanu. Ramu fell to his knees, rolling his eyes. "Stand up," the D.M. said, pulling Ramu up. Kanu stood before the D.M., shoulders hunched, fists at his waist. "You—" the D.M. poked Kanu's chest with a forefinger. Kanu took a step backward. "You listen. And you—" he gave Ramu a shake. "If he," the D.M. pointed at Ramu, "dies, then you—" he poked Kanu again, "you hang." Then he pointed at Kanu, faced Ramu, and declared, "If he dies, then, Ramu, you hang. Manasha's blessings on you. Good-bye, Dr. Sanyal," he said to the woman, touching his head with two fingers. "Enjoy your stay. Shailen-doctor, you can have the jeep, duty calls. See, all settled. I know how to deal with these criminal types."

People backed away slowly. Ramu and Kanu stood facing each other, one rolling his eyes and shaking like a leaf, the other, breathing heavily and glaring with bloodshot eyes. They didn't move an inch to either reduce or increase the yard of red earth between them. Nirmala crawled on her hands and knees toward them. She reached out to touch Kanu's leg, then withdrew her hand, crouching between them, whimpering.

The helicopter, blinding silver in the afternoon sun, rose with that same thousand-decibel whirr like a shining creature of light spreading spinning wings.

Nisha and Shailen listened to Dr. Sanyal chatter on about the New Delhi hospital while they walked to the schoolhouse. Nisha eyed Shailen warily. He was quiet, nodding occasionally, almost sullen. "Ah, I must take a good look inside," Dr. Sanyal said, poking her head in through the door. "Come, Nisha, we've a lot to talk about, too," she added before disappearing inside.

Nisha swallowed and looked at Shailen and then at herself. Dry red mud clung to their clothes, skin, hair. "She was one of my professors, and she kind of adopted me, I guess, after my mother died." Shailen paused and touched the mud on his shirt. "I wrote to her last year—" he started again, without any prompting, words tumbling out, "and then, just a few weeks back, I told her my plans, though I wasn't expecting her to turn up so suddenly, without a word, to be the replacement, not her. Anyway, I have to pack my things, show her the stuff. You'll have company—she's going to stay in the schoolhouse and you can talk about old times, I'm sure. Her things are on their way." They looked at each other blankly. Shailen rubbed his temples. "I have to show her around a little bit." Nisha swallowed again.

"Mud," she said.

"Yes. Must change." Shailen backed away a few steps, then turned and ran toward his dispensary.

Nisha entered the schoolhouse slowly. She heard the barber's wife talking to Dr. Sanyal. "Poor Nirmala, one feels sorry for her now," the barber's wife was saying to the doctor. "The woman crawled on hands and knees to her house, crawled through the bazaar, all the way down the road. Crawled to her bed, and under it. She's lying there now. Won't come out." Nisha closed her eyes. Nirmala whimpering at Kanu's feet, then crawling, as if dragging a half-torn body across an ancient battlefield. No one reached out to help her to her feet. The villagers just stood and stared at Nirmala's rolling, writhing form twisting its way through the deserted bazaar, up the red dirt road to the cluster of huts where her children stood with their thumbs in their mouths and the blankest eyes Nisha had ever seen.

Nisha slipped into her room unnoticed by Dr. Sanyal or the barber's wife talking in the next room. She picked up her journal, and holding it tightly against her chest, went inside the bathroom and closed the door. Three iron buckets of water and a wooden stool stood on the unfinished cement floor. She sat down on the wooden stool and stared at the tin can half submerged in one of the buckets. With the notebook on her lap, she began to pour water over herself.

The mud liquefied and streamed down her face. A red pool widened under her feet. Was all her blood leaving her? That eerie sweet smell again. This river-scented mud flowing swiftly down her skin, along her throat, shoulder, back. Her notebook slipped from her lap into the muddy water at her feet. She straightened up at the sound of the soft splash. Blue ink blending with bright copper. She picked up a bucket and overturned it clumsily over her head.

An hour later, Dr. Sanyal knocked on Nisha's door. "Ah," she said, "Shailen has managed marvelously. I hope I shall do half as well." Nisha combed her wet hair before the mirror on the wall. The mud was finally off. Her head felt a little heavy. Dr. Sanyal took the cup of tea from the barber's wife, who had now taken charge of the kitchen.

Nisha sat quietly for a while on her bed. "Is your work coming along well?" Dr. Sanyal asked her. She nodded. "What on earth did I arrive in the middle of?" Dr. Sanyal touched her head. "But how have you been, working here in this village? Your mother's quite worried, you know, ever since you went abroad. She wants you to get married, settle down, or so she's been telling me for the past year, since I went back to Delhi from Medical College in Calcutta where Shailen was a resident, under me, you know, such a bright boy." Nisha went to the table and picked up her mother's letter that Shailen had handed her a few days back. *If you don't come home right away, we are sending your brothers to bring you back. You are getting married this summer.* When would this nonsense end? Nisha dropped the letter in the wicker basket under the table.

"I'm sure Shailen will have a wonderful vacation in Puri," Dr. Sanyal said. "He needs it. He said he's going to stay there for at least a month, maybe even work there. He decided to leave right away, started packing, doesn't want to linger. Well, you can't blame him considering every-thing," she carried on. Nisha heard only the river.

Shailen was going to vanish, then. Nisha shifted on the bed. The afternoon felt warm and wet and sticky against her skin, as if hands had slapped that damp red mud all over her again. A red clay figure to be thrown into the river, when the south wind crossed the land, for some inexplicable blessing. A warm rosy splash, and then you were lost—those are pearls that were your eyes, of your bones are coral made—blood on latex gloves, the soil turning perfect for rice this year. And Dakhin—'the south wind piercing my heart,' her grandmother used to sing.

She had wanted to find a river, that's all. But it was as if the river had dragged her there to devour her, body and mind. She stifled a gasp. Body and mind—the river had crashed through the dam between. She had come here to write it down, neatly, write that river down, but Dakhin had rewritten her. Does text define context or context define . . . ? Sylvia Lennox, leaning back, crossing her legs, twisting a lock of her hair. Your life in your own hands, child. Her grandmother running her forefinger over Nisha's palm. Look here. In your own hands. All written in your hands.

Nisha looked down at her palms. She must get away from Dakhin's warm red waves. She must get away from that blood and mud smell, and from this roaring afternoon crashing against her ears, from this river that wanted to take everything away.

She went to the window. The river sounded like one long scream. Nisha held the bars. Had Lachmi heard it, too? The river wanted to wash away this sticky red feeling. To walk into its warmth, submerge in it, to let Dakhin take you away to that secret island. Dakhin was calling, spreading its tide out for you, rising up for you. Tell me what to believe? she had asked. Dakhin would tell you everything, make you understand fear, doubt, belief, curse, chaos. So Dakhin was calling now, Manasha's spirit rising through it, offering that incomprehensible answer.

Outside, the red dust rose up in the wind, twisted, coiled, swept forward, pulled back, scattered. A copper glaze, rising and falling, circling, engulfing.

Shailen would drive away, drive all the way down the bank, and then away, far away. She turned from the window sharply. Dr. Sanyal was still sipping her tea and smiling benignly at the trees outside.

"Barber's wife, help me," Nisha called. The barber's wife came running. "Pack." Into two suitcases she threw her clothes, shoes, books, towels, soap, shampoo, haphazardly stuffing them, two three four items at a time and what didn't fit she told the barber's wife to take. Dr. Sanyal's eyes widened. "Are you . . . ?" Nisha slung her leather bag over her shoulder, picked up her suitcases, and ran out.

She ran to the middle of the red dirt road as the jeep drove up. She would be miles away from it all soon, she felt almost sure. How long could this river follow you? Shailen braked, looking puzzled. Nisha ran to the back of the jeep and threw her suitcases in. "What?"

"You've got to take me."

"I'm going to—"

"Me, too." She climbed in beside him. She would outrun it. They would be driving away.

"The Cuttack airport, I guess. You can get a plane to Calcutta, and from there—"

"I don't want to go to an airport. Please, just drive."

"But what do you intend to . . . ? I mean, what will you . . . ?"

"Please, just drive. I need a month, just to rethink some things, that's all."

"How much money do you have?"

"Five thousand dollars—almost. I told you that before."

"Hmm, well, that'll last for a year at least—" Shailen's eyes shone with a wicked light. "Well . . . okay, get in, but let me make one thing clear, your family had better not come chasing after me with a gun and expect me to marry you."

"Nobody's going to make me marry anybody."

"A month of rethinking, hmm," Shailen rubbed his chin. "Anything can happen in a month, in a week, in a day."

"Just drive, damn it." But what if it was Shailen, and she had jumped into this jeep, but this was getting away, but what if he was . . . what was she getting away from? Nisha shook inside. Who are you, she wanted to scream, why were you here? Running from or running after—what am I doing? Tell me what to believe, she had laughed and asked that restless night. What had she received—curse or blessing? And how to know one from the other, when Dakhin with its stormy thrashing was sweeping away the hardness under her feet, when Dakhin was raging through her veins?

"Are you going to drive, or what?" she asked, her voice high pitched, cracking.

"Before something overtakes—yes, I'd better."

"Stop," she said, as they passed Lachmi's doorless house. "Why won't you say anything?" The brick house gaped at them, its interior so dark that the darkness almost seemed like a drawn curtain. "I don't know what to think, what you think, feel, what she said, how can you be so—"

"Don't ever—" He braked gently, avoiding even the most natural jerk on that bumpy road. "It's over," he said, "so let it rest. You can't possibly know everything, even think you can know everything. Let it rest. You have no idea—"

"No," she said, "I have no idea." She heard the stormy hiss of the rising tide in the distance, Dakhin climbing over the bank, pulling the land in with one giant swoop.

"You and I can only run away and hope to give that something the slip," he said, changing gears.

Red dust followed them out of the village, together with running children, "Ta-ta, Shailen-doctor, come back soon." Nisha closed her eyes as they passed the spot where the helicopter had landed. Ramu and Kanu had stood there, hunched, shaking, staring at each other, desperate with rage and fear. Ramu and Kanu sentenced to live, holding the secret of life and death in their frozen hands.

Dakhin roared under the bridge ten miles east, louder, the waters churning violently. The bridge rocked from side to side, up and down under the speeding jeep. The south wind was piling the waves higher and higher till Dakhin rose and swept across the bridge. In the rearview mirror, Nisha and Shailen saw a gigantic copper and silver wing of water leap up and shatter into a million glittering eyes.

SHONA RAMAYA was born in Calcutta, India. Her previous works include a novel, *Flute* and a collection of stories, *Beloved Mother, Queen of the Night*. She has taught literature and creative writing at Hamilton College and she was a writer-in-residence at Trinity College. Ramaya is also the co-founder and senior executive of a new literary magazine called *Catamaran: South Asian American Writing*. She now lives in Grafton, Massachusetts.

This book was typeset in Minion, a typeface designed
by Robert Slimbach and issued by Adobe in 1989.
E-mail sections were set in Rotis Serif.
Book design by Wendy Holdman.
Composition by Stanton Publication Services, Inc.,
St. Paul, Minnesota.
Manufactured by Friesens on acid-free paper.